Night Secrets

by

Shirley Martin

ISBN: 978-1-77145-252-6

Published By:

Books We Love
Chestermere, Alberta
Canada

First Print Edition

Copyright 2014 Shirley Martin

Cover art by Michelle Lee Copyright 2014

D1538638

Chapter One

A slight tug released Keriam's soul from her body. She floated to the ceiling, amazed as always that she could look down at herself in bed. With a certainty born of past experience, she knew this was no dream. Ever since her mother's death two years ago, preternatural powers had evolved within her, and she often wondered why. Was it her mother's way of watching over her from the Otherworld? These night journeys were even more recent and something she must learn to control, if only she knew how.

She drifted through the bedchamber walls, then once outside, flew over the maples and oaks that bordered the royal domain of Emain Macha, approaching the open countryside. Heading north, she traveled over the many farmsteads nestled in small groupings with their wattle-and-daub houses, the herds of longhorn sheep dotting the open fields. Here and there a hillfort guarded the country. Although it was deepest night, everything looked clear and luminous.

Maintaining her leisurely flight, Keriam approached the capital city of Moytura, its shops and stores closed, its many taverns and inns dimly-lit but alive with noise and laughter.

A heavy mist swirled around her, the night air cool and damp. She headed westward to the Plain of Sorrows, a vast land preceded by a meadow and transected by the winding Nantosuelta River. Through the fog, she drifted down among the thick clusters of oak trees lining the riverbank and smiled at the fairies who slumbered in the branches. To her heightened hearing, the rippling water of the Nantosuelata echoed like a waterfall.

The sound of hoofbeats jolted her. As quickly as her spirit form would allow, she took refuge within an earthberry bush, afraid someone might see her, even in the dim light.

Two men gathered by the river, their voices audible as they secured their horses to tree branches. Focusing her gaze in the hazy light, she recognized them as officers in her father's army, although she didn't know their names. What were they doing here at this late night hour? One bald and the other blond, they wore simple tunics and short boots.

"Gamal just returned from a mission," the bald one said. "He should arrive shortly."

Was that Major Roric Gamal, her father's courier?

Aimless talk ensued for several minutes, army gossip and tales of female exploits.

They became silent when Roric Gamal rode up, an officer she'd seen at the palace many times. He dismounted and looped his horse's halter around a tree branch, then approached the others. Younger and taller than the other two, his gait was steady and confident, like one accustomed to authority.

"Where's General Balor?" Gamal asked. "He should be present." His clipped accent told her he came from one of the southern provinces, Mag Aurfolaig, perhaps.

"Couldn't come," the bald officer explained. "The general sent me to represent him."

"Very well," the newcomer said, his baritone voice clear and resonant. "Let's get this business over with, so we can return to our quarters before dawn." Gamal raised his booted foot onto a tree stump and leaned forward, resting his hands on his knee, and lowered his voice. "No dissension now! We have already agreed we must kill him."

Kill whom? Keriam's spirit body turned cold. Merciful Goddess, these men are planning murder.

The bald man stepped forward, shaking his fist. "Do it and get it over with!"

"Think before you speak, Dothan! We must proceed with caution." Roric paused. "First, we must bribe a few government officials. Blackmail others. That will take time. The Lug Festival would be the best opportunity for killing him," he said, looking at the other two. "Don't you agree?" Receiving affirmative replies, he continued. "Gives us months to plan. And all the crowds there will make it easier for the assassin to disappear among the people and escape."

The Lug Festival, only four moonphases away. Keriam drew back, pressing her hand to her mouth, then gasped when her hand passed through her face.

Roric Gamal recaptured her attention. "We know the king intends to invite King Barzad of Elegia to Avador soon to discuss forming an alliance between the two countries. Last thing we need. If we can keep Avador weak, we should have no trouble gaining control of the realm." He set his foot on the ground and drew himself up to his full height. "But if Avador forms an alliance with Elegia, there go our plans. We must kill the king!"

Keriam sank to the ground. Her father! They were talking about killing her father! Goddess, no! They must not get away with this evil.

"Agreed," the blonde man said. "But how do we accomplish this assassination? Remember, General Balor has the final word. Anything we decide must have his approval. Got to have the army behind us."

"Of course," Roric said. "Now, I've given the plan much thought. Here's how we'll proceed."

The warble of a bird alarmed Keriam, daybreak graying the trees.

A tug pulled her spirit back. No, not now! She must discover more of their plan.

Within a heartbeat, Keriam found herself falling into her body, as if from a great height. She lay stunned, unsure where she was. At last recognizing her surroundings, she wanted to weep, so afraid for her father, her mind awhirl with panic. Somehow, she must discover details of the plot and warn him.

No one knew of her spirit travels, but what if someone found out? She'd be accused of witchcraft, a practice forbidden in the kingdom. And no one was aware of her other mental powers, of her ability to discern a person's past or see into the future by touching that person. Unfortunately, this talent often didn't work when she needed it most. By the Goddess, why couldn't she see into her father's future?

As she heard her maid in the next room, a new fear crashed through her. What if Maudina found out about her nightly trips? Superstitious girl that she was, would her maid report her to the druids? Keriam prayed she wouldn't, hoping she could count on the maid's loyalty. Like all the servants at the palace, Maudina received a sufficient wage, and well-paid servants were more trustworthy than poorly-paid ones. Surely that fact would ensure the maid's faithfulness?

The druids held great power in the kingdom, and religion ruled the lives of all of the country's inhabitants. Keriam closed her eyes, imagining her punishment should she be reported to these wise men. If found guilty, she'd be burned at the stake as a witch. Not even her father could save her, assuming he was still alive to try. Keriam said a silent prayer to Talmora, the Earth-Mother Goddess, to keep her father safe. Shifting her position, she thought hard. She must warn her father of the plot against his life without revealing her means of discovery. Would he believe her? He had to. She pushed her woolen bedcovers aside and slid out of bed, tired and groggy but determined.

No one must ever learn how truly different she was.

* * *

Keriam joined her father for the midday meal in the vast dining room with its flagstone floor and high, majestic ceiling. As was the custom in Avador, they'd left an empty place for the Goddess. Keriam enjoyed this time with her father, and she knew he did too, when they could share thoughts and concerns, a time when she could learn more about the kingdom, its people, resources, and government.

"Since I have no other children," King Tencien had once said, "you will inherit the throne. Best you learn about the country you will govern--its customs, languages, everything."

The plot against her father sent her heart pounding and drove every other thought from her mind. By Talmora, she would not permit those officers to get away with murder. She'd always found comfort in this room with its beautifully polished wooden walls, where each board was painted a different color from those above and below, so that the sides of the room presented a radiant variety of bright colors. But she found no solace this day.

"Father, you should have an official taster," she suggested as he sipped his white wine. Twisting her hands in her lap, she tried to look nonchalant, but fear for her father burned inside her. And hatred for the men who planned to kill him.

"Why, Kerry? You think someone would try to poison me?" He gave her a sharp look. "Why do you make this suggestion now?"

"It's a constant worry." Aware of her lame reply, she dipped her spoon into the spiced potato soup. Goddess, she prayed, help me save this man who means more than life to me. "You're too trusting," she said, resolved to lead into warning him of the plot.

"Not trusting, just realistic." He pressed his fingers to his temples. "A headache coming on," he murmured, then straightened up. "If someone wants to assassinate me, they'll succeed. There's nothing I or anyone else can do to prevent it."

"But of course you can! Arrange bodyguards, and--"

"Won't matter. There have always been skilled assassins, paid well, I might add.. I flatter myself that I'm popular with my people, but remember, there are those who crave power. They'll stop at nothing to get what they want."

Yes, I know! Keriam wanted to say. Tell him of the plot now, her heart urged her. She licked her lips and swallowed hard. "But what if someone--"

"Enough!" He slashed his hand through the air. "No more talk about assassination. I have a splitting headache and King Barzad is expected any day now. I have enough on my mind about the treaty."

A cold lump settled in her stomach. What had she accomplished with her ineffective warning? For now, she'd let the matter drop, but she must face--and deal with--the danger to her father. She finished her buntata soup, resolved to conceal her fear. The dining table occupied a spot close to the large stone fireplace that dominated the wall, and although heat from the burning embers drew much of the chill from the room, fright tremors raced down her arms and legs.

"Tell me about this treaty between our country and Elegia," she said, hoping to divert her mind. They both waited while the servants entered the room and served steaming plates of rice and chicken breast roasted with sage, thyme, and coriander.

"Pending treaty," he said after the servants left. "Since Avador is a land-locked country, we need a seaport to get our iron ore, lumber, and most important, our salt, safely to port and thus to markets. As it is now, brigands prey on our caravans, and we must pay Elegia for protection. A treaty to ally our two countries will benefit both."

"Can't our army provide protection for our goods?"

King Tencien shook his head. "Most of the robberies occur within Elegian territory, directly north of the border. King Barzad doesn't want our forces in his domain. He has a strong army, but often these brigands slip past his men. That situation will change if and when we sign this treaty."

"Tell me, what does Elegia get out of this treaty?"

He beamed at her. "Good thinking. The king needs a wife to provide him with an heir. My widowed sister should solve that problem. We know she can bear children."

"Father, using women as bargaining pieces between nations is an abomination of all the Earth-mother Goddess holds dear."

"I've discussed the matter with her." He reached for a bronze flagon and poured them more wine. "She has no objections."

A short period of silence followed. Desperate for distraction from her nagging worries and stymied by her father's obstinance, she let her mind flit from one subject to another.

Magic. The word crept into her thoughts like a snake slithering along the ground. Why did no one ever speak of it, as if it were a shameful secret to keep hidden away in the darkest recesses of the mind? She didn't practice the craft--the Goddess forbid! She couldn't practice magic if she wanted to. But was it wrong, and if so, why? With a cautious look at her father, she broached these questions.

"We don't speak of magic," he warned with a sidelong glance her way, "lest if, by our words, we bring the offense back to Avador."

"Why not? What's wrong with magic? Every time I've asked this question--and you know I have many times--you've put

10

me off, told me I must never mention it. Why do we never talk about it?"

His gaze swept the spacious room, lingering in every corner. He lowered his voice, prompting Keriam to lean closer. "Wizards ruled Avador with their magic over one-thousand years ago, good magic, mind you, to heal the sick and promote peace and well-being." He sipped his wine and set the bronze goblet on the long wooden table.

"After a century or so, a few evil wizards gained power, and with their power, turned good magic to bad. They executed those who defied them, starting with the good wizards. Caused such havoc and wickedness in the country that life became unbearable for those who tried to live by the words of the Earth-mother Goddess. Even suspicion of treason would send the accused to the dungeon. Informants were rewarded, so neighbor told on neighbor. Children were tortured in front of their parents." He shuddered. "A terrible time. After hundreds of years of this evil and oppression, my great-great-great-grandfather--an army officer--led a revolt."

"Yes, yes," Keriam said, impatient to hear more. "I learned about this revolt in my studies years ago, but no one ever told me how our ancestor rebelled. No matter how many times I questioned my governess, she told me the manner of rebellion was not important. Of course, it's important!"

Tencien nodded. "Yes, you're old enough to understand now. Our ancestor, Malachy, gathered a force of several thousand men, and in one final battle, defeated the evil sorcerers and their minions. The sorcerers' rule ended, and the House of Moray was created. King Malachy united all the tribes and ended human sacrifice--"

"Human sacrifice!" She clutched her stomach.

"Beheading, garroting. Now you see what evil the wizards caused.." He dabbed his linen napkin across his forehead. "Since Malachy's victory, magic has been outlawed from the kingdom, upon pain of death. Daughter, you know I am a merciful man, but anyone caught dabbling in witchcraft must be burned at the stake."

* * *

After leaving their horses at the stables on the outskirts of Moytura, Keriam and Maudina wandered the winding cobblestone streets, the young maid with wide-eyed curiosity, Keriam with a definite purpose. Shoppers, merchants, and sightseers crowded the streets on this busy day, voices of men, women and children in many accents filling the air. The scents of spices and roasting meats drifted in the breeze as food vendors hawked their refreshments. Within a short while they reached Keriam's destination, the marketplace in Talmora Square. Despite her fascination with the city, she thought hard to devise a scheme for escaping her maid's constant surveillance.

From previous trips to the city over the years, she knew her father's officials often frequented these stores and shops in their leisure time. Since today was market day, surely they would have time off, and if luck was with her, she might see one of the plotters.

Palace officials or royal guests were the only people who ever recognized her in Moytura, since the common people never expected the princess to do her own shopping in the marketplace. To be on the safe side, she always dressed plainly but in good taste, with little adornment or hint of her royal rank. Her pale blue linen dress fluttered around her ankles, and she drew her dove gray woolen cape closer across her chest, hoping the bright sun would soon chase the chill away.

They'd already passed the bakeries and candy stores, the aromas of cinnamon bread and chocolate wafting in the cool breeze. The shops became finer and more ornate as they reached Talmora Square, a section of the city dedicated to the Goddess. Sentries in their dark gray uniforms patrolled the streets to protect the citizens from robbery or other crimes. Occasional oak and rowan trees dotted the cityscape, with benches beneath: pleasant places to rest and relax.

Laid out with winding, convoluted streets to discourage foreign invaders, Moytura presented an intricate arrangement of byways and alleys that challenged all newcomers. Keriam knew every street by heart and where to make her purchases, whether it be perfume, silk scarves, or vases. Today, however, she didn't have shopping in mind.

Her head turning right to left, she passed the remaining stores without a second glance, ignoring a juggler and the dancing monkey, although at any other time their antics would have amused her.

"I'm thirsty, madam," Maudina said. "Couldn't we stop at a tavern and--"

"Yes," Keriam snapped, then quickly repented her impatience. "Only wait until I see . . . um, something I want to buy."

"Madam, we've passed all kinds of pretty clothes and jewelry, just the sort of things you like." She peered at Keriam. "Are you looking for someone?"

"Of course not," Keriam said. "Really, you have a very lively imagination. Now if you'll only "

Ah! Clad in a deep green tunic and leather belt that reflected the sunlight from its wide surface, Roric Gamal stood outside the silversmith's shop, talking to an older man Keriam recognized as a wealthy and influential merchant. Was the major enlisting his help in the plot against her father? Goddess damn this man!

A fur-trimmed plaid cloak rode his broad shoulders, billowing in the breeze, his dark brown hair swirling around his neck. A sheathed sword dangled from his belt, the scabbard expensive and finely-wrought, she could tell even from a distance. Her father must pay him a good salary, she fumed, this man who would betray him. He looked for all the world like a casual shopper, like one who had nothing better to do than while away the hours in the city. The man should be an actor! Her body tensed, every muscle taut with fear for her father and hatred for this traitor.

She had to get away from her maid, had to contrive a meeting with this betrayer.

After one more hasty glance in the direction of the silversmith, Keriam drew a copper piece from a velvet purse attached to her belt and pressed the coin into her maid's hand. "Here, take this and buy yourself a cup of tea," she said, nodding toward the Black Boar. "And buy yourself something pretty with what's left over." She made a shooing motion. "Now go. You can meet me here later."

"Well, I guess it won't hurt to leave you for a few minutes. Thank you, madam."

Thank the Goddess! Keriam hurried on, weaving her way purposefully among the crowds, almost bumping into a little boy dragged along by his mother. She kept the major in sight, wondering how much longer her luck would hold, so afraid he'd soon disappear.

She stopped a few feet from him, as he was bidding his companion goodbye. Her face set in nonchalance, she strolled in front of him. Unclasping her ivory bracelet, she let it fall to the ground.

"My lady."

She turned in feigned surprise. "Yes?"

Roric Gamal handed her the bracelet. "Is this yours?" A hint of recognition touched his face, gone so quickly she wondered if she'd only imagined it.

She smiled. "Thank you. How careless of me." Taking the bracelet from him, she pretended to lose her balance and pressed her hand to his arm to steady herself. An image of him and General Balor flashed in her head, the two of them together--scheming? A jumble of his emotions rampaged through her head--sorrow and fear, worry and guilt, but above all, determination and pride. Each emotion conflicted with the others, a fierce struggle that made her head pound.

She swayed as the ground tilted around her.

"My lady, are you unwell?" He reached for her arm, then let his hand drop to his side, a look of concern on his face.

Grappling with her dizziness, she brought her mind back to reality. "I . . . I don't know what came over me." Lightly, she touched her forehead. "A slight headache but nothing to worry about, I'm sure."

"I hope for your sake you don't have a fever." He placed his hand under her elbow, a gesture that prompted a hot rush of anger, intensifying her pain and dizziness. Talmora! Ban this man from the Otherworld. She wished she could kill him now with her bare hands, choke every breath from his body.

"Permit me to lead you to the inn," he said, nodding toward the Snow Leopard. "Perhaps their healing tea will make you feel better." He smiled her way. "We can hope, anyway."

Why not? This was what she wanted, the perfect opportunity to discover more of the conspiracy, in a clandestine way, of course. Fighting to keep her anger in check, she knew he mustn't appear too anxious.

"I appreciate your kindness, but I should go home soon." She pressed her hand to her forehead, matching her slow step with his. "Oh, my head is still pounding."

"Then it's just as well we've reached the inn," the major said, opening the heavy oak door for her. "And may I say, madam, it surprises me to see such a fine lady without her maid."

She made a dismissive gesture as he led her to a round table in a far corner. "Oh, well, the girl is somewhat flighty, wanting to see this, looking at that, stopping at all the stores. So I left her to gaze to her heart's content."

The dining room appeared dark as night after the bright sunshine, and she had to focus her eyes to get her bearings. Swallowing hard, she determined her fury would not get the best of her. She suppressed a shiver as the major helped remove her cape, then slid his cloak off, hanging them both on a rack next to their table. She didn't want him touching her.

Her glance covered the dimly-lit room, where beeswax candles burned in iron sconces and deer and elk heads dotted the walls. A stained glass window of red, blue, green, and yellow lined a far wall, the colors appearing dull now, the sunlight at the wrong angle. The aromas of ale and roast beef wafted in the air, although only a few customers patronized the inn at this mid-morning hour.

Roric looked up as the innkeeper came to their table. "Spiosra tea for the lady and ale for me." He glanced her way. "Is spicy tea agreeable with you?"

"Tea is fine." If she could drink it without choking, she fumed, her stomach knotting with hurt anger.

"I believe your excellent honey cakes might be in order, too," Roric said, looking her way again.

"Very good, sir."

After the innkeeper walked away, Roric leaned closer, his elbows on the table. "Madam, let us be honest with each other. You are the king's daughter, so no use pretending otherwise."

"I wasn't pretending. You didn't ask my name, which is Keriam.."

"Yes, of course."

"I saw no reason to give you my name or to ask yours." You traitor!

"Which is Roric Gamal," he responded, inclining his head, "formerly an army officer but now a courier for your father, since we have been at peace for so long. Although," he said with a slight smile, "I've retained my officer's rank."

"Yes, I've seen you at the palace many times." And after today, she agonized how she could bear to see him at the palace again, this conspirator who would kill the king--her father!–and wreak such havoc on the kingdom, doubtless for the gold it would garner him.

An amber pendant dangled from a gold chain around his neck, glimmering in the candleglow, and a heavy gold signet ring caught her attention. Directly above his heart a palace emblem was stitched on his tunic, evidence he served the king. As a child, she'd learned the words emblazoned there, we will keep faith. And with whom was he keeping faith? Not her father or the kingdom. May the Goddess strike this man dead!

He gave her a cautious glance from under his lashes while he drummed his long fingers on the table. "Are you feeling better now, madam?" he asked after a period of uncomfortable silence.

"Much better. I don't know what came over me." What a lie, she thought as so many sensations still roiled inside her. Her breathing came fast and hard, chills racing along her arm.

The innkeeper returned with their order, distracting them momentarily from further conversation.

Keriam disregarded the sights and scents of the dining room, aware she needed all her faculties to deal with this devious man. She reached for her cup of steaming tea, agonizing how much longer she could keep up the pretense, ready to fling the hot brew in his face.

He slid the plate of honey cakes toward her. "Please, have one of these. I assure you they are quite delicious."

She took a careful sip of the spicy tea, then set the cup down with a shaky hand. "Sorry, I'm afraid I have no appetite at this hour, so soon after the morning meal." She strove to keep her voice even, for surely her anger would give her away.

"How long have you served my father?" she asked, playing for time.

Raising the mug to his mouth, he paused. "For eleven years, since I was a lad of twenty."

Twenty, she thought in surprise. Her age.

"Tell me, what is your opinion of the king? Do you think he's a good ruler? An honest answer, please." As if he would tell her the truth! The Goddess-damned traitor! If she had a knife, she'd kill him now.

"If I considered him an incompetent ruler--which I don't-- do you think I would tell you? Or that I would serve him? Don't be naive, Princess Keriam."

"Naive?" she asked with raised eyebrows.

He dipped his head. "My apologies, princess. But if revealing my honest opinion could prove harmful to me, I would surely not confide in you, of all people."

"No, I suppose not." She gave him a level look across the table. "The king's wish for an alliance with Elegia is no secret. What do you think of this plan?"

Roric drank his ale and set the mug down. "A good idea. Such a union would greatly strengthen the country. Avador badly needs a seaport, an easy means of getting goods and supplies into the country and exporting our merchandise." He nodded. "I'm in favor of an alliance with King Barzad."

Liar! She recalled his words the night of her spectral travel, his plans to kill her father. Her turmoil increased, waves of anger pulsing through her body, her heart thudding, her hands clenched in her lap. How could he sit here and feign innocence, pretend to go along with her father's wishes, when all the time he plotted to assassinate the king!

"Madam . . ." The major leaned forward, looking worried.

Fury raged inside her, an emotion she felt powerless to control. It surged through her body, growing stronger, more intense, making her tremble, her hands shake. She wanted to call back her anger, for it would only defeat her purpose. Why couldn't she learn to harness her abilities, to master them and never let them get the best of her?

Besides, she needed time to discover more about the scheme. She relaxed her hands, trying to present a picture of cool insouciance, knowing that any minute now--

"Princess Keriam, I fear you still have not recovered from–"

--she would explode!

The mug in his hand shattered, the glass flying in every direction, ale spraying through the air.

"What--what?" Blood trickled down his hand and dripped onto the table, leaving red splotches on the wood.

Roric stared at the mug remnant in his hand, then at the spot of blood on the table. "In the name of the Goddess, how did this happen?"

Keriam pressed her hand to her forehead. Why had she let her anger get the better of her? She might never have another meeting with this traitor, another chance to discover more of the plot. Her heart sank, regret weighing her down.

Towels in hand, the innkeeper hustled over in obsequious solicitude. "My apologies, my lord." He handed a towel to Roric and sponged up the blood on the table. "I can't imagine how this happened. These are fine mugs, thick glass, the best money can buy."

"No harm done, just a cut." Roric pressed the cloth to his hand and looked her way, an anxious frown on his face. "And you, madam?"

Jerked back to the moment, she brushed at the spots on her dress. "Only a few drops of ale, nothing to consult the druids about."

The innkeeper clasped and unclasped his hands. "My lord, may I get you another mug of ale?"

"No." Roric waved him away, his gaze on her. "I'm afraid this has turned out to be a rather unfortunate encounter. I'm sorry, Princess Keriam."

"Not your fault. I'll survive the experience."

A gradual rise in temperature and a brightening in the room revealed the passage of time, the stained glass windows shining like jewels. She must fetch her maid and return to the palace, else her father would worry. He wanted and expected her to join him for the midday meal. A rush of affection for her father swept over her, coupled with regret that she was no closer to rooting out any information about the plot or the plotters. This meeting had been a waste of time. But perhaps not. It had taught her one thing: she must learn to control her power, use it only to serve her purpose.

Most important, she must save her father.

Chapter Two

Tired and dust-covered, Roric cantered his chestnut along the Royal North Road, returning from a mission to Galdina. King Tencien had sent him to this adjoining country with a message for the Galdinan king, informing him that a new ambassador would soon arrive to ascertain the country's neutrality should Avador form an alliance with Elegia...

He approached the village of Cairn on the outskirts of Moytura, a hamlet consisting of a few scattered houses and farmsteads, built around a sacred pile of stones that gave the place its name. His fears canceled all thoughts of his recent meeting. He must find a means to protect King Tencien from the plotters without revealing his hand too soon. First, he had to discover the names of the other traitors, and when the time was right, he'd turn the names over to the king. By that means, he'd deny the conspirators any chance of escape. But how much longer could he pretend to be part of the scheme? How much longer before he was discovered?

He thought of his wife and baby son, dead these many years. Goddess! How he missed them. If only he had Branwen lying beside him at night, this woman he'd loved above all others. But he had consigned them both to the past, where all painful memories belonged.

What about Princess Keriam? Despite his problems, he smiled, fully aware their meeting in the city square hadn't been an accident. He'd seen her study him out of the corner of his eye. So what was her purpose, and what–

A scream shattered the late afternoon stillness. Talmora's bones! The horse reared, and straining on the reins, Roric brought him under control. He struck his spurs to the horse's flank, closing the distance between him and an old woman who thrashed on the ground outside a hut, suffering a beating from three young thugs.

Her skirts pushed past her knees, her arms crossed in front of her face, she kicked at the bullies, vainly trying to fight them off.

He reined in the horse and swung to the ground. "Stop!" Whip in hand, he strode toward the boys. They halted their battering, their faces defiant but wary.

The old woman moaned and struggled to rise. Blood streamed down her cheeks, cuts and bruises spotting her arms.

"She's a witch!" one of the boys cried. "Everyone in the village knows she practices magic."

Magic! Like a curse, the word ricocheted through his brain and chilled his arms and legs. Ignoring his fear, he cracked his whip, the sound like a clap of thunder. "All of you be gone, before I take my lash to you."

The boys backed away, faces set in obstinacy. "You'll be sorry you stopped here," one of them said. "She'll cast a spell on you."

His heart galloped. Pretending indifference, he waved his hand. "Be off, I said."

The boys spun around and raced down the path, leaving clouds of dust behind, until they became specks in the distance.

Propped up on one elbow, the woman groaned and pushed her skirt down. "Sir, I . . ."

Roric knelt beside her. "Don't try to talk." First checking for broken bones and finding none, he carefully lifted the old woman. His quick eye noted flowers bordering the house, new shoots of corn and other vegetables sprouting in the backyard, a steam house several yards distant. He carried her to her dwelling, a wattle-and-daub hut that squatted on a small plot of farmland. The front door stood open, and he stepped inside the dark room with one lone window, his eyes needing time to adjust to the dimness. After a few seconds, he carried her over to a small bed against a far wall and carefully set her down.

Dried herbs hung from the ceiling, their spicy fragrances scenting the room. The smell mingled with the aroma of onion soup that simmered in an iron cauldron over the sweet-smelling peat fire. A quilt-covered wooden chest sat below the peg, a wash tub close by. A small but neat house, one he'd never associate with a witch.

In a far corner, a black cat jumped to its feet and arched its back, hissing before slinking through its own small door in the wall. Roric's stomach tightened. Had the boys spoken the truth? Was this cat the woman's familiar?

He headed for the stone hearth and dipped a flannel cloth into a pan of water hanging from a trammel. "Now let's tend to your wounds, madam . . .?"

"Radegunda," she replied in a raspy voice. She shoved her matted hair from her face, revealing a lump already forming on her forehead. A patched gray russet dress and shabby shoes evidenced her poverty. "The boys spoke the truth."

He paused, water dripping from the cloth in his hand. "The truth?"

She changed her position, the bed creaking. "I am a witch, but I practice only good magic."

No such thing as good magic. This sorcery had killed his wife and baby son. His chill deepened, near painful in its intensity, as if he were frozen in ice. He stifled shivers and focused on her words. The evil craft must be stamped out, never again permitted to gain a foothold in the kingdom.

He faced her, a hard set to his mouth. "Magic is an offense in the kingdom, punishable by death. You know that."

"Is it wrong to heal people?" She raised her hand to the dried herbs. "If you have a stomach ache, ginger's the thing. A headache? Nothin' beats feverfew. And I'll wager you have sore muscles from ridin'. Oregano's the best herb for sore muscles."

"Yes, yes," he said, waving a hand. "Common knowledge."

"But what if you wanna love potion?"

"I don't want to hear it!"

"Fennel!"

"Herbs anyone can use. That is not magic."

"Ah, but I c'n do so much more. I c'n–"

"Stop! Not another word!" Wringing out the cloth, he crouched down beside her, dabbing the rag across her face, neck, and arms. He worked quickly, anxious to leave, to escape the taint

22

of sorcery. "If you can practice–" He stumbled over the word– "magic, why couldn't you make the boys stop beating you?"

"Didn't get the chance. They were on me before I realized what'd happened."

"I see."

Finished with his task, he dropped the cloth beside the bed and stood. "For your own good, you must stop practicing his abomination. Heal others if you want–yes, that's all very well–but I warn you never to use sorcery again."

"'Tain't nothin' wrong with magic."

"Madam, beware how you talk." He paused, arms folded across his chest. "I could throw you over my horse and take you to the druids' tribunal for interrogation."

Radegunda cackled. "And I could change into a rabbit. You'd look mighty silly takin' a rabbit to the druids."

Like a spider, fear crept along his spine. "Don't even speak such blasphemy," he whispered. At a loss for more to say, he made a small bow. "May the spirit of the Goddess watch over you."

"I watch over myself."

"Enough!" He turned toward the door.

"Wait!"

He spun around. "Madam, you've said far too much. Consider yourself fortunate that I don't report you to the authorities." He pointed a finger at her. "But one thing I promise you. If I find you practicing magic, I shall turn you over to the druids. After your trial–in which you'll be found guilty, of course–you'll be burned at the stake."

A smile creased her weatherbeaten face. "I'm an old woman, skilled in herbs. I could end my life tomorrow, and maybe I will. But let me tell you–"

"Hush!"

Another smile, a sly one, this time. "Someday you may have need of my magic."

"Don't flatter yourself, madam."

"Well, for now, I do appreciate what you done for me, savin' me from those young boys."

"Happy to hear that," he said, not caring if she caught the sarcasm in his voice.

Blinking his eyes, he stepped out into the sunlight, heading for his horse that waited patiently, munching on the grass. Much as he dreaded the task, he considered it prudent to return in the future, to check on her injuries and warn her once more about practicing magic. Despite his horror of the craft, he had no wish for the woman to suffer death by burning. He would not wish that punishment on his worst enemy.

He thought again of his wife and baby son and often wondered if he'd ever recover from their deaths. His heart ached for both of them, even after all these years. Somehow, he must put the past behind him, learn to live again.

He frowned at the reddish glow in the east, the sun sinking below the horizon. With ten miles to ride before he reached his quarters near the palace grounds, he knew the meeting with Balor would have to wait until tomorrow morning.

Balor, the bastard! His stomach turned at the thought.

* * *

As head of the army, Midac Balor resided in a spacious house, and a fine abode it was, Roric thought as he mounted the front steps. A rambling, one story mansion with an adjoining apartment, it stood on a vast acreage, its bluestone reflecting the early morning light. But why does an unmarried man need all these rooms? Roric wondered, lifting the brass knocker. Within minutes, he was ushered into the entryway, an area as vast as a room itself, with a flagstone floor in variegated hues.

Balor emerged from a chamber down the hall and strode forward. "Ah, Gamal, what brings you to my quarters?" he asked in a harsh, grating voice. He stood tall and heavy-set, with florid skin and large-boned hands. A scar, purple and ridged, marred his left cheek. "But of course, you're always welcome here."

Offering the customary army salute, Roric placed his hands across his chest and inclined his head. "General."

"Come," Balor said, "let us forget protocol and have a drink." He motioned for Roric to follow him down the stone steps into the main room, a magnificent area with sheepskin carpeting so deep that Roric's booted feet sank into the rich texture. Floor to ceiling windows framed with purple silk draperies looked out onto a spacious lawn that led down to a manmade pond. Gold brocade sofas arranged in a semi-circled offered comfort, an indulgence Roric must deny himself, for the sooner he finished with his business and left the general, the better.

"My purpose is business," he said, measuring every word, "but it's always a pleasure to visit you." The lie nearly choked him, and he swept an admiring gaze around the room. "Charming house you have here."

"I enjoy it," Balor said, heading for an oaken cabinet. He poured a goblet of wine and handed it to Roric.

Roric spoke in low tones, conscious of the dangerous game he played. Sipping the dry wine, he kept an even gaze on the general. "Several points we must cover before we accomplish our . . . mission. May I know how the army stands in regard to our plans?"

"Need you ask? The army remains loyal to me, as always." He smirked, his dark, beady eyes leveled on Roric. "They'll stay faithful to me, if they know what's good for them. But the men are suffering from boredom–boredom!–I tell you. What's the point of having an army if we don't fight any wars?"

Roric smiled. "Good question." He wondered if the soldiers were truly loyal to the general, or if fear of Balor made them appear so. Surely their allegiance was to the kingdom, not to the man.

Balor raised the goblet and drank deeply. "The sooner we accomplish our goal, the sooner we can move against Elegia." He waved a beefy hand. "Never mind the pending treaty with that country. After I control Avador, we'll move against Elegia, annex it. That way, we gain more land, but more important, a seaport. From there, we can conquer other countries on the continent."

He slammed his hand on the table, a vase teetering. "Avador is the only land-locked country on the continent. I will remedy that situation when I gain the throne. Soon the entire continent will be mine," he said, his face flushed. "Ah, Gamal, I have such plans for the kingdom! To see it great again, as it was during the wizards' rule."

Seeking composure, Roric looked out the high gleaming windows at the many trees and bushes that added grace and beauty to the lawn. Devious bastard! How he'd like to bring him down, along with the other traitors.

He hesitated, aware he must tread with care where Balor was concerned. "Sir, if I may speak frankly–"

"You may, Gamal. Let us forget rank and speak as equals."

"Very well. Elegia has a strong army. I've spoken with their generals–"

"Not as strong as ours." Balor scoffed. "Defeating them will be child's play. And believe me, I can't hold our army back much longer." He grinned. "The soldiers remind me of pleasure women who lack customers."

Roric forced a laugh. The general was much too optimistic about Avador's military might, or did he want to deny the truth? How had this man ever become head of the troops? Hints of his hold over King Tencien came to mind, something about a secret from long ago. The secret was no business of his, but Balor's betrayal of the king was a knife twisting inside him. He had to stop him, had to defeat the plot. But how?

"Are you sure all the officers are loyal to you?" he asked, amazed at his temerity. "Might one of them tip off the king once they know our plans?" A muscle twitched in his jaw.

The general waved a beringed hand. "Never doubt their allegiance to me." He scowled. "I have ways of dealing with traitors. By the time I'm done with any who betray me, that conspirator will be sorry he ever lived. You have no idea the tortures I can devise. Why, I remember a time when I was stationed near the border with Fomoria. One of my fellow officers tried to steal a woman from me. I drugged him and with the help of a few trusted subordinates, took him out in the country where no one would find him. Staked him down near an anthill and poured honey on him." He laughed. "You should have heard him screams days later. It took him over a nineday to die."

A jolt of alarm slammed through Roric's gut. Nausea churned in his stomach, and he struggled to gain control of himself. "Didn't anyone wonder where he had gone? Did no one discover him?"

"Everyone except my subordinates thought he had deserted . . . at first. But I left it to them to spread the word. After he died, I ordered them to bury what was left of him." He grinned. "So you see, Gamal, no one gets the best of me." Balor set his empty goblet on top of the cabinet, and Roric followed suit. "Enough talk," he said, opening the door onto a stone porch leading down to a garden. "Now let me show you my roses." He smiled widely. "I'm expecting a prize in the upcoming flower show."

Roric stepped outside, shading his eyes in the bright mid-morning sun, where the aroma of roses and newly-scythed grass scented the air. He followed the general several yards from the house to the rose bushes, the grass soft and dew-laden beneath his high leather boots.

"Here, see this one?" With infinite tenderness, the general fingered a yellow beauty. Tiny dewdrops glowed like crystals on its delicate petals, its fragrance sweet and spicy. "I intend to enter this one in the show." He moved on. "But come, let me show you others, every bit as lovely."

Balor stopped, his mouth working. "Delbraith!" he snarled, the name catching Roric by surprise. "Watch out for him."

Roric slanted a look his way. "The king's secretary? Why?"

"I think he suspects us. He may warn the king."

Roric fingered the petals of an apricot-colored rose, his stomach ice-cold. "How would he know of our plans?"

"Perhaps someone tipped him off." A look of cruel cunning infected Balor's face. "Don't worry. I have my ways of dealing with traitors."

He swallowed hard, glad Balor was turned away, the general's attention on his roses. "What will you do to Delbraith if you discover he's betrayed us?"

Balor spun around. "Why, he'll suffer as any traitor would. I'll not be as lenient as our king." He placed his hand on Roric's shoulder, and the major suppressed a flinch. "Remember one thing. You're either my ally or"–He jabbed a finger at Roric's chest–"my enemy. Any double-crosser I catch will be skinned alive."

Chapter Three

"What would you like to wear tonight, madam?" Maudina asked, opening the wide clothes press.

"Let me see." Keriam thought about the vagaries of life. Only recently, she'd overheard three men plotting her father's assassination. Now she must decide what to wear for a reception. Her mind roiled with fears for her father, a torment that kept her awake at night, yet she had to pretend that all was normal. Goddess! It wasn't easy.

She snatched her mind back to the present. In her linen shift and silk stockings, she sorted through the gowns in the expansive clothes press, her hand easing through the satins, velvets, and other costly materials. She wanted to dress appropriately for the reception and dinner, since she and her father hoped to impress King Barzad of Elegia. If all went well, Tencien and King Barzad would begin negotiations to align the two countries.

She wondered if she'd see Roric Gamal at the reception tonight, then wondered why she should care. Ah, but she knew why. She must find evidence against him, expose him for the traitor he was.

"The violet silk," she said. With her light skin and dark hair, she considered it the best choice.

"The color matches your eyes, madam."

A short while later, Keriam studied herself in her full-length mirror, satisfied that she did, indeed, look her best in the gown with long sleeves and a modest neckline. Cut on the bias, the long skirt swung with every movement. She smoothed a hand along the luxurious fabric, loving its soft, rich feel. Maudina had arranged her long hair in an upswept style, with pearl hairpins and circlet confining the tresses.

Dabbing lavender water on her forehead and behind her ears, she heard a knock on the door. As she dismissed her maid, her father entered the room, beaming with pleased satisfaction.

"You look lovely, Kerry." He gestured toward a wooden bench under the window. "Let's sit down for a few minutes."

"Thank you for the compliment," she said, joining him at the bench. "You look quite handsome." She smiled, sensing his unease, aware this evening's affair meant much to him.

He rested his hands in his lap, his crimson silk tunic drawn to his knees. Gold threads ran through the neck, sleeves, and hem of the tunic, the silk shimmering with each movement. Soft leather boots reached just past his ankles.

He smiled. "I daresay you'll receive much masculine attention tonight."

She winced. Her father had broached the subject of marriage more than once lately. "Father, I–"

"I understand. You don't want to talk about marriage. But Kerry, you're twenty now, and we must discuss the matter soon. We must find you a husband."

"Very well," she said, "but let's wait until a better opportunity. Now is not the time...."

"Of course. I merely brought up the subject because you look especially pretty tonight, sure to turn every male head." He reached over to squeeze her fingers, his hand lingering on hers. With his touch, images flashed through her mind, scenes and voices from long ago.

She saw two men in a tavern, heard the noise and laughter, smelled the beef stew, the beer's malt aroma. Instinctively, she knew the men were her father and Balor, both of them perhaps nineteen or twenty. An argument over one of the tavern maids broke out between Tencien and another patron, soon erupting into a fight.

"Please, gentlemen," the tavern owner cried. "No fights!" But no one listened.

The brawl spread, involving every customer. Fists and tankards flew, chairs smashed over heads, shouts and curses filling the air. With no time to spare, Balor plunged his dagger into the assailant's back, then pulled it out, the weapon dripping with blood.

"Kerry!"

"Let's get out of here," Balor said, while the fight raged around them.

Outside on the street, Tencien heaved a deep sigh. "You saved my life."

Balor slanted him a questioning glance. "What do I get in return?"

'Anything, if it's within my power."

"Anything," Balor repeated. "I'll remember that when you take the throne."

"Kerry, are you unwell?" Her father peered at her, waving his hand in front of her eyes. "You've been in a trance for some time."

Jerked back to the present, she shivered, rubbing her arms. "I ... I had a little dizzy spell. Don't know what came over me." She pressed her hands to her cool cheeks, then drew them away, forcing a smile. "I'm all right now."

"Are you certain? Perhaps we should send for the physician."

"No need for that." She smiled. "See, my dizzy spell is gone already. No doubt I rushed around too much, getting ready." Of all the times she had touched her father, she wondered why she'd never had that vision of him and Balor before. Could it be because of her recent spirit travel, in which the general had figured so prominently?" She glanced at the hour glass atop her dresser. "Oh! It's getting late. Almost time to welcome our guests. You know how I always enjoy meeting new people and greeting old friends."

In the receiving line later, Keriam stood next to her father, greeting each person–over one-hundred–as they approached her. She placed her right hand on the right shoulder of each visitor, the guest responding likewise. Each one moved through the line too quickly for her to pick up any images, thank the Goddess.

A flute, harp, and chimes rendered soft, quiet music, with bell like tones in the background, a pleasant accompaniment to the talk drifting around her.

Keriam braced herself as Balor came into view, her breath quickening. Since overhearing the officers planning her father's assassination, she had used her special ability to spy on the general at night as often as possible. However, she couldn't always summon her power, and so far, had discovered nothing incriminating. But she would not give up.

Reeking of patchouli with its pungent, cloying scent, the general grinned as she greeted him, his gaze sweeping her body. His bushy eyebrows topped dark, ferret-like eyes that appeared to miss nothing, eyes that reflected the man's evil soul. An urge to knife him in the gut made her heart hammer in her chest, every muscle tense. A jumble of images rattled her brain, of sword fights and ants crawling over a man's body, pictures that confused her and sent her head pounding. When he moved on, she released a long sigh and offered a warm smile to the next in line, Conneid Delbraith, her father's secretary.

Roric Gamal was one of the last guests. As he approached her, she schooled her features to present a picture of warm welcome. Several inches taller than she, he was clad in a light brown tunic with gold braid at the shoulders. A dark brown belt studded with amber circled his waist. He was as handsome as she remembered, but a traitor, nonetheless. She vowed she'd find evidence against him, prove his part in the conspiracy. He smiled then, and as she put her hand on his shoulder, all her dark thoughts flew, replaced by an awareness of his maleness, the touch of his hand on her, the feel of his muscles beneath her fingers.

"Princess Keriam." Disregarding his allure and desperate to discover more of his machinations, she deliberately let her hand linger on his shoulder for a few extra seconds, and, like a never-ending cavalcade of revelations, more images raged through her mind. She saw Roric and Balor viewing rose bushes, fingering the petals. Rose bushes? The vision confused her and hurtled countless questions through her brain. All of Roric's emotions collided in her head, worry, despair, but hope, too, an amalgam that blocked clear thought. Above all, she got the impression of goodness, and she released her hand, puzzled about his intentions. She gave a slight shake of her head and returned his smile, incredibly relieved the line neared completion.

At the end of the receiving line, the men gathered around her, as if they'd never seen a woman, Keriam thought with a blend of annoyance and amusement. Should she be flattered, or were they interested only in the wealth and power she would bring to a marriage? Still, their easy talk proved a pleasant change from palace demands.

Palace officials and foreign dignitaries crowded the room, their voices mingling as everyone made light talk before moving to the state dining room. She saw Roric Gamal across the way, deep in conversation with an Elegian general. He caught her gaze and smiled. Without thinking, she returned the smile, her body warming, as if bathed in bright sunlight. She mentally chastised herself for her reaction, for this man was the enemy, and she must never succumb to his ensnarements. In her night travels, she had spied on the major, but so far had obtained no evidence against him. We are dealing with crafty traitors, she thought, swinging her attention back to her guests.

"Gentlemen," she said after a long discussion of Elegian pottery, convinced they'd exhausted that topic, "will you excuse me while I get a goblet of wine?" Thirsty after so long with nothing to drink, she wanted to get away. Besides, she saw Fergus Morrigan, the palace steward, standing alone across the room. She always enjoyed his company.

An Elegian knight made a small bow. Like the rest of his countrymen, he dressed like a dandy, clad in a gold satin tunic, his hair curled in tight ringlets, his feet encased in purple velvet slippers. Yet she knew his foppishness was only for show. Inside, these Elegian males were hard as iron.

"Princess, please permit me the honor." He spoke fluent Avadoran, but with a guttural Elegian accent. "I am ever your servant."

"Thank you, Sir Guleesh," she responded in his language, "but there is someone I wish to speak to. If you'll excuse me, gentlemen?"

Fetching a bronze wine goblet from a passing servant, she saw Fergus approach. A friend and helper for so many years, she'd always admired him.

He smiled her way. "Madam, every man in this room has his eyes on you. Surely some fortunate nobleman will ask for your hand tonight."

She laughed. "Oh, Fergus, not you, too. His Majesty said the same this very evening. But I'm not ready to marry, and when I do, I'll marry for love." What a foolish dream, she fretted, for royal marriages were most always arranged.

A trace of sadness touched the steward's face. "Ah, yes, love. That should be the only basis for marriage. I chose my dear wife for that reason." He sighed. "But since her death, I find it difficult to love another."

"Surely you will find a good woman to care for. I pray to the Goddess that you will." She squeezed his hand, and once more, a myriad of visions exploded in her brain. She saw a woman with blue eyes and silvery hair, and a split second later, the same woman dancing around a fire. Her keen intuition told her this was a vision of the future.

A warning flashed in her head. Beware of this woman.

* * *

As the last faint stars faded from the heavens and the first hint of sunrise touched the western horizon with a lavender glow, Keriam left the palace to walk outside along the graveled garden path. The luscious scent of night-blooming paconia floated through the air, the many flowers waving their heads in a light breeze. Dew glimmered on the grass, sparkling like crystal in the early morning light. The state dinner had lasted for hours, the guests only now leaving for their rooms. With much on her mind and unable to sleep, she had sought solitude away from the talk and laughter that still echoed in her ears. The breeze picked up, loosening locks of hair from the pins, her dress swirling around her ankles. Her slippered feet crunched along the gravel as she moved a few yards from the palace, heading for the small woods behind the palace grounds, and stopped to rest beside a majestic oak. Breathing in the cool night air, she closed her eyes, trying to forget–if only for a while–the threat against her father and the steps she must take to counter the menace.

All about her, tiny fairies slumbered in bushes and tree branches, their silvery wings spread out at their sides, a peaceful expression on their faces. Ah, to know such serenity.

Thoughts of Balor froze her stomach. The previous images of her father and the general continued to bombard her, scenes she'd remember for the rest of her days. Was this the hold the general had over the king, this cunning man who had once saved her father's life? This man, trusted by his soldiers and revered by the nation, now plotted to kill her father.

She may have been pampered and protected as a child, but she was a woman now. It was time to act on her own, make her own decisions. Tomorrow, she would warn her father, beg, do anything to have Balor dismissed from command and exiled, or better still, imprisoned to face trial. On what basis could she make the charges? She wondered as the rising sun gilded the landscape. She could never reveal her means of discovering the plot. It would hurt her father too much if he learned of her nightly journeys. He'd surely suspect she practiced magic.

Dismissing Balor might present difficulties for her father. How popular was the general with his troops? Was their loyalty to the man or to the country? If it was the former, she feared they would revolt at his dismissal.

On her own, she had doubled the outside palace guard, reminding these sentries to be ever alert and never permit any suspicious people past the doors. Those extra men greatly relieved her mind, but much remained to do, matters she must execute in the coming days.

What about Roric Gamal? How did the major figure into the plot? He was more than a lackey, of that she was sure. She intended to find out. And then have him imprisoned to face his punishment.

A crunching on the gravel made her spin around to see the object of her recent thoughts. Her heart fluttered and she quickly tried to suppress her excitement. If this man is the enemy, she wondered, why do I feel such excitement when he is near? She must remain strong, must never succumb to any emotional weakness. He stood in the pale early morning light, but his tall stature, his erect carriage, as if he ruled the land, left no doubt of his identity.

Roric Gamal moved closer. "Forgive me, madam. I didn't know you were here. Didn't mean to disturb you."

"You didn't disturb me, major." Ah, no? Her heart continued to beat fast, her every sense alive to his presence, his dark hair ruffling in the breeze, a slight citrus aroma clinging to him, the fit of his tunic stretched across his broad chest and shoulders." The reception lasted long, didn't it?"

"Indeed. Yet I believe it had the necessary effect on King Barzad. I feel sure he will be amenable to a treaty between our two countries."

But that's not what you want, is it? Roric Gamal would like nothing better than to see her father fail, to see him assassinated! This man is a treacherous liar, she reminded herself yet again. She must always remain vigilant in his presence. For now, she needed to be alone, needed to escape his tempting proximity.

"Time I sought my bed. Goodnight, major."

He made a slight bow. "Goodnight, Princess Keriam. May you sleep well."

Not if he continued to taunt her thoughts.

* * *

Clouds darkened the sky in the west, and thunder rumbled in the distance as Roric rode his horse along the same dirt road he'd traversed the previous week. Now would be a good time to visit that witch, Radegunda, his return from a recent mission having taken him along that route. He would see if her wounds had healed, but more important, warn her once more against practicing magic. His hands clenched the reins as her words came back to haunt him. If I wanted to, I could change into a rabbit.

Memories of his family distracted him from the pang of worry–of Balor's betrayal and the king's safety. His family, he mused with affection. Would he ever find the time to visit them again? It had been a long time since he'd last seen his parents and younger brother and sister. Why, before he knew it, his nieces and nephews would be grown, not even remembering him. But he couldn't leave Moytura now, not when the plot against the king threatened.

Above all, he missed his wife and baby son. But the child had died with Branwen on the day of his birth, both victims of evil witchcraft. Surprised to find tears streaming down his face, Roric brushed them away.

As Donn followed a curve in the road, angry gray clouds gathered above. The horse topped a hill and cantered down into a valley, where trees and bushes grew lush with springtime growth. The wind picked up, the grass and tender new crops flattening in waves, Roric's plaid cloak whipping about him. The smell of rain pervaded the air. Thunder boomed again, then raindrops fell, thick, heavy drops that soon became a downpour. Lightning scorched the sky, shortly followed by another thunderclap. Donn neighed with fear, rearing up on his forelegs. Roric patted the stallion, relieved when his destination came in sight. Within minutes, he arrived at Radegunda's property and pulled on the reins.

The house was gone, only wet, blackened timbers remaining. Scanning the grounds, Roric urged his mount closer. Who had burned the house–Radegunda herself, to escape prosecution–or one of her enemies? If it were the latter, there was no need to question why. She practiced witchcraft, no doubt arousing fear in all who knew her. But where had she gone, or had she, poor woman, burned to death?

He shuddered and dismounted, then strode among the blackened logs, his booted feet shoving aside a cauldron, pans, and iron bedstead, all her belongings that had survived the inferno. The rain came in torrents now, thick sheets of water that blurred his vision. He moved among Radegunda's few possessions, his boots squishing in the mud, all but pulling loose with every step. He raised his tunic bottom to wipe his face, a futile effort, for rain continued to pour. While he surveyed her possessions, the rain slowed to a drizzle, then stopped, the sky gradually clearing, the sun beginning to peek through the clouds. A brilliant rainbow stretched across a vast blue expanse.

From the corner of his eye, he caught a movement in the vegetable garden. He took several steps in that direction, his gaze searching among the carrots, kale, and endive, the many herbs that flourished in the rich soil. After seconds of intense scrutiny he saw the object of his search. His breath caught as he realized what lurked among the vegetables.

A brown rabbit.

* **

A few days following the reception, Keriam joined her father for the mid-day meal. This was their first time together since the gathering, because the Elegian king had stayed for several days, both men occupied with the pending treaty. In spite of her pleadings to talk to her father, Tencien had told her he couldn't spare a moment. She'd fumed for days, mindful of the passing time, of the danger than menaced. She breathed a sigh of relief now at the chance to speak to him. She must convince her father to dismiss Balor.

Candles in iron wall brackets brightened the room on this cloudy day. She picked at her food, pushing aside the lamb chop marinated in elderberry wine, one of her favorite dishes but one she couldn't abide now. How could she enjoy her meal when fear for her father and hatred for the plotters erased every other thought?

The king frowned, his expression a blend of concern and puzzlement. "What troubles you, Kerry? You've scarcely eaten a thing. You should be happy, now that we've signed the treaty with Elegia."

"When does it go into effect?" she asked, toying with her wine goblet.

"Not until the marriage between King Barzad and your Aunt Edita takes place. That will be several moonphases from now."

"Well, of course, I'm happy about the treaty." She set her fork on her plate. Her heartbeat increased with the certainty that she could no longer postpone questions about Balor. She licked dry lips and swallowed hard.

"Balor." She noted her father's startled look, heightening her anxiety. "Why do you keep him as head of the army when–"

"Why shouldn't I?" He threw her a look of challenge. "Since when have you started involving yourself in political affairs?"

Since I overheard the plotters, she wanted to say. She eased her plate aside and folded her hands on the table. "The more I see of him, the less I like him. He seems such a devious person." Spasms racked her stomach, but she affected a calmness she didn't feel.

"The man has his faults. I agree, Balor is crafty. But he saved my life once when we were younger."

Ah, yes her earlier vision flashed before her. Hatred and anger burned inside her, a wish to send the fiend to the Underworld. Goddess, the man was evil! Why didn't her father see that? Or did he, but refused to acknowledge Balor's wickedness? Her father's voice snatched her back to the present.

"So I owe him much," he said. "However, personal feelings have nothing to do with military affairs." He set his bronze goblet down with a thud.

"Father, I fear his intentions aren't honorable. Please dismiss him and–"

"Dismiss him? Out of the question. There are many factors here you don't understand. Most important, he is an excellent military tactician, a talent we will need should we have to fight another war. He inspires loyalty in many powerful people, those whose opinions matter." He sighed. "Deposing Balor could well cause civil unrest. Even if I wanted to remove him–which I don't– I'd need my ministers' approval. Kerry, we could well have a civil war on our hands. Is that what you want?"

"Of course not, but–"

"Sometimes we must make hard choices in life, do things we don't want to do but which are for the best. This is one of those times." He tapped the table. "Balor stays."

She steeled herself to give her father the harsh facts. "What if you knew Balor planned to kill you?"

His arms jerked. "Kill me? Why do you say that?"

She gave him a steady look. "Because I overheard some of his officers discussing your assassination."

"Where did you hear this?"

"In the palace," she lied. She would never reveal her preternatural experience at the time she'd overheard the men by the riverbank.

38

"And Balor? What did he say?"

Her heart plummeted. "He . . . he wasn't there."

A stunned look crossed his face. "If he wasn't there, how do you know he plans my murder?"

"The other men said he was the leader of the plot." Ah, how stupid could she be? She should have thought this through, offered a better argument.

"Who were these men? Could you point them out?"

Still confused about Roric Gamal's intentions, she paused, reluctant to mention him. "I don't know their names."

Tencien shook his head. "For Talmora's sake, you're relying on palace gossip. You don't even know the names of the so-called conspirators. So you have no proof of the general's complicity, or that of the others?"

"Not yet. But I intend to find evidence." Her jaw tightened. "Count on it."

"You do that. When you have proof, tell me."

"What kind of proof do you need, Father–an arrow through your heart? Then will you believe me?" She clenched her hands in her lap, her face flaming. What did she have to say or do to convince him?

He pointed a finger at him. "Until you have evidence, I don't want to hear any more complaints about the general."

Her father was blind to Balor's evil, she realized with a sickening knot in her stomach. Much as she loved her father–and she loved him dearly—she had to face his shortcomings. Although a good and conscientious king, Tencien could not bring himself to remove Balor from command, that evil and conniving man who planned to rid himself of the king. Or did her father fear reprisal if he brought charges against the general?

She glanced at her father from under her lashes and found a thoughtful expression on his face. From past experience, she'd learned what that look meant. Despite his dismissive words, he would consider the matter.

That was the most she could hope for, but what must she do now? Where could she turn? Ah, but she knew the answer. As always, she must rely on herself. She aimed for another spirit journey. She must find evidence against Balor.

And she must deal with Roric Gamal.

Chapter Four

Of all the holy days celebrated in Avador, Keriam enjoyed the Beltane Festival the most. It was a happy time for everyone, the end of cold weather and the start of earrach when sacred bonfires were lit throughout the country, and many sanctified oak trees were decorated with ribbons and garlands of flowers.

But this year, worry for her father overruled anticipation of the special day.

What if the assassins struck during this holy day? Keriam agonized while she headed for her bedchamber one evening. The conspirators had slated the Lug Festival for the evil deed, several moonphases away, but what if they had changed their minds?

Fearing a calamity, she spoke to the major of the guard a few days before the festival. "I want extra guards posted around the dais where His Majesty will speak, also additional guards placed throughout the crowds."

Hafgan raised his eyebrows. "Extra guards, madam? The king has said nothing of this."

"I'm telling you, Hafgan. We must prepare for any eventuality." She dared not inform him of the conspiracy. The fewer who knew of the scheme, the better. Although she disliked using her feminine wiles, she gave him a winsome smile, hoping such a stratagem would persuade him where sheer argument failed. "Do this for me."

He bowed. "Very well, madam. I will do as you command."

The special day arrived, and with a mounted escort, Keriam and her father rode their horses along the Royal North Road toward Moytura's center. At that exalted spot, the king would officiate at the festival's opening, and she would judge in the Avador Flower Exhibition. For this one day, she wanted to pretend that everything in the kingdom was as it should be, but especially that no danger threatened her father. A shadow crept over her thoughts, already erasing her resolution.

What about Balor? Surely he'd entered his roses in the flower exhibition. If given the chance, what could she say to him?

Could she influence his thinking, so that he wouldn't consider assassination?

Roric Gamal had left this morning on a mission for her father, thank the Goddess. One less fear, providing he engaged in no subterfuge while away. Yet how could she be certain? Possibly he was collaborating with other conspirators, even now. She bit down hard on her lower lip, trying to dispel her fears, hoping to find comfort in the journey's pleasant ambience.

The sun shone brightly on the ride north from Emain Macha to the capital, a light breeze lifting her long hair from her back. Puddles after a heavy rain the previous night dotted the dirt road, and occasionally, the horses splashed mud across the pathway. She inhaled the fresh scents along the roadside--lavender, lilacs, the sweet scent of peat, the fresh aroma of grass. The nearby hillsides sheltered new growth, promising a bountiful crop. Spring--her favorite season.

On the outskirts of Moytura, she turned in the saddle toward Tencien as the city's towers and spires appeared in the distance. "Look at all the people," she said, raising her voice. Hundreds lined the dirt road, waving frantically at her and her father, their cheers drowning out all other noises. Keriam and her father smiled and waved at the men, women, and children, she with a sense of pride. "They love you, Father."

But each person was a potential assassin, she lamented, her earlier fears returning.

He reached over to squeeze her hand. "They love you, too, Kerry."

She saw his head move from side to side, a pensive expression on his face, as if he were aware of the danger. Had he taken her warning seriously? She prayed so.

The voices swelled, soon becoming a roar as she and the king neared the center, their subjects crowding the city's every cobblestone street and alley. The breeze picked up, rustling the branches and leaves of the city's oak trees. For this great day, jugglers performed their tricks in the streets, and special booths occupied every spare space, the sellers hawking their wares.

Arrived at Talmora Square with its fountains and greenery, Tencien touched her arm. "I'll warrant the city's whole population is here today, all ten-thousand."

"They're happy, Father. You have ruled your people well." She prayed he'd continue to do so, for many more years.

A dais occupied the city's center, two elaborately-carved thrones atop it, with chairs for other dignitaries, including the king's ministers and the city magistrate. Banners representing the country's provinces rippled in the crisp wind, and above all the others, the turquoise and gold flag of Avador wafted in the wind. The banner bore an emblem of the goddess Talmora seated on a throne, a spear in her right hand, a lion and a squirrel at her feet. Noting the extra guards posted around the platform, Keriam gave silent thanks to Hafgan.

When the king and Keriam reached the dais, officers rushed forward to help them dismount. Tired and sore from riding such a distance, Keriam forced a smile as she reached the ground.

Flowers rained down on them, the people shouting, "King Tencien! Princess Keriam!" Accompanied by Keriam, the king mounted the dais. At his signal, a page blew on a trumpet, and the cheers ceased, all eyes on the king. A hushed expectancy came over the crowd.

He raised his arms. "Herewith begins the Beltane Festival. We thank the Earth-mother Goddess Talmora for winter's end and pray she brings us a fruitful season. Let us all remember our blessings and respect the druids, whose mission it is to help us honor the goddess and keep this country free of magic--"

A shiver raced down Keriam's spine. If he discovered her special powers, would he consider her guilty of practicing magic? Through absolute willpower, she brought her mind back to her father's speech.

"--and may we continue to live in peace and prosperity. Let no family live in want, nor any child go hungry. . . ."He spoke then of the treaty with Elegia, the benefits it would reap. Tencien's speech continued for several more minutes as he shared his plans for the country's improvements--better roads and more bridges, more secure silos for storing grain.

Further cheers erupted, prompting Tencien to raise his arms for silence. "May Talmora watch over us all and guide us in the rightful path. May happiness and good fortune reign throughout the year. Now let the festivities begin. Princess Keriam will join the other judges at the flower show."

Applause greeted this pronouncement as Keriam rose from her throne. With Donall, one of her father's officers, providing escort, she walked the short distance to a cordoned area in the square's easterly section. There, a profusion of blossoms blanketed the space, a pleasing medley of fragrances wafting on a westerly breeze. The princess joined the two other judges, sauntering among the flower displays, in low voices discussing the merits of each exhibit.

She viewed Midac Balor's rose bushes set on a mound, their delicate petals ranging in color from white to pale yellow and apricot, to pink and deep red. What a contrast to the man's ugly soul. Prompted to turn toward the crowd, she saw the general among the spectators, his gaze on her, cold and calculating. His eyes held a trace of challenge, as if daring her to refuse him an award. With a mental shrug, she turned back, focusing on the other exhibits, each one so lovely she wondered how she could make a choice.

After much viewing, the judges reached their decision--first prize for the sweet-smelling phlox, second for the clusters of blue and purple anemones, and third for the water orchids. Along with other displays, Balor's roses received special mention.

It fell upon Keriam to bestow the prizes--a small bag of gold coins for first prize, silver for second, and copper coins for third. Those growers earning special mention received a copper plaque.

When Balor came forward to claim his plaque, his warm smile made her question his motives. "Perhaps first prize next time, madam?"

Deflecting her thoughts from the general as he swaggered away, she considered the sacred bonfire ceremony tonight, a chance to mingle with her people, an opportunity she always anticipated. What if Balor appeared there, too? If so, she must learn more of his devious plans....

When night fell and a multitude of stars and planets decorated the heavens, the celebration moved to the countryside. There, a sacred bonfire blazed on the hilltop and wood smoke floated on the air. Sanctified bonfires burned on other hilltops throughout the country, many of them visible from Keriam's vantage point.

Without fanfare or prior announcement and accompanied by her maid, she rode to Knocktierne Hill, about halfway between the palace and the city. She wanted to mix with the people and get to know them better. Earlier in the day, she'd changed into a plain brown dress, a wool shawl wrapped around her shoulders. She hoped to conceal her identity, for she found people were much more willing to talk to her if they didn't recognize her as the princess.

"Perhaps you'll see friends tonight," she said to Maudina as they clambered to the top of the hill, sidestepping rocks and thick tree roots. "But don't stray far, because I intend to leave within a short while."

"Madam, I'm supposed to keep you in sight."

"Do it, then." Keriam walked away.

Women, having previously extinguished their hearth fires, gathered at the hillside to light torches at the conflagration, these to carry home to rekindle their fires. The men stood back, looking solemn, talking in quiet groups. After making light talk with several of her subjects and gauging the people's feelings, Keriam moved away from the crowd, far from the pungent smell of smoke. Next to an ash tree, she surveyed the kingdom's hills and valleys, its farms and villages. If only the country could remain at peace, if no treason threatened, if her father--

"Ah, the princess herself, come to grace the peasantry with her presence."

Keriam froze, then nodded to the intruder. "General Balor." The flickering flames distorted his features, giving his face an evil cast, a truthful picture, she thought. Yet here was her chance to learn more about him, and if she were fortunate, to gain incriminating evidence. "I trust you're enjoying the festivities."

He hooked his fingers in his wide leather belt, rocking back on his heels. "Oh, I always enjoy these spectacles. Never underestimate the gullibility of the common people, I always say."

Anger heated her face, but she refused to reveal her emotions. "Gullibility?" Her gaze covered his dark tunic with its many medals, his harsh features and facial scar, his predatory appearance.

He waved his hand at the many bonfires scattered throughout the countryside. "As if the Goddess cares what we do! As if there is a goddess!"

She clenched her jaw, then spoke in a tight voice. "General, you utter blasphemy." Talmora, forgive me, she prayed, but please rid me of this fiend. The wind picked up, fluttering her dress around her legs, blowing her hair across her face. She tucked errant strands behind her ears and assumed a neutral expression.

"Don't tell me you believe all this superstitious nonsense. Princess Keriam, I would have thought better of you."

"Then why are you here, if you don't respect the sanctity of the celebrations?"

"As I said, I enjoy these spectacles."

"But it is the Goddess who guides and protects us, who gives us rain for our crops, who blesses our families. General, I should report you to the druids." She regretted her threat immediately.

"But you won't report me, will you? You know the druids will do nothing about it. Besides, I'll deny I ever said anything." He smiled then, or was it a sneer? "But why are we arguing? This night is much too pleasant for disagreements," he said, making a small bow, his mink-trimmed cloak rippling in the breeze.

"Come," he said, "I can think of better ways to spend our time. Let us move farther back, away from the smoke. The sky is especially lovely tonight--don't you think?--with the planets Partholan and Nemed in such proximity to the moon." He offered his arm, and a bombardment of images assailed her. She saw the man in his younger days, engaged in a sword fight, his opponent's sword slashing down his cheek. She shivered.

"Madam, are you cold?"

"My shawl slipped." She wrapped it tighter around her shoulders, struck with disappointment that she'd gained no useful information yet.

Reluctant to wrangle further and mindful of the need to tread with care, she followed him, the light from the bonfire illuminating the way. She maneuvered past bushes and spreading oaks, finally reaching the eastern edge of the hill. Indeed, the stars, planets, and moon shone brightly, not a cloud in the sky. The breeze brought the sweet scent of night-blooming paconia, an aroma that never failed to cheer her . . . until now.

While he turned away for a moment, she judged the distance from the crest to the valley hundreds of feet below. If she could only push him, she would rid the land of this fiend and erase the threat to her father. But no, he stood too far back, and besides, she couldn't murder a man in cold blood.

Balor turned her way again. "Princess Keriam, there's something I've thought about for a long time, and I suppose I should approach your father first. But I find it difficult to resist you. Your presence here tonight gives me an opportunity--"

By the Goddess, what was he talking about?

"--that I can't let this chance slip by me. As you know, I have remained unmarried for all these years--"

Oh, no!

"--but now I consider it time to take a wife. Would you do me the honor of marrying me?"

A stab of alarm jolted her mid section, but she quickly recovered. She must take care with her reply. Why was he asking her, he, who had never before expressed any interest in her? Did he intend to gain control of the kingdom through marriage and not assassination? She wished she knew his intentions. She realized she shouldn't refuse him outright, for it would serve her purpose to play for time. And she must defeat him.

"General Balor, your offer comes as a surprise. I need time to consider your proposal and get my father's permission," she lied, knowing her father gave her free rein on marital matters, as long as she married into the aristocracy. And Balor belonged to that privileged group. "I must admit, your proposal is most appealing."

Another lie. She was becoming very accomplished at prevarication.

"Ah, I'm pleased to hear that. And I understand you need time to consider, Princess Keriam. We'll talk about this again soon, shall we?"

"Of course." For now, she'd accomplished nothing but postpone the inevitable. She wouldn't marry him for all the gold in the kingdom.

* * *

Fergus Morrigan, the palace steward, had an important matter to discuss with Tencien as they sat in the king's office after reviewing the palace accounts. "Sire, I should like to marry again," he said, easing his chair away from the oaken table. Bronze oil lamps hung from the ceiling, and coupled with the sunlight through the wide window, provided sufficient illumination. "Since my first wife died of the black fever years ago, I have been lonely, as you may imagine. The lady I have chosen comes from the village of Mag Bregha--"

"Lovely place," Tencien said. "Been there many times."

Fergus nodded. "Aradia is all a man could want in a wife, sweet and gentle, a true lady, so kind and thoughtful. With your permission, I would bring her here as my wife."

"By all means," Tencien said. "Would you like to be handfasted here at the palace?"

"Sire, she wants the ceremony at a shrine near her home, if that is agreeable with you. After the wedding, we will return here straightaway."

"No need to hurry." Tencien smiled. "A man needs time alone with his new wife."

"Thank you, sire."

* * *

Four days later, Fergus brought his new bride to the palace, and with her silvery blonde hair, blue eyes, and pale skin, Aradia was truly beautiful. Her sweet smile and soft voice endeared her to all the palace staff.

But Aradia was not all she pretended, Keriam discovered a few days after the woman's arrival at Emain Macha when the sound of weeping drew her to Maudina's small room. Keriam knew that her maid often suffered from a difficult moontime, and thus permitted her to rest in bed. And that time is about now, she thought with a quick calculation.

She opened the door and stepped inside. "Why, Maudina, what's wrong?" she asked, sitting down beside her maid. "Your moontime?"

Maudina sniffed. "Oh, princess, the steward's new wife--"

"You mean Aradia."

"Yes. She told me I'm so ugly no man will ever want me." Maudina gave her an appealing look. "Do you think I'm ugly, madam?"

"Are you sure you understood her correctly?"

Maudina nodded. "She said it very plainly. You should have seen the expression on her face."

"Well, of course I don't think you're ugly." Keriam stroked the girl's hair. "Haven't I seen how Traigh looks at you in the stables? And--"

"Really, madam?" she asked in a choking voice. She brushed her hand across her reddened, tear stained face, and Keriam offered her a handkerchief.

"You're not just saying that?" Maudina said, wiping the handkerchief across her eyes.

"I don't make idle comments.. Do you know, I've often envied you your looks--"

"You have?"

"Indeed. Your skin tans so nicely, while mine turns pink and peels. And your hair! So thick and glossy, such a rich shade of brown with golden lights. Ah, Traigh is not the only man who casts you covetous looks."

"Truly?"

"Truly." Keriam placed her arm around her maid's waist, and pleasant images brushed her mind. She saw Maudina and Traigh holding hands, their faces radiant. Dropping her arms, she sat back. She found it difficult to believe that Aradia would make such spiteful remarks, yet she had to accept her maid's account. "Now, promise me you'll ignore Aradia's cruel comments. I feel sure you have a greater chance at happiness than she. That kind often brings trouble on themselves."

And trouble for everyone else, Keriam found the next day.

On a mission for her father, she headed downstairs, past the main hall, then through a long stone walkway that led to the kitchen. She wanted to instruct the cook to prepare chicken broth for the king. Laid low with a feverish cold, Tencien rested in bed, and Keriam considered isean broth as good as any herbal remedy for many respiratory illnesses.

A few steps from the kitchen entrance, Keriam stopped, hearing Aradia address the household staff--cleaning women and cooks--all dwarves. Outside the kitchen, a large, well-equipped pantry provided ample room for concealment, a place where she could listen to Aradia undetected. A statue of Falgeria, the hearth goddess, warded the pantry's entrance.

"I want to tell you how happy I am to be here, as part of the palace family, so to speak." Aradia laughed a little, as though self-conscious at her pronouncement. "We can all do much to improve the palace functions, and as the steward's wife, I intend to do my share. One example, if I may express an opinion. Already, in my short time here, I've noticed many of the children idling about with books. Surely the young ones find reading a boring occupation and would rather do something useful. Much needs to be done, like cleaning, sweeping, and dusting. The children could perform these little chores or run errands. Besides, idle boys and girls can get into trouble."

Bertha, the head cook, spoke in her deep, rumbling voice. "But madam, Princess Keriam has given orders that the youngsters should spend part of the day to read and practice their letters, even if they don't have formal instruction."

"For what purpose?" Aradia asked, a trace of annoyance in her voice. "What good will learning do these children? Far better for them to perform household chores, rather than encourage them to think they can rise above their station. I fear they will be sadly disappointed to discover that all this learning will gain them nothing." Her voice took on a warm note. "Let's try things my way for now. Perhaps we'll find the children are happier performing useful tasks."

So, Keriam wondered as she silently walked away, does the steward realize what a cunning woman he's married? Tempted to confront Aradia now, she feared embarrassing the servants. Just the same, someone needed to explain things to this woman, and Keriam vowed to do so first chance she got.

That opportunity came sooner than expected, when Keriam was leaving her father's bedchamber the same afternoon. Ahead of her, the steward's wife was ascending the stairway, soon reaching the second floor.

"Aradia, I hope you have settled in here. Is there anything I can help you with?" She motioned for the woman to join her at a stone bench that hugged the wall. Statues of gods and goddesses lined the long hallway, and occasional flower vases on oaken tables added a further touch of refinement and grace.

Aradia sat beside her, a heady musk scent wafting from her clothes. Her fingers were delicately-tapered, the nails like dragon's claws. "Thank you, Princess Keriam, but so far, things have gone smoothly for me."

I'll wager they have, Keriam thought. "One thing I like about the palace's workings is that everyone does his share. You'll find--if you haven't already--that everyone is loyal to the king and eager to see that the palace runs smoothly."

"But the children . . ." Aradia hesitated.

"The children?" she prompted. "What about them?"

"Seems to me they could use their time more profitably in chores. They spend far too much time idling about."

"But they are not 'idling about', as you say. They are improving their minds, an endeavor that may help them when they get older. As a matter of fact, I hope to find a capable teacher who can guide them along those lines, teach them their numbers and letters, then introduce them to the country's fine literature."

"Dwarves--the entire household staff! I'm surprised these people aren't working in the mines, where they belong."

Keriam's face grew hot, a muscle twitching in her jaw. "They belong here because I had them brought here. Their fathers were all killed in mine accidents, and their mothers had no one to turn to. Certainly, learning to read and cipher will aid these children if ever they hope to manage a business or own a shop." Keriam stood, signaling the discussion's end.

"But, princess--"

"But that is how I want things done. Do you have any other questions?"

Aradia stood also, a hint of defiance in her expression. Pink spots blossomed on her cheeks. "No, madam."

Reluctant to make an enemy of the steward's wife, Keriam smiled and squeezed her hand. As if scalded, Keriam dropped her hand and stepped back. Images beat against her mind like lightning bolts, visions that confused her and sent her heart pounding. She saw Aradia and Balor, their heads close together, as if planning in secret. She saw a man falling to his death. Who? her frantic mind screamed. Keriam blinked her eyes, praying to Talmora that these images were only empty pictures, visions that would never come to pass.

"Princess, are you ill?" Aradia asked with a worried frown.

Snatched back to the present, Keriam forced a smile. "I'm fine." With a nod, she walked down the long hallway toward her bedchamber.

Was this the woman her vision had warned her about, this virago with the silvery hair? The words came back to haunt her. Beware of this woman.

* * *

Since she was a child, Keriam had always enjoyed the capital city of Moytura. Now that she had reached adulthood, she liked to visit the Treasury of Knowledge, a magnificent sandstone building that housed a collection of rare volumes and fine literature for children and adults–thousands of books. Gathering reading material for the palace children gave her the perfect opportunity for a visit, away from Aradia's spiteful remarks to the servants.

After giving instructions to Maudina to meet her later, Keriam ascended the steps, her walk quick and purposeful, certain the library would contain a wide choice of children's books. A slight dip in each step revealed the library's constant usage throughout the years. . . .

Aware of the passing time, she retraced her steps within a short while, a diverse choice of books in her arms. These books, painstakingly printed and illustrated by the druids and bound in the finest leather, should please the children and entice them to learn.

Mindful of Maudina's tendency to dawdle, Keriam spared a few minutes for herself, an indulgence her palace duties often denied her. She headed across Aventina Way, a broad thoroughfare that separated the cultural center of the city from the meadow and the Plain of Sorrows beyond. At the meadow, she set the books on the grass, then eased to the cold ground. She stretched her legs out and rested under an oak tree, its sacred essence protection against evil. Lost in her private thoughts, she didn't see the man approach.

"I've been waiting for a chance to find you alone."

Chapter Five

"Oh!" Keriam looked up to see Roric Gamal standing beside her, clad in a dark brown tunic and mid-calf high boots, a book in his hand. A thrill of alarm sent her heart pounding, her breath coming fast. She tried to act nonchalant, but how could she pretend indifference toward this conspirator without revealing her suspicion of him? Hatred blazed a path from her head to her stomach. She clenched her hands, then quickly released them, lest he catch her anger. To think she'd returned his smile at the recent reception. This man is a deceiver, she fumed. She must watch out for him.

"I didn't mean that the way it sounded, madam," he said in his clipped speech. "I merely meant I've been looking for an opportunity to discuss an important matter with you. As it happened, I saw you in the Treasury of Knowledge while I was fetching a book on astronomy." He hesitated. "Do you mind if I join you?"

"You're here, aren't you?" Traitor! She waved her hand. "The meadow is open to everyone."

"Thank you." Setting his book on the grass, he sat beside her, drawing one leg up, hands laced together at the knee. He brushed his cloak from his shoulders, revealing the palace emblem on his tunic, We will keep faith. Keep faith with whom? Balor!

For the first time, she noticed his sun-tanned face with its fine lines around the mouth and eyes, his sinewy fingers. Strong hands, those, capable of committing the worst villainy. She struggled to keep her breathing even.

"I've been concerned about the king," he said, his words moderating her gloomy thoughts. Her heart leaped. Did he intend to confess his part in the plot? But no, why would he do that?

"Let me put it bluntly. His Majesty is in danger."

"Danger?" She stopped herself from saying "I know," for he'd wonder at her source of information. "Explain yourself."

"There are some in the kingdom who wish your father harm, and--"

"I can't believe this," she said, still treading a wary path. "Give me their names." Besides Micac Balor and you.

"I beg of you, madam, let that remain a secret for the present. As yet, I don't know all involved in the conspiracy, but I hope to ferret out the traitors soon." His clenched knuckles showed white, a sharp frown creasing his forehead. "It would be . . . unwise to divulge any names now."

She twisted her fingers in the grass, her gaze steady on him. She knew the answer to her next question but wanted to hear his explanation. "How do you know about the plot and the plotters?"

"I'm in their confidence," he said with a level gaze, his look calm.

She tried to conceal her surprise that he would confess. "How so?"

"In my army years under Balor, I worked hard to gain his trust." He paused, drawing the other leg up. "Not because I trust him, mind you, but because I recognize his importance to the kingdom. In all that time, he's made occasional remarks critical of your father, hinting that he could do a better job as ruler. I did nothing to contradict his assessment of the king but played along with his suggestions. In the back of my mind," he said, tapping his head, "it occurred to me that I could use my pretended acquiescence to the kingdom's benefit. So this is why I'm talking to you now."

He let another moment of silence pass, as if collecting his thoughts. "Now, about the king--you have great influence with His Majesty, madam. It might be wise if you suggested a holiday, or possibly a state visit, anything to get the king safely out of Avador. For several months, if possible."

Conscious of the challenge, she shook her head. "He'll never agree to leaving the country, and certainly not for a long period of time. He's always said his place is here with his people. But he needs a rest. I must persuade him to leave."

"Indeed. Otherwise, I fear his life is forfeit. But I ask one favor of you."

"What's that?" She kept a cautious eye on him, still unsure if she could trust him.

"You must never reveal that I warned you of the danger, lest word leaks to Balor, jeopardizing my ability to stay in his confidence. This must remain a secret between us."

"And I will treat the warning as such. Major, your advice is unnecessary." Keriam paused, an obvious question forming. "How do I know I can trust you?"

"Madam, please understand one thing. I'm a loyal subject who wishes your father a long and fruitful reign. He is a conscientious ruler who has done much good for the country. For my family, too." He stared across the meadow. She studied his face while he spoke, his straight nose and firm jaw, his firm lips, then snatched her mind back to his words. She looked at his hands again, and it wasn't difficult to imagine those hands touching her, caressing her. Her face warmed, and she brought her mind back to his words. "Once, years ago, when the king was passing through our village, my father requested an audience." The major swung his attention back to her. "A distant cousin claimed land left to my father. After hearing both sides, King Tencien ruled in my father's favor. So you see, my family owes the king much. But I would be loyal, anyway, and I would not see any harm come to him or to the kingdom."

She'd been mistaken about him all along. Or was his suggestion only a ruse to lull her into believing him innocent, should an assassination--the Goddess forbid!--actually succeed? How could she find out, or would she ever?

As if reading her mind, Roric pressed his right fist to his chest. "Never doubt my loyalty, Princess Keriam. I swear by Talmora, I'd give my life for the king."

Keriam released a slow sigh; to break such an oath was to risk the Goddess's swift punishment and eternal damnation. A swell of relief dizzied her, a heavy weight lifting from her shoulders. So Roric was not part of the plot against her father. Now she had an ally in her quest to keep her father safe. She wasn't alone anymore.

But a deeper reason—one she didn't dare examine too closely—prompted this spurt of happiness.

* * *

Inside the spacious palace library, Keriam bent over to examine the few engineering titles along one shelf, hoping to learn more about building bridges. As her father had said at the Bel Festival, the kingdom--and especially the capital--needed more and better bridges to span its many rivers. The royal library housed a collection of rare books and manuscripts, but more important, engineering books. Floor-to-ceiling bookshelves lined the room, but many empty spaces remained, most notably children's books, a reminder to procure more of those whenever she had a chance.

But how could she concentrate on bridges, when Balor haunted her mind night and day? His marriage proposal returned to taunt her. What should she say if he repeated his offer? She could no longer postpone refusal. She would not marry that fiend.

Bright sunlight through the wide windows turned the tan sheepskin rugs to gold. Burnished wooden shelves and tables shone like glass, and sunshine warmed the room. The windows stood open, bringing a light breeze that wafted the green silk draperies and diffused the scent of hyacinths posing in a bronze vase.

She thought about Roric Gamal and their talk outside the library in Moytura. She stopped for a moment, reliving every moment of their time together, remembering his every facial expression, his deep voice and clipped speech, his long dark hair that fell to his shoulders. A man she could never forget. And didn't want to forget.

Glancing up, she saw someone standing in the doorway. She pushed away from the bookcase. "Conneid Delbraith," she said, beckoning to the king's secretary. "I don't see you very often anymore."

"My misfortune, princess. Please, a moment of your time."

"Of course. Close the door, please." She led him to a sofa in the middle of the room and motioned for him to join her there. Sinking into the soft leather, she gave him an inquiring look.

Although only in his late thirties, Conneid showed gray at his temples, from too much worry? Keriam wondered.

He leaned forward. "Madam, permit me to get straight to the point. His Majesty has been working very hard--"

"How well I know. He should take a long holiday." If only he would.

"My thoughts exactly, but he says he can't neglect the demands of his position." Conneid lowered his voice. "Madam, I fear the king is in danger, but he ignores the peril."

"Danger? What kind of danger?" she asked with caution. Be careful what you say, her brain reminded her. Roric's information about the plot must not be compromised.

His gaze darted about the room. "Don't trust General Balor. He wants to--" He choked on his words--"get rid of His Majesty."

Keriam pretended shock. "Balor, the head of the army! Are you sure of this?"

"As sure as I am of anything. A wily man, the general. Evil would be a better word. He ravished my sister years ago. She's never recovered from such wicked depravity." He bowed his head for a moment, his mouth tight, his gaze on the floor.

"Ah, Conneid!" Tears sprang to her eyes and she brushed them away, unable to say another word.

He shook his head, as if throwing off a burden, then went on. "But it's the present that concerns me, madam. We must rid the kingdom of this fiend who wants to overthrow your father."

"Mind you, I have an open mind, but I'd like to know on what basis you make this assumption. This is a serious charge."

"Once I came across him in a hurried conversation with one of his lieutenants. He stopped talking as soon as he saw me. Oh, I know their talk could have concerned any innocent topic, but why did his lieutenant look so guilty when he saw me? As if he were caught in a crime? Besides that, I've received warnings from others."

"Give me a few moments to consider what you've told me." Silence fell over the library while Keriam's mind worked. She must protect herself and her sources, but at the same time, must thwart Balor. Oh, to rid herself of all this pretense, to say to the world, Yes, I know Balor is a beast, and Aradia, too. But she would fight them as long as she had breath in her body. And she would defeat them both.

After a long moment, she twisted her amethyst ring on her finger, then rose from the sofa. Conneid Delbraith followed. "We must do something, and soon," she said, a hint of steel in her voice. "If what you say is true, we must work before the general's scheme comes to fruition."

"May I ask what you intend to do, madam?"

"We need evidence against the general, someone to spy on him. Can you recommend anyone?" At this point, she didn't know whom to trust. So far, her nightly spirit travels had produced no revelations.

"Princess, I fear I couldn't help you there. Roric Gamal is the man to ask. With his military background and long service with the king, he's bound to know someone who could spy on Balor."

"Roric Gamal," she mused aloud, her heart leaping. "I haven't seen him around the palace lately."

"No, madam. He's on a mission for His Majesty, to Lonan, I believe."

"Very well, I'll speak to him when he returns." She gave him a warm smile. "And thank you for coming to me, Conneid. You have ever been a good friend."

"It's been a pleasure and an honor, princess." He led the way across the carpeted floor and opened the heavy library door for her. One of Balor's officers walked past, sliding a suspicious look their way. What was he doing in the palace?

"Well, that's all I wanted to tell you," Delbraith said in a clear voice. "Just wanted to thank you for helping my wife. She's feeling so much better since you brought those herbs to her."

"Anytime I can help, Conneid." Her heart beat fast as her gaze followed the officer's strides down the long hallway, his boots clattering on the flagstones. She clenched her hands at her side until he disappeared into one of the conference rooms; then she snatched her mind back to immediate concerns. She reminded herself she must not look for conspiracies everywhere, and that most likely his appearance here had an innocent explanation. Despite her best intentions, fear gnawed at her insides. The sooner she had tangible evidence against the plotters, the better.

When Roric Gamal returned to the palace, she would launch her plan.

* * *

Free from palace duties and mindful of the need for divine protection for her father, Keriam left the palace early one afternoon to head for the Nantosuelta River. There, she would pray to the river goddess who would surely watch over her father. Perhaps then Aventina would keep her father free from harm, protect him from the plotters.

Stepping outside the back entrance, she checked to make sure all the guards were in place. She circled the palace, greeting the guards as she passed. Since she'd doubled the outside sentries, she felt more secure in protecting her father, but still she knew an accomplished assassin could commit his evil deed anywhere.

Frowning, she motioned to Hafgan. "One of the guards is missing."

Hafgan turned away for a moment, then looked at her, his face flushed. "He had an errand, madam."

"For His Majesty?"

"No, madam, a personal errand." Staring down, he scuffed his boot on the gravel.

She flinched, as if he had hit her. "And you let him go?"

"Madam, he said it was important and that he would return shortly."

She pointed a finger at him. "Listen, nothing is more important than the king's safety. When he comes back, you must dismiss him. And Hafgan, if this happens again, you will be dismissed."

"I understand, Princess Keriam.," he said, a contrite expression on his face.

She stalked away, hoping the ride to the capital would burn off her anger. After Traigh, the head stableman, saddled Laith, she rode northward to Moytura, past the crops ripening in the fields, the many farmsteads and barns along the way. Desperately trying to dismiss her fury at the guard–and Hafgan---she flipped her hair from her shoulders, thankful for the light breeze on her face. Stone mile markers revealed the many miles slipping past, and after much riding, she reached Moytura. She dismounted at the entrance to the city and walked the horse past the many shops, headed for the meadow.

In the glade, birdsong trilled from the trees, sunlight gleaming through the branches. Ash, oak, and hawthorn branches swayed, the breeze becoming stronger. Shoving her hair from her face, Keriam glanced at two squirrels playing tag in the trees. Considered sacred and protected by royal decree because they were Talmora's favorite animal, the delightful rodents ran rampant throughout the country, numbering in the millions. Aware of the need to complete her act of propitiation, she rode farther on to the Nantosuelta River and tethered Laith to an ash branch.

Keriam sat to tug off her leather riding boots and cotton stockings, then strode toward the wide, winding river, the grass warm and dry beneath her bare feet. A bridge spanned the water farther down, but her ritual would mean little if she took such an easy means of execution. The burbling sound of the rushing water cloaked all other noises--the birds' singing, the insects' buzzing. Clusters of trees lined both sides of the river.

Tucking her dress and shift inside her belt, she headed down the sandy bank where sun- light glistened on the rippling azure water.

Unlike the moderate air temperature, the river felt ice-cold when she first stepped in. She gradually became accustomed to the temperature as she waded farther out, the water undulating against her bare legs. Toward the middle, she found the river swift-flowing and deep but continued on. What would the riverine goddess think of her if she'd stopped at the shallow end, unable to brave the current? The violent force of the current nearly knocked her down, but she kept her balance. When the water reached her waist, she stood in silence for a few moments, then bowed her head in prayer.

Aventina, please keep my father safe from all danger. Guide him well, that he'll always do right by his people. Let no misfortune come to him, and let him continue to rule for many more years. Watch over our people, that they may continue to live in harmony, peace and prosperity. May we always live by the teachings of the Earth-mother Goddess, and honor her and you for the rest of our lives.

Keriam eased her gold torque from her neck and tossed the adornment out, the sunlight glinting on its shiny surface, the torque landing with a tiny splash. Praying further that the offering would satisfy Aventina, she headed back to shore, releasing her wet clothes from her belt, letting them fall to her ankles.

She brushed the soles of her feet, then retrieved her stockings and boots and sat to pull them back on, then made her way toward a rowan tree. She sat down and spread her dress out evenly across her legs, hoping the sunlight would soon dry her clothes. As always, Balor sent a shaft of hatred to her stomach, where it settled like a cold ball.

Would her prayer and offering protect her father? But Balor wasn't the only threat, she worried, shifting her position. What about Aradia? Or were the steward's wife and Balor working together?

She tightened her jaw. Aradia would bear watching.

Chapter Six

The light of a full moon shone through Keriam's bedchamber window, the night air cool with a southerly wind. Unable to sleep, she focused her thoughts on the steward's wife, fearful Aradia would bring discord to the palace . . . and the king. Indeed, she'd caused enough trouble already. A vague disquiet nudged her mind, a sensation that soon became a roaring suspicion. She had often wondered why these feelings of intuition came to her, but had gradually accepted that they were part of her strange powers. And she had learned never to doubt these warnings. What was Aradia doing now? Possibly I am wrong this time, she thought, and my fears are for nothing. No doubt the steward's wife lay in bed with her husband, where she belonged. But if she was elsewhere?

She must discover what Aradia was up to.

Closing her eyes, she kept her mind clear. She breathed rhythmically, her mouth slightly open as she lay quiescent, then drifted into a twilight state, with only a vague awareness of her surroundings. Minutes or hours later, a numbness crept over her body, her limbs paralyzed. She departed her body, and she looked down to see herself in bed, asleep.

The steward's suite occupied a portion of the floor above, and Keriam floated along the walls, then upwards until she reached their bedchamber on the next floor. After she listened outside their door for several moments, she slipped through the thick walls, stifling qualms about this intrusion on their privacy. The steward's snores told Keriam he slept soundly, but alone. Where was his wife? Outside the palace?

Quick! Find her! Chafing at her slow progress, she drifted through the palace walls, then floated above the earth. From her high vantage point, she could see the entire grounds below: the magnificent bluestone palace and the stables. Bushes, flowers, and an occasional tree bordered a lake close to the royal residence, opposite the stables. The royal cemetery occupied a small space close by the lake.

About a half-mile to the west stood the army barracks and a cluster of military housing for the officers, including Balor's, his mansion set apart from the others. A small woods of rowan, ash, and oak sequestered the palace grounds from the military housing. Meadows and open fields extended beyond.

The smell of pungent, musky smoke drew her downwards to the far edge of the woods, a smell carried north by the wind. Chanting urged her nearer, and she skimmed along the wet grass, always within the trees' concealment. To be certain no one would see her arracht she hid behind an oak. Clouds drifted in front of a full moon, hindering her vision, then gradually floated across the sky to reveal a woman beside a fire. Keriam blotted out the night sounds, all her concentration on the woman, now visible by the bright moonlight.

Aradia danced in a circle around the fire, her silvery hair streaming down her back.. Her chanting intensified, blending with the crackling of the flames. Face gleaming by the firelight, she shook a wooden rattle, her dark bedgown fluttering around her ankles. A knife glinted in her other hand. A knife! Talmora, why?

Motionless behind the tree, Keriam listened to the chant.

"Goddess of darkness, demon of the night, the night, the night! Endora, grant my wish, my wish, my wish!"

Aradia knelt and grabbed a bird from the ground. Its wing broken, it flopped helplessly in her hand, its loud squeaks echoing through the trees. Eyes aglow with menace, Aradia chanted over it in a strange language, then slit its neck. Holding it over the fire, she let the blood drip onto the flames with a sizzling sound. Flames leaped, a red cloud spewing upwards. A noxious smell, like rotten eggs, polluted the air. The wind increased, whipping Aradia's hair across her cheeks, molding her bedgown to her body. A sudden hunger flickered across her face; her eyes shone like pinpoints of light, yellow in the night blackness. Long, lank hair hung in front of her eyes, her teeth gleaming like daggers.

With feet spread wide apart, the woman raised her arms.

"I am the eagle that soars through the sky
I am the viper that slithers along the ground
I am the fox that prowls the night

I am the wolf that stalks its prey
I am the lion for courage
I am the jackal--for death!"

Keriam sank to the ground, her spirit-brain working. She must rid the palace of this evil sorceress.

She waited long moments, until much later, the fire died out and Aradia left to make her way back to the palace. Seconds later, Keriam drifted back to her bedchamber as desperate questions taunted her mind. What wickedness was Aradia planning? Did the sorceress, too, plot evil against the king? One idea after another crammed her brain, Roric Gamal's suggestion the most promising. She must persuade her father to leave Moytura, for weeks, if necessary. Her thoughts blossomed into ambitious schemes. Since it had been years since her father had left the province, they could tour the country together.

She'd propose her plan to her father the following morning. He must agree. There was no alternative.

* * *

Rather than broach her plan during the morning meal, Keriam waited until later in the day, when she found her father at the wide oaken desk in his office, a sheaf of papers in his hand. Numerous daggers and spears from many countries decorated the walls, interspersed with shields and swords. The rest of the room stood in stark simplicity, with only a long oaken table fronting a plain leather sofa in the middle of the room. Green silk draperies at the wide window wafted in a gentle breeze.

He looked up as she entered the room and set the papers down. "Ah, Kerry." Books, stacks of papers, a feather pen, and an ink bottle occupying every space evidenced the many duties that kept her father busy from dawn until nightfall, and often through the night. Of course, he had Conneid Delbraith to perform these duties for him, but such was his interest in royal affairs that he wrote many letters himself.

"Sit down," he said, holding an oaken chair for her. "Always glad to talk to you."

He tapped the vellum sheets. "A long letter from King Barzad, elaborating on the marriage agreement between him and your Aunt Edita. You may read it if you wish." He rose and moved about the room in shuffling steps, his back bent over, face set in a grimace.

Keriam frowned. "A backache again, Father?" A common occurrence lately.

Tencien pressed his hand to his back and groaned. "Been sitting too much lately." He smiled feebly. "This is what happens when you get old."

"Forty-five isn't old. You have years and years ahead of you." Goddess, she prayed, please let it be so. Tencien stood by the open window, where sunlight streamed into the room, accentuating the gray hairs sprinkled throughout his head. Aiming to cheer him, she changed the subject. "Let me explain the reason for my visit."

"You never need a reason, daughter."

"Thank you. But I've been thinking--you've been laboring so hard, what with the treaty--" She pointed to the sheets on his desk--"all your other duties. Why not take a vacation, tour the country--"

"Can't. Too much work here. We must improve the roads, as I promised during the Bel Festival. Other improvements, too. I have papers to sign, ministers to confer with."

No, her father must leave. He wasn't safe here.

Frowning, he looked out the window. "More bridges, more silos for storing grain . . ." He turned quickly, wincing with the movement. "Many of our people often go hungry, did you know that?"

"A sad situation which I hope we can rectify." She spoke in a strained voice, resigned to deal with mundane matters. "Father, I do follow the kingdom's affairs."

He opened his hands wide. "Then you see why I can't leave now. In truth, I don't know when--or if--I can." He headed for his chair, wincing again as he eased down. "May even have to raise taxes, much as I hate that possibility."

"Father, for your own good, please leave the kingdom. You have enemies here." Including Aradia, she wanted to say, but would he believe her? That sorceress ran roughshod over the women but charmed the men, who would never believe anything ill of her. "How often must I warn you?"

"Kerry, let's understand one thing. I will not run away from trouble or any imaginary--"

"Not imaginary, the danger is real."

"If I have definite proof of a plot, then of course, I'll have the collaborators arrested." He pointed a finger at her. "But they will get a fair trial. I have yet to see signs of a plot. Until I do, I will stay here. I will not be intimidated, not by Balor, not by anyone. Now, let's hear no more about it."

Yet she saw through his brave words. She'd learned to read her father well over the years, and something told her he would investigate the threat to his life, if he hadn't already.

Forcing a smile, she tried to speak in a normal voice. "Well, for now, let's see what we can do about your condition. My maid has spoken of a woman, skilled in herbs. Her house in the country burned to the ground, so she lives in Moytura now. Has a shop, makes and sells herbal lotions. Let us see what she can do about your back."

Tencien nodded, grimacing as he pressed his hand to his back. "It's worth a try. Do you know her name?"

"Radegunda."

* * *

Bright mid-morning light penetrated the window in the back room of a shop on Perfume Lane, providing plentiful light for the old woman to prepare a lotion with care. She knew that even a few drops of an ingredient could make a big difference, whether it be a burn salve or face lotion. Frowning in concentration, she skimmed off a layer of sheep's wool grease from a pot of warm water, then mixed the grease in another pan of water, aiming to warm the resulting lanolin over the hearth fire. Blended with beeswax and lavender, then stored in a stoppered bottle, this compound would make a pleasant and beneficial body cream.

Bowls of dried lavender, lilac, and rose petals awaited her attention on the wooden counter, the breeze from the open window wafting delicious scents throughout the small space. She was especially grateful for these pleasant aromas that helped erase the smells of the small stable at the end of her street.

Despite a vent that carried hearth smoke through the roof, a stifling heat enclosed the room. Radegunda raised her apron and dabbed it across her face, then continued stirring. Her legs and feet ached from standing so long on the hard stone floor, but she would never complain, she vowed, shifting her position from one leg to the other.

Since moving to Moytura, she hadn't regretted burning her house down. She'd never have found safety or happiness in her former village, where people feared and shunned her, calling her a witch. Since she hadn't been able to carry all her belongings to the city, she'd rather have her house burned to ashes than to have strangers rummaging through her things, searching for signs of witchcraft. And yes, she was a witch, but she cast only good spells, always striving to help others. If they refused her help, too bad. Their loss. Besides, what if that young man--she wished she knew his name--had turned her over to the druids for interrogation, as he'd threatened? She shuddered at the possibility

Here in the capital, she lived and worked among thousands, known by her customers as a healer, skilled in herbs. She smiled to herself, happy her shop had proved successful, thankful for her many patrons. Why, she'd even had to hire another woman to help her. Adsaluta should be here soon, she could tell by the amount of sunlight in the room.

A bell rang at the shop's front, jerking her from her reverie. She removed her apron and with a soft jangling sound, pushed back the curtain that separated the work area from the store.

A tall man stood at the wooden counter, fingering a jar of crushed thyme and honey, one of her best-selling breath sweeteners. Other products presented themselves on the counter-- lilac soap, chamomile lotion, rose water, and many other tempting perfumes and cosmetics.

Clad in a brown tunic, a wide leather belt circling his waist, the man exuded an air of importance. She noted the palace emblem on his chest, and although a trace of uneasiness churned inside her, she sought to keep her voice even.

"May I help you, sir?"

He set the jar on the counter. "Radegunda?"

"The same, sir," she said, her heartbeat increasing.

"You are wanted at the palace. I have a horse outside for you."

Her body trembled with fear, the room swaying around her. Someone must have reported her to the druids. She'd always considered the king a kind man, but the druids must enforce the law against witchcraft. She'd be interrogated, tortured--

"Madam?" He reached a hand toward her, his forehead creased with concern. "Are you ill?"

She pressed a hand to her heart. "Wh-why do they want me at the palace?"

"I shall tell you this one time, but you must learn not to question the king. He has suffered from a backache, and it's said you are skilled in the healing arts."

She wanted to faint with relief, but a new worry ended her contentment. Could her helper manage the shop alone? She'd have to; Radegunda saw no other choice.

It seemed he could read her mind. "The king will pay you well if you cure him."

And if not? She wanted to ask, but feared risking the question. Besides, she felt sure she could help the king.

"I pray you, sir, let me stop by my helper's place so's I c'n tell her. Adsaluta lives only two doors down."

"Very well." He tapped his knuckles on the counter. "Now gather your supplies and let us leave. We mustn't keep the king waiting."

* * *

Lodged at the palace, Radegunda stood outside the king's bedchamber, a tray in her hands, a jar of healing salve tucked in her pocket.

The guard at the door raised his eyebrows. "You are the king's healer?"

"You c'n call me that." After he opened the door, she shambled into the room. She found the king on his back, a grimace

69

on his face, his forehead glistening with sweat. Anxious to prove herself and help the king, she hoped she could cure his backache.

He composed his features as she approached the bed. "Ah, Radegunda--that is your name?"

"If it pleases you, Your Majesty."

"Whether or not it pleases me is beside the point. I shall address you as such, if that is correct."

"Yes, Your Majesty."

"Enough of 'Your Majesty'. You may call me 'sire.'"

"Yes, Your . . . sire," she said, setting the tray on a bedside table. "By the week's end, I hope to see Your Majesty up and walkin' again, back to normal." Oh, oh, she shouldn't use such bold talk on the king. What if he dismissed her now?

Immensely relieved he said nothing, she reached for a bed pillow. "If I may, sire, I'd like to raise you a little, so's you can drink the honey-sweetened willow bark tea." She'd added a mild sedative, but she didn't tell him that. After she raised him to a sitting position, she handed him a cup. "It's not too hot, sire. After you finish, I'll massage your back with a healin' salve."

He sipped the tea, smiling with appreciation, then handed her the empty cup with a heavy sigh.

Gently, she removed one pillow. "Now please lie on your stomach, and lemme ease your bedgown up."

The king did as instructed, a slow process that left him drenched in sweat. "I feel worse than before," he complained.

"Only give me time, sire. I think you'll see an improvement within a few days. Sometimes we hafta feel worse before we git better." Radegunda hesitated, then plunged ahead. "And sire, I don't want you to stay in bed. Tomorrow, I want you up and walkin'."

"Humph!"

She wiggled the stopper from a jar of salve and released it with a soft plop. "Your lower back, sire?"

"Yes," he said, his voice muffled.

"If I may sit on the bed, sire?"

"No need to ask."

Sitting, she dipped her fingers into the salve, then worked it into his back.

"Burns," he mumbled. "What is it?"

"Ground red pepper blended with body cream, sire. And if it burns, that means it's workin'."

For several minutes, she leaned over him, massaging his back. Convinced she'd done as much as was helpful for the first day, she set the salve aside and eased his bedgown down. "Now I want you to turn onto your side, sire, with your knees partways up."

While the king positioned himself, she spoke soothingly. She pushed the top back on the jar and gathered the tray, all the while talking in a pleasant voice. By the time she tiptoed from the room, the king slept soundly.

Day after day, she worked with him, each day showing an improvement. Within a week, he'd resumed his normal schedule, with only a slight lingering pain in his lower back, a soreness Radegunda assured him would eventually go away.

* * *

Keriam studied her father during the morning meal while the sun remained low on the horizon, and only dim candlelight provided illumination in the vast dining room.

"You look so much better, just within these last few days. When you walk, you're not bent over as before."

"Radegunda has made a new man of me," Tencien said. He finished his oatmeal with honey and shoved the bowl aside. "I wish I could speak to her before I depart the palace, but affairs in Sligo require my attention. It will take a good part of the day to ride to that city and back, so it's up to you to pay the healer woman--a goodly amount, please--and convey my appreciation."

She sipped her hard cider, enjoying its tart, fruity flavor, then looked at him with alarm. "You're going to ride a horse, after your recent back trouble?"

"Carriage," he said, "and I'll get out now and then to stretch, as Radegunda suggested."

"And outriders, Father?"

"Very well, but only to set your mind at ease."

She sighed with relief. The sun's first hesitant rays lit the room, a beam of golden light through the wide window that revealed the colorful wooden walls, the brightly-hued sheepskin rugs on the floor.

Keriam spread honey on her acorn toast. "I have a suggestion. Why don't we continue with Radegunda's services," she said as Tencien glanced her way. "We definitely need a healer since Belasaria died last year. Then, too, I'd benefit from learning about herbs and such." Toast halfway to her mouth, she looked over at him. "What do you think?"

"By all means, ask her to remain. If she's concerned about her shop, tell her we'll redeem her losses." He dabbed a linen napkin across his mouth, then pushed his chair back and stood. "Must be on my way." He bent low to kiss her on the cheek, then strode from the room, his straight shoulders and firm step revealing he had many years left to rule, to live.

If the assassins didn't strike him while he was away.

* * *

In her father's study, Keriam drew a large bag of silver coins from a desk drawer and handed the money to Radegunda, explaining her father's absence.

"Now," she said as the healer woman tucked the bag in a hidden pocket of her dress, "the king and I both recognize a need for a healer woman at the palace. The amount I gave you should cover any losses you would incur from closing your shop. Would you be willing to do that, or do you know of someone able to manage the shop in your stead?"

"Yes, I do know a woman who would be willin' to manage for me." Her face brightened. "Madam, if I could only have a place to make my lotions and such here at the palace--"

"That should present no difficulty. We have a still room right off from the kitchen, with its own hearth. You can use the herbal garden that adjoins the main palace garden. I feel sure the herbs there are the same you use in your own preparations, and the cook wouldn't mind sharing the plants with you."

"Suits me fine, madam. With your permission, I can make my lotions here and leave it to Adsaluta to take care of things in the city." She hesitated, staring at the floor.

"Something else, Radegunda?" Keriam observed the thin old woman in her torn and patched brown dress, the gray hair drawn back in a bun, her hands red and work-roughened. Tiny wrinkles tracked her face, expanding at her forehead and mouth. The healer woman twisted her hands in the folds of her dress, her lips compressed.

After a furtive glance around the room, the woman spoke in a low voice. "Madam, I have the second sight."

"Ah!" Keriam, too, threw a desperate look around the room. "Why are you telling me this?" she whispered.

Radegunda leaned forward. "Madam, c'n I speak frankly?"

"Agreed, only if what you say doesn't leave this room."

"Never!" A pause ensued. "But I . . ."

"Yes?"

"I suspect--I know!--you have the second sight, too."

Keriam gasped.

Radegunda waved her hand. "Don't worry. I'll never say nothin' about it. Why should I, when I would only bring trouble on myself? And the only reason I sense your ability is because I have the power, too." She lowered her voice again. "But madam, lemme speak plainly. Some people wish the king ill--"

"I know! And I've tried everything, even asked His Majesty to take a holiday or make a state visit. I'd give my life for him, if I could. But I don't even know the names of all the conspirators." Nor did Roric Gamal.. Odd, Keriam thought, she'd known this woman for such a short time, and yet she was confiding in her more than she ever had in anyone, except her father.

"Don't trust Aradia, Princess Keriam. She doesn't fool me. She is evil, that one."

"Very true!" Keriam stared out the window, not seeing a thing. A few moments slid past before she rose and folded her arms across her chest. Radegunda stood also. Fully putting her trust in the healer, Keriam spoke with determination. "I'll ask His Majesty to talk to the steward as soon as he returns. He must make

Fergus Morrigan see his wife as she truly is. Then Fergus must return Aradia to her family."

"D'you think the steward will listen?"

"If he doesn't return Aradia to her family, I'll ask the king to relieve him of his duties. I intend to get that woman out of the palace, out of Moytura."

Radegunda frowned. "I hope your scheme works, madam."

"It will." She twisted her amethyst ring on her finger, then nodded in dismissal. "Thank you again for all you did for my father . . . and for your warnings, too."

"It is an honor to serve you and your father, madam."

As the healer woman left the room, a premonition crept over Keriam, a sense that something would draw her and the woman ever closer.

What that something was, she had no idea. But she saw heartbreak and disaster ahead for both of them.

Chapter Seven

Keriam brooded by her window, tapping her fingers on the windowsill. Late yesterday, a messenger had arrived from Sligo with news that business in the city had extended the king's visit, but Tencien would return home within a day or two. What if the plotters killed her father in Sligo?

What would stop them from committing their evil crime far from the palace? She clenched her hands on the windowsill and gazed out at the vast countryside, as if the hills and meadows held an answer to her plight. Turning toward the statuette of Talmora that rested on her dresser, she gave the statuette a long look, and it seemed as if the Goddess returned her look, almost as though the Goddess wanted to communicate with her. This was not the first time Keriam had felt that she was in direct communication with the Goddess. Did Talmora want to tell her something? Did the Goddess sense her anxieties about her father? Ah, how she needed the Goddess's help.

She spun away and headed downstairs to the Hall of Petition, where she heard disputes and grievances in her father's absence. Early in his reign, Tencien had provided an opportunity for the people of Moytura to bring their disagreements to him, giving them a chance to find adjudication for the disputes that often arise between neighbors and antagonists. For those who lived too far from the capital, the king had established courts in other key cities, a more than adequate judicial system that served all of the people.

Outside the room, men and women waited singly, an expectant expression on their faces when they saw her, hoping they would soon be called to present their case.

Inside the vast room, floor to ceiling red velvet draperies flanked two majestic windows that looked out onto the expansive lawn and garden. Keriam took her place in the ornately-carved wooden throne, its seat and back done in the same red velvet. The flagstone floor, bare of rugs, was attractive in its simplicity. A statue of Talmora stood guard in the east corner; in the west corner the Avadoran flag caught the bright sunlight that highlighted its rich hues of turquoise and gold.

Two peasants stood before Keriam, both dressed in rough garb, one of them missing an arm. In a long white robe, Druid Cathbad stood next to the throne, his expression harsh and unrelenting, as if he'd already reached a verdict. A network of wrinkles stalked his face, his long gray hair falling past his shoulders and a beard that hung to his waist.

In gentle tones, Keriam spoke to the peasant to her right. "Please tell me the nature of your disagreement with the other man."

The man bowed low. Tight-lipped, he pointed a finger at the other man. "Your Highness, this man stole apples from my tree."

"Only because--"

"Let him finish," Keriam said to the one-armed man.

"He's done it more than once. Me and my wife seen him stealin' my apples."

She turned to the other man. "Is this true?"

"Your Highness, my children are starving. Ever since the wife died, things have gone from bad to worse. I used to be a carpenter, but then I lost my arm in an accident. I don't own land, so I can't grow my own crops. Yes, I know thievery is a crime, but I must feed my children."

"Not from my land!"

"Hush!" Keriam turned to the former carpenter. "Could you not learn another trade or find employment?"

"Your Highness, I've wanted to, but it's hard to leave the children for a long time, to go lookin' for another job."

"Very well." Keriam sat back on the throne, measuring her thoughts. "Since you have no money, I can't fine you for thievery."

"But you can punish him," Druid Cathbad said at her side. "I suggest twenty lashes, madam, in a public place."

The carpenter blanched, his shoulders slumping. The farmer gloated.

"Such punishment won't put food on his table," Keriam said. "Better if he finds employment to support his family." She

76

addressed the one-armed man. "I know a wood carver in Moytura who needs someone to help stock his shelves and tidy up his workroom. He lives on the outskirts of the city but has an empty apartment above his store, where you and your children may live. I shall speak to him, persuade him to hire you."

"No!" the farmer sputtered.

The carpenter bowed. "Thank you, Your Highness. I shall do my best to be worthy of your trust."

The druid scowled. "You would reward thievery?"

"Not reward, Druid Cathbad, just help him back on his feet. After he has earned a sufficient wage, he can repay the farmer for the apples. Three coppers sounds adequate."

Druid Cathbad clenched his fists and turned away. From past experience, Keriam knew he didn't like to be thwarted. She feared she had made an enemy for life.

Finished hearing the cases a short while later--fewer than usual--she recalled today was the day she visited the hospital in the city, to cheer the sick and injured and confer with the staff there. Best she remind someone of her mission. Leaving the throne room, she saw Fergus outside the library and motioned to him.

He headed her way, an air of distraction about him.

"Fergus, I'm leaving to visit the hospital. Just wanted you to know, should anyone ask about me while I'm away."

"Yes, of course, madam," he said, a faraway look in his eyes.

"Fergus, are you ill?" she asked him, this man who was like a second father to her.

He stared at her, as if brought back to the moment. "No, madam, I'm fine."

What was the matter with the steward? She pondered, walking on down the main hall. Normally, she considered him a conscientious helper, capable of handling any problems that might arise. Her father couldn't have a better man. But lately, he'd been acting strangely. What had made him marry Aradia? She wondered as her mind drifted in a different direction. A fine man like Fergus with a woman like Aradia? She must have truly bewitched him, Keriam thought as she rushed back upstairs and along the hallway, then opened her bedchamber door.

Sick with her moontime, Maudina lay asleep in her own small room, dosed with Radegunda's red raspberry tea. Mindful of her maid's devotion, still Keriam looked forward to being free of Maudina's constant surveillance for this one day.

Slipping on a tunic and riding trousers, Keriam saw a raven light on the window ledge. "Well, hello, little bird." She smiled in surprise, for she'd never known a bird to come so close. Its glossy black feathers shone in the early morning sunlight, its beady eyes staring. Shifting from one foot to another, it gave her an inquisitive look, as if to ask a question.

She moved closer and reached a hand toward it, then stopped, afraid her movement would frighten the bird, and indeed, it hopped a few steps to the side. Keriam frowned, filled with sorrow. "Was it your mate Aradia killed?" The raven tilted its head, as though considering every word. "Poor little thing, I'll wager so." With a spurt of daring, she inched a little closer to the bird, but as she'd feared, it flew away. The sunlight glinted on its obsidian wings, and soon it became a black speck against a clear blue sky.

What had brought the raven to her window? Did its appearance foretell good fortune? She hoped so. After changing into her riding boots, she hurried downstairs and out the back door next to the kitchen, on her way to the stables.

Her booted feet crunching along the gravel path, she saw another raven pecking at worms on the ground, while two of its friends rested in tree branches. There surely were many ravens-- No! A stray cat dashed from around the corner and caught the bird between its teeth.

"Stop that!" Keriam swatted at the cat, forcing it to release its prey and sending it scurrying back around the corner. Before she could check on the bird, it flew off, the other two joining its flight. She sighed, relieved that the bird had suffered no harm; then she hurried on to the stable.

There, she found Traigh filling the horses' feeding troughs with fresh oats. She understood Maudina's attraction to him, this tall, broad-shouldered man with light blonde hair.

He looked up and blinked. "Princess?"

"Please saddle my horse, Traigh."

He glanced around. "Madam, where is Maudina?"

"She's sick. Nothing serious," she said in reply to his worried frown. After waiting several moments, she turned toward her horse's stall, aware she was leaving for the hospital earlier than usual, thus possibly confusing Traigh. "Are you going to fetch my horse, or must I do it?"

"No, madam, I'll see to it," he said, setting the oat bucket down. "I'm just surprised . . ." His voice trailed off as he entered the gray's stall and slipped the noseband on. With a skill born of countless applications, he quickly finished saddling and bridling the horse, then led the gray from the stall. Stopping the horse by the mounting block, he offered his arm for support.

Keriam mounted the horse astride, then rode at a canter for a short distance before settling the horse into an easy gait.

Her long hair streaming behind her, she basked in the clear air, and soon the grounds of Emain Macha disappeared behind her. She rode past the fields and meadows, the gently-rolling farmland, the sweet scent of grass floating through the air. Splashes of pink and yellow dotted the hills, summer flowers blooming. She loved this time of year, when everything was fresh and green. In the far distance stretched the majestic Orn Mountains along the horizon, their snowcapped peaks lost among a scattering of clouds.

Miles of undulating hills flew by, then the land flattened. The capital beckoned, its magnificent towers and spires gleaming in the bright sunlight. From here, she could see the many houses and buildings, most made of brick or gray stone. On the outskirts of the city, the houses became more splendid, and red tiled-roof dwellings, many of them with carved wooden balconies, were spaced far apart. Nearing Moytura, Keriam breathed a sigh of happiness, eager to see the sights and sounds of the city that never failed to cheer her. Loosely holding the reins, she eschewed the city stables. Her gaze absorbed the many shops, the throngs of noisy people, the other riders on the cobblestone streets. Food aromas floated all around her, vendors selling spiced apples, beef chunks on long sticks, and so many other tempting treats.

The streets became more crowded as she approached the city square and rode past the statue of Talmora, a stone edifice warded by a stately oak and rose bushes in bloom. Impatient to reach the hospital, she swung the horse from the main street and maneuvered the winding alleys, where timber and stone shops rubbed against each other. A squawking chicken flapped in front of her horse, causing him to start. Barking dogs chased after the horse as she passed the blacksmith's, a tailor's shop, and a sword smith's shop, but soon tired of the chase.

Keriam slowed the horse to a walk as the Treasury of Knowledge came in sight, and beyond that, the city hospital.

* * *

Over the midday meal in the main dining room, she discussed the hospital's needs with several physicians, druids skilled in medicine.

She dipped her fork into a casserole of spinach and barley, seasoned with basil, pepper, and pungent coriander. "Tell me something," she said, addressing Druid Kentigern, the administrator. "Do you have enough pallets at the hospital, should any calamity arise?"

Druid Kentigern reached for a slice of oat bread and stopped, his hand halfway to the bread basket, then quickly grabbed a slice. He looked puzzled, his fingers combing his long beard. "What sort of calamity, princess?"

"I'm old enough to remember the plague that killed so many people over ten years ago."

"Madam, if the black fever should strike again--may Talmora protect us!--there is little we can do. Certainly, we couldn't care for the sufferers here. The disease is too contagious."

"So we should just let the victims die?" She swallowed a bite of the casserole, fast losing enjoyment in the noontime meal.

Kentigern squirmed in his chair. "Madam, I didn't say that. Families should care for their loved ones, and many of us–including me--would be willing to tend to the sick, help them in every way we can." He cleared his throat. "But I fear there is little we can do except alleviate their misery. As you surely must know, most of them will die." He smiled with false joviality and forked a bite of the casserole. "But surely we are anticipating a problem that

80

won't arise. What makes you think the black fever will hit our people again?"

"No real reason, doctor, unless we have a long dry spell that brings fleas." She smiled, trying to match his optimism. Why did she have the nagging feeling that a plague would strike again? "As you say, no doubt I am anticipating a problem that won't arise." She folded her hands on the table and looked at him directly. "What are you doing about a cure? Surely you are working on this."

He looked at her in surprise. "Madam, it's difficult to find a cure for this disease. The plague defies understanding."

"Well, Druid Kentigern, try to understand it, will you? And please work on a cure."

Leaving a little time for herself, she left the hospital a short while later, then rode her horse to the spacious meadow that preceded the Plain of Sorrows. She headed for the broad plain that stretched west for miles, transected by the winding Nantosuelta River. Dust blew from the parched, baked grasses of the plain, getting into her eyes, layering on her clothes. Blinking her eyes, she rode on. Reaching the lowland, she dismounted at a rowan tree and tied the reins to a branch, then sank to the ground under the tree's shade. A squirrel scampered on the ground near her feet, its dark eyes sliding back and forth. She held out her hand, but the animal darted off, racing up the tree. Tiny fairies cavorted in tree branches and played in the grass, and she smiled and waved at them, cheered by their answering waves, a welcome distraction. Insects buzzed in the grass, and butterflies fluttered near her. Fascinated, she watched the butterflies' swirling and dipping, these beautiful creatures that housed human souls.

A lovely country, was Avador. Was it true that only a vast ocean extended on all sides of the continent, and no other lands existed beyond? She supposed so. Many ships from all countries on the continent had tried exploring the ocean, but ship-battering storms and sea monsters had driven them all back.

Keriam stretched her legs out, happy to have this time to herself, even if the heat was stifling. Her damp hair clinging to her forehead, she grabbed the hem of her dress to dab across her face and brow.

The dark Gorm Forest loomed north of her, a land of sinister mysteries, for in the depths of the forest lurked the torathors, those creatures, half-human and half-monster, only whispered about among her countrymen. The threat of their horns and shaggy bodies was enough to scare children into obedience. The torathors will get you if you don't behave.

Leaning her head against the tree, she closed her eyes and focused on her problems. She must keep her father safe, and if he refused to speak to Fergus about Aradia, she'd thwart that evil woman, no matter what she must do. She'd speak to Fergus, convince him his wife caused strife and discord among the palace workers.

Time passed, the air becoming cool and humid. Keriam opened her eyes, amazed to find a fog enshrouding the plain. The air smelled wet and musty. She swivelled her head, trying to make out trees and bushes in the distance. There! She finally discerned the cluster of oaks that bordered the river. Thank the Goddess! How odd to find a fog this time of year, this time of day. What if it remained for hours? Well, then, she might have to stay here longer than intended, and they'd worry about her at the palace.

She peered through the haze, and saw--ghostly warriors. On the plain, phantom soldiers performed a nimble dance of death, hacking and slashing, hurling javelins. Heavens! Mouth wide open, Keriam sprang to her feet and pressed a hand to her pounding heart. She tried to dismiss her fears, for surely her eyes were playing tricks on her. Her horse neighed and thrashed his front hooves in the air, pulling on the reins, finally breaking free.

"Liath, no!" He galloped off, the reins trailing behind him, soon disappearing in the haze. Keriam slumped against the tree, missing the horse already.

Through the heavy mist, an old man approached. Long gray hair flowed past his shoulders, a dark robe cloaking his gaunt form. A beard fringed his face and fell halfway to his waist. Disjointed movements surfaced behind him, hundreds, thousands! of soldiers! What was happening here? She banged back against the rowan tree, her nails clawing the rough bark. She bit down hard on her lower lip. Her knees shook, her breath shallow and rapid, every muscle tense. She feared to move.

"Princess Keriam, don't be afraid," the spectral stranger said in a deep, mellow voice. "I have waited a long time to meet you. We are related, you know. Both of us belong to the House of Moray."

Somehow she knew. Her skin chilled as she tried to speak. "King Malachy?" she said after the third attempt. Shivers raced across her arms and down her legs.

He bowed low. "At your service, princess."

"How-how did you come into my world?"

"Nay, 'tis the other way around. You are now in my world, the Otherworld."

Chaos reigned behind him. Warriors whacked and screamed, shields clashing with a ringing of metal on metal. Arrows and javelins zipped through the air. Swords swished and blades clattered. The rattling of quivers and the hum and whirr of spears and javelins rent the air. Warriors in short tunics swung their swords, severing heads and arms. Was she the only one who saw and heard these images? She glanced back toward the meadow, but the fog hindered her vision. Soldiers moved with frightful agility, arms thrusting and parrying, legs moving forward, backward, and sideways. The smell of blood tainted the air, making her queasy. She fought her nausea, her attention fastened on Malachy and the soldiers.

Malachy gestured behind him. "Howbeit, I was not king-- only a general--when this battle raged. Unfortunately, these hardy warriors fear the evil wizards may yet prevail."

"But what makes your enemies continue to fight?" She risked another glance at the warriors, hoping they would all disappear. But alas, the battle still raged, as fierce as ever.

He looked toward the soldiers, too, then sighing, turned toward her. "Our enemies can't accept the fact that they lost the battle."

Much of her fear left her; her breathing came more easily now, her legs no longer stiff. "So you defeated the wicked men and became king then," she said as half statement, half question, eager to confirm Tencien's tale.

"With the Goddess's help, madam," he said, his shrewd gaze leveled on her. "Remember--you must remain ever vigilant against iniquity."

"Iniquity--yes." Keriam clenched her hands at her sides. "I must make my father understand the threat against his life."

"Indeed!" Malachy appeared as a nebulous figure in the fog that continually rolled across the plain. The haze thinned and thickened, first tiny wisps of vapor, then dense clouds. Misty shadows wrapped around trees.

A look of sadness captured Malachy's face. "Now, I fear more trouble--nay, disaster!--looms ahead for the House of Moray. Conspirators plot to kill the king."

"I know!" Blood pounded through her veins, making her head throb. "How can I stop them? What can I do?"

"Beware the woman with silvery hair. And the general--"

"Balor!"

"Just so. You must keep them apart."

"Aradia and Balor?" A picture flashed through her mind, Aradia and the general together. A question exploded in her brain. "How do you know all this?"

He smiled. "Princess Keriam, don't you understand that our worlds exist side-by-side?"

"I . . . I've heard that, but I never believed it was true." The Otherworld, a world of ghosts, wizards, and magic. A place where death was only a pause in the cycle of rebirth. But she could never find this world within the busy rhythms of the palace, nor the hustle-bustle of the city.

The battle still stormed behind them, a javelin whizzing their way. Screaming, Keriam threw herself to the ground with a hard thud. The weapon landed in the dirt beside her. The breath knocked from her, she lay motionless. Her hands and knees throbbed with pain.

Malachy reached a hand to help her rise, then drew back, obviously aware his specter was powerless. "Madam, please realize these ghostly images can cause no harm."

Bracing herself, she rose to her feet and brushed off her tunic. "Well, they seem awfully real to me." Her hands prickled with cuts and bruises, her knees stinging. A glance to the side revealed a phantom javelin, as insubstantial as the fog.

"We were discussing the palace plot," he reminded her. "Many officers conspire with Balor."

"Who? Name them!" Terror iced her stomach.

He shut his eyes for a moment. "Alas, I don't know their names."

She bent over to rub her hand against her knees, still smarting from the fall, then raised herself. "Is there no one I can trust?"

"Fergus, a good man. But he's in danger."

"Fergus--danger?" She ran sweaty hands up and down her hips. "How can I protect him? What can I do?" She licked her lips. "And Aradia--"

"You must find a way to deal with her. Kill her if you must."

"Kill her?"

"Yes, whilst you can. She won't act yet--the time is not right--so you still have time before you must act." Malachy opened his mouth as if to say more, then faded into nothingness.

"King Malachy!" Keriam's gaze swept the plain, the warriors gradually disappearing. The fog slowly lifted, trees and bushes coming into focus.

"Oh, no!" She slid down and stared at her bruised hands. Moments passed, her recent experience repeating in her mind, like a nightmare without end. Hard to believe it had all happened.

She wouldn't accomplish anything by sitting here. Time to return to the palace, but where was Liath now? She pushed herself to her feet and hurried toward the meadow, hoping to find her horse along the way. Moisture clung to her hair and clothes, her skin clammy from the humid heat. After a long trek across the meadow and past the busy streets, she found the horse grazing by the city stables, on Moytura's outskirts. The horse whinnied in greeting.

"Well, thank you for waiting for me!" After a bit of tricky maneuvering, she mounted the horse and rode past the stables, then galloped into the countryside, counting the minutes until her return.

Confusion roiled inside her as she retraced her ride. What had really happened there on the plain? Had it all been a dream?

But no; she stared at her hands, still stinging and bruised. She saw King Malachy as if he were with her now, still saw the clash of swords, the screams of warriors, saw the javelin headed her way. And oh, Goddess! the headless bodies, the severed arms. For the rest of her life, she'd remember this scene.

The palace appeared in the distance, its mellow bluestone a welcome sight, its windows gleaming in the late afternoon sunshine. Towers at each corner bore banners that hung limply in the still heat. As Keriam drew closer, she noted the lake to the west, its water glistening like crystal, and the woods behind the palace that separated it from the officers' houses and the soldiers' barracks.

Within minutes, she reached the palace grounds and walked her horse for a few minutes, letting the animal cool off. Upon her arrival at the stables, Traigh rushed out to meet her, helping her dismount.

"Madam, thank the Goddess you're back!"

"Sorry if I caused any worry. I was . . . detained."

On solid ground again, in familiar surroundings, she hurried along the path, the gravel crunching beneath her booted feet. Otherworldly images refused to leave her mind, every image fresh, as if the scene were happening now.

Inside, her boots clicked along the stone floor, her gaze searching everywhere. Everything looked the same, normal and reassuring. It seemed as if she'd been gone for an eternity, but she assumed only a few hours had elapsed. Quiet reigned over the palace, wherein the servants performed their chores, dusting and sweeping. They offered her a shy greeting as she walked past. She returned their greetings and continued on as problems tormented her, making her head throb, the blood pounding in her veins.

Crossing the main hall, she passed Aradia in an alcove with Balor. Aradia and Balor! They stood with heads close together, just as she'd seen in her vision, as Malachy had warned her. She must confront them, must keep them apart. She rushed back in their direction--and saw Aradia alone, arranging flowers in a glass vase.

She fought to keep the panic from her voice. "Where's the general?"

Aradia frowned, a long-stemmed rose in her hand. "General?"

"Yes, Balor!"

The steward's wife shook her head, her silvery hair gleaming. "I don't know this . . . General Balor."

Keriam wanted to scream. "But I just saw you with him."

"Princess Keriam, I fear you are mistaken," Aradia said with a condescending smile. "I've been by myself all afternoon."

Keriam looked into the witch's eyes--demon eyes, as if all the evil in the world had gathered in their depths, ready to loose wickedness and depravity on all mankind. For only a moment, Keriam saw flames flickering in each pupil, a hypnotizing fire that enthralled her.

Aradia raised a hand to push her hair from her forehead, and Keriam saw fur! A patch of grayish-yellow fur defiled the back of the woman's hand. She stared at the fur in horrified fascination while the foulness wavered and disappeared, as if it had never been. Canine teeth glimmered like stilettoes, then gradually became normal teeth again.

Keriam swayed for a moment. Was she losing her mind?

"Madam, are you unwell?" Aradia asked in a mock solicitous voice. "Really, if you continue to have these dizzy spells, it may be a sign of something serious. Perhaps you should see a physician."

"I think not." Keriam spun away and headed for the stone stairs that led to the second floor balcony. She dashed up the long stairway and reached the top. There, she noted a break in the wooden balustrade that separated the second floor from the vast drop to the stone floor below. Despite her anxieties, she made a mental note to have Fergus consult the palace carpenter tomorrow, to repair the balustrade.

A multitude of misgivings accompanied her with every step, from the second floor landing and down the long hallway to her apartment. She knew she'd spoken to Malachy; she remembered every detail of their encounter. His warning about Fergus returned to haunt her. He's in danger. Where was the steward now? She hadn't seen him since her return.

Breathing hard, Keriam opened her bedchamber door. Maudina looked up as she entered, frowning with worry.

The maid sprang to her feet. "Princess, where have you been? Traigh said--"

"Didn't Fergus Morrigan tell you I was leaving?" Keriam leaned against the door, her heart beating fast. "And where is he, by the way?"

"Madam, he wanted me to tell you. His lady wife--that Aradia!--sent him into the capital to fetch silk material for a dress."

"Silk material! Fergus has enough duties here without running foolish errands for his wife." Another question flashed in her brain. "Why didn't Aradia go herself?"

"She's afraid of horses, or so the steward told me. And I understand she had other things for him to tend to." An apologetic smile came over Maudina's face, as though she were to blame for the problem.

"It's not like the steward to act so irresponsibly," Keriam said, a muscle twitching in her jaw.

"I agree, madam. Fergus has always been dependable. But I fear Aradia has cast a spell–" Eyes wide with shock, Maudina started again--"well, I mean, he's a different man since he married that wit--woman."

"I fear so." Keriam pushed away from the door and slumped onto her bed. Shoving strands of hair from her face, she spoke in a harsh voice. "And General Balor, what was he doing here?"

"Madam, I don't know! I haven't seen him." Maudina's voice cracked, her eyes brimming with tears.

"Maudina, forgive my interrogation." Keriam jumped to her feet and hugged her maid. Images blazed in her head, prompting her to drop her arm. "And I forgot to ask how you're feeling. You look much better than you did this morning."

The maid's face brightened. "Oh, yes," she said, brushing her hand across her eyes. "Radegunda knows as much about medicine as any physician. I feel fine now."

"Good, I'm so glad." She nodded in dismissal. "I'll eat the evening meal in my room. Please ask Kormlada for potato soup and acorn bread."

"Yes, madam." With a nod and a swish of her long skirt, Maudina headed for the door.

As the door closed behind the maid, all the day's events returned to taunt Keriam, most especially the battle scene in Otherwhere. And Malachy; she'd never forget him. Would she see him again? she wondered, pacing the floor. Possibly he could help guide her in the coming months. Talmora knew she needed assistance.

What about Aradia? Had she only imagined the fur on that wicked woman? And those canine teeth?

Within a short while, Maudina brought her steaming potato soup and warm acorn bread on a wooden tray. Keriam forced herself to eat, although her appetite had left long ago. Yet she knew she needed all her faculties for clear thinking, and she surely couldn't think on an empty stomach. Seeking comfort in the room's pleasant normality, she stared around her room. Decorated in lavender and pale blue, with touches of rose and green, its soothing tones should have consoled her. But they didn't.

The sun sank low in the east, the last of daylight fading. The first faint stars glowed in the heavens like dim candles, gradually brightening as darkness deepened. She stood in night's blackness as frantic thoughts rampaged through her head. Where was Fergus? Had evil befallen him?

Keriam agonized over what to do about Aradia. Ah, the answer was clear. She must send her back to Mag Bregha. Thoughts of the sorceress churned in her brain, of her evil spell on the palace grounds and her ritual slaughter of an innocent raven, her unkind remarks to the dwarves and Maudina. Goddess! She had to get the witch out of Emain Macha! Anger burned inside her, an onslaught that built within her, growing stronger, more vicious. Her pulse pounded; red spots flashed in front of her eyes. She clenched and unclenched her fists, a vein throbbing at her temple. She wanted to kill the witch!

A table vase shattered, shards flying onto the rug. She looked at the broken pieces in dismay, telling herself again she must learn to control her emotions.

Her prophetic visions plagued her relentlessly. She saw a man falling--

No! She shuddered.

The railing! Fergus!

A scream gutted the night silence.

Too late!

Chapter Eight

"An accident," Tencien said to Keriam after his return from Sligo the following day. "A horrible, sad affair, but an accident, nonetheless."

"But Father, the railing--"

"I know what you told me, but it still remains an accident." He rose from the chair in his office and paced the room, then turned abruptly to face her. "Fergus reeked of spirits, did you know that?"

"No, I didn't." Taken aback for a moment, she rallied. "You know as well as I that Fergus never drank to excess."

"What are you saying, daughter? That someone pushed him off the balcony, then poured spirits on him?"

"That's exactly what I'm saying. Whose word do we have about the liquor? Who saw him fall? If the druids have prepared him for burial, they would have removed his travel clothes and dressed him in something finer. There are too many unanswered questions here."

Sighing, Tencien returned to his chair and sank down, looking as if he had aged ten years. "Questions or answers won't bring Fergus back," he said in a choking voice. "But he is now in the land of Truth and Eternal Life, a time for joy, not grief."

Keriam brushed a hand across her eyes. "You're right, but I miss him, just the same. No one can replace him." She sat in silent misery for long moments, reliving all the happy times with the steward.

"Yet we must replace him, and soon," Tencien said, sitting upright. "I've given the matter much thought, just in this short amount of time." He fingered the ink bottle on his desk, then returned the bottle to its place. "After consulting the druids, I've decided on Major Roric Gamal."

Roric Gamal! Mixed emotions vexed her. An inexplicable spurt of happiness warmed her, but she wanted no entanglements. Yet their mutual care for the king's safety would bring them together, for she intended to confer with him about a capable spy. But what if the major discovered her preternatural powers?

"He's a dependable, intelligent servant," her father continued. "Up to now, I've employed him as a courier, a position far below his capability. He's served me for years and I know from past experience that I can trust him. Indeed, I've placed him in delicate situations before, and he has acted with discretion. He'll serve the country well as the palace steward, too, not that anyone can truly replace Fergus Morrigan. Sometime before the funeral, I'll speak to Gamal."

"And when is the funeral?"

"Three days from now, but we'll have a mourning period for three days after that." He glanced away for a moment, then turned back to her, his eyes sad, the facial lines and wrinkles pronounced in the early morning light streaming through the window. "He deserves that much, don't you think?"

"Oh, yes." She plucked at the folds of her dress, a sick feeling in her stomach. "What about his widow?"

"Aradia is welcome to stay here, but I should think she'd want to return to her family. We'll provide for her, of course."

Despair gripped her stomach. They had to get rid of this evil woman.

Her mind worked hard as she searched for a way to switch the topic to her father's safety. She decided that the direct approach was best. "Father, I'm still concerned about you. Have you considered that Fergus's death may be related to a conspiracy against you?"

He sighed again, a faint rebuke in his expression. "So we're returning to that subject, are we, Kerry? Do you see schemers behind every tree, in every shadow? How can Fergus's death--a mishap!--possibly be related to a plot against me?"

"I don't know! I've thought about it again and again. In the first place, I still don't think the steward's death was an accident-- No, let me finish. I kn--" She thought quickly, remembering Roric's warning not to reveal him as a source of information. "I suspect General Balor may have designs on the throne. Father, remember I mentioned about the plot and Balor."

"Hmph! Balor has ever had ambition. What kind of ruler would I be if I saw a plot in all those who serve me?"

"A prudent one, and one who's alive instead of dead."

A pensive look came over his face as he fingered his quill pen and rearranged several papers on his desk. He switched his gaze back to her. "I'm not as trusting as you may think. There are always those who want power. I told you that once, remember?" At her answering nod, he continued. "As the kingdom's ruler, I must work toward helping my people. If I have to continually look over my shoulder to see who has a knife at my back, I can't accomplish much."

He pointed a finger at her. "Mind you, I'm not dismissing your concerns, but correspondence and business with King Barzad has kept me too busy to deal with other matters. However, I'll have Balor investigated. Does that satisfy you?"

Relief lifted her spirits. "Very much so. What do you intend to do?"

He scratched his chin. "Despite what you may think–and some things I may have said-- the problem of Balor has occupied my mind a good deal lately. But I need time to put my plans in place. Now, let's have no more talk of conspirators and no more questions. I have enough problems to deal with as it is."

"You have relieved my mind." But what would her father discover about the general? A clever one, that Balor. Of all the times she'd spied on the general at night, she'd found nothing incriminating.

* * *

After Keriam left, Tencien stood before the window, hands clasped behind his back, his mind working. He looked out over the palace grounds, to the green fields and woods that stretched beyond. Goddess, how he loved his country, how he wanted to protect Avador and all it stood for, keep his people safe and content. If he were killed, what would happen to the kingdom? To Keriam? Talmora knew he had enough concerns now--build new bridges and repair the old, construct secure silos for storing grain, provide for the people's defense. How could he do all that if he must constantly remain alert for assassination?

What if Keriam's suspicions had merit? Would Balor go so far as to kill a friend from childhood? Tencien rested his hands on the windowsill. To think Balor planned to murder him! If true, that threat hurt more than anything.

The safest thing for him would be to stay secluded at the palace, never make any public appearances. But such was not his way. He had to show himself to his people, let them know he was king, else others might attempt to seize the throne. Then Kerry's fears of Balor's machinations would surely come to pass.

Long thoughtful moments ensued before he spun away from the window. He would turn the problem over to the most capable person he knew, one he would trust with his life.

* * *

At the palace entrance, Roric saw a cluster of dwarf children kneeling on the stone floor, their excited oohs and ahhs an indication that something aroused their attention, but what? A summons from the king had brought him to the palace, but this tableau was unexpected. He strode closer, looking over the children's heads.

A brown rabbit.

Oh, how cute!" one of the children cried.

"How come we never seen it here before?"

"It'd make a tasty stew, I'm thinkin'."

"No! Don't even talk about hurtin' it."

Pressing his hand against the wall, Roric took deep breaths, waiting for his panic to subside. As the rabbit gazed up at him, he saw Radegunda's eyes.

He'd heard a new woman had been hired, but for what reason? Could this new person be Radegunda? He wouldn't bother King Tencien about the witch, but he'd speak to Princess Keriam at the first opportunity.

For now, he could at least see that no harm befell the woman. He opened his mouth. "Children . . ."

They all looked up, throwing him questioning glances.

"Leave the rabbit alone. You mustn't harm a helpless animal."

One little boy piped up. "Nah, sir, we wouldn't really hurt it. We was only talkin'."

"Yeah, just funnin'."

"We wouldn't hurt no rabbit."

Roric nodded. "Good, see that you don't."

Chills raced down his back as he walked across the main hall to the stairway that led to the king's office. His steps slowed as he ascended the stairs, his booted feet scraping on the stone. Had magic already gained a foothold in the palace, and was it destined to soon spread throughout the kingdom? Memories of his wife and baby son--both dead at a witch's hands--strengthened his determination to obstruct the practice of witchcraft, no matter where or how it revealed itself. His jaw tightening, he headed for the king's office and announced himself to the sentry. . . .

"I hope I will be worthy of the trust you've placed in me," Roric said after the king explained his new position as palace steward. "Believe me, sire, I will perform my duties to the best of my ability and help you in every way possible." He meant every word; this promotion from king's messenger to palace steward was quite unexpected, more than he'd ever hoped for.

Tencien nodded. "And I feel sure you'll do well, major, which is why I have entrusted you with this position in the first place." He leaned forward and lowered his voice. "Now I have another matter for your consideration. Word has reached me of a plot against my life."

Roric's heart jumped. Should he tell the king of his infiltration of the conspiracy? No, he quickly decided. Then the king would want to know the names of the plotters, and he wasn't ready to divulge a list yet. Such a list would compromise his investigation.

"I've been told that Balor heads the plot," the king continued, "difficult as that is to accept. I've known the general a good part of my lifetime. I'm aware of his flaws. He has ever had ambition--not necessarily a fault, you understand. But I also know there are many who would discredit the general to enhance their own position, hoping to replace him," he said, tapping his fingers on his desk. "I must know the truth of this plot, must have evidence, else there can be no accusations against the general. Find out as much as you can about the plotters, then convey your findings to me. That is all for now." Tencien smiled. "Oh, and I'll inform the princess. I fear she has worried about me."

Roric rose and bowed. "Very good, sire. I shall do my best." He paused. "And I must say it saddens me that there are those who would conspire against you."

Leaving the king's presence a short time later, he congratulated himself on his appointment as palace steward, certain he could meet the challenge but regretting the circumstances that had created the position. How he missed Fergus Morrigan, a friend for so many years.

Ideas and plans dominated his mind, ways in which he could aid the king in his new employment, but more important, ways he could garner evidence against Balor. First, however, he must return to his room in the officers' housing and clean out his quarters. Whenever possible, he intended to familiarize himself with the primary rooms in the two-hundred-and-five room palace and the dungeon below. Seldom used under Tencien, the dungeon might take on a new life if Balor--Goddess forbid!--became ruler.

A growing suspicion breached his thoughts. Had Fergus's death been an accident, as everyone thought? If not, was his murder connected to the plot against the king? Who would benefit from both? No matter how demanding his new status proved to be, he'd investigate these questions and find answers.

About to go downstairs, he heard footsteps on the flagstone floor and turned to see Princess Keriam approach, her steps quick and purposeful, her dress fluttering around her ankles. A look of pleased surprise captured her face, quickly transmuted to an expression of studied nonchalance.

Bracing himself against an onslaught of fierce emotion, he stopped by a wooden bench. How lovely she looked, a woman any man would desire. Yet, thoughts of his wife intervened. He cleared his throat. "Princess Keriam, if you have a moment, I'd like to speak with you."

"And I've wanted to speak with you. Let us go somewhere private." She motioned for him to follow her along the hallway. Several steps behind her, he noted her graceful walk, her upright posture, the flow of her dark hair down her back. They passed several stone statues of gods and goddesses, the most majestic one being of Talmora, the earth-mother Goddess. The Goddess looked confident and serene, an iron spear enclosed in her right hand, The Book of Laws in her left.

They reached a small antechamber adjoining her bedchamber, both rooms part of her spacious apartment. After closing the door, she gestured toward a chair and took one opposite.

The sun was sinking below the eastern horizon, and the brass oil lamp on her desk glowed in the fading light, casting a mellow tinge to the room.

"Please close the door and sit down," the princess said. In her pale blue linen dress–beautiful in its simplicity–her long dark hair flowing down her back, she looked quite regal, every inch a royal queen. Her dangling silver earrings swung with each movement, catching the lamplight. A sweet-spicy scent clung to her, a fragrance vaguely familiar, redolent of country gardens. He admired her hand movements as she rearranged papers on her desk, those long, supple fingers, the purple ring flashing on her right ring finger. With her ivory skin, dark blue eyes, and rosy lips, she was pleasing to look at, a balm to his troubled mind and a temptation he must defeat.

A hodgepodge of books, papers, and knickknacks cluttered her desk, a disarray at odds with her neat, concise manner. A small statue of Talmora adorned an oaken table.

He settled into the chair, giving her an expectant look.

"I need someone to spy on Balor," she said without preamble.

Shock tightened his stomach. "How do you know about him?" Delbraith, no doubt. "If I may ask."

"Someone warned me about the general."

"And you're wondering why I didn't tell you when I found you outside the library in Moytura." He changed his position and crossed his legs, increasingly aware of the dangerous game he played.

"Yes, I have wondered."

"Madam, I wanted to wait until I had more names, so we could move against all the conspirators at the same time. I wasn't withholding information for any devious reason. It seemed safer this way."

"I understand. In any event, I need someone to discover who visits him and whom he visits. Do you know of any officers or men we can trust to do this?"

I'm ahead of you, he wanted to say, having already considered several likely candidates, spies he could rely on. "Madam, there are a few officers I trust, men I've been close to for many years." He tapped his fingers on his thigh. "I'll speak to them in the coming days, as soon as possible."

"Them?" She flipped her long hair over her shoulders, sending her earrings swinging again.

"We'll need at least four men; five would be better. The ones I have in mind are quite skilled in espionage. They've spied for the king, truth to tell. I suggest they spy not only on Balor, but also on those he contacts." If that's possible, he thought, well aware of what a cunning person Balor was. Things did not always work out the way you expected, a lesson he'd learned long ago.

"Very well. And another thing–surely you are aware of Aradia, her close relationship with the general. I fear very much those two have formed an alliance."

"Madam, I share your concern." Aradia was nothing but trouble. He'd seen evidence of her troublemaking already in the short time since she'd arrived at the palace. "We must rid the palace of Fergus's widow. I suggest you send her back to her family."

"I intend to." She paused, as if gathering her thoughts. "I strongly suspect she had a hand in Fergus's death."

"Do you have proof?"

"No proof, only suspicion. But I will do everything I can to find proof. Now the other men involved in this plot–you refuse to tell me their names–" She held up a hand–"and I understand your reasons. But would any of them act on their own, without Balor's direction to . . . to get rid of the king?"

"I doubt that very much, Princess Keriam. Balor holds a tight rein. He and he alone heads the plot." He paused, marshaling his thoughts. "I do know of two wealthy merchants the general has contacted. But Balor doesn't know that one of them is on our side."

"Thank the Goddess!"

Roric nodded. "He hates Balor as much as you and I do. In return for their financial support, the general has promised them important positions in the government he intends to form with . . . your father's demise. Of course, the other one loyal to Balor will deny knowledge of the plot. I agree that spying on the general will yield the most favorable results, for now." He leaned forward, his hands clenched between his knees. "We must have evidence. Sooner or later, the spies should find incriminating information we can use."

"Let us pray so."

"Very well, Major Gamal. That will have to do for now." She hesitated. "But you had something you wished to speak about."

"If you have time, madam."

"I do."

Now that he had the chance to speak, the words stuck in his throat. "That newly-hired woman at the palace--"

"Radegunda?" The witch! "May I ask why you hired her?"

She tilted her head. "But I thought you knew. She's a healer, skilled in herbs and such. She cured His Majesty's backache."

"I fear you are gravely mistaken." He paused, considering bluntness or subtlety and decided the former was best. "She's a witch."

She flinched, as if he'd struck her. Seeing her frightened expression, he pressed his point. "You know as well as I that magic is forbidden in the kingdom. For her own sake, I beg you, send her away. Do you want her to suffer at the stake?"

"Sir, I fear you are mistaken. She has done much good at the palace. Surely she has shown no signs of practicing the evil craft." She gave him a level look. "What makes you think she's a witch?"

"She told me."

Her hands jerked. "When? When did she say this?"

He related saving Radegunda from the thugs. "She admitted to me that she is, indeed, a witch."

"Very well." She nodded and retrieved a paper from her desk, as if in dismissal. "I shall speak to her."

"That's all, just speak to her?" he asked, every muscle tense. "You must send her away."

"I 'must'?" she said, raising her eyebrows.

"What I mean is, I would want no harm to come to her." He licked his lips. "I have suffered from witchcraft. A sorceress killed my wife and baby." Would the heartache ever go away?

"I'm so sorry!" She frowned. "I didn't know you'd been married."

"A long time ago."

Keriam fingered her pearl necklace. "I find it difficult to believe she's an enchantress, with all the good she's done at the palace. I have only your word about her."

"Talk to Radegunda, then. See what she says, madam. Remember, witchcraft is illegal in the kingdom. If found guilty, she could be burned at the stake."

"Major, you don't need to instruct me in the law. This much I will do. I will investigate the matter."

He started to rise, painfully aware he could expect no more for now. Sacred shrine. Radegunda must leave the palace.

* * *

After Roric left the antechamber, Keriam breathed a long sigh, but puzzlement disturbed her thoughts. Yes, she knew that Radegunda had andhashelladh-the second sight--but that didn't make her an enchantress. She wondered why the woman would confess such a thing to Roric Gamal. And what if Roric knew she had the second sight, would he consider her a witch? There must be more here than she understood. She'd speak to Radegunda, ensure that the healer woman understood the danger in practicing witchcraft.

She glanced at the statuette of Talmora, and for only a moment, she thought it moved, as if the Goddess wanted to tell her something. Quickly, she dismissed the thought as only a figment of her imagination.

Despite her concerns about Radegunda, she laid a hand on her breast, wondering why Roric's presence always sent a warm glow through her, a quickening of her heartbeat. Recalling his deep voice, his every gesture, she smiled to herself, each image playing itself again and again in her mind. She shook her head, telling herself she dreamed idle fantasies, wild illusions that had no place in her life, longings that would forever remain unfulfilled.

Tossing aside these futile yearnings, she brought her mind back to her immediate concern–Radegunda.

Later that evening, after the kitchen staff had gone to their quarters and a peaceful quiet had settled over the palace, Keriam found Radegunda in the still room. The healer woman worked at the hearth, where a sweet-smelling concoction bubbled in an iron cauldron over the fire. Pine torches in iron sconces provided dim illumination in the dusky twilight, casting wavy shadows across stone walls that reflected the heat from the hearth and made the room uncomfortably hot.

"Radegunda."

Next to a long table, the woman spun around, as if caught in a crime; then a cautious smile spread across her face. "Princess Keriam."

Leaning against the wooden counter opposite, Keriam returned the smile, wanting to put the woman at ease. She must broach the subject of magic with care. "Is everything to your satisfaction here?" Her gaze shifted to the various wooden bowls of petals and herbs that rested on the table where the healer worked. Pleasant herbal fragrances floated through the air. "Do you need anything else?"

"All settled, princess, although I'm used to more light. But I'm not complainin', just makin' a statement." She wiped her woolen apron across her shiny forehead. The flickering candle flames caught her movements, distorting her shadow on the wall. "I make up my lotions, soaps and such every evening. Once in a nineday, my partner, Adsaluta, comes and picks them up to sell at the shop. We share the proceeds."

Keriam nodded, impatient to get to the subject, but in a roundabout way. "Have you always lived in the capital?"

The woman jerked back, knocking over a wooden bowl of rose petals. "N-no, madam." She brushed the petals back into the bowl while she talked. "I-I lived in a village on the outskirts of Moytura before I came here. M-my house burned to the ground."

"I'm so sorry! How terrible for you!" Keriam sucked in a breath, her gaze scanning the room to ascertain that there were no eavesdroppers. "Radegunda, what are your feelings on magic?"

A guilty look captured the old woman's face. "Magic, madam?"

"Practicing magic." Keriam folded her arms across her chest.

Radegunda paused, staring down at the floor. She looked up and spoke in a quiet voice. "Madam, I am skilled in the healing arts--"

"Which some may construe as enchantment," Keriam said, "but that doesn't answer my question."

"Princess Keriam, may I ask why you want to know about my-my skills? What makes you think I practice magic?" She bowed her head. "If I may ask."

"One of the king's officers has spoken to me of your skills."

"I seen him this morning! I don't know his name--"

"Roric Gamal, the king's steward now, since Fergus Morrigan was . . . uh, died."

"Oh, my," the healer said with a crestfallen look. "Back in my village, he saved me from thugs who was beatin' me. I didn't know he worked for the king. He was wearin' his cloak so I couldn't see no palace emblem." She brushed her hand across her glistening forehead. "An' I guess I was too upset to notice, even if I could see it."

"Why were the thugs beating you?" Keriam asked, although she was sure of the answer.

"They called me a witch, and--"

"And are you? Radegunda, if you practice good magic, your secret is safe with me."

"Only good magic. Never evil."

"Ah, now we are getting somewhere. As long as you do no harm--"

"Never, madam." She shook her head fiercely. "As I say, only good."

"Something I must tell you--Roric Gamal still retains his officer's rank and has influence with His Majesty. He may cause trouble, since he greatly fears witchcraft. Stay away from him." Keriam wished she could follow her own advice. But something drew her to him, as though her mind–and her heart–had no will of their own. "Best you stay away from Roric Gamal," she repeated.

"Oh, madam, I will."

Another thought hit Keriam. "If you have the second sight, why didn't you know that Roric Gamal works for the palace?"

"Like I said, I was too upset to catch that fact at the time he saved me. Anyway, my ability don't always work when I want it to. Sometimes it comes to me unexpected-like, especially in dreams."

"Ah, yes." Keriam nodded. It was the same with her, but she'd never admit it to anyone, least of all the druids, who held the power of life and death over all the people of the kingdom. Satisfied with the information she'd gathered, she pushed away from the counter. "It is agreed then. I'll say nothing of your skills, and I hope you realize it's to your advantage to say nothing of mine." She regretted the threat immediately.

"I'll keep quiet, princess. I promise."

"That's settled, then." She sniffed appreciably at the aromatic scents wafting from the wooden bowls. "Your customers must enjoy your toiletries. They surely do have tempting scents."

"Indeed, madam. I'll send some lilac soap and talcum powder up to your room tomorrow."

"Thank you. I'm looking forward to using them." She turned to leave. What if Roric Gamal discovered her powers? Even though she knew no magic, he could easily accuse her of witchcraft. What if he saw her specter on one of her nightly sojourns, or discovered she had the second sight? She shuddered at the thought. If only she could follow her advice to Radegunda and stay away from him. But circumstances and concern for her father had thrown them together. And something else she was afraid to identify, an attraction that grew stronger every day, more intense each time she saw him.

Even if Roric suspected Aradia, what could they do about the steward's widow? Since Fergus had been buried several days go, Aradia had shown no desire to return to her village. The sorceress should be an actress, Keriam fumed, recalling the woman's tears as Fergus lay in his grave. What kept her here, if not Balor? King Malachy's advice about the evil woman returned to haunt her.

Kill her if you must.

Chapter Nine

Dressed plainly, oblivious to the noise and laughter around him, Roric sat at a corner table in The Hungry Bear, nursing a mug of malt corma. Mostly farmers, drovers, and a few craftsmen patronized this clean but humble tavern where a multitude of aromas filled the air--the smoke from countless pipes, the yeasty smell of corma, the tantalizing fragrance of beef sizzling in the stone hearth. Lit glass lamps hung from wall hooks, relieving the room's somber dullness, masking scratches and burn holes on the furniture. Young and old customers, men and women, occupied every table of the common room. Narrow, worn stairs at the back of the room led to sleeping quarters above.

Talmora's bones! He needed a pleasure woman now. When was the last time he'd procured the services of one of those wenches?, If you can't remember that, you must be in bad shape, old man. Mindful of diseases, he kept a protection shield in an inside cloak pocket. Besides, he didn't want to leave any unwanted children behind.

Raising the mug to his mouth, Roric reflected on his new position as palace steward, a responsibility that kept him engaged from dawn and throughout the day, often until the early morning hours. The king had finally insisted he take a day from his duties every nineday. And that was a suggestion he couldn't refuse, he thought, setting his mug down. Still, he missed his parents and the rest of his family, writing to them whenever time permitted, enjoying all their news from home. He sighed. Maybe someday . . .

Thankful none of the military officers or palace staff frequented this tavern, he basked in his temporary anonymity. Soon enough, he'd return to the palace, once more embroiled in all its machinations. Not that he minded the obligations his position entailed, far from it. Yet he walked a perilous path as the palace steward, but also one who must pretend to join in the plot against the king. How much longer would his luck hold out? How much longer could he lead this double life? He drummed his fingers on the oaken table. Sacred shrine! What if Balor found him out?

If Balor should succeed in his assassination--the Goddess forbid!--Roric would consider a plan that had brewed in his mind for a long time. Best if he, Roric, took part in the general's government, hoping to thwart him and eventually overthrow him, then restore Princess Keriam to the throne. Possibly he could even moderate Balor's plans and tame his excesses. What would happen if the general were permitted to run roughshod over the people of Avador? His hands clenched on the table, as if wringing Balor's neck. If only he could!

Radegunda still resided at the palace, damn the witch! He kept his distance from her, but he wished Keriam would send her away. After Balor was arrested for treason--and he would be-- Roric would approach the princess again. He would convince her that Radegunda posed a different kind of threat, but one every bit as menacing.

Draining his mug, Roric contemplated ordering another. He looked around for the serving wench, a pretty, buxom lass with blonde hair and blue eyes, not to mention swaying hips that promised untold pleasures.

She caught his glance and approached his table, a beguiling smile on her face. "May I offer you anything else, sir?"

Roric grinned. "That depends on what you have to offer."

She jerked her head in the direction of the stairs. "Let's find out."

* * *

Three evenings later, Roric left the king's study after a consultation with Tencien concerning a new bridge over the Nantosuelta River, its cost estimate and feasibility of construction before the start of the rainy season, several moonphases away. Now would be a good time to explore the dungeon, while the rest of the palace slept and before he sought his own room. After he traversed the long hallway and hurried down the stone steps to the first floor, he strode past the main hall and the extended walkway until he reached a heavy oaken door beyond the kitchen, one that warded the dungeon.

106

A lantern hung on the wall outside the dungeon. Using a torch from a wall sconce, he lit the lantern, then opened the creaking door. By the dim light, he passed through and closed the door behind him. He descended the stone stairs, his footsteps cautious on the dark, mold-slippery steps. The lantern light did little to dispel the stygian darkness, the floor jolting him as he reached the bottom.

The stench overwhelmed him, all but making him gag.

Setting the lantern down for a moment, he brushed spider webs from his hair and tunic, his eyes trying to penetrate the darkness. As he moved on, rats scurried out of his way, and a rank odor assailed him, a blend of stale urine and excrement. Cockroaches climbed the walls and skittered along the floor, crawling across his boots.

Roric slapped at the pests. "Damn it, get off!" Walking on, he nearly slipped and fell on the slimy floor but caught himself. He moved more slowly, gaining time to acclimate himself to the layout of the cells.

Under Tencien, the prison had found few occupants, but wisdom warned Roric that situation would change if ever Balor gained the throne. Since the cells remained empty, no guards were posted, but he noted a chair for one guard, and a key rack nailed to the wall above .

Holding the lantern closer, he examined the row of keys, observing they were numbered to correspond with the numbers of the cells. He grabbed a key at random and headed for the matching cell. There, an iron door faced him, with only a tiny opening at the top and one at the bottom for passing in food and water. A simple twist unlocked the cell door, and he stepped inside, his gaze covering a straw pallet--flea-ridden, no doubt--next to the wall, an iron bucket in the corner, and manacles chained to the wall. Anxious to escape the cell's foul odor, he left and closed the heavy door behind him. Four more cells lined this side of the room, an equal number of cells on the opposite side.

A wide wooden door at the end of the dungeon beckoned, and his footsteps echoed on the stone floor as he headed for the door. At the end, Roric raised the iron bar and pushed the door open, only to find a long stone tunnel, reached by descending a few steps. More rats scuttled out of the way as he proceeded along, the tunnel walls dark and slimy. After walking about twenty yards, he came to another set of steps leading upward, a hinged door above his head, no doubt concealed from the outside by a cluster of bushes. With one hard push, he opened the door and caught a cool night breeze, but more than that, information that might prove useful in the future.

How many people know of this tunnel? He'd wager not even the princess knew of it, for royalty didn't concern themselves with such crude matters.

Recollections of Princess Keriam taunted him as he emerged onto the first floor of the palace and strode across the main hall, on the way to the stairs that led to the upper floors. He knew their mutual concern for the king's safety would bring them together more often in the coming days, a prospect that sent his mind racing in different directions. Anticipation grappled with reluctance, for much as her calm, confident demeanor always lightened his mood, he feared enthrallment by her charm.

And it would be a long, long time before he forgot his wife . . . if ever.

* * *

"A moment of your time, Aradia." Keriam waited by a stone statue of Seluvia, the forest goddess, as the steward's widow approached her along the hallway. Fury blazed inside her, but despite Malachy's advice, Keriam could never murder Aradia, even if murder of a witch were possible.

"Yes, madam?" Aradia raised her eyebrows, her musk scent overpowering. Her green silk dress clung to every curve of her body, its neckline much too low for daytime wear.

Keriam tensed, but she would proceed with her plan. She must get the sorceress out of the palace. "Now that Fergus is . . . is dead, I should think you'd want to return to Mag Bregha, to your family."

"Oh, madam, I find I like it quite well here at the palace."

"Well, I find I'd rather have you gone from here. Aradia, I won't pretend I've ever had any fondness for you. And I don't understand why you've remained here so long after Fergus's death." Balor, obviously. "But it's best that you return to Mag Bregha. I'm sure you'll be happier there, away from sad memories." Keriam struggled to keep the sarcasm from her voice. "So I want you to leave no later than the day after tomorrow." Keriam paused, waiting for a reaction from the sorceress, a reaction she didn't get. "Will you need any help with packing your belongings or transporting them?"

"I have few possessions, madam, my clothes and a few trinkets. I can pack them in a case and use the palace carriage, if I may."

"Yes, of course." Keriam paused, at a loss to know what more to say. She dared not touch the witch for fear of the images her touch would invoke. "Well, then, I wish you good fortune in your future endeavors," she said, looking forward to the day she'd be rid of the woman.

But what about Balor? Keriam wondered as Aradia glided down the hallway. Surely Aradia still harbored an affection for the general. King Malachy's warning about the steward's widow returned to trouble her. Keriam couldn't believe this was the end of her association with the sorceress, but apparently it was so.

Keriam frowned. Aradia had agreed to return to her home much too hastily. Why hadn't she threatened to go to the king, to ask his permission to stay? She might do that yet, Keriam considered. If so, she'd have to convince her father that Aradia must depart.

* * *

Keriam headed for the stables the following day, intent on visiting the library to obtain more books for the palace children. Maudina was busy elsewhere, thank the Goddess. She found Traigh inside Liath's stall, bent at the waist, his back to the horse, the horse's hoof between the man's legs. Frowning, he released the horse's leg and straightened as she entered. The stall smelled of fresh hay and pine shavings, with tack and saddle hanging from wall hooks.

"Madam, we have a problem with the horses--all of them." He scratched his head. "Their hooves--they all have a stone bruise and--"

"A what?"

"Madam, all the horses' hooves are stricken with a stone bruise. I can't understand it. Now and then, a horse may develop this malady--but all of them?" He brushed his hands on his tunic and shook his head.

Keriam's heart sank. What if she couldn't rid herself of Aradia by tomorrow? "What causes this--do you know?"

"If the sole of the hoof is cracked, an infection sets in."

"How can you treat this--or can't you?" Her pulse raced as she waited for his answer.

He nodded. "I can treat the ailment with salt water, but it may take awhile for them to recover."

"How long?" Keriam held her breath.

Traigh scratched his head again. "Could take two ninedays."

"Two ninedays!"

Traigh looked as heartsick as she felt. "I'm afraid so, Princess Keriam."

Keriam sighed. At least he knew a remedy. "Very well. Do the best you can." She left the stables then, her mind in confusion, her fears mounting. How could this happen? The answer hit her like a slap in the face. Aradia!

* * *

In his ornate bedchamber, Midac Balor stood by his chest of drawers and raised the lid of a jewelry box atop the chest. Made of mother-of-pearl and rimmed with gold, it had belonged to his mother, who had bequeathed the box and its contents to him. For your wife, she'd said, whenever he married.

His mother . . . Goddess, how he'd loved her. But his father . . . He gripped the edge of the chest as memories flooded his mind, images he should have dismissed years ago of that cruel, domineering man who had enjoyed inflicting pain on his oldest son.

His mother, a kind and loving woman, had appeared helpless to intercede. But she should have . . . or he should have escaped. Balor had to admit that his love for his mother was tinged with contempt, for she should have protected him from his father's fury.

Discarding painful reflections--rejections!--Balor rummaged through the many fine pieces in the box, his aim to choose an item that would most please the princess. Then, perhaps, she might prove more amenable to his marriage offer. When he became king of Avador, she'd reign as his queen, a prospect that warmed his blood and sent his dark thoughts fleeing.

After much discriminating perusal, he chose a gold bracelet of the most excellent workmanship, studded with alternating carnelian and turquoise. Dropping it into his belt pouch, he checked his appearance in the nearest wall mirror, admiring his dark uniform, the glittering medals that bedecked his chest. His high boots shone so brightly, he could see his reflection in them. Gingerly, he traced the scar on his cheek, thinking it gave him a rather dashing visage, a look that attracted the women. He turned from the mirror and opened his bedchamber door that led to the outside, then strode along a narrow dirt path to his stables. There, after having his horse saddled, he mounted the black stallion and cantered the short distance to the palace.

He found the princess speaking with one of the cleaning women--a dwarf!--in the spacious main hall, the princess's smile an indication of her easy relationship with this miserable excuse of humanity. Several dwarf children lounged in chairs and sofas, books in their laps but their rapt attention on the princess. Why were they permitted to pollute this magnificent hall with their presence? When he became king, he'd ensure they were confined to their quarters. He shot them all venomous looks, and sneaking guilty glances at each other, they quickly returned to their reading.

Princess Keriam gave him a curt nod. "I shall be with you in a moment, general. Or did you wish to see His Majesty?"

"You, madam." How dare she make him wait while she wasted precious moments on an underling? What a joy it would be to whip her now, to prove his power over her! His loins tightened at the thought.

111

The princess wore a simple gray dress trimmed in red and black plaid at the collar and hem, the silky frock revealing every curve. He imagined her without any clothes, her perfectly-formed breasts, her slender hips and long legs. His loins tightened further, and he turned away, pretending to study a vase of phlox on a side table. Catching bits of conversation, he realized she was asking the woman about her family, for Goddess's sake! Well, he'd stop that nonsense when Keriam became his wife, when she learned to recognize her master. Once they married, he wouldn't permit her to acknowledge such a creature's presence, unless to order punishment.

The dwarf waddled off, and the princess approached him in her easy, graceful manner. "My apologies for making you wait, general." Her voice was as cold as her expression, no smiles for him. "What did you wish to speak about?"

"In private, madam, if you please."

"Of course." She led him to the library across the hall, her gown fluttering around her ankles as she walked, her firm buttocks outlined against the silky material.

"Yes, sir?" she asked after closing the library door. No offer of a seat or refreshment.

He shifted his position. "Princess, you may recall the night of the Bel Festival, when I suggested that you marry me. Some time has gone by since then, so I'm asking you again, now. I would have you for my wife."

"General, I fear I can't marry a man I don't love."

"Think again, madam. Many marriages begin without love but achieve that happy state as time passes."

"But we never know, do we? We don't know if a marriage that begins without love can truly change in the course of time. Marriage is a chancy arrangement as it is, sir. Why take an added risk?"

Resolved to stifle his anger, he took refuge in argument. "You think your father will let you pick any man you want? More likely, he's already chosen a husband for you."

"My father knows my wishes, sir," she said, folding her arms across her chest. "He is in agreement."

"You are--how old, madam--nineteen, twenty? You wait many more years, and no man will want you."

"No great loss, general. Oh, I'll admit I'd like an affectionate husband and children, but if I can't marry for love, I won't marry at all. And I don't find the unmarried state a dispiriting one. There is much at the palace and throughout the kingdom that requires my attention."

A vein throbbed at his temple. "So your answer is 'no'?"

She tilted her head. "General Balor, I thought I had made that plain."

Goddess-damned slut! He spun on his heels and strode across the floor, then jerked the library door open, banging it back against the wall. A vase crashed to the floor, shattering into pieces. He marched across the vast hall, his high boots clicking on the flagstones, and left the palace by a back door. Outside, he took deep breaths, clenching and unclenching his hands as he strode toward the stable, then mounted his horse.

Astride his horse at the edge of the palace grounds, Balor plunged through the trees and bushes that comprised a small woods separating the palace from the army barracks. His muscles tense, his heart pounding, he reached into his belt pouch and grabbed the bracelet. His hand shook as he hurled the bauble into the bushes. One day very soon, the princess would pay for his humiliation.

Revenge would give him such pleasure.

Chapter Ten

"'So they married one another, and that was the fine wedding they had, and if I were to be there then, I would not be here now; but I heard it from a birdeen that there was neither cark nor care, sickness nor sorrow, mishap nor misfortune on them till the hour of their death, and may the same be with me, and with us all!'" On a sofa in the main hall, Keriam closed the book of children's tales and smiled at the dwarf boys and girls gathered on the floor in front of her. The children remained still, their eyes focused in rapt attention.

"Now that I've read you a story," she said, "it's time for you to go to bed, so--"

"One more story, Princess Keriam, please?" a young boy asked, his eyes wide open in appeal.

"Yes, another story, princess," the others joined in.

"No, children, it's getting late." Keriam set the book on a long oaken table that flanked the sofa. "I'll read again tomorrow. Now, off to bed with you, and sleep well."

After goodnights were said and the children had traipsed off, Keriam headed for the spacious kitchen at the rear of the palace to meet Radegunda. The healer woman had promised to teach her about the medicinal arts, knowledge that might well prove useful. Twilight darkened the sky, but flaming pine torches cast dim haloes in the vast main hall and the long walkway that led from the hall to the kitchen. The heat and fumes from the torches within the confined space made her eyes water and prompted her to walk faster, her long dress fluttering about her ankles, velvet slippers whispering on the flagstones.

Thoughts of Balor drove every other consideration from her mind. Why had she spurned him so abruptly? Look at the harm he could cause to those closest to her--Maudina and Radegunda, but most especially, her father. If Tencien should suffer because of her refusal, she would never forgive herself. But what other choice did she have--accept his marriage offer, then renege later? No, that wasn't her way. Ever honest, she always believed in giving a truthful answer, as gently as possible, or not so gently, as in Balor's case.

What if the general hastened his schedule for the assassination because of her refusal? Worse, what if he decided on a slow, lingering death for the king? The plotters had designated the Lug Festival for their evil deed. Even if she and Roric could foil their plans before that occurrence, what would stop the conspirators from trying again . . . and again?

Dismissing her despondent thoughts, Keriam entered the still room and greeted Radegunda, who waited by a counter near the wall. Wooden bowls of herbs cluttered the counter, and recently-built shelves lined the wall above her, each shelf filled with glass jars. Dried herbs hung from the ceiling, imbuing the room with a myriad of pleasant scents.

The woman dressed better now, Keriam was pleased to see. Clad in a deep green linen dress trimmed with brown silk piping, she looked like a successful merchant's wife. Shiny new brown leather shoes bedecked her feet, and even her face looked different, not quite so gaunt now, her cheeks fuller with fewer wrinkles.

Radegunda returned the smile. "Ah, madam, ready for more herbal lessons?"

Keriam stopped by the counter, inhaling the fresh, spicy scents of herbs and crushed flowers, aromas that always cheered her. "Indeed, I still have much to learn.."

"Happy to help, madam. I'm here to serve you and your father." Her hands moved nervously about the bowls, the stoppered essence jars, as she spoke in an undertone. "That Aradia, princess . . ."

Keriam tilted her head. "What about her?" she asked, although she normally didn't indulge in palace gossip.

"Well . . ." Radegunda twisted her hands in her apron. "Why does she stay here at the palace?" the healer woman blurted. "Madam, I hear the servants gossiping. They say Aradia's family disowned her long ago. And no wonder!" Radegunda made a sign of warding off evil: her thumb and forefinger touching, she flicked her right hand over her left shoulder. "She's wicked, that one. I fear she will cause more trouble."

"No, she won't, because I've told her to leave the palace. She can return to Mag Bregha, family or no family, as soon as the horses have recovered."

"Horses, madam?"

"Every horse in the stable has a stone bruise--an infection--in their hooves." She shook her head. "I don't understand it and neither does Traigh. But if anyone can cure the horses, it is he. Let's hope they all recover, and soon. For now, I have other concerns." She smoothed her finger along the edge of the wooden counter, carefully forming her next words. "If you can practice magic, why can't you do something about this drought? I fear this dry spell will bring fleas, and you know how many diseases those insects can cause. Think of the millions of squirrels in the country that might carry a disease. What if we have another plague like we did eleven years ago?"

"Princess, I haven't been able to summon rain since these spells take practice, you understand. I've been so busy here with my preparations, that I fear I've neglected my magic. Besides, I believe evil forces are at work here."

Goddess, don't let it be so. Keriam stifled a shiver and forced herself to deal with ordinary matters. "Enough talk. We could use our time better by dealing with herbs, don't you think? So tell me something. My maid often gets stubborn colds. What should she take for that?"

"Ah, yes, madam. There are many plants that cure colds." On her tiptoes, she reached high on the shelf and brought down a labeled jar. "Forsythia. Mix this dried flower with honeysuckle in lemon balm tea. It should cure that cold very soon and make Maudina feel much better."

The enchantress pushed the jar aside. "Gotta be careful about the use of these herbs and flowers." She tapped another jar on the shelf directly above her. "Foxglove, for instance. If given in the right amount, it c'n ease heart trouble. The wrong amount c'n cause death."

"I understand," Keriam said, now realizing how much she had to learn about medicinal plants.

"And another thing, madam. Please notice I've arranged the jars accordin' to their uses." She tapped the second shelf. "You see here? All these jars are herbal cures for the stomach, and right next to them, I have others for headaches. Now here," she said, tapping another shelf, "these here jars are for insomnia." Keriam nodded, thankful the woman had arranged the herbs in such a manner, for she had to squint to see the labels in the dim light.

Radegunda's mind was busy as she talked, rendering concentration difficult. Ever since Roric Gamal had seen her rabbit shift at her home, the memory had ruled her days and nights. What if he reported her to the druids? At the time of her last shape shift, she thought she could move quietly at an alcove in the palace entrance, to observe the comings and goings. But she hadn't counted on the dwarf children. She vowed never to shape shift again, at least, not while she lived here.

"And headaches?" Keriam asked. "His Majesty often suffers from severe headaches."

"Headaches, yes," Radegunda said, reaching for another labeled jar, setting it on the counter. "Feverfew."

She wished she could forget her fears as easily as she explained herbal cures. Further palace talk warned of a jackal prowling the nearby woods. What if that predator trespassed the palace grounds and found her in her rabbit body? No, she vowed, she wouldn't shape shift again.

* * *

"Bit of trouble, sir."

Roric looked up from the table at The Hungry Bear while one of his spies drew out a chair and sat across from him. Serving maids rushed to and fro, carrying trays laden with tasty dishes. Delicious fragrances of beef stew and apple pie wafted through the air, but Roric couldn't summon an appetite.

"What kind of trouble?" Roric asked after a long pull from his mug.

"Well . . ." The man shook his head, opening and closing his mouth.

117

Roric shoved his mug of corma toward the man. "Here, Calum, drink this while I order another." He raised his hand and caught the serving maid's attention--a different girl this time, not the pretty lass who'd given him such pleasure on his last visit--then pointed to the mug. He turned back to the spy. "Now, you were saying . . .?"

Calum gulped the drink and wiped the back of his hand across his mouth. "Well, you see, it's difficult to spy on the general at night because . . . because . . . a jackal!" he blurted, as if that word explained everything.

Roric frowned. "You're not telling me much. What's this about a jackal?"

Calum lifted the corma to his mouth and took another long gulp. "Two nights ago, I noticed a jackal--sir, I swear it's not a wolf or a dog, although it looks a little like both." He stared into his drink, as if the brew provided an answer. "Anyway, I saw this animal--like a wild dog, actually--lurking around Balor's house at night. It came from the woods toward the south side of his house. You know, there's a wide lawn between the woods and his mansion. All I can tell you is what I observe when I stand behind a tree on the west side of Balor's house. After it got there, it just . . . disappeared."

"Disappeared?"

"In the bushes. I lose the damn jackal as soon as it reaches the mansion, and where it goes after that, I don't know." He pursed his lips. "I even searched through the bushes but found nothing. Strangest thing I ever saw."

"You saw no opening?"

Calum lifted his hands. "Not a damn thing."

The maid placed a frothing mug beside Roric, and he set two copper coins on the table, his gaze never leaving the spy's face. "Jackals--don't they travel in packs, like wolves?"

"This one's a loner. She--"

"She? How do you know it's a female?" Roric gave the spy a long look, his mind in confusion. In the name of the Goddess, what did a jackal have to do with Balor?

"For some reason, I just think it is. Don't know why. She doesn't make this trip through the woods every night, mind you.

Maybe two or three times in a nineday." He scratched his head. "Don't know where the damn jackal goes."

"Have you seen any humans at the general's house--besides Balor?" Roric asked, discouraged that so far, they'd gained no useful evidence.

He shook his head. "No, sir, not a one."

A thoughtful silence followed. A sly one, the general. "Very well, Calum. Keep on as before. We're bound to come up with something." As soon as possible, he'd relate the man's findings to Princess Keriam. For now, he wouldn't tell the king of this new development, not until he had something more definite to go on.

While Calum drained his mug, Roric leaned forward, resting his elbows on the table. Questions flooded his mind. Was the jackal Balor's familiar? Did Balor shapeshift? What if the general practiced wizardry? If he did . . . Roric's mind raged with hopeful possibilities. If he could prove that Balor practiced the evil craft, he would arrest him and turn him over to the druids. But he must have evidence. It all came back to proof.

* * *

Keriam's spirit lifted from the bed as she lay sound asleep. Night after night, she'd spied on Aradia, to discover what evil the sorceress was devising. Talmora, she'd be glad when the witch had departed the palace. So far, Keriam had gained no new information, most times finding Aradia in her room, sound asleep. And where the witch went other times, Keriam had no idea. Since the steward's death, his widow occupied a small room on the third floor, at the opposite end of the hall from the present steward's quarters.

Roric's recent tale of a jackal roaming the woods aroused her suspicions, her brain focused on one person: Aradia.

She drifted upward to the third floor and slipped into Aradia's room, keeping within the shadows. Her bed was empty, the sorceress nowhere in sight. Hurry! Keriam's spirit brain warned. She must find Aradia before she left the palace, if it wasn't already too late.

Like a feather caught in a downwind, she floated toward the first floor. Step by cautious step, she slipped through the thick walls and emerged outside after one of the guards walked past. Seeking concealment, she floated toward an earthberry bush beyond the spacious palace garden, in an area that warded the woods separating the palace grounds from Balor's mansion and the other military housing.

Despite its immense size, the palace had purposely been built with only three doors leading to the outside, one at the front and two at the back on either side of the kitchen, features that helped protect the palace from intruders. Keriam suspected that if Aradia were to embark on her own nightly sojourn, she would choose one of the back doors.

Before long, she heard the heavy oaken door screech open. Aradia stepped into the full moonlight as another guard approached along the flagstone walk.

"Mistress Morrigan, it's late to be outside, and dangerous, too. I've heard tales of a jackal roaming the palace grounds at night."

Aradia laughed softly, a sweet, melodic sound. "Sir, I appreciate your concern, but I've always found that animals are shy. They leave us alone if we do the same for them. As a matter of fact, I couldn't sleep. Thought I might take a walk in the woods. I promise you, I'll be careful."

"Very well, mistress. But if you need help, please be sure to call me."

"Thank you, sir. How kind you are. I'll remember your warning." After the guard walked past, Aradia headed for the thick woods, her step quick and purposeful. Several yards away, she stopped behind a spreading oak and looked in all directions.

Hiding within the earthberry bush, Keriam observed Aradia as if it were daylight, saw her pale skin, heard her every movement. The sorceress slipped her shoulder straps down, and her silk nightgown slithered from her body in a soft heap. She raised a large rock and shoved the gown beneath it, her naked body gleaming in the moonlight.

And then . . . and then . . . Keriam stared, her mouth open in shock. A light fog surrounded the witch. Fur patches sprouted on the sorceress's body, starting on her belly and spreading outward. Hands became paws, the face elongating into a snout. Bones crunched; limbs realigned as the witch slowly sank to all fours, her feet lengthening, long hooked claws scratching the ground. A tail grew, and her hips and shoulders narrowed, like a wolf's. Her body fully covered with fur, Aradia growled, low and sharp. A strong, musky odor fouled the night air.

Keriam stayed motionless, shocked beyond words, beyond action. Goddess, she prayed, what can I do now? How could she fight this creature? Would Radegunda's magic prove a match for this witch?

"Can't a body get any sleep around here?" A sweet, bell like voice, barely audible, rose from the earthberry bush.

Who was that? Keriam spun around, her spirit heart beating frantically. She looked around, her eyes catching a fairy tucked in the curve of a branch. The tiny creature yawned and stretched her arms. Her silvery wings shone in the moonlight, curly golden hair framing her face. Clad in a pink pastel gown, she resembled a tiny doll, not more than two inches long, her eyes, nose, and mouth perfectly-formed.

Keriam pressed her hand to her ethereal heart. "Ah, you startled me," she whispered in her spirit voice. "Sorry if I disturbed you."

The fairy waved a tiny hand. "It's all right, princess. I'll go back to sleep soon enough. But watch out for that Aradia. This isn't the first time she's shape--shape--"

"Shapeshifted?"

"Yes!"

"Goddess!" A jolt of alarm slammed through her spirit body.

"Indeed!" The fairy yawned again and sank back into the branch, shimmying into a comfortable position. "Now, if you'll excuse me . . ."

"Wait! Please tell me your name."

"Zinerva," she said in her sweet voice. "Now, I really must sleep. . . ."

"Goodnight, Zinerva." Tempted to reach over and touch the lovely creature, Keriam realized her own ghostly body precluded tangible contact.

Tucking her wings across her chest, the fairy closed her eyes, and in no time, a slight rise and fall of her chest indicated she slept deeply.

Keriam cast one last affectionate glance at the comely creature. She hoped to meet Zinerva again, during the day, perhaps, when distractions wouldn't preempt a furtherance of their acquaintance. Vague possibilities claimed her mind. Was there some way she could use these lovely creatures--not only Zinerva, but other fairies that inhabited the trees--to help her? Well, something to think about . . .

Mindful of the passing time, Keriam followed the witch through the woods. When needing solitude, she'd often roamed these woods in daylight hours, thankful this wasn't the same vast forest as where the torathors dwelled. She enjoyed the experience during the day, but now her spiritshook with each step.

Keriam slid from tree to tree, always careful to keep the sorceress in sight, the thick tree roots and jutting rocks proving no impediment. Like monsters, gnarled tree trunks and twisted limbs loomed all around her. At the woods' edge, the jackal sped toward the general's house.

Keriam left the forest. She'd learned all she needed to know.

* * *

The jackal trotted along the ground, through the thick trees and undergrowth. She sniffed the rich earth, stopping occasionally to smell a rotting carcass or a strange plant. Now and then, the animal looked behind, a vague disquiet in her head, uncertain of the cause. She paused and snarled, a low, throaty growl.

Somewhere in the dim recesses of her memory lurked her lover's admonition that she must remain always on guard. Her lover . . . a flicker of joy made her heart beat faster, saliva dripping from her mouth. The heat consumed her, strong and gloriously wild.

She reached her destination and raced the remaining distance, across the wide, grassy space. Insects buzzed around her. A snake glided through the grass, its tongue flicking in and out, its head darting from side to side. So many diversions! But she raced on, her goal in sight.

A barbarous excitement raged within her, but fear accompanied her, too. What if an arrow felled her? Once more, she sniffed the air around her until convinced no danger threatened. At her lover's house now, she stopped beside a secret entrance that bordered the house, a wide opening set beneath a layer of leafy twigs, placed behind a thick bush. With her right forepaw, she moved aside a leafy branch, then wiggled and squirmed through the opening.

A few steps led her down to a narrow tunnel under the house. Aradia trotted along, her eyes keenly sharp in the darkness, the soft pads of her feet touching the cold stone floor. She paused to smell a dead rat, then ran on, impatient to see her lover. Snakes slid along the floor, and spiders dangled from webs on the ceiling, but she ignored every temptation. The jackal's brain issued a warning, something she must do, but what? Ah, yes, she must close up the tunnel opening, make it look as if no entrance existed.

Within minutes, she shifted to her human form. The fur gradually disappeared, the bones realigning again; the snout became a nose, and paws reformed into feet and hands. Human again, she returned to the hole, bending over double as she retraced her steps. There at the entrance she pushed a secret door into place, one that concealed any hint of the tunnel or the opening.

She headed back along the tunnel again and climbed the few steps to the bedchamber door. Without knocking, she emerged, naked and eager, into Midac Balor's elegant bedchamber.

He drew her into his arms. "I thought you'd never come."

* * *

Upon her return to the palace, Keriam's spirit body hid behind a bush while a guard made the rounds, a bored expression on his face. After he disappeared around the corner, she slipped out from her hiding place. Caught up in her anxieties, she failed to see or hear another man who left the stables, his high boots crunching on the gravel. Too late, she saw him staring at her: Roric Gamal!

Mind-numbing fear drove her behind an oak tree. She admonished herself for being discovered. Fool! Had Roric actually seen her? If so, what would he think of her now? Would he ever trust her again? How could she face him tomorrow? Even now, she could hear his accusations as he dragged her to the druids: witch!

* * *

Riding back to the palace, Roric thanked all the gods and goddesses that his horse didn't suffer from the stone bruise. He must have been riding it at the time the other horses were afflicted. But why should all of the horses be suffering from this malady? What was responsible? He headed for the palace, wanting solitude and sleep, to forget--at least until morning--the dangerous game he played. But he mustn't reject Calum's report of a jackal, a tale too serious to dismiss.

He strode the gravel path that led from the stable to the palace, wondering if he could sleep at all. As he neared the palace, he conceived a plan. Perhaps if he visited Balor again with more information that would prove useful to the general, it would deflect any suspicion from him.

Something moved among the trees and bushes, not far from where he walked--a spirit, as ephemeral as air. Recognition punched him in the gut. Princess Keriam! He stared, but the specter disappeared, prompting him to wonder if he'd only imagined it. Did the princess practice witchcraft? Talmora's bones, don't let it be true! He shook his head, convinced that strain and worry prevented clear perception. Or possibly tonight's drinks on an empty stomach had affected his brain? But he'd had only three mugs of corma. Perhaps three too many.

* * *

Aradia nestled in bed with Midac, warmly satiated after their lovemaking. She congratulated herself on her ingenuity. Only look at what she'd done to the horses, given them all a hoof infection. She'd stay at the palace as long as she pleased, and no stupid princess would tell her when to leave. Despite her satisfaction, a few matters rankled her, topics with which she must confront the general.

"I saw you talking to the princess recently," she said, her tone accusatory.

A short pause ensued. "Well, you see, I had hoped to marry her--"

"Deceiver!" She kicked his bare leg. "I'm only second-best, is that it?"

He laughed. "You didn't let me finish. I changed my mind about the princess after I learned to know you better. What good fortune that you came to the capital! And now that your cloddish husband is gone--"

"Thank the demoness! I married him only to escape that dreary village." She chuckled. "Even had some friends pose as my family when he visited. And he thought I loved him. What a simpleton!"

"Well, he's out of the way now. Once we're rid of the king–
"

She sat up in bed. "When?"

"Ah, getting impatient, are we? All in due time, my dear. Now, let me finish. Once we're rid of the king, you may marry me. We can rule the country together."

She sank back down and snuggled closer. "And the princess?"

"I leave her to you. I'm sure you can devise ways to make life difficult for her, so she'll be happy to leave."

Aradia giggled. "I know a few poisons."

"Save your poisons for the king." He hesitated. "Or perhaps we will eliminate him some other way. In any event, I don't want the princess dead--No," he said as she jerked from his arm, "another death is one too many. We don't want others to get suspicious." He tapped her arm. "Remember, the army backs me, if only from fear, and that's all that matters. The soldiers know what will happen to them if they refuse to obey. With the princess gone from the palace, or better still, kept prisoner there--and you'll make sure of that, won't you?--I see no threat to our position or power."

"What about the new steward?" she asked.

"Gamal? What about him?"

"Can we count on his loyalty? You told me he's on your side, but as the king's steward--"

"Just wait until I rule the country. First chance I get, I'll test his loyalty. Then we'll find out whose side Gamal is on."

"And if it's not yours?"

Balor chuckled. "If not, I have a special punishment reserved for him."

"Ooh, tell me what you're going to do to him." Her heart beat wildly. "May I watch?"

"Ah, my dear sadistic witch. We'll have many punishment holidays when I become king. And you may watch to your heart's content." He reached for her hand and placed her fingers on his groin, which she found hard as iron. "I'll even put you in charge of the festivities. How does that sound?"

"Oh, I can hardly wait," she said, fondling him. "And I'll wager you can hardly wait now."

"Ah, yes, but sex is so much better when you, uh, don't rush things." He reached over to smooth his hand along her hip. "How strong is your magic, I wonder? Is it as strong as that old crone--what's her name--Radegunda?"

"Stronger! I can make a person see anything I want him to see. But sometimes I forget myself, like the time the princess saw us together, or thought she did. And you were nowhere near." She continued to fondle him, reveling in his quickened breathing. "At the time, I was thinking of you so much, I slipped up."

"Tell me how you did it."

She laughed. "You want me to give away my secrets?"

Balor bent low to lick her nipple. She gasped with pleasure, aching to have him inside her. "Never mind," he said. "You're good at so many things. Now show me what you do best." He

126

mounted her, and with one quick movement, plunged inside her. "Make love like an animal, darling. Like a jackal!"

Chapter Eleven

"You did well this time, sir. You almost beat me."

Roric smiled as he removed his fencing mask and gloves, breathing a sigh of relief at the swift onrush of air on his sweaty face. "'Almost' is the operative word, I believe. Now tell me what I did wrong."

"You still clench your left hand when you prepare to lunge," he said with a frank look. "This betrays your intentions."

Roric wiped a handkerchief across his face. "Something I need to improve."

The instructor nodded. "You can always improve your fencing. It could be a matter of life or death."

* * *

Hours before sunrise, Radegunda stepped outside the palace, greeting one of the night guards as he made his rounds along the courtyard walk. She held a lantern in one hand, a cloth bag in the other. By now, everyone at the palace knew Radegunda and considered her a friend, one they could trust to cure their ailments.

A warm breeze carried the scents of the courtyard, the smell of dry grass and night-blooming paconia. A quarter moon floated high in the heavens, accompanied by a multitude of stars; a chain of four brilliant planets trailed across the eastern sky.

The guard raised an eyebrow. "Rather late to be out, Radegunda," he said, a question in his voice. "Or early, depending on how you look at it."

She smiled. "Heard the horses have a problem. Thought I'd check on them but didn't want to bother Traigh or any of the stable boys."

"Madam, if you can heal the horses as well as you cured my toothache, we will all be grateful. Those horses can barely

128

stand–all of them! No one's been able to ride for days." He scratched his head. "Strangest thing I ever saw."

"I'll see what I can do. Goodnight, Noland."

In a loft above the stalls, Traigh and the stable boys slept soundly, no doubt exhausted after all the ministrations they'd had to perform on the horses--soaking their hooves in salt water twice a day, day after day. On light feet, Radegunda entered the first stall to find a bay lying down, twitching his hooves.

Radegunda laid a gentle hand on his forehead, saying magical words meant to soothe, and immediately the horse settled down in quiet contentment. She held the lantern close to the horse's hooves, examining each one.

She nodded in satisfaction. "Ah, yes, we'll have you better in no time." Opening her bag, she withdrew a jar of ointment, a mixture of tar with camomile and garlic, blended with a special herb few people knew of because it grew only in the mountains. She had procured the herb, along with a magic spell, years ago from a wizard who lived secretly in a cave, high up in the mountains.

She applied the ointment to each hoof, saying her magic, placing her hand lightly on the horse's leg. The hay around the horse's hooves sizzled and smoked, a sign her spell was working. Fearful one of the guards would smell the smoke, she beat it out with her bare hands. She went from stall to stall, bestowing the same tender treatment, a blend of ointment and enchantment, until she'd ministered to each one of them.

Convinced her spells had cured the horses, she wished she could perform a charm on Balor and Aradia, completely change their natures and make them both so docile that they wouldn't threaten anyone. But her magic wasn't strong enough yet. Repetition was the answer; she had a myriad of spells she wanted to practice, but she couldn't do them here at Emain Macha. Besides her books of spells, she needed open spaces and absolute solitude, impossible to obtain at the palace.

* * *

Ravens lit on Keriam's windowledge, one by one. Smiling at their antics, she counted the lineup: ten, eleven, then another landed. Sunlight gleaming on their black wings, the birds shifted from one foot to another and tilted their heads. Their beady eyes focused on her, as if they had momentous news to impart. How intelligent they looked!

"If I spoke to you birds," she asked, "would you understand me?"

They nodded in unison.

Why, yes, they did understand! Well, this presented all kinds of opportunities, and who knew what occasions to use their intelligence might arise in the future.

Outside, parched brown grass and drooping foliage revealed the lingering drought. How she wished it would rain, not only because the grass needed moisture--indeed, it did--but also because she feared dry weather would bring fleas. Avador must remain free of the plague.

Keriam squinted in the bright sunlight, the heat blasting her face. She returned her attention to the ravens. "Well, my little friends. I must remember to leave bread crumbs for you. Or do you prefer worms? Sorry I haven't caught any of the slimy creatures for you, but you've taken me by surprise." She touched her forehead. "Next time, I'll remember." She smiled while the birds' claws scratched against the stone windowsill, and they dipped their heads from side to side. "But tell me what I can do for you. Or do you want to do something for me? Either way, I'm happy to see you."

After the birds flew away, Keriam sank onto the bench, clenching her hands as her mind returned to the ever present problem. The Lug Festival was fast approaching, but she would not wait for Balor to make a move. If necessary, she'd hire someone to kill him. In the name of the Goddess, how could she hire someone to commit murder? Such an act would reduce her to Balor's level. Yet what choice did she have? She stood and paced the floor, clenching and unclenching her hands, wishing she could wrap them around Balor's neck. Her head throbbed with worry and tension. She could not--must not--wait for the general to strike first during the festival. Desperate plans formed in her mind. Could she hire someone to kill the general? Quickly, she discarded each plan as an unfeasible scheme; she could not slay someone in cold blood, nor hire someone to commit murder.

In any event, she must speak to her father.

"Have you thought of sending General Balor on a military mission?" she asked Tencien later that day. She took a chair in his office, arranging her cotton skirt around her ankles.

He smiled. "As a matter of fact, I intend to send him with an entourage to Elegia, to help coordinate our army with theirs, strengthen the military alliance. The general speaks their language fluently. There is much we can learn from the Elegian army."

"The wedding between King Barzad and your Aunt Edita will take place soon, don't forget." Tencien sat forward, clasping his hands between his knees. "You and I will journey to Elegia for the ceremony." His smile made him look much younger. "It's been a long time since you've taken any journeys. I'll wager you're looking forward to it. You may have a whole new wardrobe, if you like."

"A journey would be pleasant." Keriam returned the smile, reluctant to tell him a new wardrobe was the least of her concerns.

"When does the general depart for Elegia?" she asked, not conscious that she held her breath until her lungs felt about to burst.

"In a few days. I fear he won't return in time for the Lug Festival. He wants to leave before the rainy season starts, while the roads are still passable." Keriam released her breath in a long, slow sigh. "Of course," the king continued, "he regrets missing the holy day, but he realizes that duty comes first, one of the reasons why I esteem him as a military leader," he said with a level look her way.

Silently, Keriam thanked the Goddess that Balor would be gone, but new fears emerged. So what if Balor would be absent from the kingdom during the festival? That wouldn't prevent an assassination. He had others to do his will, and it wasn't many moonphases until the Lug Festival, not long until--

"Kerry, sweetheart, what's wrong? Your face has gone white."

Forcing a smile, she rose from the chair. "Must be something I ate. Perhaps I'll lie down for awhile."

He rose, too, and took her elbow. "Let me send Radegunda to you."

Keriam waved her hand. "No need to bother Radegunda," she said as he opened the door for her. "I'll be fine."

He stopped, his hand on the doorknob. "Are you still worried about me? Is that the problem? I told you after Fergus's death--" He swallowed hard. "--after Fergus's death, I told you I still maintain my trust in Balor--no, let me finish. I trust the general, but I'm willing to give you the benefit of the doubt, which is why I asked Gamal to investigate the matter. For now, I'm sending Balor to Elegia. Such a trip will get him out of the country for a while."

She nodded, but who knew what would happen in the coming days?

* * *

"Ah, Gamal." Midac Balor greeted the palace steward. "Just the man I want to see."

The general sat beside a massive oak desk in his study, a spacious room across the hall from his bedchamber. A statue of the Earth-mother goddess adorned an end table set against a far wall--for effect? Roric wondered. Plain gray silk draperies hung in the still summer air, as limp as the wilting roses in his garden.

The general indicated a chair. "Sit down." He smirked. "Palace duties keeping you busy?"

"As always," Roric replied, taking a seat. He must stay ever on guard, aware he must watch every word, every facial expression. "But the day is coming very soon when I will cease serving the king. Indeed, when the king ceases this life, I will serve you."

Balor returned to his seat. "What about the silver merchant in Moytura--what's his name, Drummond Haley? Can we count on his gold?" He smiled at his play on words.

"That's why I came to see you. I visited him recently, as you requested. His support is conditional upon gaining a position in the new government, preferably as Minister of Coinage." Roric smiled inwardly at another bit of information. Drummond Haley was on his side, another ally against Balor. Should disaster befall the king--Talmora forbid!--Roric had an associate, someone who shared his hatred of the general.

Elbows on the desk, the general leaned forward, his beefy hands clasped. "Minister of Coinage? That should present no problem. I intend to get rid of the one we have now, when I become king. Never liked him." He paused. "And you, Gamal? What position do you want?"

Roric lifted his hands. "I see no reason why I shouldn't continue as palace steward, if you agree. However, I'm willing to serve as you wish."

Balor nodded, absently tracing his finger down the purple scar on his cheek. "Again, I see no problem. I must leave soon for Elegia, at the king's request--" He snickered"--to glean useful information from their military experience. As if we could learn anything from them. Once we take control of Avador, Elegia will learn their army is no match for ours."

"I beg to disagree, general. Remember I told you once, that country has a formidable, well-equipped army, not that I wouldn't wish it otherwise. Better swords, too."

"When I become king and we march on Elegia, we'll see who has the stronger army. Yes, I'll admit they have finer swords, and I intend to discover their secret. But we have far greater manpower."

"I fear manpower may count little when we lack better weaponry--"

"And whose fault is that?" Balor slammed his fist on the desk, a gesture that sent papers flying to the floor.

"The king is a weakling," Balor continued while Roric bent over and returned the papers to the desk, stifling his annoyance. Next thing you know, he'll want me to polish his boots.

"Tencien," the general continued, "has devoted all his attention to peaceful pursuits--his words, not mine--and deprived his army of the necessary weaponry. But that's another situation that will change when I become king." He grinned. "We don't have long to wait. After the festival, the kingdom will be ours."

* * *

"There now! Didn't I tell you how well I shoot an arrow?" Aradia asked Balor, a triumphant smile on her face. She nodded toward a dead squirrel on the ground, an object in the far distance, a target seemingly impossible to hit.

By prearrangement, Balor and Aradia had met in this lonely spot, each riding from different directions, Aradia with her bow and quiver of arrows hidden under her voluminous cloak.

Balor wrapped his arm around her shoulder, his fingers brushing her breast. "My dear, you're better than any archer in the army. That squirrel must be over fifteen-hundred feet away. How did you learn to shoot so well?"

"I've practiced every day since I was a child. But after my marriage to that oaf, Fergus, I had to relinquish practice. You have no idea how good it feels to resume again."

The Avador countryside spread all around them; wild animals scurrying among the surrounding trees made perfect targets. The shimmering heat and still air hung over them like thick sheepskin. Aradia's dress clung to her, damp with perspiration, and her silvery hair, now a dirty gray, hung in wet strands to her shoulders. She wiped her hand down her hips, looking for a new target.

"But how do you see the targets?" he persisted. "How do you focus on them?" He shook his head. "That squirrel--I had to strain my eyes to see it. Yet you took aim and hit it as if it were only a short distance away."

Aradia pressed a finger close to her eye. "Excellent vision, my love--"

"Ah, yes, your eagle eyes. You're a clever one, darling, able to transform to the body of a jackal but with the eyes of an eagle."

"Not to mention exceptional divination ability that enables me to find my target and bring it much closer." She thought for a moment. "It's as though I draw the object to me. I pretend it's no farther than the length of my hand, and . . . there you have it! Or I have it, you might say."

Shading his eyes, Balor gazed upward, where a lone raven approached from the east, a tiny speck in the distance. He tapped Aradia's shoulder and pointed. "Let's see you get that."

"Of course." Quickly, she drew an arrow from the quiver and nocked it. After a moment of concentration, she took careful aim as the bird flew closer, its flapping wings gleaming in the bright sunshine. She let loose, the arrow finding its mark. The raven fell to the ground with a hard thud.

Aradia and Balor rushed toward the prey and pulled the arrow from its warm, lifeless body.

Aradia grinned. "Now what do you say?"

"Without a doubt, you're the best archer I've seen."

She looked at him, bloody arrow in hand. "So?"

Balor beamed. "So you have the privilege of killing the king."

She smiled, returning the arrow to the quiver. "No poison, then?"

"I've given the matter much thought." He scratched his chin, looking off into the distance. "I fear poison is too risky. For one thing, those ugly dwarves guard the kitchen as if it belonged to them. So we can't handle his food. For another, any poison we put in the king's food would also kill the princess. No," he said, catching her scowl. "I don't give a damn about that creature, but one death is enough . . . two, I should say. Don't forget Fergus."

She snorted. "How could I forget that clod?"

"But no one must see you or connect you with the king's death. Now, as to the time of the assassination--the Lug Festival presents the best opportunity. I reached that decision several moonphases ago."

"Midac, darling, I agree. We know the king will give one of his boring speeches during the festival, right there in the city square. There are plenty of trees where I can conceal myself, far from the city square but close enough to take aim."

"But how can you escape without anyone seeing you?"

She winked. "I have that planned, too."

Chapter Twelve

In the privacy of Princess Keriam's office, Roric studied her worried face. Compelled to express his misgivings, he wished he could say something to console her. "Do whatever you consider necessary, madam. The king must not appear before the people at the festival. I fear that's precisely when the assassin--or assassins-- will strike." Roric took a deep breath. "Another consideration--we may never have definite proof against Balor. A clever man, the general. He leaves no evidence, or none that our spies have found. They have examined his desk and papers in his absence, after one of them bribed Balor's butler to inform them when the general was away from home. And to keep the other servants away from the general's office whenever the spies are there. I'm sure they've told you the same," he said with a questioning look. And as he had told the king.

Keriam nodded. "So far, we've come up with nothing," she said, turning away to stack a few papers.

By the evening twilight, a brass lantern cast a mellow glow on the room and confined the shadows to the corners. How pretty she looks by the evening light, he thought, her skin a rosy hue in the lantern light, her hair blacker than night. How he desired her, he admitted with a newfound realization, something he'd tried to deny for so long. But wanting and having were two different things. And she could never be his. Despite the urgency that colored their bond, he thought only of drawing her into his arms, kissing her lips, pressing her body close to his. Ah, to lie with her beneath him, to hear her sighs in his ears, her gasps of pleasure--

Her voice brought him back to the discussion, the danger to the king, a menace he must overcome, and Balor a man he must defeat.

"We need proof!" She pounded her fist on her desk, shaking the ink bottle. "And I'm afraid we don't have time."

Glancing toward the closed door, she lowered her voice. "I agree, His Majesty should stay home from the festival. But imagine what the people would think if he doesn't appear." She rearranged a few papers on her desk and faced him again. "Thank the Goddess Aradia is gone from the palace. No one has reported any jackal lurking in the woods."

"You are certain she's gone?" Roric had doubts the sorceress would have left so agreeably.

"I was absent from the palace yesterday when she departed, but the carriage driver assured me he took her back to Mag Bregha."

Roric lifted his hand, wanting to touch her, comfort her. He let his hand drop to his side. "Have you thought of drugging the king's cider the morning of the festival? Only to put him to sleep," he said in response to her shocked expression. "Let him sleep through the festival. The celebration can continue without him, no matter how much the people look forward to hearing him speak."

She shook her head. "He'd never forgive me."

A longing to take all her troubles on himself consumed him, an ache in his heart. Yet he must dismiss his feelings and go with hard facts. "Which is more important to you--his forgiveness or his life?"

"You know the answer to that! Why do you ask?" Her chest heaved, and she flipped her long hair over her shoulder.

"I merely want you to understand the seriousness of--"

"As if I don't understand! What have I been telling you?"

"Very well," he said, pretending calmness. "Surely you can procure an herb from that wit--from Radegunda." Even as he said the witch's name, dread knifed his stomach. Familiar with her habits now, he did everything possible to avoid her. "If I'm not mistaken, you often spend time with her in the kitchen.".

"Learning about herbs and plants that heal," she said, a look of challenge on her face.

"Ah." Or learning magic? He suppressed a shudder. His mind wrenched back to the night he'd returned late to the palace and thought he'd seen her specter. Or had he only imagined seeing it? He took a deep breath. "Then I'm certain Radegunda can give you a drug to add to the king's cider. Princess, it's a matter of life or death." Thoughts of the witch still hounded him, his fear of

Radegunda as strong as ever. But if she could help Keriam, he would set his fears in abeyance.

After a moment's hesitation, she nodded. "I'll do it."

"A solution to our problem, for now. But if Balor fails this time, I fear nothing will stop him from trying again. We must defeat him, find definite proof of his perfidy. If necessary, we can bring charges against the general and the other plotters."

"The very same thing I have worried about. If Balor fails, he will certainly try again." Keriam frowned. "But what charges? We have no proof!"

"None at present," Roric said, conscious of the challenge. "But if we imprison them--"

"His Majesty will never approve those methods."

"Then we must get the king out of the country, as we discussed earlier. Possibly when you both go to Elegia for the wedding, you can think of some excuse to keep him in that country."

"For how long? Indefinitely?"

"Let's deal with the Lug Festival for now. We'll see what opportunities present themselves after that." Roric clenched his hands. "As painful as it is to admit, we must be prepared for every eventuality. Goddess forbid that you fail in your endeavor, that you can't keep the king home from the festival. If that happens, you must have extra guards posted in the city square. We can trust the king's guards. I'll give orders to have them placed both near the dais, at every corner and oak tree, also mingling among the crowds."

"I've already given those orders, major."

"Very good, madam."

Roric thought quickly, resolved to deal with other concerns, and he chose his words with care. "I must tell you that no matter what happens, I remain loyal to the kingdom and to you."

"'No matter what happens'? What, exactly, do you mean by that?"

"Madam, I will do everything in my power to protect the king, to keep him on the throne. But should something befall him--"

"No!"

"--should something happen, I will do what I think is best for Avador . . . and for you. If I should take part in Balor's government--"

"You wouldn't!" She sat back, her mouth wide open in shock.

He nodded. "I would, if I consider it best for the kingdom, because--"

"You would conspire with that fiend?" Her chest rose and fell, her face flushed with anger.

"Not conspire, madam, but work with him for the good of the country." And for you, dear lady. I want to see you take your place as queen.

""For the good of the country'! How can you say such a thing? How can you even think of working with him? He's evil, that one. Stay away from him!"

"Madam, you must trust me. I intend to follow my conscience."

"You have no conscience!"

"Princess, I believe I can do more good by pretending to participate in Balor's government, if it should come to that. Far better for the country for me to work within the government, possibly protect Avador from any of Balor's excesses. I have some influence with him, you know."

"And be tainted by his evil!"

"Never!" He paused, struggling for calm. "Madam, let us hope and pray King Tencien remains on the throne. No matter what, I shall always remain loyal to you and the king."

"Not if you serve Balor. If my father . . . if something happens to my father and Balor becomes king, I'll consider any man who serves him a traitor."

"If that's what you think, I'm afraid there's no more to say. With your permission . . ." Standing, he bowed and left the room, sorry they'd parted with such bitter words but convinced he was right.

* * *

Persuading the king to walk with her on the palace grounds the following morning, Keriam led him to a bench beside the lake where they could talk in private. She would try one more time to convince him of the dangers that faced him. If he disregarded her advice, she would follow Roric's suggestion: she'd drug her father's cider the morning of the festival. The Goddess knew she'd tried everything else.

While the king spoke of inconsequential things, Keriam's mind swung back to Roric. If Balor were successful in his assassination attempt,would Roric actually serve under that monster? She swallowed hard. His betrayal hurt more than anything. If he served under Balor, she never wanted to see him again, never wanted to have anything to do with him. Did she really mean that? She studied her fingers, afraid to admit how much it would hurt to never see him again, to never hear his voice or see his smile. How long had she felt this way about him? How long had she yearned to be held in his arms, feel his lips on hers? Even now, after their recent disagreement, she ached for him, and in the most secret part of her body, she throbbed with a need near impossible to deny.

Aware she dwelt on impossible dreams, she snatched her mind back to the present. A warm breeze carried the sweet scent of narcissus and phlox, the garden a medley of colors and fragrances. Thankful they faced away from the bright sunlight, she sank down gingerly onto the hot stone bench, her father following.

"Father, about the Lug Festival--"

"I've discussed this matter with Major Gamal. He'll order extra guards posted and--"

"But, Father--"

"Don't interrupt, Kerry. I intend to speak to my people at that time. Nothing and no one will stop me, and extra guards should prevent any harm. It's not advisable for me to stay secluded at the palace, where the people can't see or hear me. For political reasons, I must see and be seen." He slanted a look her way, his eyes filled with love. "Nor would I want any harm to come to you. But my dear daughter, something I must say. I want you to hear me out. If anything should happen--"

"Please, Father--"

"--if anything should happen to me, you inherit the throne. You take charge of the kingdom. There are no other heirs, only my sister, who will marry the king of Elegia. I have already put this in writing, so there will be no doubt. I've had good advisors all these years. They will serve you as they have served me."

Tears flowed down her cheeks. "Nothing will happen to you, Father. I'll see to that."

* * *

Accompanied by five of his most trusted officers, Midac Balor rode northeastward to Komartis, the southernmost city of Elegia, where that country had a small military outpost. Through the Bearn Gap in the Orn Mountains, the entourage trekked over steep, thickly-wooded hills, and descended into deep valleys. The men remained ever on the alert for danger, especially from torathors--those fur-covered, horned creatures who might lurk among the trees. The horses plodded up a winding, rocky road that led through the hills, the trees changing as they rode northward, from oaks, ashes, and rowans to hemlocks, beeches, and birches.

The dense forest provided shade, a welcome protection from the brilliant sunlight that occasionally lit a patch of open ground. Venomous, furry snakes slithered along the ground and draped from trees, ready to strike with their sharp, deadly fangs should they be disturbed. Caracabs with their long, spreading wings, screeched and dived from overhead, pouncing on unsuspecting prey in the trees or along the forest floor.

Balor drew a linen handkerchief from his waist pouch and wiped it across his sweaty forehead and down his face. Perspiration plastered his uniform to his body. His gaze focused on every tree and bush, his hand resting on the ivory hilt of his broadsword. Sapphires and rubies on the hilt glinted in the bright sunlight that now and then penetrated the thick tree cover. He smacked at a cuileg on his cheek and brushed at another of the biting insects on his forehead.

Shading his eyes, he looked toward the eastern sun, gauging the hours until nightfall. He smiled, recalling the palace ceremony at Moytura, in which the king had bidden him goodbye and wished him success for his mission. The king was in for a surprise, because he had no intention of completing his journey.

On open ground now, he eased on the reins and stopped his stallion, his officers gathering around him. From this spot on a tree-studded hill, he gazed back fondly over Avador, its hills and valleys, its acres of rich farmland abundant with crops ready for harvest. The towering spires of Moytura gleamed in the distance, the Nantosuelta winding and doubling back over itself.

Soon all this would be his, yes, all this and more. Ah, he had such plans for the country--and himself. He would restore Avador to its former greatness, conquer Elegia and Galdina, then Fomoria and Partholonia. Only look at all the benefits of Avadoran civilization, its medicine and learning, its libraries and monuments. The people of the other countries were barbarians! Yes, he would extend Avadoran civilization to the entire continent and unite them all into one vast empire. Never again would Avador depend on another country to export or import goods. Of course, they had the recently-signed treaty with Elegia, but that treaty was void until the marriage took place between Tencien's sister and Elegia's king.

Balor addressed his officers. "Soon, we will connect with the road that leads to Elegia. Within a few days, we should reach Komartis. We'll rest there for a day and learn as much as possible about the Elegian army--its numbers and state of readiness. Then we will return to Moytura in time for the Lug Festival." He smiled at his men. "You wouldn't want to miss the festival, would you, gentlemen? After we've eliminated Tencien, we'll take control of the government, as we planned." A stern look captured his face. "All my soldiers know better than to disobey me. By now, they should understand the consequences of betrayal."

Lieutenant Halloren frowned. "Just the same, general, I've been thinking, and--"

"Thinking can be a dangerous occupation," Balor said, his hand on his sword hilt. "Leave the planning to me."

The lieutenant licked his bottom lip. "Yes, sir, but this seems a chancy business, killing the king. What if the people rise up--"

Balor whipped the sword from its scabbard and with one sharp slash, cut the man's head off. The head rolled several feet, finally stopping when it bumped against a tree. The headless body toppled from the horse and fell to the ground.

Resting his hands on the pommel, Balor look at the other men, his gaze covering each. "Does anyone else have any objections?"

None did.
"Very well, gentlemen. We shall proceed."

* * *

Many days later, Aradia perched high in an oak tree about fifteen-hundred feet from the city square, awaiting the king's appearance the morning of the Lug Festival. Warded by the statue of Talmora and surrounding rose bushes, the spot provided ample safeguard against detection. Darkness still covered the city, but soon the crowds would gather to hear Tencien address his people. She looked toward the western horizon, where a pinkish glow lit the sky. Not long now. Dressed in green, her face and hands painted brown, she remained concealed from prying eyes. Soon there would be guards posted at every street corner--or so she'd heard--but who would think to look this high up in a tree and at such a great distance from the dais, where the king would speak?

Midac will be very proud of me, Aradia thought, beaming with satisfaction.

After the palace horses had recovered--Radegunda's doing, no doubt--the palace carriage had taken her to Mag Bregha. In the middle of the night, she'd ridden a friend's horse back to Midac's mansion and kept the horse stabled there, with the princess no wiser. She'd stayed secluded in a small apartment adjoining the larger house, seeing Midac only at night. She'd sworn Midac's servants to secrecy. Nor would they betray her, upon pain of death.

If that wasn't clever enough, surely her trip from the general's mansion to the city last night gave ample proof of her ingenuity. After donning a dress and applying face paint, she'd tied her quiver and bows to her back, then she'd shifted to her jackal body and raced through the night, along the lone dusty road that led to Moytura. No one had seen her then; no one would see her now this far up in the tree, hidden by its many branches and leaves.

Bathed in sweat, she lifted the hem of her dress and dabbed it across her face, careful not to remove the paint. She changed her position, aiming for a more comfortable perch, and looked below at the clusters of people already gathering to hear the king. The sky turned golden, bringing the city's streets and buildings into sharp focus: the flag hanging limply from an iron pole on the dais, the chairs for the king's ministers. Brightly-colored banners festooned the many storefronts, the streets sparkling clean in preparation for the festival. Oh, these gullible fools were in for a surprise.

Time passed, and soon crowds packed the city's streets and alleys. Talk and laughter filled the air, men, women, and children joining in the celebration. Fools! They wouldn't be laughing when the king lay dead, an arrow through his heart.

Aradia's gaze settled on the dais, her every sense, every nerve, wondrously alive. She had one chance only to succeed in her mission. She would not fail.

Aradia grinned. Not long now.

Chapter Thirteen

The morning of the Lug Festival dawned bright and clear. With purposeful steps, Keriam descended the stairs to the main hall, mindful that this day was the culmination of all her thoughts and plans since she'd overheard the plotters moonphases ago. In the hall, servants hustled about, eager to complete their duties before joining in the festivities later. On hands and knees, young girls and women scrubbed the flagstone floor, while other women polished the many tables scattered along the hall length. Children placed wooden bowls throughout the main hall and filled them with an incense of gardenia, mugwort, and frankincense, creating pleasant scents.

Last night, while she slept, Keriam dreamed the Goddess had come to her room and stood by her bed. When she awoke, she wondered if it had been a dream.

Greeting the dwarves, Keriam made her way toward the dining room that led off from the hall. There, she found her father's seat empty. Where was he? Keriam wondered with a twinge of alarm. An early riser, the king usually ate his morning meal soon after daybreak, when she always joined him. Keriam stood beside her oaken chair, her fingers tightening on the back. Perhaps she should go see--

Her father entered the room, his steps slow and halting, a troubled expression on his face. "Sorry I'm late, Kerry. Had a bad night." His fingers brushed his forehead. "Headache again."

She eased into her chair and placed the linen napkin in her lap, carefully choosing her words. "I can give the speech in your stead." Fingering her moist goblet of cider, she ignored his surprised look. "A new experience for me." She aimed for levity, afraid to express the same fears she'd apprized her father of time and again.

He reached for his acorn toast. "I appreciate your offer, but I can't let my people down." He slid a look her way, a rebuke in his expression. "We've gone over this many times."

She nodded toward his bronze goblet. With Radegunda's connivance, she'd drugged his cider. "Be sure to drink your cider, then. It's a long ride to the capital. You don't want to get thirsty."

He waved his hand. "Not today. You know how hard cider aggravates my headache."

Keriam stifled her disappointment, now more determined to accomplish her goal. "Father, I beg of you, stay home. I told you I can give--"

Tencien slammed his fist on the table, making her jump. "Stop your nagging, Kerry. I've had enough!"

* * *

Leaving his horse at the city stables, Roric headed for Talmora's Square, less than a half-mile away. Hundreds, thousands! of people had assembled in the city, their excited voices drowning out all other sounds. He edged through the crowds that jammed the streets, his head turning right and left. The smell of smoked meats and spicy cider floated through the air, vendors selling refreshments. Hawkers plied their souvenirs--wooden carvings of the Earth-mother goddess, miniature flags, and special Lug buttons that commemorated the God of Light. Fathers balanced young children on their shoulders, while older children were held in place by their mothers. Would the festive mood remain throughout the day? Roric worried, or would tragedy strike?

His gaze covered every street, every corner, his hand fingering his sword hilt. Hemmed in by the multitude, he looked in all directions, grateful that extra guards surrounded the dais. More were posted at each city block and beside every oak tree. He nodded in satisfaction; yes, all the appointed men stood guard. One oak tree in the far distance caught his attention. Could a zealous archer use that tree as a base for assassination? Quickly, he dismissed that concern. Not even the most skilled archer could hit a target from that distance.

Buildings of only one story flanked the city square, not high enough for an archer, so he saw no danger from that angle.

Roric tried to relax, hoping his worries proved groundless. Goddess, he prayed, protect the king.

* * *

From her high perch in the oak tree, Aradia had a clear view of the king and the princess as they arrived, a glimpse denied ordinary mortals at this distance, since they lacked her exceptional vision. Next to the dais, the king's retainers helped him and the princess dismount.

Aradia sneered as the king and princess mounted the platform. Just look at Tencien, so full of his importance, so confident his stupid subjects loved him. And the ridiculous princess, smiling and waving at the mob! Well, that insipid Keriam wouldn't be smiling in a few minutes.

Aradia pressed her hand to her mouth to stifle her laughter. All these idiotic people cheering the king and princess, raining flowers on them! Just wait, just wait . . .

A page sounded a trumpet, then Tencien raised his arms to address the mob. The applause reached a crescendo.

The branch that supported Aradia cracked and broke, sending her tumbling. She caught herself on a lower branch, then checked a scratch on her left leg, cursing her bad luck. The lower branch didn't give her nearly as good a view. And what if someone had seen her fall? Her gaze shifted from side to side, until she was convinced no one had spotted her. She lost precious seconds raising herself to another branch above her, an absolute necessity.

Now the king turned to the side, speaking to those to his right. Damn it, would he never turn in her direction again? She must aim for his heart, only one chance granted. An eternity passed before he faced her direction again. So, now . . .

Perspiration dripped into her eyes, hindering her vision. Cursing again, she brushed her hand across her eyes. Now the king had turned in the other direction. Demoness Endora, are you not with me today?

The king faced her way. Now! Aradia reached for the arrow in the branch and nocked it. She sighted down the shaft, bringing the king into sharp focus, as if he were mere feet away. With a silent prayer to the demoness, she released the arrow.

Chapter Fourteen

"Just in time, gentlemen." Slowing his horse to a walk, Balor turned in the saddle to address the officers who rode behind him, having reached Moytura upon their return from Elegia. He raised his voice to be heard above the cheering. "Look, the king is entering the city." He lifted his hand slightly in that direction, careful to remain unobserved. Ten of the king's guards surrounded the dais, prompting a chuckle from Balor. Much good the guards would accomplish against Aradia's aim.

He thought about the productive mission to Elegia, a trip in which he had gleaned useful details about the Elegian army, its size and equipment, and why their swords performed so much better than those of Avador. Balor and his men had inspected the fort closest to the border and learned the distance from that fort to the next farther north. Yes, a fruitful trip.

The general and his men stopped by a large warehouse at the hilly northern entrance to the capital, gaining them a clear view of the city square with its fountains and greenery, the dais where the king would speak. Clusters of oak, ash, and rowan trees rose behind them, but here the hilly ground was bare, except for weeds and thick tree roots.

Cheers and applause filled the air around him, the multitude frenzied with excitement. Stupid fools! Soon they'd scream with horror, if–and he never doubted it–Aradia had succeeded in reaching the city during the night. His eyes scanned the mob, to all the men, women, and children who thronged the streets. Now Tencien and Princess Keriam mounted the steps to the flag-bedecked platform, waving at all their meek subjects.

The king's ministers and the city magistrate already occupied the wooden dais, standing and bowing as Tencien and Princess Keriam approached.

Balor's glance slid far to the right, to an oak tree warding the stature of Talmora. He focused his eyes anxious to see movement in the tree. Was Aradia preparing to shoot the arrow now? He shook his head in acute disappointment. Damn it! He couldn't see any movement that far away. Balor prayed silently to Endora that Aradia had reached her destination, that she would execute their plan any moment now. She must kill the king!

A trumpet blew, and Tencien began to speak. Balor's gaze flew to the king again.

"My fellow Avadorans," Tencien said in a clear voice, "I greet you on this first day of the Lug Festival." He turned to his ministers, recognizing each of them for the ways in which they had aided the country, then spoke on the progress he had made since the Bel Festival. "And we thank the god of light for all that he has done for us, for giving us bountiful crops. We pray that he will always bless–Ah!"

Princess Keriam screamed.

The king staggered and fell, an arrow through his heart.

"No!" The princess sprang from her seat and dropped to the floor beside him. She knelt over his body, her hands raised in supplication. "No, Father, please no!"

"Talmora, help us!" The ministers fell to their knees beside the princess and checked the king for signs of life. They crowded around each other, each one desperate to assure himself that the king. Stunned looks captured their faces.

From a distance, Balor smiled, his pulse racing with excitement. Aradia had accomplished her task well.

Shock silenced the multitude, but for only a moment. Then cries and screams erupted, everyone shouting at once.

"What happened?"

"The king is wounded."

"Goddess, no!"

"An arrow through his heart."

"He'll recover. It's not a fatal wound."

"You fool! An arrow through his heart–can't you see he's dead?"

"Oh, woe is me! The king is dead!"

Princess Keriam clutched her stomach, rocking back and forth. "No, Father, please don't die! Father, I tried so hard to save you. I did everything–" Broken sobs tore from her throat; Balor could hear her cries even from the distance separating them. Well, he'd give her something more to cry about.

* * *

Grinning exultantly, Aradia threw her bow into an upper branch and tore her dress off, tossing the garment far above her, where it snagged on a branch. Thank you, Endora, thank you.

The king was dead! A glow of satisfaction warmed her. After performing a hasty shape shift, she scampered down the tree, her agile paws flying from limb to limb. In her urgency to transform herself, she had sacrificed the finer jackal attributes–keen hearing and smell–for speed in completing the shift. She must get away! After one quick glance around, she raced off toward Balor's mansion. Her heart pounded with exhilaration, her tail twitching with excitement. No one had seen her.

* * *

Balor raised his hand, beckoning to his officers. "Now!" With him in the lead, the mounted officers guided their horses down the hill, then plunged through the mob. "Out of my way!" Conscious of the passing time, he pushed at the obstructing fools. On all sides, crowds hindered his passage, slowing his progress. Tempted to kick the clods out of the way, he thought better of it; mustn't antagonize the people at this early stage. Precious minutes later, he reached the dais.

Ah, at last. His face deliberately set in sorrow, Balor dismounted by the platform and threw the reins to one of the king's guards, then climbed the stairs, his officers following.

"Balor!" Leith Connor, the Minister of Coinage exclaimed, "thank the Goddess you're here."

"Yes, we thought you were still in Elegia," the Foreign Minister said. "But we're glad you're back."

Ignoring the princess and ministers, Balor crouched by the king's body. Princess Keriam stared at him, her face streaked from crying, her mouth open in shock. He felt for a heartbeat and found none. Thank the demoness. Thank Aradia.

"You!" The princess sprang to her feet and pointed a finger at him. Tears streamed down her face. "You did this! You're behind the murder. You and Aradia!"

Leith Connor laid a remonstrative hand on her arm but she shook him off. "No, madam, you mustn't speak like this. The general has always been a loyal servant of the king."

Another minister spoke up, his voice choked with sorrow. "Please, madam, I beg of you. Don't make the situation worse."

Men and women closest to the dais murmured among themselves, their heads turning from the princess to the general. Balor restrained a smile, inwardly laughing at their confusion. Of what did Princess Keriam speak? they asked each other. Was she truly accusing him of this wicked deed? Why in the name of the Goddess had she made such an outrageous accusation? Why, indeed.

The general stood, glancing at his officers. He donned an expression of shocked grief as he addressed his men, his eye on Princess Keriam. "I fear the princess is too distraught to think clearly."

"You bastard!" She waved her hand at him, her face red with sorrow and anger. "You're not fooling me."

"Madam, please!" the Minister of Forests scolded. "You must not speak to the general in this manner."

Balor turned toward Keriam. "Madam, I just returned from Elegia, only arriving here as the king began to speak, so—"

"Aradia! She committed this evil deed at your command. Don't deny it."

His hands on his hips, Balor spoke with stern resolve. "Madam, I fear grief clouds your thinking. I've ever been a loyal subject—"

"Liar! Murderer!" She lunged for him, but his officers restrained her. The ministers traded dazed glances and muttered among themselves. Choking on her sobs, she struggled in the officers' grasp, loosening her hairpins until her hair fell in tangled strands in front of her face. The men held her in an iron-hard grip, their faces set in determination.

Malvin Kerr addressed Balor. "General, is this restraint necessary?"

"Of course, can't you see she is momentarily deranged? Why, she might hurt someone, or even herself." He turned toward the Minister of Justice. "We can't let this wicked deed go unpunished. I charge you with conducting an inquiry into the king's assassination."

The Minister of Justice bowed his head. "By all means, general."

"Princess Keriam!" a spectator cried, others following.

"Let the princess speak."

"Yes, let Princess Keriam speak."

Keriam clenched her jaw. Her captor's concentration focused on Balor, their grip slackened, and she broke free. His officers grabbed for her again, but Balor held up a hand. "No, let her speak. Let's see what the unsettled princess has to say." Brushing the tears from her eyes, she faced the general. "Balor! You traitor! Murderer!"

He spoke in low tones, his words audible only to her. "Beware what you accuse me of, madam. I can make things difficult for you."

"So you say!" She took a deep breath; firm resolve hardened her words. "What makes you think you can fool these people for long? I'll have the druids conduct an investigation and–
"

"Investigation, madam? On what basis?"

"On the basis that you and Aradia conspired to murder my father."

"Princess Keriam, Aradia is no longer in Moytura. Don't you recall," he said in a voice heavy with sarcasm, "she left for her home in Mag Bregha." He raised an eyebrow. "Or had you forgotten?"

"I have only your word for that."

The crowds and ministers grew restless. She caught bits and snatches of conversation, hints of increasing impatience.

The Minister of Commerce stepped forward, speaking in a resonant manner. "General, Princess Keriam is the heir to the throne."

The Minister of Roads added his voice. "With all respect to you, general, I believe Princess Keriam should be heard."

"Yes," the other ministers agreed. "Let the princess speak."

Balor performed a small bow. "Of course."

As the ministers retreated, Keriam turned toward the multitude and opened her mouth to speak. "My people–"

"Poor Tencien," Balor muttered at her side. "What a painful death, an arrow through the heart."

She jerked her head in his direction. "You stinking bastard!"

"No loss to the kingdom, though," he went on, as if she hadn't spoken. "Suppose we leave his body here, shall we? And let it rot. Of course, animals will eat–"

She pounded him with her fists. "Curse Endora, Balor!" Tears of rage streamed down her cheeks. "You Goddess-damned murderer! May the Goddess ban you from the Otherworld. You . . . you . . ." She shook her head, tears blinding her vision.

Placing his hand on his sword, Balor addressed the crowd. "My good people, as you can see, the princess is overcome with grief. I assure you, she will address you in good time. For now, I think it's best if we permit her to grieve alone." He nodded to his men, speaking in a low voice." Escort her back to the palace. You know what to do if she gives you any difficulty."

"Murderer!" She screamed, twisting and struggling against her captors. "You won't get away with this, Balor. You fiend!"

"Princess Keriam!" the people cried, the cry becoming a chant.

Balor raised his arms to address them, and soon quiet fell over the square. "People of Avador! Evil lurks in the land." He gestured toward Tencien, whose body now reposed under a cloak. "At such a time, our country needs a firm hand. I fear at present the princess is not fit to rule. As head of the army, I have the soldiers of the kingdom behind me, the Avadoran army to back me." He paused, hoping they caught the veiled threat. These people are like sheep, he thought. He could convince them of anything, lead them wherever he wanted.

The prolonged pause allowed him to hear the ministers behind him talking among themselves.

"Balor would be best."

"Yes, precedence over us..."

"–the army backs him."

"...a good and loyal servant, but more important, a strong leader."

Balor concealed a smile as he continued his speech. "We need strength and resolve now," he said, his voice rising. "I fear the princess is not equal to the task. As must be obvious to all of you, she suffers from delusions." He shook his head, his face cast in puzzled dejection. "I have ever been a loyal and devoted subject. If you accept me as king, I promise I shall rule with fairness and fortitude. I shall track down the evildoer who committed this wicked deed and avenge the king's death. I pray to Talmora I do so with your blessing."

The ministers bowed their heads in acknowledgment. "King Midac."

The crowds shouted and waved their arms. "General Balor! King Midac!"

Too far away to rush through the crowd when the arrow struck the king, Roric gazed at the death scene. He had failed his monarch. Tears clotted his throat; grief tightened his chest and stomach. One question tormented him. Where had the fatal arrow come from? He scanned the city square, his glance flying from tree to tree, as if he could discover the source of the arrow long after the missile had found its target. Brushing tears from his face, he remained at the edge of the throng. Later this night, after the people had dispersed, he would check each tree in the square, well aware the assassin had shot the arrow from high up.

Sacred shrine! Why had the ministers accepted Balor so willingly? If only one of them had spoken against him . . . Roric shook his head. Too late now.

Fierce hatred for Balor and grief for Keriam churned inside him, a painful fusion that blocked all rational thought. Just think how Balor's toadies had manhandled the princess! Goddess, he'd like to kill them all! Yet me must think clearly, must devise a strategy to counter Balor's cruel betrayal, and certainly, he must see that the king's body was treated with respect and escorted back to the palace. Above all, he must pretend to participate in the usurper's devious plans. Only then could he save the kingdom. Only then could he help the princess, this woman who meant so much to him.

* * *

On the outskirts of Moytura, Keriam tried to maneuver past her captors, but hemmed in by four attendants, she found escape impossible. The horses' hooves stirred up clouds of dust and dislodged pebbles, their manes flying behind them. Dust blew in her mouth and eyes and coated her face. On the way to the palace, the group rode past towering corn stalks and clusters of strawberry bushes, many crops ready to harvest. Talmora, she lamented, how can everything look so normal when my whole world has turned upside down?

She heeled her horse, trying to maneuver past the soldiers. "Let me pass, you bastards! How I hate all of you! May Talmora punish you for your sins."

The head officer laughed. "Oh, no, madam. We can't leave you. We enjoy your company too much." The others joined in the laughter.

Now and then, the officers had to ride single file as farmers headed for the capital with their horse-drawn carts, blocking the road. She'd never escape at this rate. A shepherd led his sheep along the road, another hindrance that detained her for long minutes.

She made one more desperate attempt to shove past the officer to her right. "Let me go!"

"Oh, no, you don't!" He grabbed her reins in a viselike grip, his hand and arm muscles standing out in knots. He called to the soldier to his left. "Henwas, you know what to do."

"Right you are, sir."

While one man pinned her arms to her side and another wrapped his arm around her neck, Henwas pressed an acrid-smelling cloth to her nose.

"No!" Keriam twisted and cried, jerking at her arms, struggling to shake off her antagonists. To no avail.

* * *

Returned to the palace later, Keriam awoke to find herself on the third floor, in a small room used to house one of the head servants. Dizzily regaining consciousness, she looked about the room as it tilted and rocked around her. What would happen now? Would the people accept Balor as their new king? How could they!

And her father—would Balor leave her father's body on the platform, with no one to mourn his death? Would he really let it . . . let it rot? She pressed trembling hands to her eyes, afraid to accept that possibility. Father, father, she moaned. By the dim light of one small window above, she took in her surroundings. Besides the narrow bed she lay on, the room held a washstand and a two-drawer chest; a simple utilitarian room, nothing more.

Gripping the edge of the bed, she struggled to her feet but fell back again, landing on the bed with a hard thud. Stars burst in front of her eyes. The room spun around her: nausea plagued her stomach. She tried to rise again inch by inch, grasping the bed's edge until assured she could stand by herself. On her feet, she stood still for silent moments as she waited for her dizziness to pass. Confident she could walk, she shuffled to the door.

The door was locked.

Again and again, she yanked and twisted the doorknob, with no success. Wildly, she looked around the room, her aim to find a pin, anything to unlock the door. And found nothing. Desperately, she felt in her hair, finding one hairpin left and tried it in the lock. Still, the door didn't open. She trudged across the room and sank down on the bed to ponder her dilemma. Surely someone would rescue her. Fear hit her like a blow to the head. Did Balor intend to imprison her for the rest of her life? He wouldn't succeed, but foiling him would challenge all her concentration and energy.

A key turned in the lock, jolting her. The doorknob turned and Aradia stepped inside, a triumphant smirk on her face. Aradia, the witch, Aradia, the assassin.

The sorceress shook her head in mock dismay. "Poor little princess. I fear grief has unsettled your mind. You–"

"Be quiet, you Goddess-damned scum! Before long, the entire kingdom will learn of your wickedness."

"I could have you tortured for those treasonous remarks," Aradia snapped, eyes narrowed, arms folded across her chest. Her silvery hair was braided and coiled atop her head, her deep green gown clinging to her sensuous figure. A beautiful woman was Aradia, but her evil knew no depths. "However," she said in dulcet tones, "I'll be lenient . . . for now. But tell me something–how do you intend to inform the people of my so-called wickedness?"

"I don't need to tell them anything. You'll give yourself away in no time. Oh, I'll admit you may fool the people for awhile, but soon enough they'll catch on to your cunning ways. You can't pretend to be something you're not."

Aradia laughed, a soft, throaty sound. "I have so far."

"But how long can you maintain your deception?" Keriam's insides spasmed and she swallowed hard, fighting her sickness. The drug still fuzzed her brain and hindered concentration. She had an important question she must ask the sorceress, but what was it? "Once the people see through you, they'll discard you like a rotten apple."

"I think not. Have you forgotten that Balor rules the kingdom now? He has already declared himself king. We will wed soon, and with his support, I can do anything I want."

The question erupted in Keriam's brain. "My father's bod–
"

"His corpse? It's been returned to the palace. Even now, the druids are preparing it for burial. We'll have a period of mourning, of course, before and after the funeral."

Tears hazed Keriam's vision, but she fought her sorrow. Would they allow her to attend the ceremony? She refused to inquire, denying them the satisfaction of rebuffing her.

"Maudina–where is she now?" She didn't care about herself, but she worried about her maid's fragile nature.

"That little wench decided I can use her." Aradia leaned against the wall, resting her hands behind her. "After all, I do need

158

a maid since I sent my other one back, that good-for-nothing lazy girl."

Misery tore at Keriam's insides. "Please don't mistreat Maudina."

Aradia's eyes widened. "Why, I wouldn't dream of it." She snickered. "At least, I won't beat her if she performs her duties correctly. I promise."

The drug still impaired her, but Keriam strove to keep her eyes open, her senses alert. She saw no point in further pleading. Appeals would only thwart her. "And Ragegunda?"

The sorceress waved her hand. "I sent her away. We don't need her here."

"Sent her away–where?" Keriam forced herself to sit up straight.

Aradia shrugged. "Just sent her from the palace. Where she goes is her business, as long as she causes no trouble."

Keriam laughed with mock humor. "'Causes no trouble'? Oh, that's funny. You should know about trouble."

"I've had enough of this senseless discussion." Aradia pushed herself away from the wall. "And you'll be allowed to stay at the palace as long as cause trouble. That's why I'm keeping you in a room by yourself. You can join the servants for meals." She snickered. "I'll tell them to expect a guest. Oh, and remember to always take the servants' stairs at the back of the palace." Aradia pointed a finger at her. "Don't even think of escape. We have guards everywhere."

Shock stabbed Keriam in the gut, but she blinked her eyes in false humility. "Oh, I'll be as meek as a squirrel."

Aradia glared at her, then jerked the door open and stormed out of the room, slamming the door behind her.

Unable to fight her grief and nausea any longer, Keriam lay down in a fetal position, giving rein to suppressed tears. She mustn't cry, for the people of Avador celebrated death, when the soul returned to the Land of Truth and Eternal Life. But she couldn't stop her sobs, and the tears flowed relentlessly, streaking down her face, dampening the cotton bedcover.

What more could she have done to prevent her father's death? Now, when it was too late, she realized she should have commanded his guards to take him to a safe refuge. She should have obtained a more powerful drug from Radegunda to give him the night before the Lug Festival, one that would have incapacitated him for a full day and night. She should have . . . But 'should haves' won't bring him back, she lamented, clenching her hands so hard her nails broke the skin. Nothing would return her father to her.

She turned onto her back and stared at the ceiling, gasping for breath. What about her poor subjects? How they would suffer under Balor! Talmora, she prayed, please watch over my people. How she wanted to kill Balor, and yes, Aradia, too. She thought hard, searching for a way to thwart them both, get rid of them! But the drug still dulled her brain.

Roric Gamal remained a painful mystery, one that intensified her despair. Was he loyal to the kingdom and all her father stood for, or had he long ago transferred his allegiance to Balor? Had he truly deceived her all this time? Foolish woman! She had actually thought that he cared for her. His looks, his expressions, had surely indicated that he felt something for her, or had she been mistaken all along? Was it all just wishful thinking on her part? She wanted to drive him from her mind, but images of him refused to leave. She feared he would always remain in her heart, a deep, aching wound that would forever torment her.

Keriam pressed her hands to her throbbing head. She couldn't stay here, for she could accomplish more for her people away from the palace.

She must escape.

Chapter Fifteen

Long after the stunned, griefstricken crowds had dispersed from Moytura and darkness had fallen on Avador, Roric returned to the capital, a long ride in the late night hours. Arrived at the city square, he dismounted. He tied Donn's halter to a low-hanging oak branch at one of the many trees that added grace and beauty--but also concealment?--to the area. He stood in thought, his gaze lingering on every tree that faced the dais. Silvery moonlight pooled down on the city, aiding him in his quest. Not a cloud drifted in the sky, while street lamps cast warm yellow light on the cobblestone streets.

Could a determined archer have shot the fatal arrow from one of these oaks? Where else would the missile have come from? Not from within any of the one-story buildings that faced the square, for it was obvious that the shaft had come from a greater height. Still, he had only scant hope of discovering the assassin's identity, for he had no reason to believe the archer would have left any evidence. Indeed, most likely his search would prove futile, but he must try. To neglect a probe would be foolish, no, negligent.

Miniature flags and souvenirs littered the square, mute testimony to the tragedy that had struck this day; normally people treasured these keepsakes. Vendors' stands had long since disappeared, their merchandise packed and taken home. Not even the taverns remained open on this tragic day. Only silence prevailed in the capital, except for an occasional vagrant shuffling along the city streets.

Lips pursed in concentration, Roric gauged the distance at which he stood and considered it too close for an archer to commit the crime and escape detection. He must move farther back. His booted footsteps rang on the cobblestones as he strode farther away, to a distance of about one-thousand feet. There two oak trees, about one-hundred feet apart, gave shade in the daytime, wooden benches resting at their base.

Minutes later, a search of both trees, branch by branch, yielded no clues. Roric cocked his head, his eyes covering the entire city square. A tree about fifteen-hundred feet from the dais offered only a slim possibility as the spot where the assassination happened. He strode in that direction, doubting that even one of Balor's best archers could hit a target from such a tremendous distance. Reaching his goal, he stood with hands on his hips, his gaze shifting from the tree to the dais and back. No, an impossible target.

But wait, he'd better explore this possibility, no matter how remote. Grabbing a bottom branch, he swung himself up into the tree, then moved farther up as before, branch by branch. Almost at the top, he sighed with disappointment. What had made him think--

Now, what was this? Reaching higher, he touched a piece of silk--a dress? He loosened the material from the branch and caught a strong musk scent. Aradia! His fingers searching for further evidence, he found an ash arrow stuck between two twigs. Perched high in the tree, he leaned against the trunk, his mind raging with all the ramifications of this proof of Aradia's guilt . . . and Balor's. And hatred for them both. Sacred shrine! He could hardly see for the anger that pulsed through him. He wanted to choke them both to death.

Roric tucked the dress under his wide belt and, arrow in hand, clambered down the tree. He must tell the princess of his discovery. But when would he have the chance to speak to her again, or would he ever? He longed to talk to her, hear her dear voice, smell her sweet fragrance. He must see her again, but how?

Poor princess! His heart ached for her. In one day, she'd witnessed her father's murder and been banished to virtual imprisonment, all her activities monitored. How could she live like this? Ah, but he knew the answer. She'd face her situation with her usual composure and rise above it, emerge stronger than before. Keriam, no woman like her! More than anything, he regretted their present estrangement, but surely she'd eventually see that his pretended collaboration with Balor was the best course--for her and the country.

162

Reaching his horse, he placed his foot in the stirrup and mounted, then touching heels to the chestnut, rode away from the square, the horse's hooves clattering on the cobblestones.

The palace guards, forced to switch their allegiance upon pain of death, now served Balor. Conneid Delbraith, the king's secretary, had disappeared with his pregnant wife, and where, no one knew. So much had changed in only one day. So much tragedy. Roric passed the many stores and shops--the silversmith's, a sword shop with its fine selection on display, a fabric store with its silks and linens in the window. Would life remain the same for these merchants, or would Balor disrupt all business in Moytura, indeed, in all of Avador? What if the new king started a dispute with Elegia, prompting their government to invade Avador? Roric imagined the city in ruins, stores and businesses burned to the ground. His gut churned at the thought.

So he had evidence of the assassin now, Roric mused as he rode his horse back to the palace. Much good the proof did him with Balor firmly ensconced at the palace, his coronation scheduled for later in the nineday. But would the dress and bow serve as adequate proof before a druidic tribunal? For now, he disregarded that concern. He had his own evidence, enough for the moment. He knew a safe hiding place for the dress and bow back at the palace, at the bottom of an oak chest in his apartment.

As his horse covered the miles of dirt roads back to the palace, Roric noted the peaceful dark countryside, the farm houses nestled in the valleys, the trees and bushes that dotted the hills. How normal everything appeared, as if the kingdom remained as it always had been, ever since he could remember, with King Tencien on the throne. Talmora's bones! What would happen to the kingdom now, to the people of Avador? Would life in the country ever return to its previous tranquility under Tencien?

No, not until Balor was killed.

* * *

For one distressful moment, Keriam paused at the kitchen entrance, then entered, head high, as if she'd always dined with the household staff. Hunger gnawed at her insides, making her queasy.

Two full days without food or drink had passed since her father's murder, and she realized she'd gain nothing by starving herself. Indeed, she must eat to maintain her strength, to enable her brain to function. She needed clear thinking in the coming days.

"Princess Keriam!" Seated at a long oak table, the staff stood at her appearance, the long wooden benches scraping on the flagstone floor. The servants all looked as heartsick as she felt, but none looked overly-shocked. Apparently they'd been apprized of her new status. The dwarf children at a separate table looked up and waved a greeting, each one calling her name. She returned the greeting, trying to maintain a cheerful demeanor for their sakes. Bertha, the chief cook, had her own chair at the head of the table, and she drew it out for Keriam, her misshapen hands clutching the chairback and removing the stool set there to give her extra height.

"Please, madam, sit here." In a quick aside, she motioned for one of the other cooks to take up a plate for Keriam.

Keriam smiled. "Thank you, Bertha, but where will you sit?"

"We can make room, madam." The palace gardener motioned for the others to scoot along on the bench to make room for the head cook, who carried her stool over to the new place. Most--but not all--of the household staff were dwarves, and Keriam saw now that could create an awkward seating arrangement.

Kormlada returned to the table with a platter of roast beef and steaming vegetables, setting it down beside Keriam. The savory beef aroma tempted Keriam, reminding her how much time had passed since her last meal.

One of the chambermaids turned a tearful face in her direction. "Ah, madam, that it should come to this. What will we do now that--?"

"Please, Angharad, we must take each day as it comes. And don't worry. We'll manage." Her smile covered the assembled group. "Do you know, I consider this a learning experience. Why, I'll wager the palace staff has always saved the best cuts of meat for themselves." An exchange of sheepish glances around the table confirmed her suspicion. "So you see, I'm learning already." She gestured to the others. "Now please, go ahead and eat," she said, dipping her fork into a vegetable melange of carrots, potatoes, and broccoli, cooked in a cream sauce and spiced with thyme. "Bertha, this is delicious. You must give me your recipe," she said, attempting to put the woman at ease. And who knew? She might have to do her own cooking sometime in the future.

With a scratching of knives and forks on tin platters, the others followed her lead, none speaking. Keriam swallowed hard, wondering how much longer she could maintain this pretense, as if no tragedy had struck, as though her father had left on a royal journey and would return any day now. She stifled her tears and tried to divert her thinking to more productive pursuits.

What was Balor's and Aradia's game? she wondered. To make life so miserable for her that she'd leave the palace in desperation? Or was she, indeed, a prisoner for life? One thing she determined: she would set her own course, would not let anyone dictate her actions. If Balor or Aradia dared try to confine her to the palace, she'd find a means to frustrate them. Keriam's gaze skimmed the layout of the kitchen, studying the door that led to the outside. She hoped to soon have one of her spirit journeys, to discover the route of the guards, inside and outside the palace.

And what about King Barzad of Elegia and the treaty with Avador? If he knew of her father's assassination, would he come to Avador's aid? But he wouldn't know unless someone from Emain Macha sent word to him, a quite unlikely possibility.

Maudina still resided here, serving Aradia, but prevented from any interchange with her former mistress. I must contact her, Keriam vowed, if only to find out how the poor girl was adjusting to service under Aradia.

Painfully aware of the silence, she lifted her hand. "Please, all of you, feel free to talk." She addressed the gardener. "How do the roses and other flowers fare in this dry weather?"

Annan set his knife and fork on his plate, resting his gnarled hands on the table. His wrinkled, nut brown face evidenced his years of working in the sunlight. "I water the plants as often as possible, madam, but that's no substitute for rain. If it don't rain soon, I fear many plants will wither and die."

"Fleas, too, madam," Bertha said, "if you'll pardon my blunt talk while we're eatin'."

"Yes, and fleas can bring the plague. I pray to the Goddess that doesn't happen now. A plague is the last thing we need, what with everything else . . . ." Keriam's voice trailed off, and she took refuge in silence, an awkward silence that lasted too long. Taking a deep breath, she returned to the subject. "Only think of all the squirrels in the kingdom. What if they should carry a disease?"

The servants looked at her in shock. "But madam, what can we do then?" Bertha asked. "We can't destroy them. Since they're sacred, they're protected by royal decree. But of course, you know that." She stared down at her plate. "Pardon me for speakin' so bluntlike."

"You spoke only the truth," Keriam said. She smiled brightly. "But perhaps we see trouble where no trouble exists, or will exist." She had enough to deal with now.

* * *

She must get through this day. Keriam viewed Balor and Aradia--recently crowned and married yesterday--as they stood before her father's open gravesite for his burial service. As was the Avadoran custom, the ceremony took place at dawn, while the sun was beginning to crest the western horizon, turning a bluish gray sky to lavender, then pink, and finally a golden burst of light illuminated grass, trees, and flowers, the palace in the background. A cool breeze blew across the royal cemetery, stirring up clouds of dust and bringing a hint of autumn.

Three bearded and sandaled white-robed druids presided over the grave, each performing his own function. Dunlang rang a clear bell, its tones imbuing a solemn atmosphere to the ritual. Tuathal swung an incense bowl, a strong myrrh scent wafting through the air. A third druid, Mothla, murmured an incantation over the grave.

The kingdom's ministers had gathered here for her father's burial service, and Roric Gamal, still the palace steward, had joined the others. Dressed in red, the color of mourning, Keriam stood alone, opposite the royal group, refusing to mingle with any of them. Struggling against her tears, she gazed at her father, embalmed in cedar oil, as he lay in his deep grave. She wanted to throw herself into the pit and hold him close one last time. But no, she wouldn't give Balor and Aradia the satisfaction of witnessing her sorrow. Her gaze scanned the ministers across from her, for the most part the same ones who'd served her father, for only a few of them had refused to work for Balor. How she missed her father's secretary, Conneid Delbraith, absent from the palace since the king's murder. What was he doing now? she wondered, and how did his wife manage, this lovely woman who was expecting a child within another moonphase?

Her father's precious possessions reposed with him--his sword and bronze shield, his bronze scabbard and drinking cup, even his carriage. All these things he would take with him to the Otherworld, to give his soul joy throughout eternity.

Yesterday evening, she'd swallowed her pride and asked one of the servants to procure vellum and a feather pen, so that she could write a letter to her mother. This her father would deliver when he joined Brenna in the Otherworld. Overjoyed to make contact with her mother, Keriam had written of her life in Avador and how she missed her. Now, she held the letter reverently to her lips and kissed it, then tossed it into the grave close to her father.

Keriam wrenched her attention back to the ceremony as one of the druids began speaking over the grave. Mothla spoke of the joys of the afterlife--"for the king's soul is returning to the Land of Truth and Eternal Life. We beseech you, Talmora, accept our sovereign's soul and grant him safe passage to the Otherworld. Let us not grieve or weep over the death of our beloved king, for this is a time of joy. A soul is returning to its home. King Tencien is now joined with our dear Queen Brenna, to live with her in happiness until his next earthly incarnation."

Keriam took a deep breath, so fearful she'd soon lose control of her emotions, break down and cry. Despite her efforts, tears streamed down her cheeks.

Looking up, she caught Roric's sympathetic gaze on her, and a slight shake of his head, as if he wanted to convey a message. She turned away, wanting only to escape his presence, wishing he would leave the palace, the capital, the kingdom. Traitor! She never wanted to see him again, this man who served Balor. He had fooled her all along. Her heart hammered in her chest, every muscle taut with anger.

What would happen to her now? Unless she found a means of escape--a scheme that had so far eluded her--she was destined to spend her remaining years at the palace, confined to live and dine with the servants. Or did Balor and Aradia have a different fate planned for her? A shaft of fear hit her midsection, turning her body to ice. Did they intend to put her on trial and convict her--of what? They had no basis for arraignment, for no one knew of her preternatural powers . . . no one except Roric Gamal. Radegunda knew of her second sight, but something told Keriam the enchantress would never betray her.

Had Roric really seen her spirit that fateful night she'd spied on Aradia? He had never said a word of the encounter, so perhaps her fears proved groundless. She hoped and prayed so. Visions of her burning at the stake penetrated her sorrow, but she dismissed her fears, too heartsick to deal with anything but her father's death.

She fixed her gaze on Balor and Aradia, the fiends! Anger pulsed through her, a muscle twitching in her jaw, hands clenched at her sides. Recognizing the need to conceal her emotions, she relaxed her position and unclenched her hands. She'd get them both, no matter what she must do or how long it took. They would not get away with murder. Someday, Balor and Aradia would both receive punishment for their sins, and she'd gain her rightful place as queen. Fearful that Avador would suffer under these unlawful rulers, she silently wept for her country. She'd save her people from the bastards if it was the last thing she ever did.

Watching as the druids shoveled dirt over her father's body, she realized--as if she needed the reminder--that she had no one to help her, no one to depend on, certainly not Roric Gamal. Very well, then. She would accomplish this mission herself.

* * *

"How long do you think she'll last here?" Midac Balor crawled into bed beside Aradia and pulled the silken sheet up to his chin, deeply inhaling her musk scent, an aroma he never tired of.

"The princess?" Aradia chuckled. "Or former princess, I should say. So far, she's shown no sign of resentment against our treatment of her. She lives with the servants, eats with them. Earlier today, I saw her outside with the gardener, pulling weeds beside the rose bushes." She giggled. "She surely doesn't look like a princess now with her grubby clothes and roughened hands. Since we've forbidden her the use of the library--and believe me, that woman likes to read--how else can she spend her time, unless it's housework? Do you know, she tried to organize a class to teach the stupid dwarf children, but I stopped that nonsense. You haven't seen them idling about with books lately, have you? I've got plenty of jobs for those ugly oafs."

Balor caressed her breasts, excitement burgeoning inside him. "Good for you, darling. I'm so proud of you. But to go back to my question--how long do you intend to keep her at the palace?"

"I want to see how much misery she can take," she said, easing her thigh over his. "Maybe after awhile I'll consider releasing her, but not yet. You have no idea how happy I am to get even with that woman after all the insults I suffered from her." She paused, tracing her fingers across his chest. "Why don't we just kill her?"

He shook his head. "Not a good idea. We already have two murders behind us--have you forgotten Fergus? One more assassination might make the people a bit suspicious. More to the point, I fear it would definitely arouse resentment against me. Just the same, it would relieve my mind to get her out of the palace soon. If we keep her here much longer, she'll become a disrupting influence. We'd best let her go, eventually."

"No!" Aradia shifted her position. "She might stir up trouble among the people."

"She'll cause no trouble away from the palace. My men have orders to quell any uprising, stamp out the first sign of rebellion. And remember--I have spies everywhere. If she attempts a revolt, she'll learn the true meaning of punishment for a traitor. If she even speaks a word against either of us, she'll be skinned alive. That threat alone should cure her of any treasonous ideas."

"And teach her who runs the country now. But Midac, darling, one thing you must promise me."

"Whatever you want." His fingers traced a path across her stomach, then trailed down to the moist juncture at her thighs.

"Permit me to supervise her execution," she purred.

He rose on top of her and whispered in her ear. "How can I deny you anything?"

Chapter Sixteen

"She'll get what she deserves, and the sooner, the better. Both of them." Hands on her hips, Bertha stood in the steaming hot kitchen, supervising the cooks as they prepared a beef and vegetable stew for the evening meal. Rich aromas filled the room: the stew bubbling in an iron cauldron over the hearth, and acorn bread baking in the brick oven. Two wide windows flanked the east wall of the kitchen, the sun sinking below the horizon.

We all know who Bertha is talking about, Keriam fretted as she leaned against a wooden counter to cut up carrots. The head cook's face and arms revealed a mass of black and blue marks, a result of Aradia's complaints about the palace food--"too hot or too cold, too spicy or too bland--" Bertha enumerated the criticisms, kicking a stool for emphasis, as if she wished it were Aradia's head. The other cooks went about their chores--setting the tables, fetching butter from the larder, settling the dwarf children at their own table--now and then nodding in agreement.

Apparently, Aradia didn't mind where Keriam labored, as long as she worked, and as long as she was under the watchful eye of a palace guard. Her life had settled into a predictable routine-- helping Annan with the garden in the morning, and preparing meals in the late afternoon. How she missed reading to the dwarf children, tending to their needs when their mothers were too busy. And how she missed her father. Goddess! She needed him. For a moment, she stared off into space, her thoughts far away, to all the happy times she and her father had shared. Brushing the back of her hand across her eyes, she returned to her job.

She set the carrot pieces aside, then started slicing two stalks of celery, lining them up in a row on the cutting board. Finished a few minutes later, she scooped up the carrot and celery pieces into a bowl, then dumped the vegetables into the cauldron, where the beef already cooked in a rich, dark broth. The fragrant bouquet of thyme and coriander rising from the pot whetted her appetite, since she'd eaten her mid-day meal hours ago.

Long-handled iron spoon in hand, Ula stood by the wide stone hearth, stirring the stew. Her face shone with perspiration, wet spots staining her dress. Past experience had taught the cooks not to leave the kitchen door open to get a cool breeze, for then the flies swarmed in mercilessly. At the far end of the hearth, Kormlada drew out loaves of acorn bread from the brick oven. A yeasty, nutty aroma floated through the room, further whetting Keriam's appetite. Ula gave the stew one final stir, then set the dripping spoon on a wooden counter and grabbed a ladle from the rack. "Stew's done," she announced to the other servants who waited outside the kitchen. They traipsed into the room, each one casting ravenous looks at the hearth. "Everyone get a bowl for yerselves before I take up a helping for the royal bastards." She smiled at Keriam while the servants lined up in order of precedence and fetched a wooden bowl from a stack on the counter.

After the other servants ladled up their helpings, Ula looked around. "Well, it looks like we all have ours. Now I'll add a bit of extra flavoring for the bastards." An exchange of amused glances followed this pronouncement. Keriam smiled, too, although a guilty flush warmed her face as Ula threw in the day's collection of dead flies--those that had slipped into the room with each opening and closing of the outside door--and cut-up cockroaches she'd saved for the occasion. A few minutes later, two giggling servants with trays left the kitchen and headed for the palace dining room.

Placed at the head of the table, Keriam raised a spoonful of stew to her mouth, the beef and vegetables salted and spiced to perfection. "Very good, Bertha. You outdid yourself this time." She reached for a slice of bread and passed the platter along to the others, to the only family she had now.

Bertha took a slice and chewed, then looked at the others gathered at the table. "Looks like I won't see my brother much anymore," she said, seeing she had everyone's attention. "He's a miner, ya know. Visited him last Sacredday. He told me the king's set new hours for the miners--fifteen hours a day!"

"Fifteen hours!" Ula expressed everyone's shock.

"You heard me." Bertha gulped her cider, then set the mug down with a hard thud, spilling drops on the table. "And that ain't all. He's givin' them only one-half day off a nineday."

"Goddess!"

"Things is like that all over, so I've heard."

"Yeh, everyone's complainin'."

The group sat in silent commiseration, a sorrowful expression on their faces.

After a few moments, Bertha broke the silence. "That's the way it is all over the kingdom, or so everyone tells me. That bastard Balor hasn't even been on the throne one moonphase, but I can't remember when the people's been so unhappy, even when we had the black fever all those years ago." She lifted her hands. "But what can we do? What can anyone do?"

Glum expressions around the table provided the answer. The head gardener spoke for the entire group. "Nothin'."

Oh, no, Keriam mused. You are so wrong. There is plenty we can do, and I intend to do my part.

* * *

"Aradia has lost no time in spending palace funds," Keriam remarked to Kormlada as the two of them opened crates and boxes in the vast storage room next to the pantry, searching for new silver drinking cups the sorceress had ordered for royal dining. The money could have been better spent on the Avadoran people, Keriam fumed, shoving a heavy box out of the way.

"Oh, madam, you should see the new silk draperies in the royal bedchamber, and bedcovers to match. I sneaked up there while the king and queen were away one evening." Kormlada frowned. "I didn't see nothin' wrong with the draperies they already had." With a pry bar, she cracked open a wooden crate and drew out a silver cup. "Ah, here we are." She held it up, and even in the dim light, it shone brightly.

"Pretty, but unnecessary." Keriam looked around her, at the immense quantity of items stored in the room--new sheepskin rugs and blankets, boxes of spermaceti candles especially made for the palace by a candlemaker in Moytura. She spied a long coil of heavy rope stashed in a corner, for use in lifting bluestone to replace broken stones on the second floor of the east side of the palace. Fergus had arranged for their delivery shortly before his death.

Her breath caught, an idea forming in her mind. The rope! If she could only elude the guards, she could simply walk out of the palace late at night. But if she had to, she might need to lower herself down from her room. She hoped and prayed she wouldn't need the rope, but it might be good to have it, to be on the safe side.

Kormlada broke through her thoughts. "Arad--the queen wanted these cups especially for the reception they're gonna have soon. Hundreds of guests supposed to come."

"Reception?" Hundreds of guests? How could she ever escape the palace?

"Yes, madam, didn't you hear? Most of them should arrive any day now and stay for days. I heard tell from one of the other servants that all kinds of activities are planned. People will be comin' and goin' all hours of the day and night."

Keriam's spirits plummeted, but just as quickly, her natural optimism came to her defense. Somehow, she'd escape. And she might have to use the rope after all. Still, if she were to get away, she couldn't get far or procure a place to live without money. Balor and Aradia had usurped the palace funds, and she had no money of her own. Her jewels? Aside from the amethyst ring she kept hidden in her room, only the Goddess knew what had happened to her other rings, bracelets, and necklaces, for she surely didn't. No doubt Aradia was sporting her sapphire ring this very minute.

And if anyone knew she was the escaped princess, he would not risk harboring her.

Ideas played in her mind, a means of fleeing the palace, solutions just out of reach. But she'd think of something. Sure as the Otherworld, she wouldn't stay here for the rest of her life. Cups in hand, she left the room with Kormlada, her heart much lighter than it had been in a long time.

* * *

That night while she slept, she had one of her nightly journeys, that special time when her soul wandered throughout the palace, or even roamed the countryside. She spied on the guards, those inside the palace and out, surveying their movements and habits, judging when--and if--she could safely slip past them when she attempted escape. She vowed she make these nightly journeys as often as possible, for one trip alone would do little good.

And Roric? Her spirit brain urged, don't you want to see him? Ah, yes, more than anything, she wanted to see him again, and never mind her doubts about him. As quickly as her spirit body would take her, she floated upward to the steward's quarters and drifted through the walls. Roric! He slept soundly on his side, one muscular arm close to his chest, the other stretched out in front of him. Bare-chested, he had never looked so appealing, a mat of curly hair trailing from just below his neck on down to his stomach--and from there? She smiled to herself, her thoughts flying to places she had never dared consider. She gazed at him for long moments, and even in her corporeal state, a flush spread over her body, an insistent desire to lie in bed with him, to feel his body on hers, to know his kisses, his caresses. With more regret than she cared to admit, she left him and returned to her room. If only she could forget him, drive him from her mind, for he served Balor now.

* * *

On a clear morning with no clouds in sight--and no hope of much-needed rain--Keriam pulled weeds in the palace garden, working between clusters of red chrysanthemums and purple asters. A hummingbird darted about, sampling the irises. A light breeze brought the sweet scent of pink peonies in a batch to the far right, but the leaves and petals of all the flowers drooped in the dry spell. Earlier in the day, she'd placed a wreath she'd made from these flowers on her father's grave, although it had taken much discrimination to find presentable blooms.

The sun was warm on her back, but the air carried a hint of cooler weather to come. Now and then, she flexed her fingers to get the kinks out, or stood and stretched. She dabbed a handkerchief across her perspiring forehead, then inched along on the ground, headed for the phlox.

But oh! when would it rain? Thinking hard, she looked out across the clear lake. How about an irrigation system? she wondered with more than idle speculation. Since the lake bordered the palace garden, such a system seemed a feasible solution for watering the flowers and bushes. She'd speak to Annan about it first chance she got.

Because the gardener's assistant had run away a few days ago, Keriam found plenty to keep her busy here, a chance to divert her mind from her worries. From Roric Gamal.

She found herself thinking of him more and more, and warmth stole over her body with each thought of him. Yet painful doubts persisted. Did he truly serve Balor, or had he remained loyal to her? A heavy weight settled over her heart, and she wondered if she would ever know.

Returned to her task, she jerked at the weeds with a vengeance. A raven lit on the ground beside her, looking at her intently, as if it wanted to say something. Two more ravens landed on the grass beside the first, all of them seemingly in quiet communication; then five more alighted.

"Well, hello there, my feathered friends." She reached for her handkerchief to tuck it in her pocket but couldn't find it.

"My handkerchief," she murmured, looking all around. "Where did I put it?"

One of the ravens hopped along the ground, back to the spot she'd just left. Grabbing the piece of linen in his beak, he hopped back to her and dropped the handkerchief in front of her.

"Well, what do you know! You understood me!"

Smiling with surprised delight, she edged closer to them, but they flew away at her approach. For a few moments, she raised her head to watch their flight, pondering when she'd see them again, or if she ever would. What if they were trying to tell her something?

"Princess Keriam!"

Keriam looked up to see Maudina approach along the gravel walkway that led from the courtyard to the gardens, the girl's steps quick and purposeful, her comely face a welcome sight.

"Maudina!" Keriam dropped the weeds and rushed toward her former maid, brushing her hands on her brown cotton dress. Fighting imminent tears, she hugged the young girl. Countless images of the maid and Traigh flooded her mind, pleasant visions but ones she determined to ignore, wanting to concentrate on the here and now. She vowed from hereon to suppress this preternatural ability, for this continual bombardment of pictures often hindered clear thought.

"Maudina, I haven't seen you since . . . since . . ." She wiped a hand across her eyes. "Ah, dear Maudina, it seems like such a long time."

Tears streamed down the girl's face. "I know, princess," she said in a wavery voice. "That bit--Aradia won't let me out of her sight, except at bedtime. But she and Balor--excuse me, King Midac--rode into the city today on some business--don't ask me what." She snorted. "As if they'd tell me!"

Taking her hand, Keriam led her to a stone bench and sat, resting her hands in her lap. "How is she treating you? The truth, now."

"Aradia?" the maid said with a rueful smile. "All sweetness and light, everything a true lady should be. Why, I have only a couple of black and blue marks now, so I guess I'm improving. At the beginning, nothing I did pleased her."

"Ah, Maudina." Keriam gave her a quick hug. "I'm so sorry." She thought quickly. "Suppose you had a chance to escape the palace--"

"Not much chance, madam, if you'll pardon me for interrupting."

"But suppose you did. Or suppose--may the Goddess guide us–something happened to

Aradia. Do you have a place to go to?"

"I have a sister who lives south of Moytura, madam." She gazed down at her lap. "Much good that does me now."

Dabbing the handkerchief across her forehead, she gave the maid a hopeful look. "But if something should happen to

Aradia--you know what I mean-- you could live with your sister, couldn't you?"

"I've considered that, but I suppose Aradia will live to be one-hundred." Maudina scoffed. "Only the good die young."

"If you have the opportunity, please go to your sister. Later, when I gain the throne–and I swear I will--I hope you'll return to the palace. For now, I hate the thought of what you have to endure from the usurper queen."

"Don't be sorry for me, princess. My situation is nothing like what you're going through. Pulling weeds," she said, gesturing toward the garden, "working in the kitchen . . ." She shook her head. "I shouldn't complain."

Keriam smiled. "All good practice, nothing that will kill me. Why, if ever I have to find a position, I'll warrant all this work--" She waved her hand, indicating the garden and the palace--"will serve me well."

Maudina spoke quickly. "Madam, I must leave you soon. I lied to the guard, told him I had a message for you from Aradia. If I stay too long . . ." She shrugged her shoulders, a worried frown on her face. "And I will go to my sister, if I ever can. Believe me, if you gain the throne--and oh! madam, I pray that you do--I shall come back to serve you."

"Good! Now, dear Maudina, best you go back." Keriam stifled her disappointment, so happy to see her maid again, to talk to her, discover how she managed. "I don't want you to get into trouble." When would she see her again?

"Madam, I wanted you to know, since this is the first chance I've had to talk to you--before Radegunda left the palace, she urged me to tell you that if you can escape, you're always welcome to live with her, so--"

"Radegunda's--that's the first place Balor would look." Surely Aradia had told Balor about their herbal lessons, for Aradia never missed much.

"She's considered that, madam. If you go there, she intends to leave right away for her brother's farm in the country, north of Moytura."

"Very well, if I can escape." Keriam pounded her fist in her the palm of her other hand. "I must get out of here, not for my sake, but for the kingdom. I could do more for Avador away from the palace. If I can inspire a revolt among the people--"

"A dangerous gamble, madam. I fear you'd be severely punished."

Desperate plans rampaged through her mind. "As it is, I'm sure they don't know that . . ." She swallowed hard--"that the king was m-murdered, unless someone from here got word to them." She frowned. "Not likely, though." She pressed her hands to her face. "My father and I were to attend a royal wedding in Elegia the next moonphase. Goddess, what will they think, when we don't appear?"

"I don't know!" Maudina stood. "Madam, forgive me, but I must leave. Only remember--Radegunda. She lives at 15 Perfume Lane, keeps the key hidden behind a loose brick, fifth brick from the bottom, to the right of the front door."

Keriam silently repeated the directions. "I'll remember. And thank you for coming to tell me. Much as I enjoy visiting with you, I fear you will only bring trouble on yourself if you come see me again."

"Don't worry about me. I'll try to visit whenever I can. Goodbye, madam."

Keriam rose and gave her another warm embrace. "Goodbye, Maudina."

The maid rushed off along the pathway, her dress fluttering around her ankles, until she became a small figure in the distance. After one final wave, she opened the wide oak door at the back courtyard, then disappeared inside the palace.

A guard stood by the door, prompting Keriam to worry if he'd report Maudina, or if he'd accepted her story. Kind, dependable Hafgan had always served her and her father well, but Balor had wrought so many changes within the palace, creating shifting loyalties and arousing suspicions among the servants. No one knew whom to trust.

Keriam returned to the bench, resting her hands in her lap. The wind picked up, cooler now, wafting her hair about her face. She brushed a strand of hair from her cheek and hugged her arms, weighing her few options, painfully aware that for the first time in her life, she was at the mercy of others.

No, she wasn't! She would determine her own fate. Maudina had given her much to think about, and there had to be an answer to her plight. Ideas and possibilities churned through her mind, each one quickly discarded. Countless moments slid past as she remained in quiet but busy contemplation, until a scheme struck her like a flash of light. Dare she try it? She had nothing to lose.

Smiling, she resumed her task, eager to put her plan into action. She felt better than she had in a long time, if only her scheme would work. She would persevere, and she would triumph.

Chapter Seventeen

"We must raise taxes," Balor said,. presiding over a long oval table in the Blue Royal Conference Room. "We'll need more money. I fear war will be forced upon us."

War with whom? At a loss for words, Roric stared down at his hands, then raised his eyes. Balor had better explain himself.

While Balor pontificated to his eight ministers and the steward, Roric., the usurper's eyes shifted from one man to the next, as if he were daring anyone to challenge his legitimacy. And that is a valid concern, Roric agonized, his gaze on this upstart. Roric's look slid to the other men in the room. What was going through their minds? Was their loyalty only a pretense, as was his? Four had served under Tencien, their sudden switch of allegiance to the new king a shock to him.

A stack of vellum rested in front of Balor, his thumb and forefinger ruffling the pages. Feather pens, ink wells, and papers sat at each man's place, the oak table polished to a shine. Discarding his uniform for all the trappings of his new kingly role, Balor sported a long-sleeved purple velvet tunic, a gold pendant adorning his neck, a gold-link belt circling his waist. A gold ring flashed on his right ring finger, two bracelets of the same dangling from his left wrist--enough of the precious metal to feed a family for several years.

The other men, including Roric, wore simple tunics of gray, brown, or black, with wide black or brown leather belts buckled at their waists. Soon the impending cool weather would necessitate woolen trousers and cloaks.

Since Balor didn't permit any weapons in the palace--aside from the swords carried by the guards--Roric had had special high boots made with a hidden sheath for his dagger, and thus kept the weapon with him at all times.

As palace steward, Roric always joined this group that met at least once every nineday. Did Balor value his opinion, or did the new king simply want to keep an eye on him? If it was the latter, Roric knew he was in trouble. Having served faithfully first as courier and then palace steward under Tencien, Roric feared he could well be an object of suspicion under this king murderer. Only one moonphase had passed since the fiend had gained the throne; his changes had already caused misery within the palace and throughout the kingdom. Only look at all the men out of work, newly-made vagrants roaming the streets of the capital, robbing honest men and ravishing respectable women.

Surely the caravans to Elegia had brought word of Tencien's assassination and of Balor's takeover of the throne. Would the Elegians come to Avador's aid and help overthrow Balor? Roric wondered if he could persuade King Barzad to assist Avador, if only he could travel there. For now, he didn't see a chance to leave the country, since any extended absence would arouse Balor's suspicions. Above all, he must work toward placing Princess Keriam on the throne. He clenched his jaw, determined to make that happen. His thoughts dwelt on Keriam, to all the lovely things about her, everything that made her a desirable woman, a woman he might some day learn to care for, and one he thought about night after night. Yet he hadn't had a chance to talk to her since the king's assassination, hadn't had a chance to comfort her and assure her of his devotion. Stifling his anger at the usurper, he returned his thoughts to the discussion.

"Sire, the people will surely object to a raise in taxes," Drummond Haley, the new Minister of Coinage, offered after the king had silently read a few messages. One of Roric's recruits, Haley harbored the steward's hatred of Balor. Both men anticipated the right moment--if it ever came--to overthrow the new monarch and establish Princess Keriam on the throne. The two men played a dangerous deception, a duplicity that could well result in torture and death.

"Let them object!" Balor scowled, looking up from his messages. "What can they do about it? We need money for palace repairs before the east side falls apart. We must build additional monuments to our gods and goddesses. But most important," he said, his finger stabbing the air,"we must manufacture more swords and shields for our soldiers. Elegia has made aggressive moves, reinforcing their southernmost garrison. We must prepare for war."

Stunned looks greeted this announcement, and Roric questioned if surprise or disbelief prompted the shock. Any knowledgeable person knew that Elegia was a peaceable country, wanting only to live in harmony with its neighbors. The only reason that country kept a well-equipped army was because of Avador's bellicosity in the past, before Tencien's reign.

"Still," Haley persisted, "the poor people may find it difficult to pay more money to the government, when so many of them can barely support themselves and their families." Absently, he brushed a flea from his sleeve. "For the rich, of course, the increase will present no problem. Sire, perhaps we can--"

"Perhaps we can tax everyone equally, rich and poor alike," Balor finished for him. "Let every citizen know that he is participating in his country's welfare." His eyes lit with anticipation. "Gentlemen, I have such plans for our country, to restore it to its former greatness. I look forward to the day we no longer depend on any other nation for getting our goods to market, or for importing goods from elsewhere. And we must rebuild our army, so that no other country ever threatens us again."

Roric suppressed a sneer. Sacred shrine! No country threatened Avador now, or was Balor thinking of events from long ago? He sifted ideas through his mind, striving to present a means of lessening the burden on the impoverished.

"Sire," Roric said, "have you considered taxing only unnecessary items, such as jewels and silks? That way--"

"That way, only the rich will pay taxes," Balor said. "No, I want this tax to be equally distributed among the people. Besides," he said with a sly grin, "I want everyone to gain satisfaction from knowing that they are helping to support the country. After all, if we go to war, it's to everyone's benefit to contribute to Avador.

"Which brings up a second point," Balor continued. "We must conscript more men for the army." His finger tracing the puckered scar on his cheek, his glance shifted to Gareth Egmond, Minister of War. "Put this order in effect tomorrow. Draft every able-bodied man between fifteen and forty. And one thing you must understand, gentlemen--I still retain my position as head of the army. Let there be no question about that."

While the new monarch shuffled the vellum sheets, Roric and Haley exchanged uneasy glances; then they quickly looked away, lest others suspect their connivance.

Balor retrieved a paper from the stack. "Now, another matter. Word has reached me that the former king's secretary, Conneid Delbraith, has been inciting the people against me. Foolish man! Surely he knows the penalty for treason. And he should know that we have spies everywhere." He waved the paper. "I have here a letter that Delbraith sent to one of Moytura's leading citizens, but was intercepted by one of my men. It was written in a code that was easy to break," he said with a deprecating grin. "I shall read the translated version to you."

My dear Kevan, Greetings and best of health to your dear wife and children. I fear the good times we enjoyed under King Tencien—may the Goddess rest his soul—are in the past. Balor has brought suffering and misery to the Avadoran people. The people will not contend with this situation for long. You and I and everyone who feels as we do—and there are many, my friend—must do our part in resisting his malicious rule, with the goal of eventually overthrowing him. Let us begin by establishing committees of resistance, corresponding with each other and enumerating our grievances. Let each of us enlist others who share our concern about the new government, those who are willing to work toward its ultimate overthrow. By that means, we can establish a cadre of fellow objectors.

Balor slapped the paper on the table. "Treason, gentlemen!" His cunning eyes moved from one man to another. "This is but one example. Word has reached me of a secret society composed of those who conspire against me. Doubtless Delbraith belongs to it. Let us never forget. The people chose me as their king!" He crumbled the letter, the sound like thunder in the quiet of the room. "But we will ferret out these traitors, starting with Delbraith. I will not countenance betrayal within the realm. And we all know the penalty for treason, don't we?"

Balor should know about treason. He was the vilest traitor of all. Afraid of revealing his rage, Roric studied a marble statue of

Talmora that commanded a far wall. He wanted to kill the king now, end the country's misery, but he'd never murdered anyone in cold blood, and he couldn't--wouldn't--do it now. Roric had heard tales of this secret society: farmers, merchants, and others planning to overthrow Balor and place Keriam on the throne. But how strong was this underground? And what were its chances of success? He could contribute much if he joined this society, but he already walked a thin line with his deception, serving as Balor's steward while hating the man he served, longing to overthrow him sometime soon. Best he didn't jeopardize his position.

The king smiled venomously. "Let's see how bravely Delbraith talks once he's captured--and he will be captured, never doubt it--when he is skinned alive."

Sacred shrine! Roric quelled a shudder, surprised by Conneid's temerity and fearful for his life. Always diffident and self-effacing, the former secretary had taken a huge chance, indeed, had risked his life, indulging in this seditious correspondence. Yet Roric gave him his due, full of admiration for Conneid's bravery, and for the man.

Afraid Balor's planned capture and torture of Delbraith was but a prelude of calamities to come, Roric mourned for Avador. For the present, he saw nothing he could do, no way to resist Balor's evil rule without inviting suspicion on himself.

But there would be a day of reckoning. He'd see to that.

Chapter Eighteen

Back at her shop on Perfume Lane, Radegunda tended to her last customer, tired after standing for so many hours, thankful her busy day was ending. Soon the sun would set and she could close her shop, tally up her sales. And a profitable day it had been--not counting the new taxes the king had imposed--well worth her aching joints.

"Oh, and I'll take a few of your soap bars, too," the customer--an elderly, well-dressed matron--said, looking over the counter display.

"Very good, madam, what would you like--lavender, lilac, chamomile?"

"Rose soap," she said, brushing a flea from her sleeve.

"Madam, I'm sorry I'm out of the rose, but I should have some tomorrow."

The customer scowled. "Well, two lavender soaps, then."

"Of course." After making change and setting the woman's purchases in a cheesecloth bag with thin leather handles--a little extra gift for her customers, made by a local craftsman--Radegunda shifted her position as the woman left and closed the door. Behind her, shelves offered a tempting variety of herbal remedies--rosemary, valerian, yarrow tea, fennel, and many others. Miniature lilac, chamomile, and lavender topiaries attached to colorful ribbons hung from the ceiling, adding their pleasant scents to the room.

Her mind drifted in another direction, her thoughts on magic.

Ah, magic. Why, only look at how skilled she'd become in the art since her return from the palace. Born with innate magic, she had perfected her talent over the years. Not even her helper, Adsulata, knew of her special skills. She could best that sorceress Aradia any day. She still had much to learn, mind you, and she couldn't always practice in the room above her shop, for many of her spells were much too dangerous to initiate in such a small space. .

186

Hours later, while the rest of the city slept--except for the vagrants, pleasure women, and tavern patrons--Radegunda headed for an isolated place by the Nantosuelta River where no one would disturb her, a long walk for her sore feet but worth the effort. She looked warily in all directions, ever on the alert for criminals who prowled the city. Oak branches tossed in a cool wind, fallen leaves rustling on the cobblestones. She heard a tramp shuffling along the street in the distance, and hiding in the shadows of a sword shop, she waited until he traipsed off.

She passed many other shops along her route, finally reaching Aventina Way. After crossing the wide avenue, she traversed the plain and headed for the river, where clusters of trees lined both banks of the raging, frothing waters. She stood still, worried about any idlers that might lurk among the trees and bushes.

Certain she was alone, she removed her shoes and padded down to the riverbank, the sandy soil squishing between her toes. She stayed motionless for long moments, gathering all her strength and power within her, letting her spirituality flood her being.

Facing south, she raised her hand and chanted, "Hail, you who dwell in the temple of the brilliant ones, you beautiful rudder of the southern sky.

> Grant me what I want
> What I desire
> Give me this wish
> And give me fire!"

She flung her hand out, her fingers extended. A burst of fire erupted from her fingers, singing her skin, lighting the river with an amber glow. She dropped her hands to her side, and the flames disappeared. Blowing on her burnt fingers, she reminded herself to apply a healing salve when she returned home.

That spell was enough for tonight; she must conserve her magic and ration her power. Yes, she thought as she walked back to her shop, she was becoming quite skilled with magic. But she still had much to learn.

* * *

So many things could go wrong. After observing the coil of rope in the storage room recently, Keriam had planned her escape with care, allowing--she hoped!--for all eventualities. Since Balor had tripled the outside guard, she saw many difficulties ahead. Above all, no harmful recriminations must fall on any of the staff, once she was free of the palace.

No matter her duties--in the kitchen or the garden--Keriam schooled herself to act normally, and never by word or expression give herself away. The household staff remained loyal to her, despite their forced submission to Balor and Aradia. But how long could anyone withstand having their fingernails pulled out to gain information? Surely even the bravest man or woman would succumb.

Already, guests had started to arrive for the reception and all the festivities Balor and Aradia had planned. If she wanted to escape, she'd better do it soon, for time was running out. And she feared she'd have to lower herself down by the rope, since earlier in the day she'd seen people at the stables, so many Balor had hired extra stable help. She couldn't simply walk out by either of the back entrances.

That evening, she paced the floor of her room, scarcely able to wait until the remainder of the palace slept. She eased her bed to rest under the open window high on the wall, a task she'd saved for her final night here. What if someone had walked past her room earlier and seen the bed's altered position? That would certainly arouse suspicion. Her hand pressed against the wall for balance, she stepped up onto the bed and looked out the window to the back courtyard below. Talmora, what a long drop! But she wouldn't let distance stop her. She vowed that nothing would stop her.

Stepping down, she nodded to herself. She could do it. She could escape.

Still, descending from her window to the courtyard below solved only one step of her scheme. She must also elude the outside sentries. Here, Radegunda's lessons in herbs provided the answer: she would drug the men.

Hours later, confident the rest of the palace slept, she set out for the storage room, for once grateful she was relegated to the servants' staircase. In total blackness, she descended the three flights of slippery flagstone stairs, feeling her way with each step. By now familiar with the habits of the first floor's only guard, she knew he took several minutes to patrol the entire area. A few steps before reaching the first floor, she waited until she heard the sentry move off to the other end of the main hall. With one hand clutching the iron handrail, she pressed the other hand against the wall, the stone slimy beneath her fingers.

Once she reached the main floor, rushlights in iron sconces enabled her to see. Hugging the wall, she made her way the short length from the stairs to the storage room, and there, she tugged open the heavy oak door, praying she could elude the sentry.

Darkness cloaked the huge storage room, only the dim hall light providing illumination. Leaving the door slightly ajar, she waited a few minutes for her eyes to adjust to the blackness; then the room's multitude of boxes and crates gradually came into focus. She moved about in the semi-darkness, touching crates and sidestepping barrels as she shuffled over to a far corner to retrieve the rope. Rats scuttled across the floor, spider webs draping the corners.

Rope in hand, she prepared to-- Booted footsteps rang on the flagstone floor of the main hall. No! A stab of fear knifed through her, and she ducked behind a large crate. Her heart pounded so loud, she heard each beat in her eardrums.

"Who's there?" the sentry barked by the open door. There's one thing that's gone wrong, she worried. What if he found her here? Her mind worked frantically, devising a plausible reason.

A ring of steel pealed in the darkness. Sword in hand, he stepped inside the room, shoving boxes and crates aside. His head turned from side to side, his footsteps sounding like thunder in the room's silence.

Keriam crouched behind a crate, every muscle tense, holding her breath until she feared her lungs would burst. Countless moments dragged past, a torture of waiting. After what seemed like hours but was probably only minutes, he left, closing the door behind him.

What could she do now? She didn't dare get up to see if the guard had left, for he might have remained close by. Cramped muscles plagued her, and she changed her position, still fearful to leave. Absolute blackness surrounded her. Nothing but silence enclosed her in the dreary room. A spider crawled across her bare arm, and with a shudder, she flung it away.

Tempted to cry from disappointment, she sensed the passage of time and realized she couldn't escape this night. Too much time had elapsed, and she chided herself for waiting too long before her trip to the storage room. Convinced the guard had left, she unwound from her stiff position, her muscles cramping, her fingers tingling. She dragged the rope from the room, finding it heavier than she had imagined. Midway up the first flight of stairs, she paused to rest, then stopped occasionally until she reached her room, where she shoved the rope under the bed. Already, dawn lightened the sky. Now, she must face the same agony of waiting the next day.

Performing her duties as if her life remained the same--as if she wasn't planning one of the greatest moves in her life--proved a challenge every minute of the following day. Was Kormlada giving her distrustful glances? Keriam agonized while she peeled potatoes. Did the outside guards observe her every movement while she worked in the herb garden, as though they expected her to flee from the grounds any minute?

And the visitors! They spilled out from the Blue Reception Room, filling the main hall, arriving by the back entrance, coming and going at all hours, as Kormlada had predicted. Keriam stayed out of their way, fearful someone would recognize her. Balor and Aradia had spread the rumor that the princess was too disturbed to rule and had to be confined to her room. And now, word was there would be a grand dinner for all the guests tomorrow evening. Keriam had no intention of staying around for that.

That night became a repeat of the previous one, a long trek down the servants' stairs, this time to the kitchen, evading royal guests along the way. Surely with the nights becoming cooler now, the guards would appreciate a mug of hot tea. And if she added a sedative--only enough to put them to sleep for a few hours--she could escape undetected.

Inside the kitchen, darkness greeted her again, but she felt her way past the tables, counters, and stools, familiar with the complete layout of the room. Even from here, she heard the noise and laughter of the guests in the main hall. She stopped by the hearth, where a few embers still burned, and an iron cauldron hung from a hook. She blew on the embers, and wisps of smoke soon curled up from the hearth as a cluster of orange flames blossomed among the logs. Accidentally brushing her hand against the cauldron, she jerked her burnt fingers back. At least it wouldn't take long for the water to boil, she mused as she retrieved nine mugs from a shelf on the other side of the room.

Now for the herbs . . . Since Radegunda had left with only her clothes, not being permitted to take anything else, the herbs and crushed flowers remained on the stillroom shelves, each jar neatly labeled. It took several tries for Keriam to find the jar of crushed poppies, for each time she had to hold a jar by the hearth fire to read the label. Steam rose from the cauldron, heating her face. She strained to lift the pot, then poured the water into the waiting mugs, along with a spicy tea from a kitchen shelf. Now to measure the correct amount of crushed poppies . . . Her hands shook and she knocked a large stirring spoon onto the stone floor, the sound magnified inside the quiet room.

The outside door burst open, and a guard rushed inside. Keriam jumped, but quickly relaxed and fixed a calm expression on her face.

"I heard noise," he said, "something breaking? And pr— madam, may I ask what you are doing here this late hour of the night?"

She eased in front of the counter where the mugs waited. "Since the weather is turning cooler, and I couldn't sleep, I decided to make myself a cup of tea. I accidentally knocked something to the floor." She affected a coquettish look. "Would you and the other guards like a cup of tea?"

"Why, that's mighty thoughtful of you." He nodded. "Tea sounds like a good idea."

"Only wait a few minutes outside, and I'll have the tea ready for you and the others."

As he closed the door behind him, Keriam breathed a long sigh of relief. Lips pursed in concentration, she measured out the necessary amount of poppy. She added this to the hot water and spicy tea and waited a few minutes, then grabbed a wooden tray from another shelf. Leaving the door open, she set the heavy mugs on the tray. The mugs started to slip, but she caught the tray in time and stepped out of the warm kitchen.

Outside, a cool wind lifted her hair from her shoulders and molded her dress to her body. Shawlless, she shivered in the cold, the tray shaking, jiggling the mugs. She followed the stone courtyard until she found the back sentries and asked them to fetch the others. Shortly after, the other guards joined them.

"Ah, madam." A sentry reached for a mug. "Just what we need on a night like this."

Another raised the mug to his mouth.

"Drink it slowly," Keriam advised. "I'm afraid it's quite hot."

"Very good, madam. I feel warmer already."

Bidding them all goodnight, Keriam headed back inside to the kitchen and set the tray on a counter. So much for that part of the plan . . . if it worked.

Taking the three flights of stairs in the dark, she tripped and fell in her haste, bruising her hands and shins. She brushed her hands off and returned to her room, there to wait for an endless time, each minute an hour. A breeze blew through her open window, and she shivered with cold and worry. Had the poppy taken effect already? If given in the right amount, it shouldn't take long for the flower to work. But had she given the guards enough . . . or too much?

Convinced adequate time had elapsed, she pushed the bed against the wall and tied the rope securely around a bed leg, then pulled the rope hard to test its hold. Her heart beat frantically with the passing time, her teeth chattering. With a silent thanks to the Goddess that her bedchamber faced away from the stables, she prayed she'd escape undetected.

She gathered up a small cloth bag she'd filched from the storage room days ago, her few possessions making it light and easy to manage; then she tied its end strips around her neck and stepped onto the bed. A few days ago, she had sewn her amethyst ring in the hem of her dress, something valuable she'd always have with her, to pawn if necessary.

Now comes the tricky part, she fretted, afraid of losing her courage. She thrust one leg out the window and then the other, onto the ledge that extended out from the palace wall, a ledge that provided enough room for her to sit. She held on tight to the windowsill with her left hand, the rope with her right. The wind picked up, swirling her hair, whipping her dress around her body. Gripping the rope with both hands now, she eased off the window ledge and down the rope.

She stared down to the ground below and swallowed hard. She mustn't look down. She'd never make it if she did.

Grasping the rope, she descended, foot by foot. What if someone discovered her? But no, she'd make it. She would escape. The rough rope chafed her bruised hands, but she ignored the pain.

What if the rope slipped from her hands and she fell all the way to the bottom? What if the sentries awoke and came after her? I'm not going to make it, she agonized while the wind buffeted her and fears wracked her brain. Despite her vow not to, she looked down again. Such a long drop! She focused on the palace wall, anything to divert her mind from the distance. Her hand and arm muscles ached, the rope slippery in her moist hands.

After an eternity, she reached the ground . . . and found someone waiting for her.

Aradia.

Chapter Nineteen

Agonizing over Princess Keriam, Radegunda could scarcely focus on her customers, especially since her keen intuition hinted that the princess might attempt an escape very soon. Before leaving the palace, Radegunda had snitched a handkerchief the princess had left in the kitchen during one of their herbal lessons. From time to time, she fingered the scrap of linen, thus enabling her to perceive how the princess fared. She found the answer depressing, indeed. Visions of Princess Keriam peeling potatoes in the kitchen or pulling weeds in the garden sent her spirits diving. Ah, that it should have come to this!

For reasons Radegunda couldn't explain, many details of the princess's life remained hazy, or worse, out of reach, creating an additional worry.

After the store closed, she trod the stairs to her left, then opened the door to her small apartment. There, she eased out a dresser drawer, and reaching under her nightgown and shift, retrieved Keriam's handkerchief. Do you have good news for me, madam? she asked, sitting on the bed. No escape for her yet, she realized after a few despairing moments. A vision of the princess pacing the floor of her solitary room sank into the witch's consciousness. She wondered what that image meant.

Fears about the princess kept her awake for hours, a time of tossing and turning in her narrow bed. In the early hours of the morning, she sighed with exasperation and threw back her covers to rise from the bed. She retrieved the handkerchief from the drawer again and touched its soft fabric.

She closed her eyes as fresh pictures flashed in her brain. Ah! She saw the princess lowering herself on a rope, much time passing before she reached the ground below.

She saw--No! Aradia waited at the bottom, but after a long moment, the sorceress shimmered and disappeared. Frowning, Radegunda opened her eyes. What did the vision mean? Surely Aradia's appearance was a false picture, meaning nothing. But if not? For the first time in years, Radegunda prayed to the Earth-mother Goddess. Please keep the princess safe.

* * *

Keriam landed on the walk and released the rope, the heavy cordage swinging back and forth, bumping against the palace wall. She flexed her sore fingers, hoping Radegunda would have a soothing lotion for her bruised and burned hands. But that was the least of her problems. Drawing a deep breath, she turned . . . and saw Aradia. In a black nightdress, the sorceress stared at her, her eyes cold and calculating, a sly smile on her face. After all she'd been through--all her planning, stealing the rope, drugging the guards, then her dangerous descent from the fourth floor--was this where it all ended?

No! Hatred burned within her, deep and merciless. Keriam clenched her hands, her fingers itching to strangle the woman. A dagger glinting in her hand, the sorceress lunged for her. Stifling a scream, Keriam dashed away. She tripped and fell on the gravel, her breath coming hard and fast, her heart thudding. She jumped to her feet and looked behind her--and Aradia faded away. Weak with relief, Keriam knew she mustn't linger, afraid she'd see Aradia in the flesh. No doubt her own fears had created this image of the sorceress. Never mind the cause! No time to lose!

She peeked around the corner of the palace and found the guards at the far end of the courtyard, fast asleep. Darkness cloaked their sleeping bodies, and she said another silent prayer that their slumber--and her absence--would not be reported for hours. She heard the noise and chatter of all the visitors inside, another party being held in the Blue Reception Room. Keeping away from the busy stables, she rushed past the palace gardens, heading for the Royal North Road to Moytura. She had to cover a distance of over twelve miles and reach Radegunda by early morning.

Keriam wanted to shout with relief. She was free! Ahead of her beckoned Moytura and refuge.

Tempted to leave the road and make her way through the meadows and farmland that bordered either side of the highway, she rejected that idea, confident she would make quicker time this way. And time--besides safety--was very important.

Thankful she wore her most comfortable leather shoes, she ran faster than ever, racing toward the dirt road, reaching it minutes later. She looked up at the sky, alarmed to find thousands--millions!--of stars decorating the heavens, a full moon frosting the countryside with a silvery glow. Anyone could see her, since few trees or bushes lined this empty stretch of road. She hoped and prayed--

Hoofbeats pounded behind her. Her heart lurched, and she glanced all around, her eyes searching for sanctuary, but only grassy meadows flanked the open road. The horse drew nearer, the hoofbeats like a clash of cymbals. Why hadn't she considered a disguise, anything to conceal her identity? She resisted the temptation to look behind her again.

The horse galloped past, stirring up dust, the rider no one she recognized and obviously no one who knew her.

"Whew! He had me worried, too."

Keriam jumped, staring around her; then she raised her head. "Oh, it's you! Zinerva, you shouldn't startle me like that."

The fairy hovered above her, whirling and dipping in graceful gyrations. Her silvery wings shone in the moonlight, her pink dress fluttering with every movement. "Sorry, princess," she said in her bell-like voice, "but I was so afraid for you after your escape from the palace." She flew nearer, until she floated in front of Keriam's eyes.

Keriam smiled at the fairy's childlike face, the tiny mouth and nose, the golden curls. "Have you been following me?"

Zinerva landed on her shoulder, a barely discernible tap, and plopped down. "As a matter of fact, yes. An owl hooting woke me up, and I saw you from my perch in the tree. I saw you lower yourself all the way on the rope. Oh, my! Madam, I'm so proud of you." She hopped across to the other shoulder, tiny feet padding across Keriam's upper back, and sat again. "I don't blame you for leaving, but why didn't you take your horse from the stable?"

Keriam gave the fairy an affectionate pat with her finger and switched her cloth bag to her other hand. "A horse would have made things much easier, wouldn't it? But it would also get Traigh in trouble. You know Traigh, the stable--"

"I know who Traigh is, and I know he's sweet on Maudina. Madam, there's not much we fairies miss." She sighed, her breath a soft caress on Keriam's neck. "So where are you walking to, the capital?"

"True, Moytura, where else?" The road became hilly now, trees growing in clusters along the roadside. The highway, wide enough for four men to ride abreast, winded through hills and valleys, past cultivated farms. Often, she had trouble seeing ahead as she followed the twists and turns of the road. Stone mile markers along the way revealed she still had much distance to cover. In silent procession, clouds drifted in front of the moon; how she wished that bright orb would remain concealed.

Grabbing branches for support, Keriam strained her legs to ascend the steep incline, her body bent forward until she reached the top several minutes later. She brought her mind back to Zinerva's question as she began her descent, taking cautious steps on the rock-strewn path that swung far to the right, nearing the village of Clontarf.

"Zinerva, much as I appreciate your company, please don't feel you must go with me. It's a long way to Moytura, and this is your sleeptime, after all." Hers, too, but there would be no slumber for her this night.

The fairy laughed. "Won't tire me, madam, not when I can ride on your shoulder, and I can nap tomorrow. But it occurs to me--maybe I can help you."

"Help me--how?" Keriam turned her head so quickly, she nearly dislodged the fairy. Zinerva caught herself in time, her tiny fingers clinging to Keriam's collarbone.

"Well, I know what a bitch--pardon my language, madam, but she is--"

"Yes, yes, go ahead."

"Well, when Aradia wakes tomorrow and finds you gone, she's going to be very, very angry."

"I realize that, Zinerva. And you know something? I don't care. I only worry that Maudina or the guards will get in trouble."

She recalled the note she'd written, absolving the guards of blame. Surely the message should satisfy Aradia, but then again, with the sorceress, you never knew. "I won't forgive myself if someone should suffer because of me."

"Maybe I can create a di--di--"

"Diversion?"

Zinerva snapped her little fingers. "Yes, that's it. I can create a diversion so that when Aradia wakes up, she won't even think of you, at least not for a while."

"Umm. What kind of diversion?" Neat wattle-and-daub houses lined both sides of the road now, rich farmland spread out for miles.

"You know that gold necklace with a diamond pendant that Aradia always wears?" Zinerva asked.

"Do I know it! It's my necklace."

"Well, she takes it off at night and leaves it on her dresser. My, how it shines in the dark. Well, anyway, me and my friends can fly in her room at night and steal the pendant."

"And get Maudina or one of the household staff in trouble? Not a good idea."

"No, no, princess. We'd return it the next night, but if it disappears tomorrow morning, that will be enough of a dis-dis--"

"Distraction?"

"Right, a distraction so that Aradia won't notice you're gone 'til later. And I'm thinking none of the servants would tell her right away that you've disappeared."

"How do you know all this--about the pendant and where Aradia leaves it at night?"

The fairy giggled. "Princess, me and my friends often fly around in the palace at night. We come in through the open windows." She folded her arms across her chest. "No one sees us, honest. We know how to e-e--"

"Elude?"

"That's right, madam." Zinerva shook her head. "These big words give me trouble."

"Elude isn't a big word."

"No, but it's un-un--"

"Unfamiliar?"

198

"Yes, that's it. Anyway, we know how to elude the sentries. The inside sentries guard only the bedchambers and the first floor at night."

"Yes, I know."

Zinerva bent her little head to give Keriam a close look. "So what do you think?"

"You promise to return the pendant the next night?" Keriam didn't care about any anxiety Aradia might suffer, but as always, she feared for the servants.

"Of course, madam. We don't want to get anyone in trouble, either."

Still considering every aspect of the scheme, Keriam shoved her hair from her face and tucked the strands behind her ears.

"So what do you think, huh? What do you think?"

"Go ahead, then. Zinerva, I'm greatly indebted to you, but I fear daybreak will come soon, so best you return to the palace." She patted the fairy again with her finger. "Goodbye, dear friend."

Zinerva sprang from Keriam's shoulder. "Goodbye for now, princess. But I hope we see each other again soon." She flew away, waving her hand.

Keriam returned the wave. Missing the fairy already, she trudged on, her legs and feet tiring, her fatigue more noticeable now without Zinerva's engrossing presence. She brushed the dust from her hands and dress and bent to remove a stone from her shoe outside the village of Bearaigh. Not far to the capital now.

The air smelled sweet, filled with the scent of ripening wheat and corn. Ahead of her, a fox raced across the road, attended by two other foxes. Somewhere, a dog barked, and a chorus of howls reverberated through the still night air. The breeze picked up, clouds continually drifting across the sky. Trees swayed in the wind, tossing their branches to and fro. Cool night air washed over her, molding her dress to her body, blowing her long tresses across her face. Shivering, she hugged her arms. A rooster crowed in the distance, a signal of the imminent dawn.

Had they discovered her absence at the palace already? I mustn't get caught, she fretted again and again. If captured, what would they do to her? She'd heard tales of Balor's cruelty. He and Aradia are a perfect match, she agonized, her mind frantic with all the punishments they might devise.

So concerned about possible capture, she hadn't noticed how far she'd come along the road to Moytura. She glanced ahead, so glad her journey neared its end. She would not think about capture, she vowed, determined to be optimistic. Things would work out for her.

The ground leveled after a short while, the city's spires and towers visible in the distance, the spire of Talmora's temple rising above the others. But she still had several miles to cover, and she didn't dare stop to rest. Despite the cool breeze, perspiration beaded her forehead and trickled down her back and between her breasts. Tempted to run and save time, she feared that exertion would only heighten her exhaustion and thus defeat her purpose. Best to maintain a steady pace.

Miles later, she reached the city's southern outskirts, the large warehouses and cheaper shops coming into view. Robins warbled from the trees, and a pink glow lit the western horizon.

What if Balor or Aradia had already sent soldiers after her? She glanced behind her but neither saw nor heard anyone. Just the same, so much could happen before she reached the safe anonymity of the city's streets. A soldier on horseback might be on her trail already, now ascending one of the steep hills along the way, able to make much better time than she on foot. Keriam rushed on, continually glancing over her shoulder, expecting to be caught any moment.

Weary and footsore, she reached Warehouse Street, thankful as never before for the city's convoluted layout. Aches and pains taunted her from her neck and shoulders to her hips, legs, feet, and toes. Worse, thirst tormented her, a torture aggravated by the dust that layered her mouth and throat. Not far to Perfume Lane, she thought, walking faster as she wove her way among Moytura's streets and alleys, her shoes slipping on the dew-slick cobblestones. Despite wearing comfortable shoes, blisters plagued her feet, and she removed her shoes and carried them, stepping warily among the garbage.

She approached Radegunda's street and stopped, edging back toward the storefront of a shoe repair shop.

Ahead of her, the city's sentries swarmed over the cobblestones, swords drawn, talking excitedly among themselves.

Heartsick, Keriam wanted to weep. How had the sentries already learned of her escape? Who had betrayed her? Zinerva? No, never!

Behind her, she saw only the empty street. Cautiously, she backed away, still pressed against the storefront. If she could only--

Too late! Glaring, a sentry raised his sword. "You! Come here!"

Chapter Twenty

Caught! Now return to the palace--to the dungeon!

Keriam looked in every direction but saw no escape. Suddenly mindful of her cloth bag, she slipped her hand behind her and dropped the incriminating evidence of her flight. The bag fell among piles of garbage that awaited disposal by the city's refuse collectors. She wanted to scream, kill the guards, race away from the city--and then what? Eventual capture. Questions hounded her. How had the sentries recognized her in her torn, faded work dress? Who had betrayed her and how had these men learned of her disappearance already?

Despite the frantic beating of her heart, she tightened her jaw, flashing the guard a defiant look. If these men intended to seize her, she'd fight them every step of the way.

But wait! He'd addressed her as "girl", giving no hint he suspected her royal lineage.

"You, girl!" Lowering his sword, the sentry motioned her closer. Even in the dim early morning light, she saw the one silver ash leaf that glinted on his collar, evidence of his lieutenant's rank. She headed his way, taking her time about it, resolved to make this encounter difficult for him, whether or not he suspected her of any crime.

The officer looked her up and down, an appreciative gleam in his eye, but spoke with a serious mien. "A man has escaped, a traitor to the king. We're questioning everyone who comes this way."

Inwardly, she sighed with relief, a short-lived contentment, for her mind brimmed with anxieties. Traitor? Who? Not Conneid Delbraith!

"We've hunted him for too many Goddess-damned ninedays." The guard slid his sword into the scabbard, the gleam in his eye replaced by tight-lipped fury. "So tell me, wench, have you seen any man leaving the city with his pregnant wife--a man about thirty, medium build, some gray hair?"

Conneid! Who else could it be? Her stomach clenched. Look how fear of Balor had warped so many attitudes in the kingdom. Formerly patient and polite, these city guards had become brutes under Balor's harsh rule, inspiring fear and hatred in Avador's citizens.

"Hurry up and tell me what you know! I've wasted enough time with you."

Ideas crammed her mind. If she could throw him off . . . "Why, yes, lieutenant. I saw a man and his pregnant wife riding southeast in the direction of Sligo, as if all the demons of the Underworld were after them." Her face assumed a stern cast. "I hope you catch these traitors."

The lieutenant turned to shout orders to the guards. "Southeast, hurry! Get horses from the city stables. I'll catch up with you."

"Right, sir! We're on our way!" The guards dashed from the street.

The lieutenant pulled her close, his hand brushing her breast. His breath stank of ale and onions. "Thank you, sweetheart. Don't think I'll forget your help. If we find our man, I'll pay you double. Where's your, uh, place of business?"

He thought she was a pleasure woman! Careful to hide her distaste, she gave him a beguiling smile. "Number 9 Pleasure Alley. And lieutenant, you'll get your money's worth from me."

The officer grinned. "I'm sure I will." He released her and raced on, soon disappearing around a corner.

Keriam breathed a long sigh of relief as the sun's first hesitant rays erased night's darkness and touched the streets of Moytura with a pale glow. Here and there, industrious shopkeepers mopped the cobblestones in front of their stores with soapy water, and vendors set up their wares on three-tiered wooden stands. Beggars slept within the concealment of dark storefronts, heads resting on their cloth sacks, snoring in careless oblivion.

Retrieving her bag from the garbage heap, she brushed it off, then replacing her shoes, rushed on to Perfume Lane, painfully aware of the passing time. With desperation lending her speed, she dashed through the city's many byways, but slowed down when early-morning proprietors cast her suspicious glances. Shifting to a more sedate pace, she covered the distance to 15 Perfume Lane, where a sign hanging in front of the store revealed three large bars of soap, proclaiming its merchandise. She found the key where Maudina had indicated and unlocked the front door.

* * *

Even as night's darkness surrendered to the sun's first pale glow, and farmers' carts filled with produce and freshly-plucked chickens rattled across the streets, sleep still held Radegunda in its somnolent grip. Normally an early riser, she'd slept late this day, after staying up until the early morning hours to await Princess Keriam. Unable to keep her eyes open any longer, she'd finally yielded to sleep, terribly disappointed and worried about the princess. Through a slumberous fog, she heard someone knocking on the door.

"Radegunda!"

Radegunda jerked awake and stared around the room, surprised to find herself in bed, faint sunlight lifting the darkness from the room. Her mind still hazed by sleep, her eyes gritty and aching, she raised herself on her elbows.

Someone was knocking on the door. Fear bridled her movements, for surely a caller at this early hour meant trouble--a summons from the new king, questions about the princess--yet she realized that refusal to answer would only intensify her dilemma. She threw her covers aside and--

"Radegunda, are you there?"

Princess Keriam! She breathed a long, slow sigh. "Madam, come in. The door's not locked."

She rose from the bed, bare feet touching the cold wooden floor, and slipped into her woolen robe, then hustled to greet the princess.

"Ah, Radegunda!" Princess Keriam entered, her appearance a far cry from the refined noblewoman the healer remembered. Her dark hair hung in tangled strands down her back, her stained dress torn, her shoes scuffed and dusty. Protocol forgotten, the two women rushed together and hugged, both fighting tears.

204

With watery eyes, Radegunda drew back, shocked by the princess's calloused hands, her tanned face, her sinewy build. "Madam, you have no idea how worried I've been about you, how glad I am to see you now!"

Brushing the tears from her eyes, the princess set the key on a table. "And I've missed you so!" She frowned, a note of distress infecting her voice. "But I can't stay here; it will only bring trouble on you. I fear Balor will send soldiers after me, so--"

"So we go to my brother, as I told Maudina we would. Since I lent him money and delivered his children--now grown, by the way--he owes me a few favors. Gimme but a few minutes to git my things together, then we'll be on our way. Just wait . . ." She threw her a questioning glance. "I'll wager you'd like somethin' to drink."

"How did you guess?"

Radegunda poured a large mug of water from a brass pitcher and handed it to the princess. "Drink as much as you can, since I don't have no water bag." While the princess drank, Radegunda rushed about, opening and closing drawers, throwing underclothes and dresses into a leather bag.

The old woman gave her a frank look. "Madam, you're gonna need a cloak. I got an extra one here, besides a couple of dresses I c'n alter later to fit you. Ain't no trouble, madam," she added.

"Thank you. But as for you . . ." Setting the empty mug on the table, Keriam looked heartsick. "I know what Maudina said about your brother, but you don't need to stay there with me." Her gaze covered the small room, her eyes darting from corner to corner. "Your store . . . you'll need the money."

Radegunda closed the leather bag with a sharp click. "Adsaluta can manage the store. She's a widow; she c'n use the money, since I let her keep half the proceeds. I told her I may visit my brother one of these days--didn't tell her why. She don't know about my offer to help you." She gave her a reassuring smile. "Don't worry, madam. I got this all worked out. But we gotta hurry!"

"Of course!" Fatigue enervated Keriam. She wanted only to lie down and sleep for the rest of the day. But she mustn't tarry, could not surrender to the exhaustion that seeped through every bone, every muscle of her body.

Several minutes later, Radegunda looked around the room. "Well, I guess that's all. Let's leave now, if you're ready," she said, heading for the door.

Only dim sunlight washed across the windowless second-floor landing and the steps leading downward. "I'll go first," Radegunda offered, preceding Keriam to the first floor. The wooden steps creaked under the witch's heavy tread, the newly-polished steps slippery and smelling of beeswax. Keriam grasped the wooden railing with each cautious step, anxiety courting her the entire distance. What if the king's officers waited outside the front door this very minute, ordered to return her to the palace for punishment? And Radegunda, too. Regret tightened her stomach; she should never have come here, should never have endangered this kind, helpful woman.

They reached the first floor, a room filled with delicious fragrances and tempting products, merchandise that would have lured Keriam in a less crucial situation.

"Mustn't forget this," the healer said, reaching for a silk rose that rested on the counter. "When I put this in the window, that's a sign to Adsaluta that I want her to manage the store." She tied the rose to a string that dangled in front of the window above the door, then looked around one more time. "Can't think of anything else."

She led Keriam outside. "Adsaluta's got a key," she explained, locking the door behind her.

Both of them strolled the streets, outwardly carefree, as if this day were like any other. Still, fear dogged Keriam's footsteps, a terror she tried to hide with casual talk and an occasional smile. A few early-morning travelers roamed the cobblestones; now and then a drunk lurched from the city's many taverns, staggering past. Even now, her mind worked as she agonized over how she could overthrow Balor and restore the House of Moray to the throne. As yet, no ideas came to her.

The two women wove their way among the intricate streets and alleys, past the swordsmith's shop and the tailor's, soon reaching the many warehouses that ringed the city. Once beyond Moytura, they increased their pace but dared not run, lest their haste invite suspicion. Balor--curse Endora!--had spies everywhere.

Ragegunda's breathing came in gasps, her free arm hanging at her side. "Not far to go," she said as they left the city behind and entered farm country to the east of the forest, its gently-rolling hills sheltering crops ready for harvest. The Gorm Forest loomed miles to their left, this land of torathors, those monsters that inhabited its depths. Its dense growth of oaks, hickories, and pines ranged over hills and valleys, an endless procession of greens and yellows, its colors changing with the season. "Should be there soon."

Dark, angry gray clouds scudded across the sky, a sign of imminent rain? Keriam hoped. The temperature dropped and sharp gusts tugged at her hair, the wind whipping her clothing to her body. Corn stalks bent in a wind that flattened grass and vegetables to the ground, but the grass in the fields remained brown and dry, begging for rain.

Keriam forced a smile, then bent over to empty pebbles from her shoes. "Your help means more to me than you'll ever know. Some day I hope to repay you." The blisters on her feet burned with every step, her shoes' rubbing a continual torment. Visions of a long soak in warm water tantalized her, a wish she suspected would remain unsatisfied. She'd settle for a place to sit and a mug of hard cider. And even that's probably expecting too much, she thought as she ran her tongue across her dry, cracked lips while clouds of dust swept across the road.

Radegunda waved her hand. "Forgit about payment, madam. I'm happy to do whatever I can, payment for what you already done for me. But . . ."She frowned.

Keriam stopped and slanted her an anxious look. "Radegunda, what is it?"

The old woman stopped, too, meeting her gaze. "Princess, I'm thinkin' that yer fancy talk is gonna give you away. Can't you talk, well, like me?"

Keriam bit her lip, faced with this unforeseen problem. "This is the way I've talked all my life. I fear I can't change now." She sighed, considering all possibilities, when an inspiration brightened her voice. "What if I pretend to be mute?" She gathered strands of hair from across her face and tucked them behind her ears, then resumed walking.

An expression of pure relief came over her face. "You think you c'n do that, madam? You'll have to remember to never say a word, no matter what. Yer life depends on it, mine, too, come to think of it. Oh, I know my brother wouldn't turn you in, ordinarily. But if the king's men come snoopin' around, askin' questions and makin' threats, one of the servants might betray you if faced with torture. Much as the people love you, madam--and they all do, with the exception of Balor's lackeys--it takes a very strong person to withstand havin' their nails pulled out."

Keriam's stomach knotted. "Then I'll become the best actress you've ever seen. As for threats to the servants, I won't let it come to that. I'll turn myself in before anyone suffers because of me." Turn herself in, and then what? Imprisonment? Torture? She shivered, deliberately shifting her mind to other matters.

The dark clouds blew to the west, replaced by a blue sky and brilliant sunlight. The temperature rose. Perspiration streamed down Keriam's back and plastered her clothes to her body. And still no rain!

"There!" Radegunda pointed ahead. "There it is, my brother's farm." An old farmhouse hulked in the distance, large but weatherbeaten, its once white wooden frame now a dirty gray, its wooden shingles loose. The surrounding farmland appeared neat and well-tended, Keriam observed as they neared the property. Countless rows of ready-to-harvest corn waved in the breeze, and fields flourished with other vegetables--kale, endive, lettuce, and onions. The sweet scent of strawberries floated their way, making her mouth water, her stomach rumble.

A narrow dirt path flanked by a yardful of scraggly grass and weeds led up to three sagging wooden steps, the boards loose and creaking. A narrow porch fronted the house, enclosed by a railing that lacked more boards than it held. Two small windows on either side of the door greeted the sunlight, their surfaces clear and shiny, in defiance of the house's decrepit facade.

Keriam and Radegunda mounted the front steps. Careless with exhaustion, Keriam nearly tripped on a loose board but caught herself in time.

The enchantress raised her hand to knock on the door.

"Radegunda!" A tall, burly man with nut brown skin and white hair emerged from the side of the house, his unbelted linen tunic tattered and stained, his feet clad in short leather boots. Raising a foot up on the porch, he swung himself over the railing, heedless of the board that broke off and fell to the ground.

"What you doin' here, not that I ain't glad to see ya." His glance covered Keriam, a welcoming smile on his face. Brother and sister hugged, then Radegunda introduced Keriam. "Gwern, this here's Deirdre. She's had some bad luck, poor girl. Thieves robbed and killed her husband, took all the money they owned. Now she can't pay the rent on their shop and got nowhere to go. I brought her here 'cause she wants to earn her keep, if that's all right with you. But she can't speak," she said, as if in afterthought. "The shock of seein' her husband killed took her voice away."

"Madam, I am so sorry!" Gwern greeted her in the traditional Avadoran manner, his right hand on her right shoulder. Keriam responded likewise, bombarded by images of the farmer toiling in the fields and talking to his wife, but no noteworthy visions enlightened her, certainly nothing to arouse suspicions that this man might betray her. She intuited Gwern was a man she could trust, and the Goddess knew she needed that kind of person.

He smiled and nodded. "Pleased ta meet ya, Deirdre."

Keriam smiled in return, wondering how long she could remember to maintain her silence, how she could prevent giving herself away. She must never forget her new role, for carelessness could well mean death, not only for her, but for these kind people who offered her sanctuary.

The front door opened and closed, and a small, neat woman with frowsy gray hair stepped outside, wiping her hands on her woolen apron. A network of tiny wrinkles stalked her pink face, but she gave the newcomers a pleasant greeting. Her green cotton dress, ragged but clean, scraped the floor, as if made for a taller woman.

"So, Radegunda! I heard the commotion out here and figured we must have company." Introductions ensued again, the healer repeating the same tale of Keriam's--Deirdre's--misfortune and her inability to speak. "Come in, come in. You two walked all the way from the capital? But I guess you did, seein' as there ain't no horses or carts in front."

She opened the door and Keriam stepped inside a small room, its dimensions only a portion of her office at the palace. A sagging horsehair sofa hugged a far wall, two dilapidated chairs nestling the opposite wall. Keriam glimpsed a kitchen beyond the sitting room, with a small stone fireplace, a table, and four chairs, these two rooms completing the first floor. Delicious aromas wafted from the kitchen, of baking bread and roast beef, and her stomach responded. Wooden stairs to the left led to the bedchambers. Judging from the first floor space, she doubted if the chambers above numbered more than two. A tiny but functional house, and not a speck of dust anywhere.

"Got some hard cider for ya," Gwern's wife, Wynne, said, "just the thing after that long walk from the capital." She indicated the chairs. "Take a seat, take a seat. Be right back."

Gwern made a small bow, his hand on the doorknob. "You'll excuse me, ladies. Gotta return to the fields to supervise the workers. We was just pickin' tomatoes and endive to take to the capital tomorrow." He shook his head. "Good workers is hard to find nowadays. The new king keeps draftin' young men. Don't make sense. We need workers on the farms, or else the produce will rot in the fields." He sighed. "Well, who am I to argue with the king?"

Wynne's arrival with the cider offset Gwern's departure as she handed the mugs to the guests, then flopped onto the sofa.

A mundane dialogue ensued--discussion of neighbors and crops, but especially palace gossip. Wynne drained her mug and set it on the floor. "The new queen--I hear she's quite beautiful."

Beautiful on the outside, ugly inside, Keriam wanted to say. She sipped her cider, tempted to down it with one gulp. The tart, fruity drink was just what she needed, but her stomach still begged for food.

Radegunda exchanged glances with Keriam, an indication that they shared the same opinion of Aradia. "The queen?--I guess she's not lackin' for looks."

Wynne smacked her hands on her knees and rose from the sofa. "Well, no doubt you two will wanna git settled. I'll show you to yer room, then best I return to preparin' the midday meal."

Oh, yes, Keriam thought. Her stomach growled again, her feet tired and aching.

The farm wife preceded them up the creaking stairs, then led them to a small room at the end of the hall. Only one bed graced the room, a narrow one pressed against a far wall, its wooden bedstead cracked and chipped. A long oak chest that occupied another corner completed the furnishings, except for a table under the room's lone window. The table held a tin lamp with a half-burned candle, sharing space with a washbasin of water. At least the room's clean and neat, Keriam mused, steeling herself to get used to life's uncertainties. She'd had plenty of experience already.

Wynne smiled apologetically. "One of you will hafta sleep on the floor. Got plenty of blankets to lay down, so the floor shouldn't be so hard." She rubbed her hands together. "Well, git settled then, and I'll have our meal ready soon."

After she left, Radegunda and Keriam traded looks, Keriam's face set in deliberate nonchalance.

"I'll sleep on the floor," Keriam whispered, dropping her bag beside her.

Radegunda shook her head. "You'll do no such thing. Yer my guest, and the princess, after all."

"Thank you." Unable to resist the bed's beckoning comfort, Keriam sank onto its hard surface, yielding to her bone-weary fatigue, if only for a few minutes. As the enchantress lifted the chest lid to stash her clothes, Keriam caught a sweet lavender scent, her favorite fragrance and a reminder of her life before all the changes. She fought to keep her eyes open, aware she had hours to endure until bedtime.

Her mind brimmed with dire possibilities. What if someone discovered that this innocent farmer and his wife harbored the fugitive princess? Worse, what if these good people were punished for their kindness? A spirit of resolution determined her mood. She would not let anyone suffer for her sake.

* * *

The days passed, Keriam learning something new each day. I'd make someone a fine maid, she thought one morning as she swept the front room and dusted the furniture. Who would recognize her now?

A little less than one nineday after her arrival at the farm, Keriam went to bed one evening as a cold north wind ushered in autumn, a time when trees traded green leaves for red, gold, and brown. She huddled under her blankets, soothed by Radegunda's soft snoring. She considered she'd managed well so far, not only in her pretense of a deaf mute, but also as a servant, capable of performing any household task.

Despite her utter weariness, sleep was long in coming, for Roric intruded on her musings. No doubt he remained privy to Balor's every decision, never sparing a thought for her. Well, she would always remember him--as a traitor! Even though he'd vowed loyalty to her, she considered anyone who served the usurper a double crosser, and yes, that charge applied to several of the ministers, too. She sighed and turned over, her mind still on Roric. She remembered his deep voice with its clipped speech, his dark hair and eyes, his every facial expression. Why couldn't she drive him from her thoughts? She imagined him holding her, kissing her . . . .No! She changed position again and stared wide-eyed at the ceiling, wishing sleep would come.

Night sounds echoed around her--frogs croaking, crickets chirping, an occasional dog barking.

Tangled thoughts yielded to sheer exhaustion, but when she fell asleep, she dreamed of dead squirrels . . . and the plague.

Chapter Twenty-one

"Princess Keriam, you can't be serious! Please tell me you don't mean this."

"I've never been more serious in my life." A day had passed since Keriam's dream, and now, in the silence of their shared bedchamber, she and Radegunda discussed the dream and its significance. Since today was Sacredday, quiet had settled over the house, everyone else having gone to the city temple to pray or to visit friends.

Side by side, they sat on the narrow bed as a swarm of conflicting emotions burgeoned inside Keriam. "Radegunda, I've had many dreams in the past that have proved prophetic."

"Don't tell anyone that," the woman muttered. "The gift of prophecy itself is considered a sign of witchcraft, punishable by death." She gave her a stern look. "And I'm sure you know what the punishment is. I don't doubt you have this gift. So do I. But I would never admit it."

"Nor I. But my dream--so real! I saw people with big black spots, men and women dying!" Keriam shuddered. "And look at the dry weather we've had," she said, waving her hand in an expansive gesture. "All these moonphases, with no rain. Surely this drought will bring fleas--if it hasn't already--so I must warn--"

"I'm not doubtin' yer word," Radegunda said, in her anxiety forgetting that she interrupted the princess. "But to place yerself in danger again, just when you've found safety with me and my brother. So you warn the people, order them to kill all the squirrels. Don't you realize you'll get caught?"

Keriam sighed, fearful of capture but convinced she must proceed with her plan. "In the first place, I can't order the people to do anything. I no longer have any regal standing in the kingdom, remember? All I can do is remind the Avadorans of the consequences if we don't rid the kingdom of squirrels."

"Sacred animals, protected by royal decree!"

Keriam lifted her hands. "No choice, Radegunda. Certainly, I will leave this house and the sanctuary your brother and his wife have so kindly given me. Will you please give them an excuse for

213

me? Tell them I'm leaving to visit my sister in Gairech. I fear this will seem ungrateful, after all they've done for me. But I must leave to accomplish my task."

"And then where will you go?" Radegunda asked with a worried frown.

"To the capital. I'll speak to anyone who might listen . . . the merchants there, for instance," she said, the idea just coming to her. "They surely would heed my warning, if only from a mercenary standpoint. Look at all the business they'd lose if the plague strikes again, like it did all those years ago. And don't forget, none of them will recognize me as the princess." Keriam's gaze covered her torn and stained dress, the scuffed shoes. "No one outside the palace recognized me, even when I dressed in my fine clothes." Except Roric. She examined her calloused hands and brown arms, laughing without humor. "If I told anyone in the city that I'm the princess--which I won't--they'd only laugh and tell me I'm touched in the head.

"I can't be true to myself and ignore the meaning of my dream." She clutched the witch's hand, desperation infecting her voice. "Hundreds of people may die from the black fever, thousands! I can't have that catastrophe on my conscience. If I'm able to do something to prevent this calamity, then that's what I have to do."

"Madam, listen! Let me perfect my magic first, see if I can rid the city of the plague, if it comes to that. I haven't had a chance to practice my talent here at the farm, but whenever I go back to Moytura, I swear I'll work riddin' the city of the plague." She scratched her head. "Never been able to understand it, but fer some reason, it's easier to control the elements than it is to destroy a plague. Guess the demoness don't care about the rain or snow, as long as she can kill people with a disease. And I ain't even been able to practice controllin' the elements, or we would've had rain in the first place." She paused. "Something tells me I can defeat this sickness, if given enough time."

"Radegunda, we don't have time! I fear this epidemic will hit very soon."

"Madam, you are taking such a big chance. What if someone recognizes you?"

"I already said no one will."

Radegunda sighed. "At least, let me dye your hair. I c'n color your hair a drab brown. You'll be less likely to be noticed."

"Very well, but I still feel sure no one would recognize me." She nodded. "I know it!"

"And take a dagger for protection. I keep one here that you c'n use."

"But what if you should need it?"

"Madam, you need it more than me." Radegunda stood and paced the floor. "But where will you live?" she asked, fixing her gaze on Keriam.

Keriam smiled with wary confidence. "There's much I've learned about survival within the last few moonphases. I'm sure I can live on the city's outskirts and manage on my own, especially if I have your dagger." She gave her a steady look, much of her confidence slipping, but determined, nonetheless. "Better that I face capture and . . . and death than that thousands of people should succumb to the plague. If I can prevent this epidemic--"

"But can you, madam?" Radegunda came and sat beside her again, speaking in low, earnest tones. "What if the black fever has already infected the people? You know how quickly the disease spreads."

"I've made up my mind."

* * *

"Your Majesty, we have Delbraith!"

After gaining admittance to the Blue Royal Conference room, two city sentries announced the capture of the former king's elusive secretary. In the midst of a meeting with his ministers and Roric, Balor looked up from his papers, a savage gleam in his eyes.

A shaft of fear drained the blood from Roric's face. A sickening surge of horror roiled in his belly. He must save Conneid, but how?

Always cautious of Balor, Roric steeled his features against showing his emotions. He sat to the right of the king in this meeting with the ministers that had lasted throughout the evening into the late night hours. The light from low-hanging oil lamps suspended from black iron chains cast wavy shadows across the room and revealed the somber expressions of the men.

Balor's gaze circled the table, and his face held a look of immense satisfaction, as if to say, No one escapes me. He addressed the sentries, a lieutenant and a sergeant, and motioned them closer to the table. "Well, then, where is he?"

The officers stepped forward, the lieutenant speaking. "Your Majesty, we took him to the dungeon. We drugged him when we first caught him, but by the time we reached here, the drug had worn off. By then, the man was somewhat, uh, difficult. We needed the outside guards to help subdue him."

"The dungeon." Balor nodded, clearly pleased. "You did right."

"Sire, we caught his wife with him." Hesitation crept into his voice, and he licked his lips. "Sh--she's in labor, sire."

A sly smile flitted across Balor's face. "In labor, did you say? Take her outside and tie her to a tree. Make sure her legs are close together."

"Sire?" The sentry leaned forward, looking worried and fearful.

"You heard me!" Balor barked. "Don't make me repeat my orders."

"Yes, sire."

Goddess, no! Roric exchanged glances with the ministers and knew their shocked expressions mirrored his own.

"After that," Balor said, tapping his fingers on the table, "instruct the dungeon guard to proceed with Delbraith. The guard knows what to do." He grinned. "I'll be down shortly. Wouldn't want to miss the fun."

"Wait!" The Minister of Forests cleared his throat. "Sire, what about a trial?"

The sentries stopped, looking from one man to the other.

Balor slammed his hand on the table, scattering several papers. "A trial! Isn't his guilt evident? Don't you recall the seditious letter he wrote? We know he's guilty. We must stamp out

216

treason." Balor gave him a withering glance. "Don't speak to me of trials."

The Minister of Roads spoke up. "Sire, perhaps we should wait--"

"Wait for what?" Balor pointed a finger at the minister. "It might be well for all of you to remember I can make life difficult for your wives and children. Need I say more?"

Roric recalled the warning Balor had given shortly after gaining the throne, that the wives and children of anyone who thwarted him would suffer punishment. He clenched his hands in his lap. Kill Balor! Kill him now! He thought of his dagger in a hidden boot compartment, but prudence prevailed. No matter how the ministers felt about the new king--and that remained a question--none of them would countenance his murder.

In a swift change of expressions that characterized Balor, the tyrant smiled pleasantly at the sentries. "After you instruct the dungeon guard, go to the library and have a glass of wine from the bottle in the cabinet. You've earned it. Oh, and invite the outside sentries, share with them," he said in a rare magnanimous gesture.

"Yes, sire. Thank you, sire."

They left the room, their booted footsteps echoing down the hall. Balor returned his attention to the ministers, as though there had been no interruption. He spoke with Drummond Haley about taxation problems for several minutes, then folded his hands on the table. "One further consideration I must introduce. By now, everyone knows of the princess's escape some time ago. I had thought she'd be captured by now, thus eliminating this discussion." His glance circled the table again, and it seemed to rest on Roric a moment too long, or was that only his imagination? Roric's gut clenched, but he maintained an untroubled expression. "Make no mistake, gentlemen. My men will catch the princess. Only a matter of time. And when they do--" His features hardened--"she'll suffer like Delbraith. Never doubt that--"

Screams from the dungeon rent the air, heart-hammering, blood-curdling screams, horrible cries like nothing Roric had ever heard, not even in battle. His gut spasmed, his heart beating faster, faster. He stared at Balor, tempted to kill the fiend this moment, and never mind the consequences. Uneasy glances and nervous coughs encompassed the table. Everyone else is as disgusted and heartsick as I am, he lamented, but what can any of us do? They had to do something!

The screams bounced off the wall, filling the room, reverberating in his ear drums. Roric's stomach churned; his head throbbed. He clenched his hands so hard the muscles ached. A continual refrain beat through his head: Kill Balor!

Balor raised his voice, shouting to be heard. He pounded his fist on the conference table. "Damn the son of a bitch, I can't even think!" He snapped his fingers at Roric. "Gamal! Go to the dungeon and stuff something in the scum's mouth."

Roric shoved back his chair, nearly knocking it over in his haste, but he caught it in time. "Yes, sire!" He left the room, an overwhelming relief speeding his steps. Balor was testing him, he knew, still searching for a way out of this dilemma. The general had never trusted him. And with good reason.

Once away from the room, he slowed his walk. He had to rescue Conneid immediately but first, he had to devise a plan. His mind worked the entire way, from the conference room through the main hall, past the pantry and storage room, until he reached the dungeon door. The door stood open, accidentally or on purpose? He dashed down the steps. Torches stuck in brackets along the wall cast a dim light and revealed the open cell at the far side of the dungeon.

Sacred shrine! The screams rose to a crescendo, all but breaking his ear drums, mind-numbing wails that threatened to drive him crazy. The screams from the cell blended with moans from outside, to where Conneid's wife was tied to a tree.

As he strode along, he bent over to release the dagger compartment in his boot. His heart pounded in his chest; he bit his lower lip so hard he drew blood. He reached Conneid's open cell and saw the man's arms raised above his head, his wrists and ankles manacled to the wall. His chest was a mass of bloody, torn skin, his face shining with sweat. He flashed Roric a look of grateful recognition, then closed his eyes, as if fearing to hope for salvation.

218

"Let's silence this scum," Roric said, drawing the dagger from his boot.

The guard raised his hand. His face, hands, and tunic were covered with blood. "Stop! You're not going to kill him, are you? The king--"

"Kill you!" Roric drove his dagger into the guard's chest, then jerked it out in one quick movement.

"Ahhh!" After the guard staggered to the floor and fell with a loud thump, Roric spoke to Conneid. "Quick! We must hurry!" He bent over the body and fumbled with the key ring on his belt, finally getting it loose. Cursing the minutes that slipped past, he tried several keys before he found the one that unlocked the manacles.

Conneid gasped, his bloody chest rising and falling. "My wife . . ."

Roric propped up Conneid's slumping form, his hands coming away stained with blood. "We'll get her but we've no time to lose. Balor will be on us in minutes. When I don't return . . ." Blood streamed from Conneid's chest, down his clothes, dripping onto the floor. Releasing Conneid for one moment, Roric knelt to cut the tattered tunic from the guard's body. He handed the garment to Conneid. "Here, hold this against your chest."

His dagger tucked under his belt, his arm around Conneid's waist, Roric supported the secretary's body as they struggled to the end of the dungeon, soon gaining the door that led to the tunnel. "Wait, I'll tie this around you." Roric grabbed the tunic from Conneid's hands and wrapped it around the man, his hands shaking with impatience, his movements jerky as he secured the garment in back.

Roric raised the iron bar and opened the door, every step an effort while he supported Conneid. In absolute darkness, they descended the steps and trekked the narrow tunnel's slimy floor.

Conneid panted, his feet dragging. "Where are we going? Never . . . never been here before."

"This tunnel leads to outside. Few people know about it." Frustrated with their slow progress, his tunic and cape soaked with Conneid's blood, Roric could only match his steps with the secretary's and pray they could escape before an alarm was raised.

Yet they still had to rescue his wife. His heart thudded against his chest, and he swallowed convulsively. If they were caught . . . He saw himself manacled to the cell wall, his skin torn and bleeding. He imagined the pain, the gut-wrenching agony of having his skin sliced and peeled.

Roric ignored the stench, the skittering rats and draping spider webs, his only thought to gain the outside . . . and freedom, if they could elude any outside guards who may have stayed, if they could rescue the man's wife . . . Too many 'ifs.'

"Conneid, we must hurry!" No time for sympathy now; they couldn't waste a second.

The secretary groaned but increased his speed.

An eternity passed before they reached the steps at the end, with an abruptness that caught Roric by surprise. Nothing but night's blackness awaited them on the outside, no sunshine to light their way. Good thing it's nighttime, Roric thought as he released Conneid for a moment and slowly raised the hinged door above his head. He checked for outside guards but assumed they were still enjoying their wine. Seeing no one, he dashed up the steps and turned to reach for Conneid, then pulled him up all the way.

The cool air greeted them, and silence, a silence soon broken by a low wail several yards distant, where Conneid's wife suffered, tied to an oak tree.

"Malvina!" Conneid whispered, his face twisted in anguish.

"We'll get her, but we must hurry!" Roric's thoughts sped at a frantic pace, his aim to rescue Malvina. At the same time, they had to evade the guards, should those men return soon. And the guards would return.

The escapees rushed a few yards ahead to a cluster of trees and understory, and Roric shoved Conneid down behind a bush. "Stay here while I release Malvina. If I'm caught, run for your life, go--"

"And leave Malvina? Never!"

"We're wasting time." Roric left him and crouched forward, keeping to the edge of the woods that bordered the palace. He stopped now and then, on the lookout for the sentries' reappearance.

Precious seconds passed before he reached the pregnant woman, who struggled against her bonds and moaned, shaking her head back and forth.

He approached her from behind and drew the dagger from his waist. "Quiet! Not a sound!" Two quick cuts broke the tie that bound her to the tree and the one around her legs. She slipped forward, and he stepped around to grab her, supporting her as he had her husband.

"Now we--"

A clamor erupted outside the palace, shouting and cursing as the two city sentries burst from the palace, followed by additional palace guards.

"We'll catch the bastards!"

"Can't get far . . ."

"Right, not on foot, with the woman pregnant . . ."

"What about the woods?" A guard pointed in the fugitives' direction. Behind a tree, Roric sucked in a deep breath and held it until his lungs felt about to burst.

"Not the woods! You think they'd be dumb enough to go there, just waiting for us to find them?"

A few moments of consultation among the guards ensued, Roric catching an occasional word.

". . . north to the capital."

"No, not there . . . south!"

"I still say the woods."

"No, they've escaped the woods by now, if they were there."

". . . after them. Saddle up!"

"Remember," Roric whispered, his gaze on the sentries about one-hundred yards distant, "not a sound." One question pounded through his brain. What would he have done if Balor hadn't sent him to the dungeon? The answer came quickly. He would have killed the fiend, no matter the consequences.

Minutes later, the horsemen rode away, two in each direction. Roric tapped Malvina on the shoulder. "Now we can go to your husband."

"Oh, yes!"

Within the trees' sanctuary, Roric led the silent, trembling woman away, soon gaining the spot where Conneid waited.

"Malvina!" Conneid stood and gathered her in his arms.

"My darling!" Sobbing, she fell against him, her swollen belly pressed to his bloody form. "What have they done to you!" Then they both sank to the ground, pain and exhaustion written on their faces.

"Quiet! Back farther in the woods," Roric said, leading them away. And then what? They had to escape the palace grounds. "We'll stay here for now." He wiped the bloody knife on his tunic and returned it to the boot sheath. "Later, we'll see." He sighed. "Give the guards time to get far from here."

The forest's dense foliage offered refuge, but how long could they stay here? He thought frantically, sweat dripping down his face. They must get away. Night insects buzzed around their heads and crawled on their bloody tunics. Roric dared not swat at them for fear of attracting attention, should any other guards appear.

Conneid had collapsed against the trunk of an ash, still pressing the filthy tunic to his bloody chest. Malvina sat shoulder to shoulder with him, her legs spread out in front of her, her hands resting on her protruding belly.

Malvina and Conneid panted, their faces haggard. "You know best, Roric," Malvina whispered. "And some day, if we get out of this with our lives, we will repay you for your kindness."

"Indeed." Conneid reached for his wife's hand. "We owe you our lives."

"You're doing me a favor," Roric said, trying to make light of their dilemma. "Glad to escape the palace and Balor." He turned an anxious glance on Malvina. "How far apart are your pains, can you guess?" He tried to remember his wife's labor.

She shifted position, easing up closer to the trunk. "About fifteen minutes, I suppose." Her voice caught. "I . . . I . . . Roric, what are we going to do?" she asked, her voice rising. "How will we--"

"Ssh, I'll get you out of here."

"But she's right." Conneid gasped, his breathing labored. "We. . . can't stay here. Malvina . . . give birth, where?"

Roric spoke in low tones. "Here's what we'll do. We'll travel cross country, through the farmland, to Moytura."

"Moytura?" Conneid sucked in a breath. "Guards . . . bound to look there. Long walk, they'll find us."

"Not if we take the back route, away from the highway. We won't walk. Steal horses, two of them."

"Don't know if I can ride . . . or Malvina."

"You can ride, both of you." He tried to inject confidence in his voice, a confidence he didn't feel. "Your wife will ride in front of me. Draft horse would be best for Malvina and me, broader shoulders and back, easier for her." He looked up at the sky, at the full moon's position. "Time to leave! Guards should be far away by now. Daybreak will come soon."

Conneid wiped his arm across his glistening forehead. "After Moytura, where do we go?"

"We'll keep to the edge of the city, continue north to the Gorm Forest."

Conneid wrenched back. "Monsters in the forest! They'll kill us."

"He's right, Roric!" Malvina threw him a frantic look. "We must go somewhere else."

Roric pushed to his feet and gave them both a stern look, reluctant to admit he shared their fears. "Let's quit talking." He motioned to them. "Have to leave." He crouched beside Malvina and helped her rise, his arm around her waist, at the same time keeping a cautious eye on Conneid as the man struggled to his feet.

"The forest!" Conneid persisted. "Can't go there."

"So what would you rather do?" Roric asked, "return to the palace, face torture again? Think of your wife, what they'll do to her! We can't ride in any other direction. It's all open land, warded by the sentries who have, no doubt, spread word of your flight." His voice gentled, a note of calm reason in his tone. "Listen, we don't really know how many torathors dwell in the forest, or if any live there at all. Perhaps it's only a story to frighten children. We'll just have to take a chance."

Grateful for the few gold and copper coins in a purse attached to his belt, he nevertheless knew money would gain him nothing in the forest. He hoped their stay there would be short. And if it wasn't? Never mind about that. He had enough to deal with now.

Malvina moaned, another pain coming on. After moments, she spoke with resolution. "Let's leave, then."

Roric led them through the cool woods, and within minutes, they emerged by the grounds of Balor's former mansion, now deserted. Here, to the west of the lawn, the trees were spread farther apart, offering scant concealment. Keeping to the fringe of the woods, they followed a winding path through the trees until they exited close to the Royal North Road that led to the capital.

They cut through the open meadow, where isolated huts dotted the land, and the grass grew to their knees, hindering progress. Supporting Malvina and glancing in all directions in search of a barn, Roric maintained a steady pace. He hoped Conneid and his wife could keep up with him. They had to; there was no alternative.

"Stop," Conneid gasped. "Stop and rest."

Roric sighed, dropping his arm from Malvina's waist. "A few moments, that's all." Dread chilled his stomach. They would not reach the capital before daybreak. If Conneid had to rest now, when they'd only started, how could he cover the remaining distance, especially if they weren't fortunate enough to find horses? "Can't waste time."

"Let us trust in Roric, dearest," Malvina said, in a surprising proof of her fortitude. She laid her hand on her husband's arm and spoke in patient tones. "I know it's not easy but we must keep on. If we're captured again . . ."

Recapture? Roric shuddered. No!

His gaze covered the meadows that preceded the farmland. "Have to find a barn, get the horses. Be easier for everyone then."

Conneid nodded. "You're right, Roric. Forgive me."

"Nothing to forgive, Conneid." They trudged on through the rolling meadows and entered the farmland, where picket fences hindered their passage. Every time they came to a fence, they had to walk far around it, a process that added precious minutes to their time. Hundreds of sheep slumbered on the grasslands, another hindrance they must bypass.

Under the moonlit sky, they skirted bushes and plodded through plowed farmland, the soil rough and uneven. Sandals on Malvina's swollen feet slowed her down, and she often lost her balance, but Roric caught her each time. When Conneid slipped and fell in the rough soil, Roric released Malvina to help him rise again. Silence accompanied them each step of the way, save for the ragged breathing of the escaped captives. They had to stop often as another pain hit Malvina, a time to help her bear the agony.

How much longer could they continue like this? They'd lost vital minutes already from the time he'd left the royal conference room.

"Roric." Conneid sank onto the rough ground, holding his face in his hands. He looked up and spoke in a trembling voice. "Can't go on . . . any longer. Take Malvina, save her . . . and yourself. Leave me here."

"Let's have none of this foolish talk," Roric snapped, hating himself for his harsh words. This was no time for pampering. "We'll keep together, find safety before the night is over." Despite the cool air, sweat coated his face and trickled down his back.

Grimacing, Conneid struggled to his feet and they continued on in silence.

"There!" A short while later, Roric pointed to a barn in the distance, this one large and substantial. "Let's pray to the Goddess they have horses."

The Goddess must have heard their prayers, Roric thought after the three fugitives sneaked far behind a spacious farmhouse and reached the barn. A double side door led them into the interior, where they found four standing horses, dozing in their stalls.

Leaving the door slightly open, his eyes now accustomed to the dark, Roric made a quick appraisal of the animals as he strode past the stalls while Conneid and his wife rested against the wall next to a ladder. He found a draft horse, tall but broad-shouldered, in the second stall and opened the door, wincing when it squeaked.

"You're going on a trip tonight," he murmured to the horse, stroking its neck. A glint of metal against a wall caught his attention. He grabbed the bridle and slipped the noseband on, all the while speaking to the horse in quiet tones. Too well aware of the passing time, he soon brought it from the stall. "Best without a saddle," he whispered as he stopped by Malvina. No time for saddles, anyway.

He bent over and began lifting Malvina to set her sideways, but her bulky condition hindered him. He turned to Conneid, who stood against the wall, looking as if he wouldn't last the night. "Need your help. Here, raise her legs while I support her upper body. Let's make sure she's centered back far enough, so she doesn't slip off." Despite his weakness, the man did as told, both of them setting his wife securely on the mount.

"Now for you, Conneid . . ." Moments later, Roric found a sleek riding horse in another stall and made the same friendly gestures with it, then led the bridled horse from the stall, so grateful both were docile animals.

"Need something to stand on," Conneid said with a cautious glance at the horse.

"Here, use this." The ladder provided a prop, and with help from Roric, Conneid mounted the horse after several tries. Immediately Conneid slumped forward, resting his head against the horse's neck. With a worried glance at the other man, Roric stood on the ladder and mounted behind Malvina, an awkward procedure that took time. Then he wrapped his arms around her waist.

"Let's go!" He pressed his heels against the horse's side and rode through the open door, Conneid following. On horseback, Roric quietly closed the door. Someday, he'd return these animals, but horse thievery was the least of his concerns now.

He supported Malvina with his left arm, his right hand holding the reins. With his eye on Conneid, he kept the horses at a moderate pace.

In front of Roric, Malvina moaned again, one hand pressed across her stomach, the other clenched in the horse's mane. His arm around her waist, he felt her stomach muscles tighten, and his heart ached for the suffering she must endure.

Up steep hills and down into deep valleys, past spreading oaks and bushes they persisted, the uncultivated land rocky and uneven. They couldn't gallop the horses, not in Malvina's condition. Even this speed was probably harmful for her. This was a night for choices, and before daylight he'd know whether or not he'd made the right ones. A cold wind sprang up that sent tree branches swaying but cooled their bodies. Time and again, Roric's gaze was drawn to the moon's sweep across the sky, an agonizing reminder of time's passage.

Past trees and fences that continually confronted them, they drifted into a walk, prompting Roric to slap the horse's side. "Come on, faster!" A glance at Conneid's drooping body, the horse's slow pace, sent a shaft of fear bolting through him. They'd never reach the Gorm Forest before dawn. "We must hurry!" he called to the other man.

"Trying to." Conneid sat up straighter and dug a heel into his mount's side, and the horse increased his speed to a canter.

Pain and worry etched lines on Malvina's face. "We're not going to make it to safety, are we, Roric?"

"Of course we are!" But he feared Malvina spoke the truth. Images of recapture and torture roiled inside him, a fear so terrible it blocked every other thought. Sacred shrine! What would they do to Malvina, to her baby? And Conneid--would they finish skinning him alive, or would all three of them suffer death by burning at the stake?

Malvina's pains came more often, more intense, too, Roric could tell by her taut muscles straining against his arm. She moaned aloud and bit down hard on her hand. Bile rose in Roric's throat, his stomach clenched. He swallowed again and again.

Conneid reached over and caught Roric's arm. "We must stop. My wife--"

"Stop?" Roric exploded. "Stop, you say? And then what? Have your wife give birth here and now, so that we have a newborn baby to carry?" He regretted the words immediately. "We'll keep going," he said in quieter tones. "Can't stop." Despite his gut-churning fear, Roric injected a note of certainty in his voice. "We'll make it."

A barking dog emerged from a farmyard and raced after the horses, but soon tired of the chase. Cocks crowed and birds sang from the trees. A rising sun lit the western sky with a lavender glow. Roric's breath came faster, his heart thudding.

"Roric." Malvina groaned, her face twisted with pain. "I . . . I can't go on much longer," she whispered. "The baby . . ."

"You'll have to hold on a while longer," Roric ground out. He pointed ahead. "Look, there's Moytura. Not far now."

The city's towers loomed in the distance, and the ground leveled off. The travelers still kept to the back country, past clusters of houses that edged the city.

"Ahh." Malvina moaned, tossing her head back and forth, thrashing her legs. Talmora's bones! What if she couldn't last until they reached the forest sanctuary? Giving birth was difficult enough--Roric remembered his wife's labor--but suppose they had to stop before they reached the woods? And even if they gained the forest before she gave birth, what then? His frantic gaze swept the area. He looked for an isolated tree, any place away from human habitation, where Malvina could safely have the baby. He saw nothing but wattle-and-daub houses, packed close together, clustered on the city's outskirts.

"Roric." Conneid shot him an anxious look. "We must stop! She's ready to give birth!"

"He's right," Malvina groaned. "Can't last much longer. The baby is about to come." Her waters broke, a gush of warm liquid that drenched Roric's tunic and trousers and ran down the horse's flank. "Oh, no!"

Panic invaded Roric's voice. "Can't you see we can't stop here? People all around us! Dawn is coming. Malvina, you'll have to wait." He ground his teeth and gripped the reins so hard his fingers ached.

Shouts and curses reverberated about a quarter mile to their left, mounted sentries on Warehouse Street. Malvina grabbed his arm, her grip like an iron band.

"Roric, no! Don't let them capture Conneid or me. Kill us first!"

"No one's going to get killed!" They couldn't get caught here! If one of the sentries looked their way . . . Praying as he never had before, Roric kept to the right, soon coming to three parallel alleys that led away from the city. Blocked from the sentries' view by an aggregation of shops, they rode single file along the alley farthest east from the sentries.

Leaving the cobblestone streets behind, they came to a long dirt path lined with trees that preceded the forest's edge on a hill. Closer to their destination, Roric increased their speed, knowing they had nothing to lose now and everything to gain by this hurried evasion. More night insects buzzed around them, an irritation he ignored.

"Goddess, Goddess, Goddess!" Tearing at her hair, Malvina whimpered and moaned. She bit down hard on her hand, tears streaming down her face. Roric could only guess at her misery, the tremendous courage it took to hold back her screams. They must find refuge soon, must rest in a secluded place where she could safely give birth.

Within minutes, they reached the forest's southern boundary, a massive growth of maples, oaks, and hickories, with only the pale early morning light to guide their way.

Still in fear of pursuit, aware the sentries were bound to cover every possible road, they plunged through the forest, hemmed in by trees and thick underbrush.

"Roric, please! The baby is coming!"

"Stop here!" In a sheltered spot under a giant oak, Roric raised his leg and slid from the horse, then landed on the ground with a hard thud. He reached for Malvina. She writhed and twisted in his grasp, her contorted face revealing her pain.

Without aid, Conneid raised his leg over the horse but slipped and fell in reaching the ground. "Malvina, dearest!" He stumbled over to her, the bloody tunic visible in the faint light.

Thrashing her legs, fingernails digging into the ground, Malvina moaned continuously. "Ahhh!" She tossed her head back and forth, her face and body shiny with perspiration.

Grunts erupted from the trees. Bushes parted and strange giants burst forth.

Torathors!

Chapter Twenty-two

Fear curbed Roric's movements and chilled his blood. The three of them would prove no match for these giants, should any conflict arise. And the situation was ripe for conflict. Barefoot and clad in deerskin breechclouts, their eyes dark and wide-set, the two outlanders stared at the three fugitives. Roric returned the stare. Was their skin really so dark, or did the dim forest make it appear that way? The torathors' frowns blended bewilderment with challenge. At least two heads taller than his six feet, with hairy bodies, still the torathors resembled humans; no horns in the middle of their forehead.

Why, they're not monsters at all, Roric observed, releasing a pent-up breath.

Munching on tufts of grass, the two horses looked up at the strangers, then returned to their meal. If only he could share their nonchalance.

"Ahhh!" Malvina's moans wrenched his attention back to her suffering. Conneid knelt beside her, his hand under the crying baby's head, his other hand attempting to ease the slippery baby out by the left shoulder. Roric glanced back to the spot where the torathors had stood--but found they'd disappeared! He feared--knew--this was not the last he'd see of these creatures.

"I have a son," Conneid said in a solemn, satisfied tone. "Your knife, Roric!" Conneid yelled over the baby's cries, raising his outstretched hand.

"Here." Roric leaned over to hand him the knife, then watched anxiously as the man cut the cord that bound the newborn to its mother. Malvina lay in silence now, breathing deeply, a puddle of blood surrounding her. He marveled that Conneid could perform this loving chore of delivering his baby, after all he'd been through and all the blood he'd lost.

Painful memories clutched at Roric's heart, of his own wife and baby, both dead soon after Branwen had given birth. A sense of helplessness mingled with agonizing nostalgia, but anger, too, at the witch who had killed them both. He wondered if he would ever find happiness and contentment again. He berated himself for his self-pity, for surely Malvina had suffered more than any woman should. Only think of her agony since leaving the palace, and now giving birth under these primitive conditions, where threat from the torathors still loomed. And why had those creatures disappeared so quickly? Surely, the giants didn't fear them.

His gaze swept the forest, his mind already planning escape. They couldn't wait here for the giants' return, but how in the name of the Goddess could they move Malvina and the baby?

As soon as he'd cut the cord, Conneid collapsed on the ground, exhaustion etched on his face. With an unsteady hand, he wiped the dagger on his tunic, and glanced around. "Where did they go?" he asked, handing the knife back to Roric.

Roric bent over and slipped the dagger back in his boot. "Who knows?" He grimaced. "But I fear they'll return. We can't stay here; we'll have to leave again. Do you think Malvina—"

"She's in no condition to move! We'll have to take our chances. Maybe they won't be back."

Roric snorted. "Don't count on it." He knelt down by the woman as she blinked her eyes open, the sleeping baby lying across her chest. Even by the dim forest light, Roric saw she'd bitten her hand all the way to the bone. "Your hand . . ."

She opened her eyes and smiled. "Do you know, I scarcely feel any pain there. We made it, didn't we, Roric? Without your help . . ." The sentence remained unfinished as the three fugitives rested within the trees' sanctuary, silent as long minutes slipped past.

The bushes parted again and the torathors reappeared, this time with a woman in tow. Upon seeing Conneid's blood-drenched tunic in brighter light, their eyes widened and they talked excitedly among themselves in a strange, guttural language. And their hair! The woman's black and shiny locks hung to the waist; the men wore theirs in pigtails. Clad in a knee-length dress of deerskin, the woman approached Malvina. She held cattail puffs in one hand and deerskin cloths in the other. The two men clutched a deerskin litter stretched between two poles. Muttering unintelligible words, the woman squatted down by Malvina and reached for the baby.

"No!" Malvina clutched the newborn tighter to her chest, her eyes wild with panic. The child began crying again, disjointedly waving its arms and legs, while the giantess looked on with an expression of puzzled affront.

"Dearest." Conneid knelt to clasp Malvina's hand. "I believe she means to wrap the puffs around the baby, like a diaper. Please let her," he said calmly. "She's only trying to help." He sank back on the ground. "We have no choice, do we?"

"You're right, we don't." Malvina motioned for the woman to take the boy and watched with a troubled look as the woman lifted him. With soft, cooing noises, the giantess held the baby, her hand under his head. First placing him on the ground, she cleaned him with the deerskin cloth. With a smile of satisfaction, she wrapped the puffs around his bottom, then wrapped a layer of deerskin around the baby's stomach and wound it around his thighs to hold the puffs in place, tying the deerskin. After handing the baby back to Malvina, she raised the woman's dress and placed another puff under her to absorb the blood.

Averting his gaze from Malvina, Roric kept a wary eye on the torathors. He still wondered how they could evade these giants, or if Malvina had recovered enough to be moved. His mind worked hard as he sifted all their options—precious few—and wondered if they could, indeed, trust these strange creatures.

The giantess stood and tapped her chest. "Lari," she said, then indicated the two giants, the litter on the ground beside them. She pointed to the closest one. "Mord," she said, then pointed to the other. "Kell." The outlanders inclined their heads, a slight smile on their faces, as if guests acknowledging introductions at a palace reception. Between them, they lifted the litter again.

"Wait!" Struggling to his feet, Conneid threw Roric a worried glance. "Listen! We don't know a thing about these creatures. So far, they've seemed peaceful enough, but how do we know what they intend? Once they get us to their settlement, they might murder us."

Roric made a staying motion to the strangers, speaking in low tones to Conneid. "If they had wanted to murder us, they would have by now. We need their help, so let's go with them.

What would you rather do, stay here with no shelter against the rain or cold?"

"You're right." Conneid rubbed his forehead. "I'm not thinking straight. Too much--"

"Too much has happened this day," Roric finished for him. "It's a wonder anyone can think. Come, let's go," he said, nodding toward the strangers.

Lari motioned for the fugitives to follow her. Roric reached down and handed the baby to Conneid, then as gently as possible, lifted Malvina and placed her on the litter. She grimaced in pain but immediately smiled an apology. Seeing her settled, Roric took the baby from Conneid and set it across her chest again.

"Ah, dear baby!" She eased her arm around the little boy and looked up at Roric. "How can we ever repay you?"

"Nothing to repay, Malvina. Glad to be away from the palace."

The party plunged through the forest, Roric and Conneid leading the horses by the reins.

They walked single file along a path that meandered through the woods, shoving low-hanging branches out of their way, stepping across gnarled tree roots. Branches and undergrowth scratched at his hands, but Roric ignored the discomfort. Red, gold, and orange leaves littered the forest floor and slicked the ground. Tall trees with thick trunks stretched to the sky, screening the sunlight. Animal sounds echoed from the trees and bushes-- squeaks, screeches, and howls. Strange green birds with long beaks and wide wings shrieked from upper tree limbs. A brown-furred snake, at least fifteen feet long, slithered along the forest floor, its bulging green eyes darting back and forth.

Apprehension accompanied Roric with each step. He shared Conneid's fears, no use denying it.

Talmora's bones! What had they gotten themselves into?

* * *

Unable to find Midac within the palace, Aradia stepped out onto the back courtyard, smiling in smug satisfaction as a guard stood at attention and pressed his hand to his heart. Yes, she and Midac had wrought many changes in the palace routine; none of the friendly mingling with the servants, as when Tencien and Keriam had ruled the land. The princess! Aradia seethed, her mind devising punishments for the princess--former princess, she corrected--whenever the fool was caught. And oh, yes, she would be caught.

Squinting in the bright sunlight, she headed past the palace garden, then through the woods, finally seeing Midac in the back lawn of his former mansion. And I suppose he'll be there all afternoon, she fumed, wondering what fascination a grown man-- the king now!--found in his Goddess-damned roses. Minutes later, she emerged onto Midac's back yard. A cool breeze molding her dress to her body, she walked at a leisurely pace, swaying her hips, shoulders thrown back to emphasize her full breasts thrust against her silk bodice.

Shears in hand, Midac glanced her way, a frown of annoyance on his face. She knew he hated interruptions while he tended to his roses, but she didn't care. Precious little time he'd spent with her lately. The scent of roses wafted her way, more of a stench, she thought, heartily tired of their smell and the time he spent away from her.

Midac dropped the shears to the ground and swiped his hand across his forehead. "What is it this time, Aradia? Can't you see I'm busy?"

"Well, is that any way to greet your wife? Here we've been wed not yet two moonphases and already--"

"Just tell me what you want! The demoness knows I have enough on my mind. That damned Keriam has made a fool of us." He sneered. "But don't worry. We'll catch that woman or--"

"And that's what I wanted to talk to you about. What progress are you making in catching her?"

He examined a yellow rose and brushed a beetle from its leaf. Picking up the shears again, he resumed pruning, his scar more pronounced than ever in the bright sunshine. "Only a matter of time before we catch her. I've offered a generous reward for her capture--five gold pieces. That should prove an inducement." Midac smirked. "That's the tenth time within the last nineday that you've asked me about that woman. Have you got nothing better to do than--"

"I have many things to do. Surely you know that--supervise the cooks, direct those oafish dwarves, refurbish the palace--"

"And that's something else! You are spending far too much money on new drapery material and whatever else you're buying for the palace. We must watch our money because--"

"Because you intend to go to war against Elegia." With no cloak, Aradia shivered in the cool air but refused to hug her arms. She would not reveal any weakness. "Yes, Midac, you've mentioned the war many times. And we've strayed far from the subject, haven't we? We were discussing Keriam Moray."

"Oh, we'll get her, never doubt it. I told you, only a matter of time." He grinned her way. "You must learn patience, my love." Did a note of sarcasm creep into those last two words, or had she only imagined it?

A biting sensation jerked her attention to her feet, a place by her ankle where several fleas nibbled at her skin, drawing blood. She bent to brush them off and scratched her foot, then raised herself. "Very well. When we catch her, I want to make a spectacle of her punishment, make sure no one else even thinks of defying you, such as Gamal and Delbraith," she said in a needling tone.

He snapped the shears too close to a rose, snipping its petals off, and cursed under his breath. "I've got a special punishment reserved for those two. They'll burn at the stake, and that should serve as an example to anyone who dares defy me." He shook his head. "I knew I shouldn't have trusted Gamal."

"Then why did you?"

"Thought I could keep an eye on him. Thought if I had him under my thumb, it would keep him out of mischief." He shook his head again. "How wrong I was." Clutching the shears at his side, he stared off in the distance. "I had so many hopes for the kingdom. I still have hopes for my country--restore it to its former glory, conquer the rest of the continent, spread the benefits of our more advanced civilization to the other countries. Yet now I find myself occupied with catching criminals, traitors to the kingdom! I'd like to see a world where--"

"I'd like to see a world where no one dares to challenge us, where no one revolts against our rule. Let's concentrate on these goals for now, my dear, and worry about glory later." She smiled primly. "Midac, you must learn priorities. Besides, you worry too much."

"I don't worry at all, madam, and the last thing I need is a lecture from you." He glared at her. "Suppose you let me handle the problems of the kingdom and you attend to running the palace, such as instructing the head cook--whatever the dunce's name is-- on how to saute trout. Demoness! That trout last night wasn't fit to eat."

Resolved to change tactics, she smiled again. She lowered her eyelashes in mock submission. "Of course, Midac. You are absolutely right. From now on, I'll let you govern the country as you think best--"

"Well, thank you!"

"--and I'll supervise the servants."

He gave her a curt nod. "See that you do."

"Goodbye for now, Midac." With a smile pasted on her face, she turned and left him, shoulders held stiffly as she stalked back to the palace. She had hoped she and Midac would have a joint reign, but now she found herself relegated to the role of a glorified housekeeper.

That evening, when Midac crawled into bed beside her, she lay on her side away from him, feigning sleep. His scoldings from earlier in the day still riled her, but more than that, his lovemaking often bordered on the sadistic. A little rough foreplay appealed to her; indeed, the roughness added a bit of spice to their lovemaking. But Midac overdid it. She had enough black and blue marks on her breasts, arms, and legs to prove his cruelty.

Grabbing her arm, he pulled her toward him. "I know you're not asleep, so no use pretending."

"Well, of course, I'm not asleep. You woke me up," she snapped.

He eased her nightgown up, his fingers tracing a path along her legs. "I can think of better things to do now. You can sleep later."

"No, Midac!" Demoness! She wanted to scratch his eyes out. "It is not the time."

Midac squeezed her breasts so hard, she knew she'd have another bruise. "You told me that two weeks ago. You think I can't count, you stupid bitch!"

She gritted her teeth. "I'm tired. I've had a busy day."

"Have it your way." He turned over on his side, away from her. "But don't complain if I look elsewhere for comfort."

As if she cared!

* * *

Deep in a drug-induced trance, Radegunda stared into a bowl of clear water, her calloused hands embracing the bowl as she waited for a vision to appear. Silence enfolded her in the bedroom, everyone else visiting on this Sacredday. In her more lucid moments, she scolded herself for forgetting Keriam's handkerchief back at the store, an oversight that had denied her a means of keeping track of the princess. Now, after one nineday of practice and much diligent concentration, she'd learned to discern the princess's movements by gazing into the bowl of water. Too bad crystal balls were outlawed in the kingdom. She knew such a contrivance would achieve much better results than the bowl of water.

First, she'd achieved a trance state by drinking a poppy infusion, but she hoped to eventually dispense with that drug and obtain the necessary stupor through sheer application of her senses. She would dispense with that drug, she vowed, fearing addiction. In time, she hoped to discover not only the princess's activities, but those of other people, as well.

After several moments, images swirled in the water, at first so unfocused she couldn't detect a definite picture. Moments later, the visions coalesced, forming a distinct picture of Princess Keriam inside a goldsmith's shop.

Radegunda set the basin on the table and slumped back on her bed. How much longer would the princess's luck hold out, before someone learned of her identity and turned her in? Radegunda had heard of the reward for the princess's capture, an inducement that would surely increase her chances of seizure.

Another fear jolted her. What if some drifter ravished the princess, or worse still, murdered her? At least she had the dagger, but how much protection would that be against a determined criminal?

And if Princess Keriam continued with her plan to warn the merchants of the plague--and advised them to have the sacred squirrels killed--it was only a matter of time before she'd be arrested for blasphemy and brought before a druidic tribunal. Her royal rank wouldn't save her. Blasphemy alone could earn her the death sentence, most likely by garroting. But if it was also discovered that she was the escaped princess--and it would be; how could she deny it?--then surely she would suffer a horrible fate.

The plague, if indeed it did afflict Moytura, was a problem Radegunda knew she must eventually deal with. Ridding the city of this epidemic would demand a very powerful spell, and at present, she lacked the skill to perform such a feat. She must practice late at night, while everyone else on her brother's farm slept.

For now, only the princess seemed concerned about the possibility of the black fever striking the city. But what if she was right?

* * *

"Sir, what must I say to convince you that the black fever may well strike the city? If enough people die from this plague--a tragedy in itself--you might lose so much business that you'll have to close the store for good." Keriam hoped to appeal to the goldsmith's mercenary inclinations, if not his humanitarian spirit. She ignored the fine bracelets, pins, and necklaces in their showcases, her only aim to convince him of the coming affliction. She thought of last night she'd spent in an alley, a cloth bag for a pillow, her dagger close at hand. Precious little sleep she'd had!

The gold merchant frowned at her across the wooden counter. "Listen, madam, I don't know your name and I don't care. But let me tell you one thing. If you persist in your argument that a plague will strike the city--an event no one else foresees--you will only bring trouble on yourself. And you tell me we should kill the squirrels! Madam, are you out of your mind? Don't you know these are sacred animals, protected by--"

"I know that, sir."

"Don't interrupt me, young lady. There are thousands of squirrels in the city, protected by royal decree. How do you propose that we kill them?"

"Enlist the help of the city sentries, or even all the vagrants that roam the city. Either club the animals to death or set poison in the trees." Seeing him about to protest, she spoke quickly. "I realize both means of killing them sounds cruel. But it would be worse if thousands of people died from the black fever. If we can prevent this epidemic--"

"Madam, I will give you this one warning," he said, wagging a finger at her. "Cease your senseless talk of a plague, one that nobody will take seriously. Find some useful employment--as a seamstress, perhaps?--because it's obvious you have too much time on your hands."

"That's not true! Sir, I'm only trying--"

"I'm not interested in your motives. I am telling you to stop this blasphemy. You will only bring trouble on yourself. Now good-day to you, madam."

Keriam turned and left the store, stifling her discouragement. Figol Murchadh was the first merchant she'd visited, but there were many more in the city. She would not give up. Returning to the place in the meadow she'd claimed as her new home, she was flooded with recollections of her former life at the palace before Balor had usurped the throne. Memories of her father sent a shaft of pain to her heart, as if an arrow had felled her. She could still smell the lavender-scented sheets in her bedchamber, could see the profusion of flowers in the palace garden, the little knick-knacks in her room and the lovely view from her window. The servants she'd befriended came to mind, the only family she'd known since losing her beloved father. And Roric, always Roric, whom she would never forget. A tear trickled down her cheek, but she brushed it away, refusing to accept any weakness.

* * *

Edan Kane moaned in bed as a fierce headache and backache wracked his body. He raised his hand to touch his forehead, finding his skin hot and dry, the sweat-drenched sheet proof of his fever. If only sleep would come, he might feel better, but how could he sleep with his throbbing head? Although it was mid-afternoon, he lay in semi-darkness, his wife having drawn the heavy draperies earlier in the morning. Today was his second day of illness, and if his condition didn't improve by tomorrow, he'd ask his wife to fetch one of the druid physicians from the city hospital.

Recollections of that crazed woman who'd visited his store only a few days ago, warning of the black fever, heightened his worry and drove him to despair. Did he suffer from the black fever now? If he suffered from that plague--and oh! Talmora, don't let it be so--had that woman cast a spell on him? She must be a witch, he agonized, wondering why she'd chosen him to practice her evil magic on. May the Goddess punish her for her sins!

He moved his legs, a sudden pain jolting him. Gingerly, he touched his groin and--no! A thick cyst! When had that happened? He closed his eyes and prayed. But what else could it be?

His wife entered the room, a cup in her hand. She set the cup on the bedside table, then returned shortly with a pan of water. Smiling, she sat on the bed and placed the pan on the floor. "How do you feel, dearest? Any better?" She smoothed her hand across his forehead, brushing a lock of hair away.

"The same," he croaked. "No, worse!"

"Ah, Talmora!" She pressed her hand to her heart, then dropped it to her side. "You'll get better; I'll see to it. I made you some willow bark tea," she said, reaching for the cup. "Here, I'll help raise you." She raised him to a sitting position, then handed him the cup. "It's not too hot. You can drink it all now."

After he finished the tea, she retrieved the pan from the floor and dipped a cloth into the water, then wrung the cloth out. She sponged his face and neck, all the while murmuring words meant to comfort. "Darling, you are bound to get better soon. Perhaps you suffer from working too hard. Haven't I said you should rest more, not work in the store such long hours?" Her outspread arm indicated the spacious bedroom with its rich furnishings. "The Goddess knows we don't need the money. Only look at how you've prospered within these last few years. A wife could not want a more industrious husband. But the children and I need you at home more." She smiled. "I fear we'll forget what you look like." After easing his sheet back, she sponged his arms and lower legs, then set the pan on the floor and raised the sheet up again.

He grasped her hand. "Gilda, if I'm no better by tomorrow, you must fetch a physician from the hospital. I . . . possibly it's more than just working too hard. Why should I have a fever now?" he asked, his voice rising. He swallowed, his throat raw and sore. "A woman came into my store the other day, warned me about the plague. I swear she put a spell on me."

"No!"

He nodded, the movement sending a shaft of pain through his head. "Even told me the squirrels in the kingdom must all be killed. Did you ever hear of such a ridiculous--no, blasphemous--thing?"

"But fleas can bring the plague," she reasoned. "We all know that."

"Yes," he rasped, "but how did she know this would happen now? Not even the learned druids foresaw this disease, if that's what it is. No doubt she cast an evil spell and thus spread fleas on the squirrels." He closed his eyes for a moment, exhausted after this short discourse. "We've had droughts before, and yes, fleas, too. So what has made it different now?"

Gilda shook her head. She had no answer.

"One thing I want you to do for me." He shifted position, grimacing with the pain. "The merchants guild holds its meeting one nineday from today. If I'm no better--"

"Oh, but you will be!"

He lifted his hand. "If I'm no better, I want you to go in my stead, warn the merchants about this witch. From what she said, I gather she's spoken to others before me." He focused his gaze on her. "Promise me you'll warn them!"

Tears filled her eyes. "Yes, of course, dear husband. But you'll be better by then, I just know you will. You can attend the meeting, warn them about this witch."

Edan raised himself up on his elbows, a fresh agony torturing his back. "If I have something contagious, I fear you and the children will get it. Ah, Gilda! That you and the children should suffer!"

She bent low to kiss him on the cheek. "You worry needlessly, sweetheart," she said, her tears belying her hopeful words. "Surely you'll be back to normal by tomorrow."

"Let us pray so." He sighed. "And one more thing--I want you to sleep in another room tonight, for fear of contagion. You shouldn't even be here now, much as I appreciate it."

"But darling, I want to be with--"

"Promise!"

She nodded. "Yes, of course, if that's how you want it."

"Good." He closed his eyes, waiting for sleep to come. On the verge of sleep, he heard his wife leave the room and softly close the door behind her.

Hours later, as the sun sank in the east and the room dimmed in the early evening, he awoke again. Through his pain and misery, he heard his children playing outside on the lawn, heard his wife calling them to the evening meal. He tried to swallow but couldn't; then sleep claimed him again. Sometime later, he heard his wife return to their bedroom to ask if he felt like eating, but he found it too difficult to answer.

He heard the strike of flint on steel. "I'll keep the lamp burning low," she murmured, "so you don't wake up in the dark." With quiet footsteps on the sheepskin floor, she left the room again.

He looked around at all the familiar furnishings, all the things that had come to mean so much to him over the years: the tall chest of drawers, the bedside table with the brass lamp, the bronze statue of Talmora that rested on another table.

He awoke again during the night, his body burning up. In desperation, he ran his fingers along his arms, feeling large cysts, black and painful. His hands shaking, he felt his face and legs-- lumps everywhere! He tried to call his wife but no sound came. Cold panic sent his heart thudding. Despite his panic, his absolute mind-numbing terror, he tried to convince himself he'd recover soon. Gilda would fetch a physician tomorrow. Surely one of those learned druids would bring a healing medicine. Yes, if he could only hold out until tomorrow.

If only he could.

Chapter Twenty-three

Does Roric Gamal serve the new king? In her trancelike state, now induced through sheer concentration, Radegunda gazed at the bowl of clear water. Concern for Princess Keriam had prompted her to leave her brother's house, so for the second time within the past two moonphases, she had returned to her store on Perfume Lane. Here in the city, she could better follow the princess's movements, hear any rumors concerning her sovereign.

And yes, she'd heard an occasional account of a strange sickness, she recalled with a stab of alarm, words uttered in shocked whispers. The plague? She didn't know, for the news was garbled. If it was the black fever, she must perfect her spells. Her books on witchcraft had revealed something she'd suspected for a long time: learning to conquer the elements was easier than getting rid of a plague. The demoness Endora was at work here. Even conquering the elements had proven an insurmountable task--so far. If she'd been able to bring rain to Moytura, there would be no talk of an epidemic now, for rain would have ended the drought that had brought the fleas.

Ever since Tencien's assassination, Radegunda had wondered if Major Gamal only pretended loyalty to the new king. Too bad she hadn't had a chance to speak to him before Aradia forced her from the palace. She smiled, recalling the major's fear of her, his hatred of anything that even hinted at witchcraft. He wouldn't have spoken to her if she'd offered him the kingdom.

Having left Adsaluta in charge of the store for this morning, she remained in her apartment, her gaze focused on the water, her every thought on Gamal. She waited for the palace to appear among the hazy images coalescing in the bowl. But--no palace!

She closed her eyes in concentration, every breath, every thought, focused on Roric Gamal. She repeated his name again and again, projecting pictures of the major, of his face, his body, his every gesture. Vague images swirled in the water, visions of trees, of a dark forest. Changing her position on the bed, she stared, refusing to believe what the water revealed.

244

She blinked her eyes as gradual pictures emerged, of a large woods--the Gorm Forest!--and Roric Gamal outside a cave, talking to another man. Delbraith? Ah, yes, Conneid Delbraith, the former king's secretary. Well! So they had both left the palace. Had they been banished, or had they escaped? The Gorm Forest, she mused, a land of dark mysteries and monsters. And if they dwelled in the forest, what about the monsters? Had parents passed along tales of the torathors merely to scare their children into obedience, or did such creatures exist? So maybe-- No, wait! She saw one now! A strange being stepped out from a cave, such a tall creature, but he bore no horn in the middle of his forehead.

Intrigued by her findings, Radegunda gazed at the water, expecting to see more visions, but after long moments, the water cleared. With acute disappointment, she set the bowl aside, hoping to be more fortunate next time.

Her intuition told her she'd soon see Major Gamal in the flesh.

* * *

"I intend to do this, Conneid, so don't try to change my mind." Outside a cave deep in the Gorm Forest, Roric's attention slid from Conneid to his new friends who had gathered outside another cave a short distance away. Settled on the ground, several torathors worked with long skeins of cordage, making fishing nets. Roric stood in the shadow of a gigantic pine tree, his gaze swinging back to Conneid.

"Listen!" he continued, not liking Conneid's frown, "we need to know what's happening at the palace. And what about the princess?" he asked, afraid to admit, if only to himself, how much he thought of her, of the times he lay awake at night recalling everything about her, wondering when--or if--she'd be caught. Goddess, he prayed, please take care of her. She means so much to me.

"We've found refuge here," Conneid replied a few paces away. His chest wounds were slowly healing, thanks to calendula poultices Lari applied every day. "And refuge is enough for me. I don't need to visit the capital."

"But I do." Roric nodded toward the cave where an outlander clan had offered shelter to him, Conneid, and Malvina. "I'll always be grateful for the home these folks have provided us. But we can't shut ourselves off from the rest of the kingdom."

"Why not? Roric, can't you see how dangerous a visit to Moytura may be? What if someone recognizes you? Only a little over one nineday has passed since our escape." Conneid shook his head. "You're stretching your luck."

Roric laughed, his gaze sweeping over his stained gray tunic, his dusty boots. "Who's going to recognize me in these clothes?" Although he'd rinsed the tunic and cloak several times in the river since their arrival here, the bloodstains persisted. He fingered his chin. "And with this stubble? I'll borrow a rabbit hat from one of these fellows, wear it low on my head. I need to find out what's happening in Moytura and the rest of the kingdom. When I served under Balor, I had no opportunity to leave the palace. And I should think you'd want to know--"

"Not anymore." Conneid waved his hand dismissively. "That's in the past. My life is here, with Malvina and little Keenan." A look of bitterness captured his face. "Once I thought I could help overthrow Balor." He snorted. "Foolish dream!"

"Not so foolish, which is why I intend to go to the capital, catch the people's mood. I've learned a bit about diplomacy over the years. I can ask subtle questions that lead people to divulge information. We have to discover how things are at the palace, how the people feel about Balor and Aradia. If they are ready to revolt--"

"Hah! As if they are, as if the populace could make a difference! Balor commands the army, and whoever controls the army controls the kingdom."

Roric surveyed the dark forest that enclosed them, the tall evergreens that reached to the sky, creating a perpetual dimness over much of the woods. A network of caves honeycombed this part of the dense woods, each cave chamber occupied by an outlander clan.

A short walk from his forest home, the frothing Deuona River twisted through wooded hills, heading southward. A rocky embankment, thick with grasses and understory and studded with trees, led down to the river. Roric had bathed in the ice-cold water this morning, a hasty ablution he was only too happy to complete. Columns of pine trees blanketed the hills, interspersed with birches and hickories. Smaller streams fed off from the river, yielding lush agricultural land that furnished bountiful crops of fruits and vegetables.

With much grass to graze on, the stolen horses remained tethered, except for the times Roric or Conneid rode them to exercise the animals. Wild goats roamed about, browsing among the meadow grasses, avoiding the horses.

"We've found contentment here, even if we have no purpose," Conneid said, wrenching him back to the moment. "Right now, peace and happiness are enough for me." He sank down at the cave entrance, as if to emphasize his need for quiescence. Roric joined him on the cold limestone floor, drawing his knees to his chest, clasping his hands around his legs. Smoke from a fire inside the cave drifted his way, its sweet scent blending with the aroma of pine. Dried herbs hung from wooden stands inside the cave, adding their fragrance.

"Peace and happiness?" Roric nodded, his eye on a poisonous snake that slithered through the grass a few feet away. He stared upward, where a caracab, with its long-spreading wings, soared in the sky. "Yes, contentment is enough for the time being. But we must work toward Balor's eventual overthrow."

"How?" Conneid threw him a sharp look. "Tell me that."

"No plans for now, maybe not even in the near future," Roric said, aware he wasn't telling the entire truth. If he could only get to Elegia, would King Barzad be willing to help? Did he even know of Tencien's assassination? "But we must rid the kingdom of Balor, must put Princess Keriam on the throne." His body warmed at the mention of her name, a myriad of enticing images flooding his mind.

"The princess." Conneid sighed. "I support Princess Keriam too, but how do we even know she's still alive?"

Fear stabbed Roric, a quick cold blade between the ribs. Nothing must happen to her, for if it did, his life would be empty without her. When would he see her again? He must see her again.

"Balor and Aradia are clever executioners," Conneid went on. "Surely you know that." He gave Roric a close look. "You don't really think Fergus's death was an accident, do you?"

"One more reason why I must return to Moytura, to discover how the princess fares," Roric said, suppressing a shiver. He clapped his hand on his friend's shoulder. "My mind's made up."

* * *

The tall trees hid much of the sunlight as Roric trod the rocky path that led from the forest to the city outskirts. A rabbit cap on his head, he strode for miles through the dark woods. Tempted to take the sleek riding horse, he decided against it, on the very slim chance that the owner might visit the city this same day. His eyes scanned the trees and underbrush, ever on the alert for wild animals. Thorns scratched his hands and tugged at his cloak. He worked the cloak loose and shoved the thorny bush aside, then walked on, watching out for venomous snakes that slid along the uneven forest floor.

He recalled his first few days among the outlanders, a time of adjustment for everyone. It hadn't taken him long to acquire a few words of their simple language, then gradually expand his vocabulary. As much as possible, he and Conneid spoke the outlander language among themselves, a practice that aided him when speaking with the forest creatures. He, Malvina, and Conneid had made friends with these folks, surprised to find that they weren't the fierce monsters their reputation suggested. Besides treating Conneid's chest, they'd applied poultices to Malvina's hand, and they pampered Malvina's baby every chance they had.

One question had puzzled him ever since their first encounter with these people. After he'd felt fluent enough, he posed the question to Mord.

"Do you fellows usually trek so far from your homes here in the forest? I mean, you were close to the city's edge when we first met you."

"Ah." Mord had smiled. "We do it all the time. We are dark, we hide behind trees. And you people," he said, stabbing Roric's chest with his forefinger, "are afraid of us." He nodded.

"Admit it, yes, you are. So your people never come so far into the forest. Like you did when we first met."

Brought back to the moment, Roric saw a gradual illumination that revealed the forest's fringe, where the trees thinned to scattered clumps, and a slight hill overlooked the capital. Closer to the city, the path changed from a dirt road to a cobblestone street. The warehouses and small shops of Moytura came into view, the city spread out before him.

Arrived at Storehouse Street, Roric pulled his cap over his forehead, his gaze covering these warehouses and shops that formed the northern boundary of the city. So many stores, closed and boarded up, so few people on the streets! What a difference from the bustling city under Tencien's rule! As he strode the cobblestones toward the city's center, the shops became more ornate, those establishments that catered to the wealthy. Most of these stores had remained open, for only the rich could afford the jewels, silks, and fancy swords, the ornamental bags and decorative belts.

He stared in the window of a sword shop, the few but finely-crafted weapons a reminder that he would need a sword when the time came to overthrow Balor. Now was as good a time as any, he decided, and since he'd never frequented this store, the proprietor wouldn't know him.

He stepped inside the shop, and a bell rang, bringing the owner from a back room.

"Yes, sir, can I help you?"

Roric's gaze covered the scanty selection. "Are these the only swords you have?" Besides those weapons, the store stocked dirks, daggers, and pikes, but again, only a meager selection.

"I'm afraid so, sir. As you probably know, the best swords come from Elegia, but we've had trouble procuring them."

"How so?" Alarm squeezed his gut. He felt certain of the reason but wanted to hear what the man had to say.

"Sir, the trade caravans can't get through. Indeed, they don't try anymore. Brigands rob the merchants, often kill them. Word is that King Balor doesn't pay Elegia for protection, as . . . as the former king did. Trade was safer under--" He stopped and bit his lip. His eyes widened in fright.

Under Tencien.

The owner spoke quickly. "But these are good swords, sir, the best there are. Take this one, for instance." He withdrew a steel sword from under the wooden counter, then set it on the countertop. "Only look at this fine weapon. It's light and fast, and can be swung easily with one hand as well as two. Has a wood grip covered with leather. Good for cutting and thrusting, but most important, it's made of the very best tempered steel." He pushed it toward Roric. "Here, hold it and swing it. See how easily it maneuvers, as if it's part of you."

Roric grasped the sword by its hilt and stepped away from the counter. He swung the sword, liking its feel, its easy grip. Moving back to the display case, he looked over the others on the shelves but realized this was the best of the lot, and was, indeed, a fine sword.

"How much?"

"One gold and two silvers, sir. You won't be sorry you bought it. This will serve you well, even though the country isn't at war--" He stopped again, his face flushed.

Isn't at war yet.

"Scabbard comes with it," he quickly added.

"Yes, of course." Roric set two gold pieces down, and while the proprietor made change from a wooden box under the counter, he unbuckled his sword belt and adjusted the scabbard, then slid the sword inside with a ringing sound. Satisfied he'd made a good purchase, he bade the man goodbye and stepped out into the bright sunshine.

Roric passed the Snow Leopard, and painful memories touched his heart. It was here he'd first spoken to Keriam on a bright spring morning when she had "accidentally" dropped her bracelet. He'd often wondered why she had 'arranged' their meeting but feared it would forever remain a mystery. He saw her now as if she stood before him, she of the fair skin and deep blue eyes, and hair as dark as midnight. Tremendous sadness overcame him, the very real fear that he might never see her again, talk to her, hear her voice. If only he could have her with him now, reach out and touch her, he would never ask for anything more.

Sighing with his loss, he soon reached another tavern, The White Eagle. By now thirsty and hungry, he entered the dimly-lit common room, noting in a quick appraisal that only a few customers patronized the place at this busy hour. He removed his cloak and hung it on a rack, then pulled out a chair at an empty wooden table. With little adornment, it was a simple tavern, clean and serviceable.

A tavern maid approached, her face lined and careworn, her white apron ragged but clean. "Yes, sir?"

"A mug of corma. What are you serving today?" His stomach growled.

"Lamb stew, sir, same as every day."

"Lamb stew, then." He stretched his legs out under the table and glanced around the room again. A few drovers occupied the other tables, their expressions glum, their clothes tattered.

The waitress returned shortly, carrying a wooden tray laden with the corma and steaming stew, along with a few slices of oat bread. Roric caught the tempting aromas of the stew, his stomach growling again.

He looked up as she set his order beside him. "Surprised to see so few people here. Business usually so slow this hour of the day?"

An astonished look crossed her face, quickly replaced by one of sadness. "Things are bad now, sir, except for the rich. Pah! Those people never have to worry about money. But the king–" She clamped her mouth shut.

"Go ahead," Roric prodded. "The king?"

"He's drafted so many young men, there ain't no one to work the farms," she said in low tones. "No one to work in the shops, either." She shook her head. "Bad times for everyone, not enough to eat, people goin' hungry. And something else . . ." Another pause ensued.

"Yes?" Roric dipped his spoon into the soup. Thick with onions, carrots, and potatoes, the soup tasted of bay leaves and chervil.

"I heard tell of a few cases of the plague."

"What!" He sat up straight. "The plague?"

"I fear so." She twisted her hands in her apron. "Not really sure if that's what it is. But there's been a lot more deaths than usual. Just in case it is the plague, the king has forbidden travel from the city. All the roads are guarded. But the dead--their families wrap up the bodies and bury 'em right away. No mournin' period. So what else could it be?" she said, her voice rising.

She leaned closer and lowered her voice again. "And if that ain't strange enough, some woman's been roamin' the city, warnin' of the black fever. No one paid any attention to her before, just thought she was crazed or somethin', but now talk is . . ." Her voice trembled.

"The talk is . . .?"

"Talk is, she's a witch that brought the plague on us."

A chill raced down Roric's spine, but he forced himself to speak in calm tones. "She'd better beware, then, before she's caught and put on trial, burned as a witch." Despite his fear of witchcraft, he dreaded the notion of a woman suffering at the stake. There hadn't been any such executions in his lifetime, nor for years before that.

"What about the princess?" he asked, his voice level. "Any news on her?" His heart pounded; his hands stilled.

"Ah, sir, the king's offered a reward for her capture--ten gold pieces. Was five before."

She was alive! His heartbeat increased. Princess Keriam had to elude Balor. The alternative didn't bear consideration. Where was the princess now--in the city? Would he see her today? Not a chance in a thousand. Goddess! How he wanted to see her again, hear her dear voice, and if only he could, take her in his arms and kiss her to drive them both out of their minds. Foolish dream!

"So far, no one knows where she is," the waitress went on. "Everyone always talks about her, thinkin' how badly she's been trea--" She shook her head. "Poor princess. Her father bein' killed, her escaped from the palace and hunted down like some criminal . . ."

Obviously afraid she'd talked too much, the waitress walked off, leaving him to the meal and his morose thoughts. Where in the city was the princess now? He regretted the angry words between them, her suspicion that he was loyal to Balor. He tapped his fingers on the table, his every thought on Princess Keriam. By now, his stew had cooled and his appetite had gone, but he finished his meal and dropped two copper coins on the table, then left the tavern.

Mindful of the sun's slow descent toward the east, still he decided to linger in the city. A few hours remained before darkness. Everywhere he looked, he saw beggars, men out of work. Roric wanted--needed--solitude before he returned to the forest, to the cave he shared with several families.

Sacred shrine! How he hated this idleness, this lack of purpose in his life. Within the forest, he helped the outlanders fell trees and chop wood for the coming winter, but he longed to rid the kingdom of Balor. Assured now that Conneid and his wife remained in good hands, he decided to leave for Elegia soon, to try to persuade King Barzad to aid Avador.

Needing quiet, Roric headed southwest, toward the Treasury of Knowledge, and beyond that, the meadow that bordered the Nantosuelta River. Ahead, he saw the tall spire that graced the top of Talmora's temple, a spire that reached to the sky. A short time later, he crossed Aventina Way and reached the meadow, the grass burnt and dying, the trees losing their leaves. Red, gold, and orange leaves crunched beneath his boots and blew in a cold gust that swept across the glade. The winding river glinted in the bright sunlight, its waters rippling with silvery flashes. A barge floated past, laden with lumber, headed for the southern provinces.

He sank to the ground and stretched his legs out, lost in his thoughts of the princess, fearing that Balor might yet capture her. He gazed off in the distance toward the temple and saw a young woman enter the sacred building. Who could she be? he wondered with idle speculation, this woman who sought comfort in these tragic times. For just a moment, he closed his eyes, his every thought on Keriam, missing her like a physical ache, wanting to touch her, hold her in his arms. He opened his eyes, too well aware he dreamed an impossible dream, so afraid he'd never see her again. A shiver of fear raced along his arms and legs, and the very real chance she might be caught and put on trial drove all pleasant memories from his mind. *Ah, Princess Keriam, if only I could see you again, hear your voice, see that lovely smile of yours . . .If only I had you beside me, I'd never wish for anything else.* Time slid past and Roric rose to his feet, brushing leaves and bracken from his tunic.

He turned to leave, saddened by the changes in the city since Balor's ascension to the throne, worried about the threat of the black fever. As for Balor, Roric itched to drive that tyrant from the throne.

Hunger, misery, and disease prowled the streets of Moytura.

* * *

Keriam ascended the steps to Talmora's temple, a grandiose sandstone building that commanded a massive space beyond the city hospital. A tall stone statue of the Goddess herself guarded its entrance. Keriam pulled at the gleaming gold handle of the wide oaken door, her worn shoes flapping on the flagstone floor as she stepped inside and approached the altar against a far wall. At the altar, an eternal flame burned before another statue of the earth-mother Goddess, this one smaller but more ornate, with solid gold shoes and sapphire eyes. Her white robe glittered in the firelight, an iron spear clutched in her right hand, the Book of Laws in her left. Her face appeared serene, near lifelike in its compassionate smile. A selection of fine white tapers rested on the altar, awaiting petitioners' prayers.

Hungry and frustrated, Keriam hoped to gain much-needed solace and inspiration from the temple. What had all her warnings accomplished? Nothing, save ridicule. Two worshipers walked past, casting her disparaging glances. Her gaze covered her ragged dress, her scuffed shoes. Why, she looked like a beggar.

Aside from the white-robed druidesses, only a few other people walked the temple's wide corridors, murmuring quietly among themselves. The polished wood ceiling shone like glass, and numerous bas reliefs of the Goddess adorned the white stone walls, interspersed with sandstone pilasters. The fragrance of frankincense floated in the air.

Keriam lit a candle from the eternal flame, then knelt in silent prayer. She prayed for her country, that Balor would be defeated. Head bent, she continued, including in her silent entreaties all those she knew and cared for. She prayed for Radegunda and Maudina, all the palace servants. And Roric Gamal? An inner voice whispered. What about him? She didn't know. If he were truly loyal to her, would he still serve Balor? Watch over Roric Gamal, was all she could implore. Sadness overcame her, near painful in its intensity, a desire to see him again, to learn–once and for all–if he remained loyal to her father's memory, or if he truly believed in Balor. Will I ever see him again? She wondered, afraid to accept that he was gone from her life forever.

About to stand, she looked up at the statue--and gasped. The statue had moved! She looked again and wondered if she'd only imagined it, for surely the statue was in the same position as before. She leaned against the altar and took deep breaths. Yes, only your imagination, she assured herself. How could a piece of stone move by itself, sacred though it was? She stayed in the same position for long moments, waiting for her breathing to return to normal. Rising to her feet, she brushed a tear from her eye, only then realizing how her emotions had wrought such havoc within her. And maybe that was what had caused her to think the statue had moved--only her emotions.

A druidess approached, her soft velvet slippers whispering across the floor, her white robe billowing behind her. A white veil covered her hair and flowed down her back, a gold diadem holding the veil in place. "Child, would you like to come to my private prayer room and tell me what's troubling you?"

"No, but I thank you, druidess." If only she could! And if she revealed her identity, that information would ensure her the death penalty.

After a few quiet words with the druidess, she left the temple, wrapping her dirty woolen cloak around her against the late afternoon chill. A gust whipped her hair in her face and blew dust in her eyes. Tree branches tossed in the wind, scattering their dry leaves on the street. About to head east again to the city center, she stopped, staring across the way, toward the wide meadow. A young man strode across the grass, his walk quick and confident. Something about him--his dark hair, the way he held his head and shoulders--resurrected painful memories. Could it really be Roric Gamal? What was he doing here at this time of day, instead of toadying to that treasonous fiend, Balor, back at the palace?

She pressed a hand to her thudding heart, moving quickly behind Talmora's statue. She kept her gaze on him as he headed east. Mixed feelings churned inside her, a blend of joy at seeing him after all these ninedays, but at the same time, hatred for this man who had allied himself with the usurper. Ah, yes, he had assured her his loyalty lay with her, but how could she believe his assurances when his actions belied his words?

Keriam waited long moments until Roric disappeared; then she walked on, convinced by now that her warnings of an epidemic had accomplished nothing. Already she'd heard of dead squirrels . . . and possible plague deaths.

Several stores ahead of her, two sentries stood outside a fabric shop, looking her way, their expressions stern. A thrill of alarm raced through her, and hoping they focused on someone else, she glanced behind her, but saw no one. She kept her head down, forcing herself to walk normally, although every instinct told her to run. Desperately, she prayed they wouldn't recognize her with her dyed brown hair.

She stopped to stare in a jewelry window, not seeing a thing, acting as if she had nothing better to do than gaze at all the wares the city offered. Out of the corner of her eye, she saw the sentries in the same spot, their focus still on her. If she could only walk past them . . .

The sentries approached her, each one grabbing an arm. "Come with us."

* * *

256

Careful to hide his distaste, Balor looked up as Aradia joined him for the evening meal. Without a word, she lifted her silver wine goblet, her brightly-colored fingernails curved like claws. Adorned in a deep blue velvet gown, a gold pendant around her neck, she was truly beautiful. But her constant nagging, her domineering ways, tempted him to violence. Although he'd long since lost any affection for her, he didn't want anyone carrying tales of marital discord behind his back. He and the sorceress must appear a happily-wedded couple, capable of producing children to carry on the royal family line. The House of Balor. He smiled to himself, liking the sound of it. And why wasn't she pregnant yet? It wasn't for his lack of trying, so the fault must be--

A knock at the door interrupted his accusatory musings. He frowned, hating the intrusion but aware he couldn't ignore it. The palace staff knew that only the most important news warranted disrupting him while he ate.

He dabbed a linen napkin across his mouth. "Come in."

A gray uniformed city sentry opened the door and stood at the dining room entrance. "Your Majesty . . ."

Balor motioned him forward. "Come in, I said. I don't feel like conducting business across such a distance. And this had better be important."

The sentry nodded. "Yes, sire, I believe it is. We've captured Pr--, er, Keriam Moray."

Aradia gasped, clapping her hands. "Just wait 'till I--"

"Hush!" Balor turned back to the sentry. "Well, it's taken you long enough. Let's hope for your sake you have a good reason for the delay."

"Yes, sire. For several days, a young woman has been warning the people of Moytura about a plague. At first, no one took her seriously, just thought she was crazed. But sire, we suspect the plague has already afflicted the city. Lately, there has been a number of mysterious deaths. So one of the local merchants tipped us off. She must have cast a spell, to cause all these deaths from the black fever, so--"

"Get to the point, lieutenant! How do you know it's the prin--, former princess?"

"Sire, at the time of her arrest, one of your ministers was in the Magistrate's Hall. He saw the woman in our custody and recognized her as Keriam Moray."

"Ah." Balor sat back in his chair, arms folded. "So where is she now--in the dungeon, I hope."

"In the dungeon at the Magistrate's Hall. We wanted to bring her back here, but she gave us some, uh, difficulty."

"Very good, lieutenant. I'll see that you and your men are well-rewarded for this day's work."

"Thank you, sire."

Balor made a gesture of dismissal, then turned back to Aradia. "Well, does that make you happy, my dear?" he said after the door closed behind the sentry.

"Does that make me happy?" She clapped her hands again. "Does the sun rise in the west? Has the demoness blessed us?" She dipped her fork in the baked chicken stuffed with almonds, a satisfied smile on her face.

He sat in silent contemplation, his forefinger tracing his scar. "Unfortunately, we must first have a trial."

She slammed her fork on the table. "A trial? Whatever for? She's a witch, causing all those deaths. We know she's guilty."

"Guilty or not--and it's obvious she is--the people will not allow us to execute her without a trial. We may have a revolt otherwise." He sighed. "Say what you want about her, she's still popular with the populace." He sneered. "Or has been popular. If it's proved that Keriam Moray brought the plague to Moytura, the people's affection may well turn to fear and hatred. People are fickle, you know."

"What do you care about a revolt? The army's behind you. You can easily suppress any rebellion."

He drank his elderberry wine and set the silver goblet on the table. "I've heard of grumblings from the people, some complaints about food shortages. Not that I really care if the people starve, but too many unhappy people can cause trouble." He nodded. "She'll have a trial."

"Even though she's brought the black fever to Moytura?"

He shrugged, chewing on a slice of Fat-hen bread. "Many people may not be aware of her predictions, the farmers, for instance. We shall have to prove that she is, indeed, a witch." He threw her a fiendish grin. "Something you should know much about."

She returned his grin, apparently unabashed at his accusation. "So she's found guilty--how should we do away with her?"

He waved a bejeweled hand. "Why ask me? I thought I'd left that sort of thing to you."

"Ah, that's right, Midac. So you did." She remained silent for a moment, pressing her fingers to her cheek. "How about impalement?" Her eyes glinted. "I think that might be fun to watch."

"Whatever you decide."

She sipped her wine, then set the goblet down with a thud, spilling a few drops on the oaken table. "And the druids? Although they are normally harsh, what if they take pity on her and declare her innocent?"

"They won't." He picked at his teeth. "One word from me will assure us a guilty verdict."

"Ah, Midac! You're so good to me!"

Chapter Twenty-four

"Best that I leave now, before winter snows make the trails impassable." Outside the cave he shared with a torathor clan, Roric checked his deerskin bag to ensure he had the necessary supplies-- dried meat and baked bread, dried fruit--for his long journey to Elegia. A goatskin water bag held his water supply for his journey northward, to be supplemented by the Deuona River and streams along the way. He glanced in Conneid's direction, not liking the frown that creased the other man's forehead, a frown that reflected the same misgivings he harbored but dared not express. Close by, several children played hide-and-seek among the evergreens, their laughter a sharp contrast to his anxieties. Above him, hundreds-- thousands!--of birds darkened the sky, heading south for the winter.

"What makes you think King Barzad will help us?" Conneid looked his way, bridling the sleek riding horse for his friend. "Does he even know of Tencien's assassination?"

Roric checked the dagger in his boot. "As for your first question, two reasons: the mutual friendship we've shared over the years when Tencien ruled. Also, I hope to convince him it would be to Elegia's benefit to eliminate Balor. Our so-called king has made no secret of his desire to conquer the entire continent." He frowned. "And your second question--I doubt very much that he knows of Tencien's assassination."

"In Talmora's name, why not?"

"The trade caravans have encountered much trouble between here and Elegia," he said, relating his conversation with the sword shop proprietor. "How can any news get through if the caravans can't reach other kingdoms?"

Conneid slanted him a worried glance. "What makes you think you'll get through?"

"A chance I have to take. I won't travel the main roads. My route will lengthen the time it takes to reach that country, but in the long run, it will be much safer. If I find a path through the forest-- and I feel sure I can--there should be no brigands along the way." He looked at the sun's position in a cloudless sky, on this cold day with strong northerly winds. "If only I could get word to the princess, tell her everything I did was for the good of the country, and for her." Finished bridling the horse, Conneid smiled. "You can tell her after we've overthrown Balor."

"That's the kind of talk I like to hear!" Roric said, although it would be many moonphases before they could battle Balor, for the harsh winter would intervene.

He led the horse toward a large boulder and mounted, an awkward maneuver without stirrups. "If all goes well, I should be back within two ninedays."

And if all did not go well? What if he never reached the Elegian capital? What if he failed to elude the robbers and brigands who preyed on travelers? Then he would never see his country again, never see Keriam.

* * *

"The druidic tribunal brings the charge of witchcraft against Keriam Moray." Three white-robed druids occupied a long bench in the front of the tribunal room, their faces stern and unyielding. Keriam sat in the docket, several feet to their right. A wooden railing enclosed her, accentuating her imprisonment. She slanted a look at these wise men, resolved to present an image of serenity and innocence. She'd never reveal that her heart pounded against her ribs, nor that perspiration streamed down her back and dampened her palms, despite the courtroom's coolness.

Her gaze shifted around the room, where worn wooden benches extended to the back of the room, every bench filled. Other people stood at the back, beyond the benches. Apparently morbid curiosity about the princess's trial had overcome the people's fear of the plague. No doubt many of these spectators were witnesses for the druids, all of them against her. She caught sight of Radegunda, then quickly looked away, lest she bring trouble on this woman who had offered her help and shelter when she'd needed it. Just the same, her heart leaped with joy, especially when she saw Radegunda's smile of encouragement.

Stringy gray hair fell to the druids' shoulders, their beards trailing to their waists. A long oaken table stretched in front of them, its worn surface covered with feather pens and inkwells, sheets of vellum, and law books.

Stray, unbidden thoughts of Roric, painful in their intensity, taunted Keriam. Bits and snatches of talk she'd overheard among the guards had revealed that he had escaped the palace with Conneid Delbraith. Where was he now? Despite her anxiety about the trial and fear of its outcome, a warm sensation engulfed her, a swath of happiness wrapped around her. She should have accepted long ago that Roric Gamal had served only her. Now he, too, was Balor's enemy. She might never see him again. For only a moment, thoughts of the trial drifted away, replaced by memories of Roric. She saw his smile again, heard his voice, remembered his straight and confident walk. Sighing, she stared around the room again.

The Avadoran flag hung limply in one corner, a statue of Talmora in another. Small windows at two opposite walls permitted scant sunshine, but even that little light exposed the room's shabbiness, its worn and scratched benches. Dark wooden walls added to its somber appearance, and iron lamps dangling from the ceiling cast wavy shadows on the walls.

"Keriam Moray, how do you plead?" Next to Druid Cathbad, Druid Tulchinne dipped a pen in an inkwell and scratched on a vellum sheet.

Her own counsel, Keriam stood and spoke in a clear voice. "Innocent of the charge of witchcraft, Druid Cathbad."

Gasps and murmurs erupted in the tribunal room.

Cathbad shook a brass bell, its loud tinkling silencing the mob. "Let us have quiet here. Keriam Moray is charged with the crime of witchcraft, an evil punishable by death." He waved a bony hand at Keriam. "You may sit."

Keriam sank onto the chair, her hands held loosely in her lap. She allowed herself another glance throughout the room, trying to gauge the people's mood. She must get through this day, and how many more days after this one? The trial had only begun. What chance did she have of an innocent verdict? Even if the druids were sympathetic to her--and knowing them, she doubted that very much--would Balor allow the druids to reach a decision on their own? Not likely.

"Let us call the first testifier." Cathbad nodded toward a man in a fine dark blue woolen tunic and black plaid trousers who rose from his place in the front row, soon reaching a bench across the room from Keriam. I remember him, she thought, searching for his name. He had expressed disbelief at her warning of an imminent plague and had advised her to keep quiet about the squirrels. Despite his appearance here, he had seemed kind and understanding at the time. His presence at this trial offered a conundrum that heightened her torment.

Cathbad addressed the man. "Give the tribunal your name."

"Angus Connor." Squirming in his chair, he threw an anxious glance at Keriam. What had prompted him to testify at her trial? Had the druids managed to find all the merchants she'd warned, and had they used coercion against these shopkeepers?

A confused look came over the man's face. "Druid, it's only recently that I learned the accused's identity. How was I to know--?"

"The accused's identity is not important," the head druid declared. "This woman is charged with witchcraft. It doesn't matter if she is the princess or the lowest scullery maid in the kingdom. Now, let us hear your evidence."

"She came into my store," he said in a voice scarcely above a whisper, "and--"

"Speak louder, sir. We can't hear you."

Angus Connor cleared his throat. "The pr--the accused came into my store within the last nineday. She told me . . . she warned of the black fever, said it would afflict the city if we . . .if we. . ."

"Yes?" Druid Cathbad prodded. "Go on."

"If we didn't kill the squirrels."

Moans and gasps broke out among the spectators, like the angry buzzing of bees. Shocked glares swept Keriam's way, overladen with expressions of strong condemnation. Tempted to return their glares, Keriam lowered her head submissively, knowing she didn't dare antagonize the people. She needed their support, however futile that support might be.

Druid Cathbad rang the bell again. "We must have quiet here. This woman's sacrilege stuns the tribunal as much as it does the people. But we can't conduct the trial amid confusion." He gazed at the witness again, his look hard and unrelenting. "Angus Connor, you may proceed." "Druids, I advised her against this irreverence, for I knew no one would countenance the killing of these sacred animals." He paused, biting his lip.

"And?"

"And I told her she must stop this heresy. I feared she'd bring trouble on herself." He rested his chin in his hand, a glum expression on his face. "As I see she has."

Silence reigned in the tribunal room while Tulchinne continued to scribble. The third druid spoke. "Would you say she cast an evil spell over the city?"

Keriam sprang to her feet. "Permission to speak!"

Druid Nialle nodded, combing his long beard with his fingers. "Granted."

"Druid Nialle, I must protest that question." She looked toward Angus Connor. "The testifier is in no position to judge as to whether or not I cast a spell--"

"Are you denying his testimony?"

"No, Druid Nialle. I'm only pointing out that I merely warned him of the plague. I didn't cause it."

Cathbad spoke. "Strange, isn't it?--that there were no cases of the black fever, a disease we haven't seen in eleven years, until this woman--" He pointed a bony finger at Keriam--"came here and cast a spell."

"Druid Cathbad, I didn't cast a spell!" Still on her feet, Keriam realized the futility of her argument but considered she must make the effort. A slim chance remained that she could explain her position and thus absolve herself. "Druid Cathbad, I knew this plague would strike--"

More gasps erupted throughout the room.

"How?" Druid Cathbad scowled. "Tell us how you knew."

Keriam swallowed hard. "I dreamed it." Goddess, why had she said that? Fear froze her stomach. She had just condemned herself.

Screams and cries filled the tribunal room. One woman fainted and had to be carried out, a disruption that caused further delay. Another ringing of the bell brought a gradual silence.

Cathbad's voice exploded with shock. "You dreamed it! That in itself is a sign of witchcraft. The demoness entered your mind while you slept, told you to cast a spell, and perform her evil deeds for her."

"Druid, no!" She'd gone this far; she had no choice but to proceed, but she harbored little hope of success. Strict religion, not reason or compassion, guided the druids' thoughts and actions. "I often have prophetic dreams."

"Is there any doubt of Keriam Moray's guilt?" Druid Nialle's gaze covered the tribunal room, as if daring anyone to contradict him. "But lest any question remain, we have more testifiers to present our case against the accused. Angus Connor, you may return to your seat. Now we want to hear from Druid Kentigern of the Sacred Hospital."

Surprise collided with panic inside Keriam's head. She clutched her chair arms. Why was Druid Kentigern here? What in the name of the Goddess did he have to say?

"Druid Kentigern, relate Keriam Moray's questions when she visited you at the hospital several moonphases ago."

Druid Kentigern looked her way, his expression unreadable, his long white robe touching the floor. "The accused visited me at the hospital during Seluvia's moonphase. She asked if we had enough pallets should any calamity, such as the black fever, strike."

"And how did you reply?"

"I told her there was little we could do in the event of a calamity, but that it was very unlikely that the black fever would strike again."

"What did she say?"

He twisted his fingers together, then stopped, sitting up straight. "She asked me if we were working on a cure for the fever."

"And you told her--?"

"I told her we had no cure."

Keriam rose again. "Druid Cathbad, I'd like to reply to these statements."

"Proceed."

She ran her tongue along her lower lip. "When I asked Druid Kentigern about a possible plague outbreak, I was merely expressing my worry, should such a tragedy occur. For several ninedays before my visit and a few moonphases after, we have had a drought. Everyone knows dry weather brings fleas, and fleas can bring the plague."

Druid Cathbad spoke. "Again we must say that no one else considered the possibility of the plague, because there was no possibility until you came and cast your evil spell." He pointed a finger at her. "Admit it! You brought the plague on us by collaborating with the demoness." He made a broad sweep with his arm. "You have many deaths on your head, Keriam Moray. Worse, you have released evil from the Otherworld."

"No! Only because I saw--"

"Only because you dabbled in sorcery!" He shook his head. His eyes gleamed with hatred. "Wickedness enough!"

Aware of the hopelessness of further argument, Keriam returned to her seat. Had Balor threatened these druids, to make them turn against her? But no, perhaps Balor's threats had not been necessary. The druids had always been stern and uncompromising, governed only by their faith. These learned men apparently believed their accusations. In spite of her admonition not to, she stole a glance at Radegunda and saw the woman's heartsick expression, a look that surely must mirror her own. Panic threaded through her body, a cold, numbing fear that halted all rational thought.

"We have one more testifier." Druid Cathbad nodded toward a woman in the first row. "Gilda Kane, please come forward."

Keriam jerked with surprise. Who was Gilda Kane? Ah, yes, she remembered talking to Edan Kane recently. But why wasn't he here today? He must have turned timid, sending his wife instead. Then she observed what her initial shock had prevented her from seeing: Gilda Kane wore red, the color of mourning. Alarm rippled through her. Visions of burning at the stake tormented her, the stench of burning flesh, her screams and cries of pain. She'd heard that if the executioner was compassionate, he could light the fire in such a manner that the condemned would quickly die of smoke inhalation. Goddess, she prayed, let it be so with me.

Keriam vowed she would continue to plead her case. She would not accept defeat.

"Gilda Kane," Nialle addressed her as she took the testifier's seat. "Explain why you are here today instead of your husband." Tulchinne looked up from his writing, his pen poised in the air.

"My husband is dead!" She waved her hand at Keriam. "This witch killed him!"

Keriam jumped to her feet. "No! All I did was warn him--"

"You killed him! A kind, loving husband, a caring father." She dabbed her eyes in genuine grief, then addressed the druids. "I know our religion celebrates death, and truly, I am happy my husband is now in the Land of Truth and Eternal Life. But I miss him," she said in a trembling voice. "He was in good health until she came, with her sinful bewitchment. This witch killed my husband, my children's father." She pressed her hand to her eyes, her shoulders shaking.

Keriam wanted to weep, too. All the affection, the goodwill she had developed with the people over the years had been erased with this charge of witchcraft. She recalled the times she'd appeared before her people on occasions such as the Beltane Festival, when she'd scrupulously avoided flaunting her royalty. She remembered the many times she'd mingled among the people, in the Treasury of Knowledge, the stores, riding her horse in the streets of Moytura.

A sudden realization stopped her cold. At those times, they hadn't known she was the princess. And now, clad in a plain brown dress, she surely didn't project a regal image, not that her former royal position would save her.

She spoke quietly. "Madam, you haven't explained how--"

"Isn't it obvious? He died of the black fever. He had a high temperature, large black pustules all over his body. Dead within three days!"

Over her heart's thudding, Keriam struggled to stay calm. "Madam, I'm so sorry about your husband's death. But I repeat, I didn't cause it. I merely--"

"He was in good health until you came into his shop, bringing your evil sorcery!" She glared at Keriam. Tears streamed down her face. "You killed him!"

Druid Nialle spoke in a low voice, his tone sympathetic. "Madam, you have suffered enough. You may leave now, go home to your fatherless children." A man came forward to lead the woman away. Her eyes puffy, her cheeks red, Gilda Kane turned to throw one last venomous look in Keriam's direction.

A tense silence settled over the assembly. Men and women dabbed at their eyes and blew their noses. Shifting shadows revealed the passage of time.

In hushed voices, the three druids conferred among themselves. Keriam had no doubt of their verdict. Images of burning at the stake returned to torment her.

After a short time--too short, Keriam agonized, Cathbad spoke. "As the tribunal room can see, there is overwhelming evidence against Keriam Moray. We find the accused guilty of practicing witchcraft. We give her two days to ponder her sins, to pray to Talmora for forgiveness. But we fear her prayers--if she prays at all--will be in vain. We know the demoness is even now preparing a place for this sinner in the Underworld, where she will suffer eternal damnation. On the morning of the third day from this one, Keriam Moray will die from impalement."

Goddess, please, no!

Queasiness churned inside Keriam, her skin cold and clammy. The room spun like a leaf caught in a whirlwind. She felt the blood drain from her face, and the floor came up to meet her.

* * *

Dizzy and sick to her stomach, Radegunda left the tribunal room in the Magistrate's Hall. Voices droned around her, the words meaningless. She lurched down the stone steps, afraid she'd trip and fall. Her head lowered, she fought her nausea.

She must rescue the princess, but she couldn't act alone. Schemes played in her mind. She needed Major Gamal's help, but would he aid her? Ah, she should never doubt his devotion to his princess.

Could she rid the city of the plague now? Was her magic powerful enough? Throughout the last few moonphases, she'd practiced that very spell but feared she hadn't developed enough skill. For now, she needed all her talent, every bit of power, to save the princess. After that, she must free the city of the black fever.

Her mind made up, her dizziness gone, Radegunda headed for Perfume Lane. She knew she would have few customers, so she'd closed the shop this one day. Voices continued to hum around her, the words distinct now.

"Princess Keriam! Whoever would have thought she practiced witchcraft?"

"So say the druids," another woman countered. "They gave no proof—"

"But the plague—"

"She is innocent!" argued another. "She is a good woman. She must not suffer this terrible punishment."

"But how can we save her? The druids have the final word."

Radegunda drew her shawl closer around her shoulders, the voices fading as she passed the silversmith's shop, the sword shop, and the other fine stores, reaching Perfume Lane a few minutes later.

She unlocked the door and hurried inside, then dashed up the stairs. She had work to do. Tossing her shawl over a chair, she sat on her bed and reached for a bowl of water on the bedside table, then closed her eyes. She must clear her mind of all worries and misgivings, must concentrate on her task. Only then could she summon the desired images, only then could she bend Roric Gamal to do her will. What if she couldn't draw Major Gamal to her? Assuming that she could, what if he refused to help her? No, she must never doubt his devotion to Princess Keriam.

Cares drifted away as Radegunda entered a trancelike state. She stared at the bowl of water for long moments, desperate to see the major's image. Focusing on her task, on past images of him in the forest, she waited . . . and waited. Hazy visions of torathors appeared, gradually forming a clear picture. She saw their tall, hairy bodies in a forest meadow, felling trees. Bent low in the river, several women washed clothes.

But no Roric Gamal.

Where was he? Still she waited, until the forest pictures faded away, and only lucid water shimmered in the bowl. Her hands shaking, she returned the bowl to the table. Distress lanced her heart, her head pounding.

She must find Roric Gamal.

Chapter Twenty-five

She would not give up. Roric Gamal must return to Moytura.

Mindful that her sickening anxiety prevented concentration, Radegunda aimed for calm and closed her eyes again. Quiet moments later, taking even breaths, she found tranquility in a near hypnotic state. She stared at the water for a long time, projecting every thought, every image she could conjure of the major.

Densely-wooded hills gradually coalesced in the water, a horse clambering up a rocky slope. Ah, there he was! Roric Gamal guided his mount, a sheathed sword riding his waist, a deerskin bag draped over the horse's back. Clusters of pine trees, hemlocks, and birches dotted the hill, and boulders were imbedded in the soil.

Where was he headed? How far away was he? No matter! She had to bring him back.

Radegunda took a deep breath, then blew out with all the force she could muster. Again and again, she performed this magic spell, rewarded when she saw a strong wind tossing tree branches to and fro. Other ideas commanded her attention, additional means of forcing the major to come home. She'd try them in turn. Roric Gamal must come back to Moytura.

* * *

Roric maneuvered the mare up a steep, rocky incline, the ground thick with shale and limestone. Accustomed to taking the familiar and oft-ridden Royal North Road in the past, he tensed with every sound--a bird's warble or a deer's frightened cry--knowing that any moment, a band of brigands could challenge him. Still, he considered his journey worth all the dangers, for he must convince King Barzad that Avador needed his help in defeating Balor.

Stones tumbled down the steep hill behind him, and he leaned forward to keep from slipping, not for the first time cursing the lack of a saddle. He felt a brittle nip in the air, the coming of winter. To the north, mountains stretched far into the distance, a neverending alternation of peaks and valleys. Surrounded by dense clusters of birches and evergreens, he continued northward on the rocky, treacherous ground, where gnarled tree roots and low-hanging branches hindered his passage. The evergreens' deep green hue broke the monotony of the leafless trees, whose scrawny branches laced together high overhead and blocked much of the sunlight.

The dim forest enclosed him, a strange woodland where every sound became magnified in the stygian stillness. A long red snake with shiny scales and huge black eyes slithered in front of him, rustling the dead leaves that layered the forest floor. The horse neighed and rose on his forelegs, forcing Roric to struggle to restrain the sorrel. Patting the beast's neck, he brought it under control, his gaze taking in every tree and bush, the caracobs that darted from tree to tree and soared high overhead. A sudden gale whipped tree limbs and chilled the air. Roric tightened his cloak around him, then shoved his hair back from his face. Tree branches cracked and broke in the fierce onslaught.

*I * *

Back in Moytura, Radegunda dipped her fingers in the water and flung the droplets out, performing this charm repeatedly.

Without warning, raindrops fell, thick, heavy drops that plastered his clothes to his body and soon turned the ground to a morass. The thick mud slowed him down, each step an added difficulty for the horse. The rain pelted him, coming down in thick sheets, drenching his clothes, hindering his vision. It had better stop soon, or he'd be way behind time in reaching Elegia.

The downpour stopped a few minutes later. Roric swiped his hand across his eyes and focused his gaze in the forest gloom. Shivering inside his wet clothes, he cursed whatever quirk of nature had brought these obstacles. He doubted the ground would soon dry here in the dark woods where the sunlight rarely penetrated.

* * *

With one final spurt of determination, Radegunda waved her hand back and forth over the forest images in the water, immensely satisfied when a fog settled over the bowl, and only nebulous images remained.

* * *

Roric patted the horse's neck again. "We're not making good time, are--" A thick fog rolled in, obscuring the dense foliage, and the temperature plunged. He looked around, the fog condensing until a thick murk covered every tree and bush. The fog stuck to his hair in tiny droplets and coated his clothes with a sticky moisture. An eerie silence enfolded the forest, as if all life had died. Sacred shrine! He wouldn't make any time at all at this rate. There was no way he could proceed, for a thick haze covered everything. Twisting around, he looked behind him and clearly saw the foliage, the woods as it had been moments ago. Ahead, the murk confronted him, as impenetrable as a stone wall.

He saw nothing to do but retreat a short distance and wait until the fog cleared. With no way of knowing the time, he judged it early afternoon. He'd hoped to reach a secluded spot in a clearing before nightfall, preferably one near the Deuona River or a stream where the horse could eat and drink, a place where they could both rest for the night. He raised his legs and slid off the horse, his booted feet sinking into the mud. He fought to jerk his feet free, nearly pulling his boots off. Each step was a struggle, the thick mud sucking at his boots.

The fog might last for days, making it difficult to reach Moytura. And as always, Keriam dominated his mind. Where was she now? What was she doing? Goddess, he prayed, keep her safe. If she were captured . . . sacred shrine! It didn't bear thinking about. If only he could see her again, hear her soft voice, know that she was safe, he would be content for the rest of his life.

He leaned against a hemlock, his arms folded across his chest. Fuming at the delay, he sought distraction. With nothing to do but think, he recalled his recent discussion with several of the

273

outlander elders. Knowing only that Princess Keriam had escaped the palace, he'd wondered if the outlanders would accept her as their queen. Only yesterday, he'd posed that question to the men. He often wondered if these folk even knew of Princess Keriam, so he proceeded carefully with his queries.

"Do you know who Princess Keriam is?" he'd asked the chief and elders while they lingered, cross-legged, around the fire in the evening.

"Princess?" the chief, Dorn, had asked. The firelight played across his somber face. "What is that?"

Roric explained who Keriam was and that she would be their queen, a ruler over all the people in the kingdom.

"We have no princess or queen," Mord said with a nod toward Dorn, "only the chief."

"But if you had a princess here among you," Roric persisted, "would you accept her as the future queen?"

Much talk and argument followed, increasing Roric's gut-wrenching worry about Keriam. If ever he discovered where she lived, he must help restore her to the throne. These outlanders would be a great help in that endeavor.

"She would have to prove herself," Dorn replied after long moments.

Roric leaned forward. "Prove herself? How?"

The chief shrugged. "She must show us that she has special powers." He stared at Roric, his expression solemn. "Why should we accept her as our queen if she is no different from our people?"

Talmora's bones! Discouragement roiled inside Roric. Would the princess ever gain her rightful place as queen of Avador? Even if she did, would these people accept her? Not unless she proved she had special powers, a seemingly impossible task.

Jerked back to the present, he looked around him, finding the fog as thick as before.

Fate was not with him today. He hoped for better luck tomorrow.

* * *

Outside the officers' quarters, Captain Fintan Davies rested beside an oak tree, resolved to present a clear argument, in spite of his anger with Balor. "When is the last time we got leave to see our families?" For days, he'd looked for a chance to talk to another officer who he suspected shared his discontent with army life under King Balor, an assessment that included most of the officers in his battalion. When he'd seen Burton striding past, he grabbed the opportunity to speak to him. Clad in a black tunic with one gold rowan leaf on his collar and black trousers encasing his legs, Fintan groused to this fellow officer in the Avadoran army.

"Hush!" Burton looked around fearfully. "Do you want to get us both in trouble?"

"Who can hear us?" Fintan said. Who, indeed? "I have a wife and children," he went on. "I haven't seen them in moonphases!"

In the quiet period after the evening meal, the sun was a bright ball in the eastern sky, firing the horizon with a crimson glow. A cool north wind swept across the grounds, stirring up dust, bending bare tree branches. The officers' quarters, a splendid building of sarsen stone, offered a stately contrast to the soldiers' utilitarian wooden barracks.

Adair Burton scowled. "Just don't gripe to anyone else. In this army, you don't know whom to trust."

Fintan waved his hand. "As if you need to tell me. But we've strayed from my complaint." To be safe, he lowered his voice. Another officer strode past, and both men spoke of inconsequential things.

"King Balor wants no distractions for his men," Burton said moments later. "All he thinks about is war or preparing for war. You should realize that."

"What I realize is that Balor will soon have no army at all--"

"Lower your voice!"

"--if he doesn't let us visit our families." Fintan spoke barely above a whisper. He shifted his position, easing the pressure on his left leg, having broken it a little over three moonphases ago. "Of course, his elite guard gets whatever they want."

"No surprise there."

"And now," Fintan said, "there's talk of a war against Elegia."

"A senseless war, so far as I can see. When has that country ever done us any harm?" Adair stabbed him on the chest with his forefinger. "But we keep our mouths shut, you understand? We fight; we don't ask questions. We don't have a choice, do we?"

Ah, but we do have a choice, Fintan mused, afraid to express his thoughts aloud. A career soldier, he remembered serving under Roric Gamal years ago, before the major became part of the palace staff, and remaining friends with him, even after that. He wondered where Major Gamal was now, since he'd escaped the palace. Despite the danger inherent in his plan, he'd contact the good major, if only he knew where to find him.

* * *

Aradia moaned, her head aching, her back in torment. Endora! She'd never been so sick in her life. Naked, she tossed and turned in her wide canopied bed with its satin sheets, trying to find a comfortable position, praying to the demoness she'd feel better by tomorrow. She had to recover; Princess Keriam's impalement was two days hence. She wouldn't miss that spectacle for the world.

What if she had--no! She wouldn't even think about it. Despite her resolution, fear seeped into her mind. Endora, she prayed again, don't let my illness be the black fever. She glanced at her hourglass on the bedside table and saw it was late afternoon. Where was Midac now? The lout was never around when she needed him. And Maudina? How did that stupid slut always manage to evade her? Aradia stared out her wide bedroom window with its blue satin draperies, wishing she were well enough to check on the lazy, good-for-nothing servants.

Determined to escape her confinement, she turned onto her side and tried to raise herself on her elbow. Groaning, she sank back down, her head throbbing worse than before. Every muscle ached, her skin on fire. If she could only sleep for awhile, she knew she'd feel so much better, but her aching back prevented even that consolation.

A knock on the door brought in Maudina. "Madam, what would you like to wear for the evening meal?" Her eyes widened, a look of alarm flashing across her face. "Madam, are you ill? You're usually not in bed at this--"

"Oh, hush, you stupid ninny! If I want to rest in bed, that's my business. Just slightly indisposed, that's all. I'm not going downstairs for the evening meal. Bring me a glass of wine and bread." She ran her tongue along her lower lip, her throat parched and dry. "Where is His Majesty?"

"Madam, I haven't seen him all day," Maudina replied, her feet anchored in place, keeping her distance from the bed. She twisted her fingers in the folds of her dress. "I'll get your wine and bread, madam, bring them right up."

"See that you do, and be quick about it."

"Yes, madam." She rushed from the room as if only too happy to get away. Serve the girl right if she got sick, too, Aradia thought, sneering.

A few minutes later, Maudina returned and set the wine and a plate of bread on the bedside table, all but dropping them in her haste. Aradia was tempted to grab her wrist, but the girl dashed back.

"Will there be anything else, madam?"

"No. Now get out."

"Yes, madam." Maudina rushed for the door, then opened and closed it as if a pack of wolves pursued her.

Aradia snickered. She tried to reach for the glass of wine, tried and failed. Panting, she fell back on the bed. If only she could sleep . . .

Hours later, Midac banged the door back and strode into the room, waking her from a sound sleep. "Curse Talmora! Have you lain in bed all day?" He frowned, his bushy eyebrows meeting across his forehead, his small, dark eyes focused on her. "What ails you, woman?" Torchlights from the hall lit the room, and even that small bit of illumination hurt her eyes, intensifying her headache.

"A backache," she improvised. Well, it was partly the truth. Her mouth and throat felt as dry as the parched grass outside, every word an effort. "Bent over the wrong way when I opened my dresser drawer. I'll recover by tomorrow."

"You'd better." Scowling, he stood by the bed, hands on his hips, his scar livid even in the faint light. "Don't forget a delegation of merchants is coming for dinner tomorrow. Tax complaints," he said, his scowl deepening.

"I haven't forgotten." But would she be recovered enough by then to entertain their guests?

He rocked on his heels. "I'm going out for awhile. Don't know when I'll be back."

To another woman? She couldn't care less where he went, what he did. She breathed a long sigh of relief when he shut the door behind him and cut off the light. Closing her eyes again, she sought sleep.

Much later, she awoke, her head pounding, her body hotter than ever. She touched her head--and gasped. Pustules blotted her face. She ran trembling fingers along her hands and arms. Large black pustules everywhere! Frantic thoughts raged through her head. What could she do? Midac must not learn of her illness. She must conceal her condition from him, but how?

A restless night of pain and worry provided no answer.

Midac returned as the morning sun tinted the western sky a light coral, and palace sounds resumed again--guards talking outside her door, servants hustling to and fro. She pulled the blanket up past her face and said a silent prayer to the demoness that he'd leave her alone.

"You still in bed? In Endora's name, what's the matter with you?" He strode toward the bed and whisked the blanket back. He stared at her, a look of fear twisting his features. "You have the plague!" With frenzied movements, he rubbed his hands up and down his tunic. "Get out of this room, curse you!"

She moaned, shoving sweaty hair from her cheeks. "No, Midac. I'm too sick to move. Go to another room. Let me stay here."

"Oh, no, you don't. You're not even staying in the palace." He jerked his thumb. "I want you out of here, now!"

Tears flowed down her pustule-marred face. "Midac, I can't move. I'm too sick."

"You'll feel even sicker if I get the guards to throw you out. I'd grab you myself, except that I don't dare touch you."

An inspiration lightened her mood. If she could shift to her jackal state . . . "Leave me now. I promise I'll get out of the palace." She smiled with false optimism. "Give me but a few minutes."

His face registered surprise. Apparently, he hadn't expected her easy acquiescence. "A few minutes, no more." He turned on his heel and strode from the room, his heavy tread shaking a vase on a table.

Aradia sighed with relief, mulling over her plan. Since jackals were night creatures, could she change to a jackal body now, this time of the morning? Would her illness prevent the shift? And if she did shift, would her black fever disappear? She had to try; she saw no choice.

Wracked with pain, she forced herself from the bed, each movement an agony. On her feet now, she grasped the bed post, the room spinning around her. She waited long moments as she strove for balance and composure. She needed all her faculties, every bit of concentration, to make the change. Resolved to ignore the hideous blots on her body, she closed her eyes and concentrated on her task. A crackling sound, a realignment of bones, revealed the shift was working. She dropped to all fours, greatly satisfied when fur splotches appeared on her body . . . appeared, then stopped. She waited, her heart thudding, every muscle tense.

Her silvery hair draped from her head, nearly touching the floor. Demoness, no! What had happened to her shift? She looked at her paws on the rug . . . and saw hands with fingers, long and tapered, part fur and part skin, tipped with claws. Her head throbbed with pain, her body burning up. She was too sick to complete the shift!

Shaking with fright, she padded over to her dresser and grabbed her mirror, awkwardly holding the looking glass in her furry hand, bracing her other hand against the dresser for balance.

No! She jumped back and fell flat with a hard thud. The mirror shattered, and excruciating pain gripped every bone, every muscle of her body. Pain exploded in her head. She forced herself to rise, a long, torturous process that sent her falling back twice again before she could stand. Refusing to believe what she'd seen, she stared in the broken mirror once more. A monster, half-human, half-jackal, covered with black pustules and dotted with fur, stared back at her.

Wait. Only wait. She must give the shift more time, she lamented, forced to realize she should never have tried the change during the day. Yes, that was it; as usual, she must learn patience. And what about her sickness? Damn it! That alone was enough to prevent the alteration. Aradia waited and looked again. Ah, no! She cried, tears flowing down her furry face, her hairy shoulders shaking. Why had she tried to change her body now? Why hadn't she told Midac to give her until tonight? Or was her illness the hindrance? Too sick to leave the room, she pondered how she could depart the palace. Tears dampened her face, plastering the fur to her cheeks and forehead. In the name of the demoness, what could she do?

The door jerked open and Midac burst inside. "I thought I told you to--" His eyes widened with horror. "No!" He stepped backwards, banging up against the wall, making helpless sounds in his throat. He screamed, a wail of fear and terror.

A sentry dashed into the room. "Sire, what is--" A look of horror flashed across his face. "What-is-it?"

Balor cocked his head in Aradia's direction. "Kill it!"

Aradia braced herself for the lethal strike. She had nowhere to go, no place to hide. She cringed against the wall, her paws pressed close to her chest, her heart pounding with fear. Her last thought was that she'd miss the princess's impalement.

Chapter Twenty-six

Swept along on a floodtide of euphoria, Keriam soared above the city, the many shops and buildings shining below, as though it were daylight. Ah, freedom! Drifting ever westward, she reached the meadow and the Plain of Sorrows beyond. Catching movement below her, she drifted down and stopped under a rowan tree.

On the vast plain, ghostly soldiers fought again, throwing javelins, their swords hacking at arms and legs. Cringing, she saw headless bodies toppling to the ground. The stench of blood made her gag.

Clad in a long purple robe, King Malachy approached, as if he'd been waiting for her. Long gray hair fell to his shoulders, his face tracked with wrinkles. He bowed low in welcome. "Ah, Princess Keriam!"

"Princess no longer!" she exclaimed, surprised as always that she could speak in her spirit form. "Haven't you heard that Balor has usurped the throne?"

He nodded, his face set in grief. "But you are still a princess, and rightfully the queen!"

"If only I were the queen! If only that usurper, Balor, didn't sit on the throne. Ah, King Malachy, he has caused nothing but trouble and heartache in the kingdom!" But wishes would get her nowhere now. She jerked her head in the direction of the soldiers. "How can they fight in the dark?"

"Madam, there is no darkness in the Otherworld. We occupy the same space as you, but in a different dimension."

"But how long will they continue to fight?" Her glance covered the ghostly warriors, and she saw the slow movements of swords, saw men falling to the blood-slick ground. Moans, groans, and curses reverberated around her, as if the soldiers fought in the real world, the world of the here and now. She wrung her hands as mixed emotions collided in her mind. Immensely happy to be free of her cell and fearing to return, still she wanted to escape this nightmare battle scene, this slashing of arms and heads, of blood-staining tunics, the awful reality of death. She threw a desperate look at Malachy. "How long?"

He sighed and looked their way, then turned back to her. "Until they realize that they have won, that good has overcome evil."

"Will that day ever come?" She tried to keep the bitterness from her voice. "Will good ever overcome evil?"

Malachy smiled. "Let us hope it comes soon."

"And do they fight here every night? When I saw them last, it was during the day--in my world--when a fog hung over the meadow."

"Not every night, madam." He shook his head. "Who can say why they fight when they do? All I know is that I must accompany them, try to convince them the battle is over. It is won."

"And the evil wizards still won't admit that they lost the battle?"

He shook his head. "I fear they never will."

A thought flashed through her head. "My father--"

"He is happy with your mother now, madam. He speaks lovingly of you all the time. Perhaps someday soon he may visit you, too."

"Oh, yes!" Even in her spirit, tears flooded her eyes, and she brushed them away. "Please tell my parents I miss them so much."

"You will see them both some day, in a land where there is no sorrow."

Birds sang in the trees, a bluish gray tinge coloring the western horizon. Not time to go back, already!

His look was filled with sadness. "Madam, I fear dawn will arrive soon."

"No! King Malachy, I won't go back!" She never wanted to return, not to the fate that awaited her.

"Madam, nothing would make me happier than for you to stay with me. But your soul must not remain separated from your body. You must go back, go back, back . . . ."

Keriam moaned. She awoke, her face wet with tears. Wrenched back to the real world, she stared around at the cold stone floor and barred windows of her cell. After long moments, she tossed her dirty blanket aside and struggled to her feet, then trudged over to her barred window. She gripped the bars while anger, fright, and despair roiled inside her, a powerful blending that shook the iron bars, then bent them. One of the bars snapped in her hands, but even if she broke all of them, it would gain her nothing. High up on the third story of the Magistrate's Hall, it was a far drop to the bottom, with sentries warding the area. She gazed out on the city, its splendid greenery, its many fine shops, the spires that reached to the heavens. She looked again--

And saw the steel stake. Recently erected, it thrust up from the city square, like a malevolent beast. Raw terror flooded her brain.

With a sharp cry, she turned away, clutching her stomach. Sobbing brokenly, she fell on her knees to her straw-filled sleeping mat and rocked back and forth. Talmora, she prayed, give me the strength to bear it. Tomorrow she must face death without flinching, must hold her head high as the guards led her to the execution site. She must act like a princess. But she knew she would scream and beg for mercy, would try to tear loose, try to escape.

Slowly, she shifted to a sitting position and eased over to the wall, then leaned against its slimy surface. She sat with her knees drawn up to her chest and rested her head in her hands. She reached for the dirty prison blanket and wrapped it around her, shivering in the cold air that blew in through the barred window. If only she had someone to talk to these last few hours before her death . . . Her mind overflowed with recollections of Roric, and how she had misjudged him. Regret swamped her, and despite her efforts, fresh tears streamed down her face. To see him once again, to touch him, hear his dear voice, ah, that would be happiness. Too late, she realized how much he meant to her. She recalled their every meeting, playing each encounter in her mind, his every word, every gesture, every expression.

A movement by the window caught her attention. A raven sat on the window ledge, tilting its head, tapping its beak against the bars, as if it wanted to remove that barrier and free her. Its beady eyes moved back and forth, finally resting on her.

"Well!" Keriam tossed the blanket aside and stood as more ravens landed next to the first, filling up the entire space. No sooner did those fly away than others took their place, or are they all the same ones? Did they want to tell her something, or had they merely come to visit? If only they could talk . . .

Moments later, the birds flew away, and Keriam, too, turned from the window. She paced the cell, this stinking, dirty room that had been her home since her arrest. Her stomach knotted as she thought of all the people she'd miss, like Maudina, and she wondered if her devoted maid still dwelled at the palace, or if she, too, had escaped. And Radegunda, the dearest friend she'd ever had.Zinerva came to mind, that endearing fairy.

"Princess Keriam!"

Keriam jerked in surprise, looking around the room. Had she imagined the voice?

"Madam, here at the window!"

"Zinerva!" Keriam covered the short distance to the window again. Clad in her pink dress, the little fairy slid between the bars and perched on the windowsill, her silvery wings folded at her side, her tiny feet dangling. Keriam touched her with her forefinger, delighting in the soft, warm skin, the silky locks of hair. "Zinerva, you flew all the way from the palace? You must be very tired by now."

Her face solemn, the fairy nodded. "I stopped to rest now and then. But madam, I had to see you. I heard talk about you at the palace. They said you were in the Mag--Mag--"

"Magistrate's Hall."

"Yes, that's it. But I didn't know where the . . . hall was. So I asked Traigh since he's always been nice to me. He told me how to find the building. So here I am!"

Keriam smiled. "Thank you for coming. I haven't had any visitors--" Her voice broke-- "no visitors, nothing to read, only my own company." And the ravens.

"Traigh," Keriam said. "That reminds me of Maudina. Is she still at the palace?"

"Madam, after Aradia died–"

"Aradia died?" Relief overwhelmed her, but questions, too. "How did she die?"

"She was sick, madam. The plague, I think they called it." Zinerva folded her arms, a satisfied smile on her face. "She deserved it, too. She was mean to everyone."

"The plague! So Maudina–?"

"Right after that, Maudina left to stay with her sister in Sligo. Traigh told me."

"Ah, I'm happy she had a place to go to."

"Madam, is it really true that you . . . that--" She dropped her arms and stared wild-eyed at Keriam, looking as if she wanted to cry. "Princess Keriam, please say it isn't true," she pleaded.

"It is true." Chills raced over her arms and legs and down her spine. Her stomach spasmed with gut-wrenching fear, with a terror she'd never known. Faintness swept over her, but she fought her sickness, swallowing again and again, so afraid she'd retch. Tears brimmed her eyes, the room spinning around her. She clenched her hands around the bars and bowed her head.

"Oh, princess!" Zinerva held her little hands to her eyes, tears flowing down her pink cheeks. "If only I could save you. If only I could help some way."

Fighting her weakness, Keriam brushed the back of her hand across her eyes. "There is one thing you can do for me--"

"Anything!" The fairy raised the hem of her dress to her eyes, then stared at Keriam with teary eyes. "Tell me!"

"Well, you remember Radegunda, the healer who lived at the palace? She's back in the city now--"

"I know, princess." Eagerness transformed her tear-streaked face.

"She has helped me so much, a true friend like you, Zinerva. She lives alone. Would you visit her? I need her help! Surely her magic can save me! Her store is 15 Perfume Lane."

Her face forlorn, the fairy bowed her head. "Madam, I can't read." A fresh tear trickled down her cheek.

"Oh, I forgot. Well, here's one way you can find the store," she said, pointing out the window in the direction Zinerva should take. "There's a sign hanging in front of the shop that shows three bars of soap. When you see that sign, you'll know you're at Radegunda's. If she's not downstairs, look on the next story." A desperate hope beat inside her, but just as quickly, terror overwhelmed her again, and her faintness returned. How in the name of the Goddess could Radegunda save her?

Zinerva smiled, clapping her hands. Happiness shone in her green eyes. "Then it shouldn't be difficult to find."

"No, it shouldn't." Keriam bent over and kissed her on the cheek, then brushed her forefinger over the fairy's golden curls. "Dear friend, I wish you could stay longer. But I think you'd better leave now. I . . ." She fought for control. "I don't have much time left." She dropped her arms to her sides and bowed her head against the cold bars.

The fairy twisted her tiny hands together. "Don't worry, princess," she said in a trembling voice. "I'm sure Radegunda can save you."

Keriam's eyes filled with tears, hazing her vision. "I'll miss you, too. You'll never know how much."

* * *

Unable to concentrate on even the simplest task, Radegunda fussed about in her workroom behind the store. Outside, the sun's first hesitant rays drove the last of nighttime from the sky and lit the streets with a dim glow. Proprietors mopped the cobblestones in front of their stores, and hawkers set up their wares. Sentries called to each other, laughing and joking, as if they hadn't a care in the world. The city was coming alive again.

By the light of an oil lantern, she dusted and tidied the shelves, checking her supplies of herbs and spices. Sleepless throughout the long night and on her feet since early morning, she fiercely dreaded the new day, the princess's last full day on earth. Tomorrow she would suffer a horrible death, a torture so terrifying Radegunda dared not think about it. Princess Keriam would die, unless Roric Gamal returned in time to save her.

She grasped the edge of her work counter and wept as she hadn't cried in ages, tears of sorrow and fear, of a terror too great to be borne. What more could she have done to bring Roric Gamal back to Moytura? she agonized. What more could she do? She'd used her most powerful spells that had prevented the major from continuing his journey. But the officer had remained in the forest, neither proceeding nor retreating, apparently to wait for the fog's dissipation. Well, the fog would not disappear for a long time. She had made sure of that, determined to hold him back. But the thick murk hadn't sent the major back to the city, either. And time was running out! Curse Endora! She should have gone after the major herself, even if she'd had to cover every mile of the vast forest. She shook her head as fresh tears filled her eyes.

She pressed her hands to her tear-filled eyes. Talmora ,help me.

A tap on her workroom window jolted her, as if the Goddess had come to answer her prayer. She dared a look out the glass. "Oh!" A fairy hovered on the other side, her silvery wings beating furiously.

Radegunda raised the window and the fairy flew in. "Well, haven't I seen you around the palace?" the enchantress said. Tears choked her voice. She took a deep breath and tried to speak normally. "Seems to me you've visited the stables often. And if I'm not mistaken, I've seen you flyin' inside the palace when you thought no one was lookin'."

The fairy perched on the countertop, resting her tiny hands in her lap, prompting Radegunda to look down. "Well, are you goin' to introduce yerself? I'm Radegunda, by the way."

Banging her feet back and forth on the counter, the fairy smiled. "Yes, madam, I know your name." She tapped her chest. "I'm Zinerva . . . like you, a friend of the princess. I just visited her." She raised her little arms and cried with despair. "Madam, you must help her!"

Radegunda dug her handkerchief from her apron pocket and pressed it to her eyes. "If only I could save her! I can't let her suffer that horrible death, I just can't!" She blew her nose, fighting for control. "I've done everything. What more c'n I do?"

Zinerva pressed a finger to her cheek. "I'd help you, madam, if there was anything I could do. But I don't see how--"

"Yes!" Radegunda bestowed a satisfied smile on the fairy, new hope bursting within her. She pulled a stool out from under the counter and sat down.

The fairy blinked her eyes. "What is it, madam?"

"Call me Radegunda. None of this formality." She bit her lower lip. "I'm afraid this will involve a lot of flyin' for you, but . . ." This had to work.

"But?" Zinerva rested her hands in her lap and stared up at her.

The enchantress clasped her hands. "You must fly over the Gorm Forest and look for Roric Gamal!" She frowned. "You know who I mean?"

"Madam, uh, Radegunda, I know everyone at the palace and those who aren't there anymore. I remember him and that other man--"

"Conneid Delbraith."

"Yes, when they escaped with Conneid's wife."

"Well, if you c'n fly over the lower part of the forest, not too far from the city--"

"I can do that!" She smiled with sweet satisfaction.

"Then we have no time to lose! If Major Gamal returns by tomorrow morning, I think--I know!--I c'n save the princess."

"Oh, Radegunda, you must!"

Radegunda sprang from the stool. "Then leave now, Zinerva! We've no time to lose. Search all over the forest--he's riding a horse--and find him. Tell him he must come back here, to my place. He must save the princess."

"Yes!" Zinerva hopped up from the counter. "Farewell, Radegunda." She flew off, her silvery wings flashing in the sunlight.

"Goodbye," Radegunda cried. May the Goddess help and guide her.

Minutes later, Zinerva flew north toward the Gorm Forest, skimming the trees, the wooded hills spread out below her. In flight almost continually since early morning, her wings ached, her eyelids drooping. She descended, now flying among the trees, twisting and darting between evergreens and bare tree limbs, maneuvering her wings so they wouldn't snag on the branches.

Her sleepy eyes searched the forest, her little ears perking up for the sound of a horse. A caracob bounded toward her, and she cringed, her tiny heart beating. The huge, scary bird grabbed a wiggling snake from the forest floor, then soared off with its prey, high above the trees.

Zinerva sighed with relief, frightened of the forest dangers but determined to continue her hunt.

Overcome with sleepiness, her eyes closing, she started to fall, but caught herself before she hit the ground.

What if she never found Roric Gamal? She had to find him, had to! People depended on her, and she had to prevent the princess from suffering a terrible death. Chills raced down her back and tiny arms and legs, just thinking about that horrid stake. The fear drove her on, more determined than ever to save the princess.

After a while, her eyelids drooped again, her wings tired and sore. Her left wing scraped a sharp branch, and pain flared inside her. Resting on the branch, she twisted her head to examine her wing as best she could, relieved she saw no tears in the gossamer fabric.

She'd better rest for a while. The Goddess only knew what might happen if she tried to go on without repose. She found a little niche in the curve of a low branch and stretched her legs out. How good it felt to give her weary muscles and joints a short rest, if only for a short while.

Yes, only for a little while. Closing her eyes, she leaned her head back against the tree trunk. She listened to the forest sounds-- clucks, screeches, and howls, happy she was high in the tree, free from all danger, as long as the caracobs stayed away. She inhaled the pine scent, the earthy smell of the woods.

Shutting out all sounds, she let her thoughts drift, her mind on her own home on the palace grounds and all her fairy friends. She thought of her human friends, too--Traigh and Maudina, and her new friend, Radegunda. Above all, she thought of the princess she would help save this day. Zinerva took a deep, contented breath, crossing her legs in front of her.

And fell asleep.

* * *

Roric paced back and forth, slapping his hands together, his boots sinking into the muck with each step. He stared ahead, disgusted to see the fog hadn't lifted but remained as heavy as ever.

It was, he thought, as if . . . as if something was telling him he must return to Moytura. But why? Had some misfortune befallen Conneid or Malvina? Or the princess! Had she been caught? Not much time had passed since he'd last visited the city, but had Keriam been captured within that time? If so, where was she now--at the palace dungeon? Talmora's bones, no! He pressed his hand against a tree trunk and gazed in the direction of the city, a gradual realization telling him he must return. If only he could see Princess Keriam again, if only he could assure her of his loyalty.

Her voice repeated itself in his mind, her every gesture, her smiles, as if she stood with him now. Goddess, he prayed, please don't let the princess be in danger.

But if she was? He had to leave the forest, now!

A quick search took him to a tree stump. He led the horse by the bridle and mounted the animal, then turned back toward Moytura. Squeezing his knees against the horse's flank, he rode at a canter, taking every twist and turn with a skill honed by years in the saddle. He shoved tree branches out of the way, his eyes always on the way ahead.

Tempted to take reckless chances, he kept his mount at an even pace, his good sense overruling his need for haste. The ground dried as he proceeded southward, no rain evident in this area of the forest. Strange how the rain had fallen only on the part of the woods he'd just departed. Stranger still how the fog had divided the woods in two, a sharp line, like a curtain. A line he wasn't meant to cross?

Again, he wondered why. What was the meaning of it all? Was the Goddess telling him something, urging him to return?

Skirting tree stumps, jumping over fallen logs, he kept the horse at the same pace along a certain route, as if some force guided him, telling him which way to go.

Loud squawks, then a scream, jolted him from his thoughts and sent his gaze to a tree branch a short distance ahead. There, a mob of blue jays wheeled, dipped, and dived around an object in the tree, something hidden from his view. Roric trotted his horse closer, across the bracken and fallen leaves, raising himself to see over the birds.

And came face to face with a fairy! Although he knew these tiny creatures resided in the trees--especially on the palace grounds--he'd never seen one this close before, this pretty little girl with a pink dress and golden curls.

Eyes wide with fright, she made shooing motions, as if she could chase the birds away. She looked at him--and blinked. "Roric Gamal?"

After waving his sword in the birds' direction, he inclined his head, surprised she knew his name. "At your service."

"Major, you must come with me!"

Chapter Twenty-seven

Roric surveyed the tiny creature. "How do you know my name? And what is yours?"

"Zinerva." She sat up straighter. "Radegunda sent me after you."

"The witch!" Fear grabbed his stomach and turned him ice cold. Not Radegunda! He wanted nothing to do with the witch.

"A good witch, major." She nodded with a smile of assurance.

"There's no such thing as a good witch." Sacred shrine! He must stay away from her.

A defiant look crossed her face. "Radegunda is a good witch. But sir, we must hurry back to Moytura. The princess--"

"What about her?" He held his breath, his hand clutching the reins.

"She's been captured. She's going to die tomorrow--"

"No!" A trembling overtook him, but he fought against his panic. He must not surrender to his fear of witchcraft, not if he had to save the princess's life. He took deep breaths and forced himself to remain calm.

"--unless you and Radegunda can save her."

"Save her--how?" He shook his head, conscious of the passing time. He tapped his shoulder. "Here, ride with me. And tell me where we're going." Radegunda's words came back to haunt him. Someday you may have need of my magic.

The fairy hopped onto his shoulder with a light plop, her feet dangling over his collarbone, and clutched folds of his cloak. "To Radegunda's, where else? She knows how to save the princess, but she needs your help."

He shuddered. But he'd disregard his fear of the enchantress, make any sacrifice to save Keriam. He dug his heels into the horse's flank, maneuvering his mount through the dense mass of trees, shoving sharp branches out of his way.

Visions of Keriam burning at the stake sent chills raking his body. "How . . . how is she supposed to die?"

"By impalement, major. Please--" Her voice trembled--"please don't let that happen."

"By the Goddess, never!" Terror invaded his body, a fear like nothing he'd ever known. He increased his pace, the scenery blurring past, and guiding the horse past thick trees and bushes, he jumped over tree stumps and boulders.

Zinerva grabbed folds of his cloak. "Major, I know we must hurry, but I'm about to fall off."

"My apologies." He reached and dropped her into his tunic pocket. For safety's sake, he slowed down. In spite of his horror, he sought to fill in the missing information. "How did you know where Radegunda lives?"

Her head peeked up over the top of his pocket. "I visited the princess in her cell this morning, and--"

"Her cell--at the palace?" He pushed a birch branch away.

"No, sir, at the Mag--Mag--"

"Magistrate's Hall."

"Yes, major, I couldn't say that word. She sent me to Radegunda for help."

They descended a hill now, and he slipped forward, maintaining a careful perch on the horse. He placed his hand at his pocket to make sure Zinerva hadn't fallen out. Satisfied she was secure, he spoke again. "So you went to Radegunda's . . ."

"When I got there, she sent me after you." Zinerva paused, her finger in her mouth. "But I don't know how she knew where you were."

"Witchcraft, no doubt." He shuddered. "When we reach the city, you must direct me to Radegunda." He must save Keriam. But he still didn't know how. Talmora's bones!

Despite his nerve-blasting worry, the view of Moytura from a distance soothed him, as always. On a slight, sparsely-wooded hill that overlooked the city, the sorrel trotted down the rocky slope, side-stepping gnarled tree roots, sending rocks tumbling ahead.

The sun was a coral glow sinking below the eastern horizon as they reached the outskirts of the city. Thank the Goddess they were here! Tempted to gallop, Roric kept at a canter for safety's sake, also reluctant to arouse suspicion. The streets were near empty, most of the stores boarded up and only vagrants trudging the dirty streets. Following Zinerva's directions, they reached Radegunda's shop within minutes. By now, the fairy had left his pocket and was firmly ensconced on his shoulder again.

Still mounted on his horse, Roric pounded on the front door.

The door jerked open, and the witch stared at him, as though afraid to believe he'd actually come. Then a smile transformed her face. "Major, thank the Goddess you're here."

"Just tell me what you want! Is it true that the princess–"

"Yes, we'll talk about it shortly. First, take your mount to the stable," she said, indicating the place at the end of the street. "Give the boy there a copper coin, and he'll take good care of your horse. Hurry!"

As if he would linger! Leaving Zinerva behind, Roric rode to the stable. His hands clenched, his heart pounded every step of the way. What did Radegunda have to tell him? He stifled his impatience as he reached the clean and well-tended stable, where he made sure the sorrel had adequate food and water. Then he hurried back to the witch.

Waiting for him by the door, she ushered him inside and led him up the stairs. Inside the apartment, Zinerva was already settled, the fairy sitting on the edge of a table. With one glance, he took in the main room of Radegunda's residence. Plain and utilitarian, it held two tables, a dresser, and a bed against the wall: a small room that led off to an even smaller kitchen.

She began without preamble, "Now listen to what we're going to do . . ."

* * *

"Eat, major." In the tiny kitchen, Radegunda set a bowl of vegetable soup and oat bread on the table in front of him, followed by a mug of corma. "Won't do fer you to go hungry. You'll need yer strength fer tomorrow." Steam rose from the soup, the aromas of carrots, beans, and coriander wafting through the air. But he couldn't eat.

Earlier, she'd told him how she'd been able to locate him in the forest. By witchcraft, of course! "And that's how I knew you didn't have a saddle," she'd said, nodding to the beautifully-crafted leather saddle in the corner. Grateful to have the accouterment, still he must pay her for it, a further depletion of his dwindling money supply.

More important, she'd explained her plan to save the princess: witchcraft again. Was Radegunda's spell strong enough? If it failed, well, he didn't want to think about that. No, he corrected, if her spell miscarried, he'd rescue Princess Keriam himself. If he could save her--ah, if only he could--he'd risk eternal damnation, do anything to deliver the princess from that hideous death.

The room darkened, and Radegunda rose to light an oil lamp on the counter, then headed for the main room to light another lamp. The lamps gave off but little light, the rooms remaining in partial darkness. Returning to the kitchen, she pulled out a chair and sat across from him. Zinerva perched on the counter, daintily eating bread crumbs.

Squirming in his chair, Roric shoved the bowl aside. "Not hungry. I wish we could save her tonight."

She shook her head. "Spell won't work tonight. Have to wait 'til tomorrow, no matter how hard the waitin'. Now, eat, major." She dipped a spoon into her bowl, a cautious eye on him.

Sighing, Roric followed her example. "Very well, and I thank you." Although his appetite had left long ago, he saw the sense of the witch's logic; he needed all his strength for tomorrow, and he couldn't think well on an empty stomach. He dipped his spoon into the soup, not tasting a thing but forcing himself to finish his repast. Then he drained the corma and set the mug down, viewing Zinerva from the corner of his eye. The fairy drank from a thimble, a satisfied smile on her face, and wiped her mouth with the tip of a napkin.

Soon finishing his meal, Roric scraped his chair back and stood to stretch his muscles and clear his head. He clenched and unclenched his hands. What if Radegunda's magic wasn't strong enough? Then he would save Princess Keriam himself, as he had vowed to do.

"You c'n stay here tonight, major," the old woman said, gathering up the dishes and setting them in a large iron tub of soapy water on the kitchen counter.

How could he sleep? Roric headed for the main room and paced back and forth within the cramped space. A short while later, the witch joined him, two blankets clutched in her arms.

"Git some sleep, sir." Setting one blanket aside, Radegunda flipped the other blanket open and stretched it out on the floor. "We have a busy day ahead of us tomorrow."

Roric shook his head. "Can't sleep."

"Rest then. I'm goin' to bed now, and you'll only keep me awake if you keep pacin' back and forth." She smiled with encouragement. "Things will work out."

He shoved his hair back from his forehead. "A thousand things can go wrong."

"But won't. Have faith in me, Roric Gamal, in my good magic." She turned toward Zinerva, the fairy now hovering above a vase of fragrant hyacinth. "And you, Zinerva, c'n sleep on the table, if you like. You c'n use a pot holder as a mattress and a towel as a blanket. Unless you want to return to the palace?"

The fairy landed on the table with a light tap, her arms stretched out for balance. "No, Radegunda! I want to stay here with you. I want to see the princess tomorrow."

"Good. She'll want to see you, too, after we've saved her," she said with a knowing look in Roric's direction. "Tomorrow, the princess will be free!"

Roric wished he shared Radegunda's confidence.

* * *

"Now stand behind me," Radegunda said to Roric the next morning as crowds gathered by the execution site. The stake! His heart thudded with fear and horror. Sleepless and stiff, he had retrieved his horse from the stable and saddled it shortly after waking. He gripped the reins, his fingernails digging into his palms. On his shoulder, Zinerva clung to his cloak, eyes wide with terror. The trio stood back far from the execution site but close enough to hear the murmurs among the people. Next to a hat shop, Roric waited behind Radegunda. His heart pounded faster, faster, faster. If the witch failed to save the princess, he knew now what he must do. The dagger in his boot! Why hadn't he thought of that? If Radegunda failed, he'd stab the princess to death, save her from this horrible execution. And then he'd kill himself. He could do it! He'd shove through the crowd and reach the princess before anyone could stop him.

Standing by a chair she'd brought from her apartment, the witch turned and gave him a look of frank appraisal. "No matter what happens, stay right here. Don't move until I tell you."

Roric nodded, loath to take orders but willing to do anything for Keriam's sake. The sorrel, now well-fed and watered, occasionally nuzzled him, as if to give comfort. He studied the spectators and noted that most of them looked sad, an air of resignation on their faces. They dared not fight the druids or the usurper. Yet here and there he caught defiant expressions, too, dark looks that matched their angry words.

"She brought the plague to our city."

"No, she's innocent. If only we could save her! What a horrible way to die!"

"But there is no way we can save her."

A hush fell over the crowd. Trying to see, Roric craned his neck, forced to stand on his tiptoes. Goddess, he prayed, please help Radegunda save the princess. He caught his breath at this first sight of her after all these moonphases. His heart pounded so fast, as if it would burst from his chest. Clad in a plain brown dress, her unkempt hair--also a dull brown--falling to her shoulders, she was still as lovely as ever. She looked around in all directions, as if hoping to recognize a friend. Sacred shrine, how he loved her! He'd give his life to save her. But before this day was over, they might both lose their lives.

Sentries moved among the hundreds of people, pushing them back, making way for Keriam. Grim-faced, a sentry on either side gripped the princess by the arm and led her from the Magistrate's Hall to the broad courtyard where the stake menaced. Balor followed with a look of smug satisfaction, his scar livid in the sunlight, his dark hair slick and falling to his shoulders. The chief magistrate and three druids came after him, their faces sober and unforgiving. More people had gathered now--thousands, Roric guessed. The sound of weeping was heard throughout the crowd.

Keriam blinked her eyes in the bright sunlight, her steps faltering as she neared the stake. Terror was written on her face, a face gone white. Roric clenched his hands, his stomach taut with tension. How he loved this dear woman. If only he'd had the chance to tell her. Goddess, he prayed again, save her. Be with Radegunda this day.

Keriam addressed the guards, words Roric couldn't hear. Then her gaze covered the crowd, and she opened her mouth to speak in a loud, clear voice. "My beloved people of Moytura, please believe that I did not bring the plague to this city. I–"

"Then who did?" someone in the crowed shouted, but the rest of the people hissed him to silence.

"Remember, stay behind me," Radegunda whispered fiercely to Roric. "And help me up on the chair." She planted a quick kiss on Zinerva's cheek. "Goodbye to you, Zinerva. Thank you for helpin' me." Roric offered the witch his arm, and she mounted the chair, pressing her hand against the storefront for balance.

Radegunda drew her magic from deep within her, letting it build and strengthen, waiting to be released. Every breath she took, every beat of her heart, revolved around her skill.

"I feared that this black fever would kill many," Keriam continued, "if nothing was done to prevent this terrible sickness. And it has killed too many. People of Moytura, you must know that I have always loved you." Done speaking, she nodded to the sentries on either side of her. Looking as if she would faint, she bowed her head.

"The princess speaks the truth!" Radegunda shouted from her high position. She raised her arms, the power singing in her veins. Men and women turned her way, looking bewildered. Roric stared in Keriam's direction and saw disbelief mingling with hope on her face.

Sentries frantically glanced in all directions, trying to locate the speaker.

Radegunda raised her arms. "The princess speaks the truth," she repeated. "She did not cause the plague. Fleas on squirrels is what caused the black fever. And if anyone who is not here tries to tell you otherwise, you will tell him that the princess is innocent."

One of the sentries pointed to Radegunda. "There she is! Arrest her!"

Too late!

Radegunda flicked her upraised fingers, and a green mist spread over the people. She flicked her fingers in all directions, until she'd reached everyone who'd come to view the execution. Features set in bewilderment, the crowds exchanged glances and drew back, as if they could escape the drizzle.

Then Roric saw–The Goddess! He knew people would talk about this sight for years to come. An apparition of the Earth-mother Goddess glowed on the ground before them, her body nebulous but her voice as real as anyone's.

"The princess is innocent!" Talmora said. "Never doubt it. Let no one say she is guilty, for such an untruth will cause me distress. Remember, my people, that I am always with you, to help and guide you, to rid your country of wickedness." The specter of the Goddess slowly dissipated in a haze, and soon she was gone as mysteriously as she had come.

Stunned by Talmora's appearance, the spectators had little time to react, for Radegunda's spell was already affecting them. They sniffed the air, mothers gathering their children close. In no time, men, women, and children closed their eyes and slumped to the ground, soon fast asleep. The sentries, too, released Keriam and tumbled to the ground, stretched out on their sides. The princess swayed, then dropped in a graceful heap.

"The Goddess!" Roric breathed. "How could anyone doubt the princess's innocence?"

"She has Talmora's blessing!" Radegunda gasped.

Overcome by Talmora's apparition, it took several seconds before Roric or Radegunda moved. After the Goddess had drifted away in a haze, and the spectators slumbered around the execution site, the enchantress stepped from the chair and faced Roric.

"Now git the princess! Ride off, back to the Gorm Forest. I'll stay here."

"Yes!" Needing no further prompting, Roric strode forward, shoving through the crowd. He stepped over the somnolents, hundreds of them, and pressed his hand to his tunic pocket. "Hold on tight, Zinerva." Driven by haste, he soon reached the princess. He bent to lift her from the ground and enclose her in his arms, then retraced his steps. Precious minutes passed until he reached Radegunda again as he eased his way among the crowds, keeping his goal in sight.

With infinite care, Roric set Keriam facedown over the horse, the princess lax and easy to manage. Relieved to have a saddle now, he placed his foot in the stirrup and mounted, easing the princess closer to his body. He bade goodbye to Radegunda, his voice deep with happiness and gratitude. He would never forget this day, never forget Radegunda. He wished he had more time to reveal his appreciation, but he had to move. Urging the horse on, he headed away from the city, toward the forest.

Once past the warehouses that bordered the city's northern edge, he bent his head to address the fairy. "Zinerva, I could never have rescued the princess without your help. And I'm sorry you can't speak to her, after all."

"I can wait, major. Now it's time to return to the palace grounds," she said. "I miss all my friends there, human and fairy."

He patted her head. "Of course you do. And I hope to see you again soon."

"Right, sir." She crawled out of his pocket, her tiny fingers gripping his tunic material. "Please tell the princess how much I love her, and I hope to see her again soon. You, too, Roric Gamal." She jumped a little, then flew off. She turned to wave at him. "'Bye, major."

He returned the wave. "Goodbye, Zinerva."

The horse cantered past the warehouses on the city's outskirts. Keriam remained fast asleep as they clambered up a wooded hill that preceded the forest, then entered its woodsy depths, where leafless trees and evergreens hemmed them in. With the princess's body so close to his, wild thoughts taunted him, desires too long stifled.

Free of the city, Roric thought of Radegunda's rescue of the princess. Witchcraft!

Radegunda had told him the spell would save Keriam from execution and proclaim her innocence, yet she remained a fugitive from Balor. She dared not risk capture again. He resolved to dismiss his apprehensions. After all she'd endured, she surely could adjust to life in the forest, too.

But for how long? She must be restored to her rightful place as queen. And Balor must be eliminated. Roric squared his jaw, determined to make it happen.

* * *

Mindful of the need for haste, Radegunda watched Roric ride away, then faced the crowd again. Silently, she thanked the Goddess for Zinerva and Roric Gamal. She could never have rescued the princess herself. Besides, she liked to see the princess and the major together. Maybe something would come of their proximity in the forest.

The crowds stayed on the ground, a few showing signs of awakening. Now she must remove all traces of the execution site. Saying a special invocation and gathering her magic within her in one final burst of power, she aimed her arm toward the steel stake, then flipped her arm back. At first nothing happened, except a crackling sound and a wobbling of the stake. She repeated her spell, projecting all her skill in this one enchantment.

With a hiss and a cloud of smoke, the steel stake rose from the ground and sailed overhead. Radegunda waved her arms in the direction of the Orn Mountains, miles away. The stake, flashing in the bright sunlight, soared over the city and continued flying north. In the far distance, it landed on a sandstone outcrop, scattering rocks in all directions. An eagle squawked and flew away, its wings beating wildly.

After the stake disappeared, Radegunda used the same spell to remove all evidence of the execution site. Happy beyond her wildest imaginings but exhausted, too, she turned and plodded back to her store, her strength depleted. She smiled to herself, immensely satisfied with all that had happened this day.

Chapter Twenty-eight

Keriam moaned. Awkwardly, she raised her head, wondering why she lay facedown across a horse. A wooded, rocky hill loomed ahead, leading to the forest. The forest--no! Can't go there. Preceding the woods, a path wound through dark clusters of trees, the hard ground studded with shale and limestone. Vague thoughts hazed her brain, recollections just out of reach.

"Madam?" someone asked in a voice heavy with concern. She heard booted feet landing on the ground, then someone grasped her by the waist, his hands strong but gentle.

"Princess Keriam," he repeated, easing her off the sorrel, setting her on the ground.

Roric! Happiness and puzzlement collided inside her, combined with a strange, inexplicable lassitude.

She turned her head from side to side. "What happened? How did we get here in the forest? Why are we here?"

"Madam, Radegunda cast a spell--"

She pressed her hands to her burning cheeks, her terror returning. "The stake!"

He gave her a smile of assurance. "But you are safe now, madam."

Like a bolt of lightning in a midnight sky, it all came back to her: the plague, her trial and sentence of death by impalement. The last thing she remembered was being led to the stake, then a green mist that dizzied her and sent her toppling to the ground.

She shivered. But was she safe now, despite Roric Gamal's encouraging words? Would she ever be safe?

Roric undid the bronze clasp that held his cloak in place, then draped the wrap around her shoulders, his hands warm and comforting. "You are cold, madam. My apologies for not giving you my cloak sooner." He waited in silence as she fastened the clasp in place. "Radegunda proclaimed your innocence and convinced the crowds of it. And something I'll never forget--the Goddess appeared before the people and declared your innocence, too."

"Yes, the Goddess! Oh, I remember!" From now on, she would never doubt that miracles could happen. And that the Goddess would appear to save her was more than she had dared to wish for.

Roric frowned, twisting around to look back in the direction of the city. "But madam, you still remain a fugitive from Balor. We must seek sanctuary in the forest."

"Not there! Monsters!"

"No, madam." He reached a hand toward her, as if he wanted to touch her, then dropped his hand to his side. "Believe me, there are no monsters in the forest. A different kind of creatures, yes, but they are good folk. I already told them about you, told them I'd try to bring you here, if I could save you."

"And I haven't even thanked you for rescuing me. If it hadn't been for you . . ." She shuddered again, unable to say more. You and the Goddess. I'll never forget this day.

"Rescue, yes. I'll save that story for another day. For now, suffice it to say that Radegunda and Zinerva are true friends. But madam, we must hurry! One of the city's sentries might come after us. Best if you ride in front of me."

"Then let's go!" Trembling from her recent ordeal, Keriam disregarded her shock. Her fury at Balor overrode every other emotion. She wanted to kill him now.

"Here, let me help you." He lifted her on the horse, making sure she was back far enough, then placed his foot in the stirrup and mounted again. He heeled the sorrel into a canter, skirting towering trees and thick understory. She slid back against his hard chest as they ascended the hill, but Roric maintained a firm perch on the animal, slowing the horse to a trot. They plunged through the dark woods, sending a doe and her fawn scurrying, their white tails bobbing.

"For now," Roric said, "it's best if you stay with us in the forest. Believe me, these forest people won't hurt you." He smiled. "I'm a fugitive from Balor, too. And Conneid and his wife–"

"Conneid and Malvina . . . in the forest?" she asked, her voice rising, surprised to discover they were so close, and that she'd soon meet them again. She smiled, happier than she'd been in a long time, to know that she'd live here among friends . . . and

Roric. And Roric, she mused, surely he was a friend. More than just a friend, a secret part of her heart reminded her head.

"All three of us," Roric said. "We've been living with the outlanders--our name for them--since we escaped the palace." He nodded. "So I'll be here, along with Conneid and Malvina."

She looked at him closely, as if seeing him for the first time. "And you--you have a beard." She longed to reach out and touch him, feel his skin beneath her fingers, know the strength of his arms. If he took her in his arms now, she could never resist him, could never refuse him. In spite of her recent ordeal, all she'd endured since her capture, Roric and he alone claimed her every thought, her every desire.

He fingered the nascent growth. "Good disguise, this beard. I think I'll keep it for awhile." He paused. "For now, we must all live in the forest. Until we overthrow Balor–"

"We must!" She diverted her mind from thoughts of Roric, for surely they were futile wishes, a longing that could never come true. "We can't permit him to rule . . . misrule the country." If only they could rid the country of this evil usurper now, imprison him and put him on trial, and pray that he'd get the death penalty. Then send him to the Underworld!

"Overthrow Balor, yes, as soon as we can. I've been on your side all along, madam," he said with a wry smile. Dead leaves and bracken crunched beneath the horse's hooves, skeletal branches swaying in a cool breeze. Oaks, maples, and hickories surrounded them, their tangled branches reaching to the sky. A dense undergrowth of golden hay-scented fern carpeted the forest floor, its aroma mingling with the dank smell of the woods. Strange, long-winged birds tenanted the upper limbs, winging from branch to branch, squawking in the cool air.

Stirred by the sights and sounds of the forest, she brought her mind back to his query. "Major, I hated you serving that fiend, Balor." She gave him a questioning glance. "Why did you do it?"

"I was doing it for the good of the country." He shoved a low-hanging branch out of the way, holding it back for her as he maneuvered the horse past. "As hard as it may be to believe, I was serving you, too." He sighed. "Princess Keriam, please understand one thing. My allegiance is to you and you alone, always has been, always will be. I would give my life for you–"His voice broke, and he turned away.

She squeezed his hand, speechless for several moments, more grateful than she could ever express that she had earned such devotion. "I understand, major." She kept silent then, busy with her thoughts, hearing the muffled clop of the horse's hooves on the packed pine floor. She wondered what the torathors looked like, these creatures that inhabited these woods. Did they speak her language? Would they accept her their future queen?

"Something I must tell you." Roric steered the horse among the thick clusters of trees, his strong hands clasping the reins. "These folk may not accept you as their princess at first."

She gasped, as if he could read her mind.

He jerked his head around. "Madam?"

She adjusted her position on the horse. "So I must win their trust." But how?

"Princess, I fear there's more to their acceptance than that. They told me you must prove that you have special powers, that you can do something extraordinary they can't do."

"Then they have set an impossible task for me," she lied. Could she finally use one of her abilities to her benefit, or to theirs? For a long time, she'd suppressed her ability to read others' minds by touching them, because the bombardment of images had often proved difficult to absorb. Was it time to resurrect this power? She'd wait and see what transpired, what opportunity arose.

"Let us not worry about the matter now," Roric said in his encouraging way.

Much later, a burst of sunlight, coupled with talk and laughter, told Keriam they'd reached their destination as Roric pushed aside an oak branch to reveal a vast meadow. She heard the rushing waters of the Deuona River in the distance, but thick groups of pines along both banks hid the river from view.

"Here we are." At the edge of the grassland, Roric slid off the horse, then reached for her, his hands warm and gentle around her waist. His face held a look she wished she could fathom, one of deep intensity. She landed on the hard ground, her dress falling to her ankles. Staring around her, she saw the limestone caves to her far right, the caverns backed by grassy mounds.

At their arrival, men, women, and children emerged from the caves, the tallest creatures she'd ever seen, talking in a guttural language she hoped to learn. The women wore plain sack dresses of deerskin, the men wearing shirts and leggings of the same. Young children clung to their mothers' legs, giving her bashful glances. And their hair! The women wore their black and shiny locks to their waist. The men wore theirs in pigtails. Soon, several hundred people had gathered in the clearing, forming a half-circle, their eyes wide with interest.

A stocky man she assumed was the chief approached them, speaking to Roric in a strange language, a staccato speech from deep in the throat. After Roric answered him, the chief looked her up and down, a doubtful frown on his face, then spoke again in his language.

Keriam glanced from one to the other, wishing she understood their speech. However, she got her answer soon enough.

"The chief, Dorn, tells me that the women have prepared a cave for you," Roric translated. "Hardly an abode fit for a princess, but it will have to do for now. Even though they don't accept you as their ruler, as an unmarried female with no relatives here, you must live by yourself. An odd regulation, I'll grant you, but we must abide by their customs."

"Yes, of course. After what I've been through these last few moonphases, I'm sure a cave will suit me fine." A cool breeze sprang up, fluttering her dress around her ankles, blowing her hair across her face. Tucking the locks behind her ears, she flashed a smile at all these strange creatures, hoping her countenance proved a first step in gaining acceptance.

Roric turned and spoke to Dorn in the torathor tongue. The chief nodded, apparently satisfied with the answer. The other villagers remained unmoving and stared at her, their gazes traveling from her head to her feet as they chattered in that strange staccato language.

Two familiar humans headed their way, the most welcome sight in a long time. Besides Roric.

"Conneid! Malvina!" Keriam rushed forward to greet them. "And your new baby!" Dismissing formalities, they all hugged each other, everyone speaking at once.

So glad to have her friends with her, Keriam felt she'd made a good start on adjustment. But this was only her first day. Much time remained that she must stay here, until they destroyed Balor.

If they could destroy the fiend.

* * *

Two days after the princess's rescue, Radegunda felt she had regained her magical power enough to rid the city of the plague, a purification spell she should have performed long ago. If only her skill had been great enough then, she would have prevented the plague in the first place and saved the princess from her shameful trial and imprisonment. She could have saved hundreds of people from a painful death, she lamented, since poring over her books on magic.

Long after darkness had fallen on the city, she sat in her kitchen chair and worked by the light of an oil lamp, fashioning a doll out of cloth scraps she'd collected over the years. She painted eyes, nose, and mouth on its face, then painted large black spots on its body to represent the black fever pustules. She wrapped a leaf of angelica around it and tied it with a string to keep the leaf in place, heartened by the herb's sweet fragrance. Would it work? It had to!

Satisfied with her creation, she left her apartment in the deepest hour of night, while the rest of the city slept, except for the tavern dwellers, pleasure women, and vagrants who roamed the streets. Clouds blocked the moon and hid the stars, conditions that greatly aided her purpose. With resolute strides, she headed north to the warehouses on the city's outskirts. Looking in every direction, she prayed she'd elude the city sentries. If she were captured . . . No! She wouldn't think about that. Her heart beat fast with every step, her thick shoes scuffling along the cobblestones.

She clutched the doll, crushing the leaf until she was forced to ease her grip. At the end of Perfume Lane, a mongrel dog rummaged through overturned garbage, growling at her. She hastened on until she came to Pleasure Alley, the women there roaming the street while calling out to the occasional man. Past the many shops, then on past countless other side streets and alleys, she finally reached Warehouse Street, next to a wide oak and a clump of earthberry bushes.

Holding the doll aloft, she invoked the fire spell, one she'd practiced again and again by the river. Magic quivered and sang inside her, a living thing, a powerful entity.

Ragegunda waited long minutes as the doll grew warm, then sizzling hot in her hand. The smell of smoke filled the air; then smoke drifted upward, and soon the doll burst into flames. Yet she waited a while longer before releasing it, until it singed her fingers. She ignored the pain, and with one last surge of power, tossed the doll onto a wooden warehouse that claimed a large portion of the street.

The witch raised her arms, her voice rising to the sky.

Aithnea, goddess of fire
Cernuna, goddess of healing
Let this fire perform its magic
Destroy the plague and save the people

I beseech you in the name of the Earth-Mother
Goddess who rules over all.

The building grew hot, the heat intense from where she stood. Dull embers became crackling flames that leaped from its walls, in no time spreading to other structures. Clouds of smoke wafted heavenward, driven by a strong northerly wind. Aided by the dry air, the conflagration widened, and minutes later, flames neared the city's finer shops, these made of sandstone, bluestone, and sarsenstone.

Radegunda watched in gratified fascination, certain the smoke would destroy the pestilence. At the same time, she prayed that her magic was strong enough to stop the spell she'd begun. Now she would--

"Fire!"

"The city is burning!"

Drunkards stumbled from taverns, and sentries cried in fright, their voices infused with a sense of helplessness. Doors banged back, light spilling onto the cobblestones. People rushed onto the streets, crying and pointing, praying to the Goddess. Soon howling, fearful mobs filled the streets, shouting and pointing, glancing in all directions.

About a block from Warehouse Street, a sentry looked her way. "You! What are you doing here? Did you start this fire?" Drawing his sword from its scabbard, he raced in her direction.

Goddess, give me time. Radegunda raised her arms again, then abruptly dropped them to her side. The fire slackened, then stopped, until only the stench of smoke and a few gray wisps tainted the air. Blackened boards toppled to the ground, falling onto the street with a crash. But the insides of the warehouses remained intact, their contents untouched, protected by her magic.

"After her!"

"She must be a witch. Get her!"

Shouting and screaming, the townspeople joined the hunt, their footsteps ringing on the cobblestones.

Fear consumed Radegunda as the men rushed toward her. Fright and fury infected their faces. With scarcely a minute to spare, she hid behind a bush and shapeshifted to a rabbit. The darkness obscuring her brown fur, she dashed around a corner, soon disappearing from sight.

A sentry reached the bush first, staring wildly from side to side. "What?" His sword drawn, he slashed at the bush and sent leaves flying in all directions. "By Endora, where did she go?"

Others joined him, talking excitedly among themselves. Some grabbed incinerated boards and waved the weapons in barbarous rage. Banging, shouting, and cursing filled the streets.

"Where is she?"

"How could the witch disappear so quickly?"

"If we catch her, she'll burn at the stake."

Afraid to look behind her, Radegunda raced through the streets. Her pulse raced, her gaze darting from right to left. If they caught her, they'd cook her for stew. She must hurry! She darted

310

around winding alleys, following the twists and turns of the city's many side streets.

At last! The back entrance of her store came in sight. Gathering her strength, she hopped high onto the windowsill, thankful she'd left the window open, and landed on the floor below with a soft thud. Safe once more, she changed back into her human form, doing this in a leisurely fashion.

In the coming days, she was aware she must conceal her identity, in the unlikely chance someone would recognize her and connect her with the fire. She dyed her hair blonde and, still bound by caution, kept to her shop. She sent Adsaluta to purchase food or needed supplies, giving a stiff and painful knee as her excuse.

The smell of smoke hung over the city for days, but warehouse owners soon rebuilt their establishments.

And the plague vanished from the city.

* * *

On a cool morning shortly after Keriam's arrival, Roric found the princess sitting on a boulder in the river, clad in deerskin like the outlander women, washing a brown cotton dress. A tremendous wave of happiness overcame him, and for a few moments, he stopped to stare at her, even though the deerskin hid the alluring soft curves of her body . The blue, foaming waters of the Deuona glistened in the bright sunshine, its waters lapping up onto the shore. Evergreens towered along its banks, and tall grasses and wildflowers flourished in the sandy soil. Pine needles coated the hard ground, the scent of pine carried by a strong northerly wind.

Pleased to see her hair restored to its lustrous black, he regretted that her hands remained rough and calloused, her skin a deep tan. Yesterday, he'd risked another visit to the city, and now he was eager to tell her the news.

First tugging his boots and socks off, he splashed through the water and sat on a boulder beside her, forcing himself to speak in a level voice. More than anything, he wanted to take her in his arms, hold her close. "Madam, I visited Radegunda yesterday."

Dripping wet dress in hand, she looked up from her washing. "How is she? She has done so much for me!"

"And for everyone, the city, all the people. She has rid Moytura of the plague. One of her . . . spells. She didn't tell me what kind of spell and I didn't ask."

The princess closed her eyes for a moment. "Thank the Goddess," she breathed. "It's enough that she did it. If only she could have performed her spell sooner . . ." She gazed off into the distance, then sighed. "Well, at least it's over." Standing up, she motioned for him to head for the riverbank again, she walking alongside him. Back on the bank again, she wrung the water from her dress and spread it on the ground to dry. They both sat down on the dry grass, she with her legs stretched out. He looked her way, at her long legs and slim body, her full breasts straining against the bodice of her dress. He yearned to lie with her on the grass, to make love to her as he'd wanted for so long, too long! Forbidden thoughts taunted him and reckless desires warmed his body. If only she were not the future queen, and if he were not her servant. His imagination soared, his yearnings telling him that he could love again. But love for the princess? A hopeless love; far better to dismiss his longing for this woman, so far out of reach. He shifted his position and forced himself to act normal, to pretend she meant nothing to him.

"And you, madam, how are you managing here? You seem to be adjusting."

Smiling, she indicated the garment she wore. "A child's frock. The women's are too long for me. I hope to learn the tasks they perform so well, such as making clothes out of deerskin and sewing them with deer sinew. But I spend little of my time in the cave, except in the late evening and at night, when I sleep."

Wiping her wet hands on her skirt, she gave him a worried glance. "They tell me the chief's daughter is sick. Do you know anything about this?"

"No, only that her illness is recent, within the last few days or so," he said, settling back on the cold ground. "She is fifteen, I believe. They say the sickness is in her head. Won't eat but what they spoon feed her. Won't talk, just stares off into space."

Braced on her elbows, the princess leaned back, frowning. "Strange. I must visit her, see if there is any way I can help." She sighed. "But I don't know how, especially since I don't speak their language well. If only I could do something for these people, repay the many kindnesses they have afforded me . . ."

Reflecting on her life within the past year, she thought of all that had happened to her. So many changes!

But she would overcome all hindrances, do anything to rid the kingdom of Balor and gain the throne.

* * *

That evening, while darkness descended over the settlement and the air chilled with a fierce north wind, Roric left his cave dwelling to visit Princess Keriam again, needing to spend time with her, listen to her voice, see her smile. This woman had come to mean much to him, more than he wanted to admit. He hoped to find her alone.

Minutes later, he sank down on the cold limestone floor of her cave, across the smoldering fire from the princess. A small cavern, it had a beauty of its own. Streams of calcite draped from the ceiling to the floor, an adornment that never failed to awe him. Colorful paintings from long ago decorated the walls, of wild animals known only to the Gorm Forest.

The firelight flickered across her face, casting a golden glow on her dark hair. His gaze rested on her hands, those once delicate fingers, now rough and calloused. He'd give anything to take her from this crude habitat, to see her restored to the throne at Emain Macha. Yet she accepted this primitive home without complaint.

She changed her position on the cold floor, drawing her legs to the side, her dress demurely covering her ankles. "It seems I have many loyal followers." She inclined her head toward the other caves. "The torathors--but we can't call them that, can we?"

"I call them outlanders, for lack of a better word."

"Ah, yes, the outlanders." She tilted her head, as if thinking it over. "If we ever overthrow Balor--"

"We will, madam. Never doubt it. Conditions will not always be so, princess. Someday you will take your place as rightful queen." And he would do everything in his power to aid her, to restore her to the throne. And then what? Leave the palace, he agonized, for it would hurt too much to see her day after day, to know there could never be anything between them.

She tucked her long hair behind her ears and edged closer to the fire. "I'm willing to wait, major, but not for long. For the good of the people, we must soon rid the kingdom of Balor."

"We can't do it alone," he said. "If we can acquire King Barzad's aid--"

"Do you think he'll help us, since the treaty is now invalid?"

"I hope to persuade the Elegians that it's to their benefit to defeat Balor. We all know he has designs on the whole continent." He turned away for a moment, then focused his gaze on her. "But they may not know of your father's . . . assassination."

She sat upright. "They don't know!" She pressed her hand to her breast, a baffled expression on her face. "How could they not?"

"Trade caravans can't get through because of brigands that prowl the trade routes. Possibly Balor has lied to the ambassadors from other countries on the continent. No doubt he's told them of King Tencien's death due to natural causes."

"The fiend!"

"My thoughts exactly, princess. Within the next nineday, I intend to journey to Elegia, convince King Barzad that Balor has killed your father and usurped the throne."

"Major, you must." She eased back. "To think he doesn't know the truth!" She sighed. "If only I could go with you, I would, but if there is any way I can help cure the chief's daughter, then it is better for me to stay here. I would want to do help her anyway, for the child's sake, but in addition, it is important that we gain the outlanders' goodwill."

Roric stretched one leg out. "I'll do my best to convince him otherwise. But we can't fight the tyrant Balor until spring, at the earliest."

She nodded. "When we overthrow Balor, you should persuade these outlanders to help defeat him. The main reason why I should stay here."

"You've got a good point there. And as for their aid, I've already thought about that. They have a weapon--they call it a sling--"

"Yes!" Enthusiasm brightened her face. "I've seen them with it."

"Looks easy to use. I can see them employing this weapon in battle."

"A battle." She shook her head in helpless confusion. "We have no army, nothing to match Balor's manpower." She stared at the embers, then slowly switched her gaze back to him. "Surely by now there is much discontent among the soldiers. I've heard that they're confined to their barracks for many moonphases, never allowed to visit their families. I've heard, too, that Balor has promoted his friends and overlooked the more deserving soldiers."

He grimaced. "His political friends who know nothing of fighting, can't even handle a damn sword!" He bit his lip. "Pardon my language, madam."

"I feel the same way, major. And by now, the soldiers must be ready to revolt." She aimed a level gaze at him. "Don't you agree?"

He nodded, hoping to inject confidence in his voice, an assurance he was far from feeling. "There is much we can build on, and I intend to work on this in the coming moonphases--making contact with any of these soldiers I commanded in the past . . . if I can."

"You're taking a big chance, major. You risk capture again. If you are captured . . ."

"Let us talk about something else, madam." He stared around her habitation, at the paintings on the wall. "Do you keep busy here? I know idleness never suited you."

"Ah, yes." She twisted around to indicate a series of limestone shelves behind her. "You see these pottery jars? The women here have been helping me prepare dried vegetables and herbs for the coming winter." She nodded. "I do keep busy."

The cave grew colder, prompting her to wrap her robe tighter around her and stir the embers with a stick. The flames leaped, the cave brighter now.

"Do you mind if I ask you about your wife?" she said, catching him by surprise. "She died several years ago? Please," she said with a wave of her hand, "perhaps I'm being too inquisitive. If so, forgive my questions."

"Not at all, princess." He thought for a moment, stifling painful memories that still clutched at his heart. "She died in childbirth. Soon after, my son sickened and died."

"Ah, Goddess! How . . . how did your wife die?"

"She bled to death." He bowed his head as conflicting thoughts raged through his mind. "A witch delivered the baby. I've always blamed their deaths on sorcery. Now, I don't know." Roric thought about Radegunda and the magic spell she'd employed to save the princess. Had he been mistaken about witchcraft all these years? He must reconsider his fears of magic, but he dared not express an opinion, since the craft was outlawed in the kingdom.

"I had a cousin who bled to death in childbirth." Keriam's voice was soft and low. "Perhaps it's not that uncommon, as tragic as it is for the family."

She scraped a stick back and forth on the floor. "When I gain the throne--"

"And you will."

Keriam gave him that heartwarming smile that made him long to take her in his arms. "When I gain the throne, I intend to establish a tribunal of druids who will issue rulings on witchcraft. We both know there are those who practice evil bewitchment," she said, reminding him of Aradia, "and they must not be permitted to practice their wicked craft. But it's just as true that witches can do much good. We should encourage them in their endeavors."

She glanced at him from under her eyelashes. "Perhaps this is the time for confessions."

"Confessions, madam?"

"I must tell you that I have preternatural powers, but I don't practice witchcraft," she said quickly. "However, I've always feared people might mistake my powers for that very thing. For one thing, I can spirit travel--"

"Then it was you I saw when I returned to the palace at night, several moonphases ago."

"Yes, I was spying on Aradia. I saw her . . . saw her change into a jackal."

"Ah! I'd heard about that sorceress, about her shapeshifting." He paused. "Something I've wanted to tell you for the longest time--Aradia was your father's assassin, so--"

"Goddess!" She tilted her head at him. "I suspected her all along, but how do you know it was Aradia?"

He told her about discovering the dress and arrow the night of the assassination. "No doubt in my mind. Balor and Aradia conspired to murder your father. May they both rot in the Underworld!"

She covered her face with her hands. "If only I could have prevented my father's death! If I could have stopped them in time . . ."

"Madam, you did everything possible. No one could have done more," he said, expressing his own regrets, hoping to alleviate hers.

"Aradia is dead now, either from the plague or killed by a guard. I've heard different stories." Her expression hardened. "And you know what? I'm glad she's dead! My only regret is I didn't kill her first!"

"I should have killed her long ago!" He broke a stick in his hands, a vein throbbing at his temple. Damn the bitch!

Silent moments passed, a time when Roric wanted to give her the comfort he knew she longed for. She had borne her burdens herself for far too long. Ah, to hold her close, kiss those lips, make love . . .These longings will get you nowhere, he lamented, for she is so far above you. "I have to learn to get past my father's murder," she said. "Better to think about getting rid of Balor and returning to Emain Macha." She fixed him with a level gaze. "But I wanted to say something else about my abilities. Several moonphases ago, I saw you with other officers by the meadow--"

"No wonder you thought I plotted against the king! But you understand now--"

"I understand you only pretended to take part in the plot. Actually, major, I came to that conclusion a long time ago. It was only that I resented--very much--your serving Balor. But I see now that was for the best. If you hadn't resided in the palace and served Balor, Conneid Delbraith would never have escaped." She spoke in a rush of words then, explaining her "accidental" meeting with him in the capital long ago. She told him how her emotions often get the best of her, "as when your mug broke in the tavern," she said, finally clarifying so many things he'd puzzled over for a long time.

"I must learn to control my talents." Keriam bit her lower lip. "Perhaps curses is a better word. I often wish I didn't have these abilities."

"But they have served you in good stead." Seeing the fire dying, he reached to a pile of logs behind him and placed another one on the fire. The flames wavered and caught, then increased again.

"When I am queen, I shall rule that good magic be permitted in the kingdom."

When Keriam is queen, he repeated to himself, determined to do all in his power to make it happen. And then what? Would he be able to attend her, even if she needed his help? He wondered how he could bear to see her day after day, to know that she ranked so far above him, to see her marry another. If she required his services, he had no choice but to stay, if only he could bear seeing her day after day, longing for her so. Otherwise, he'd leave her, return to visit his family in Mumhain and later become a mercenary.

And never see her again.

Chapter Twenty-nine

"Madam, I fear I failed in my mission to Elegia. King Barzad does not recognize the danger from Balor. I tried to convince him of Balor's hand in Tencien's murder, but he didn't believe me. Our false king reached Elegia ahead of us. He had already sent a messenger to that country saying King Tencien died of a heart attack." Roric shook his head. "Sacred shrine!"

Keriam's stomach knotted with hurt anger. "Why should I be surprised? It's as we suspected." Tears of fury filled her eyes. She brushed them away and sat up straighter.

Inside her cave, Keriam looked at Roric across the fire, saw his dark eyes, his dark hair falling to his shoulders, but more than anything, his look of exhaustion. Returned from Elegia only an hour ago after a trip of over two ninedays, he sat cross legged on the limestone floor, drinking a mug of her chamomile tea. The firelight cast wavy shadows across his tanned face, a face etched with fatigue and disappointment. In spite of her anger, she couldn't get enough of him. He had never looked so wonderful, and she realized now, as if she needed a reminder, how much she had missed him during his absence.

Roric opened his hands wide. "I offered every possible argument for overthrowing the usurper. But Barzad told me--and these are his words, madam--that Balor has always appeared a trustworthy and honorable man." Roric snorted. "Trustworthy! Honorable!"

She bunched her fists. "What is the matter with King Barzad? Why can't he see the danger that faces him?" She waved a hand. "No need to answer, major. We all know Balor is a liar. And that is the least of his sins." She drew a deep breath, shifting her position on the cold, rocky floor. "You did your best. No one could expect more."

Inside the cave, she stirred the fire and wrapped her bear robe closer about her shoulders. Comfort was difficult to come by, for although the fire warmed the front part of her body, cold air vexed her back. A vent overhead drew out much of the smoke, yet a smoky haze stung her eyes. Darkness cloaked the forest, the firelight providing scant illumination.

"I expected more," Roric said bitterly. "What does it take to make Barzad see the danger from Balor? Does he intend to wait until the fiend marches on Elegia? Without Barzad to help us defeat Balor--"

"Without Barzad, we must try something else." She sipped her tea, giving her time to think, time to get her emotions under control. Damn Balor to the Underworld! May he rot there for all eternity."

"Try something else? Like what, madam? The other countries on the continent remain weak."

"You spoke once of a possible mutiny within the army." She could tell the major's exhaustion prevented clear thought. Any other time, he wouldn't sound so discouraged.

"A rebellion . . . yes, if I can contact any of my former men now serving Balor." Roric scowled. "A chancy thing, that, attempting to get in touch with any of Balor's officers. I might as well return to the palace and shout, 'Here I am, back again.' And get captured by the palace guards."

"You must not endanger yourself." She turned away for a moment, thinking hard, but a reasonable scheme for Balor's overthrow eluded her. "Major, I understand your discouragement, but I'm certain by tomorrow you will be your confident self again."

He sighed. "Let us hope so. Right now–"

"You've had a tiring, upsetting journey." She nodded. "Together, we'll work something out." She sipped her tea again and dabbed a cotton cloth across her lips.

Outside, rain fell, beginning as a sprinkle, audible inside the cave, soon becoming a torrent. The bearskin cover at the entrance vibrated in a cold wind. Raindrops dripped through the limestone ceiling, forcing Keriam and Roric to move to another spot. Thunder rumbled in the distance.

"We have many moonphases to prepare, a long time to work out a plan," she said after a pause. She hesitated, then reached for his hand. The feel of his skin seemed so right, so good,

320

hinting at some nebulous thing she'd waited for all her life. He squeezed her hand in response, and they exchanged a smile. "Things are bound to work out for us, major." Suddenly self-conscious, she withdrew her hand. She felt cold, bereft, as if the fire had gone out, as if complete darkness had descended on the cave. "The Goddess will not permit evil to reign for long within the kingdom."

"You will forgive me if I do not share your optimism. I have seen much wickedness in this life."

"But the Goddess always prevails. And good wins out over evil." Even while she said the words, she realized how childish, how naive she sounded. She feared life didn't always work out that way.

"Then let us hope the Goddess prevails against Balor. And that by this time next year, you'll have gained your rightful place as queen of Avador." He gave her a wary glance. "And as queen, you must choose a husband . . . a nobleman, perhaps, from one of the other countries. You must continue the royal line." He made a dismissive gesture. "Please forgive my bold words. I fear I'm not thinking well tonight."

She stared into the fire, then raised her head to look at him again. "No, let us speak of it. I can't marry a man I don't love." She recalled her parents' marriage, a happy one, filled with love. If only she could marry for love . . . Not a chance!

"What does love have to do with a royal union?" he asked. "I daresay few royal marriages are formed on that basis. But it's also true that love often follows marriage. If not love, then mutual affection and respect."

Affection and respect! She wanted more than that from her husband. What a dull and lifeless marriage it would be, otherwise. She wanted a passionate love that would last for the rest of her life. And that's a foolish wish, she fretted. As if a passionate love would ever come her way!

"Once you gain the throne, madam, there will be ample opportunities to meet noblemen from other countries. You will not lack for suitors," he said with an encouraging smile, but a look of sorrow crossed his face, too, or did she only imagine his expression?

"If I loved a man, it wouldn't matter what station in life he held." She drew her robe ever closer against the evening's biting chill. "I won't marry a man I don't love and who doesn't love me." She glanced across the fire and caught his gaze on her, his look clear and direct. And full of promise? Now she was dreaming a foolish dream. She worked her hands under her robe, wrapping her arms around her waist.

She squared her jaw. "But first we must overthrow Balor. After that, I shall gain the throne."

Roric nodded. "To do that, we need the army behind us." He stood, easing his cloak around his shoulders. "Forgive me, madam, but best I seek my own cave now. These past two ninedays have been tiring, not to mention upsetting. I fear I am not good company now."

"Good night, Roric." And you are good company anytime. I could never tire of seeing you, talking to you. If only I could kiss you...

As much as she hated Balor, as much as she wanted to gain the throne, Roric was all she could think of, his presence still alive in her memory. Long after he'd departed into the rain, she wished she could draw him back and hold him, keep him with her throughout the cold night. But her wish would forever remain out of reach.

* * *

Kneeling down on the cold limestone floor beside the girl, Keriam raised her eyes to the chief, a strong-muscled, stocky man of middle age who stood next to his wife. Both of them looked heartsick, their faces haggard with worry and fatigue. She must cure their daughter, for the child's sake and theirs, but also to gain the chief's trust. She must have him on her side in any future confrontation with Balor.

"What is your daughter's name?" she asked in their language.

"Lina," the wife replied. "Ah, if you can help her! We have tried. Our healer can't do anything." She shook her head, staring down at the floor.

322

The girl lay silent and still, staring off to a place only she could see. Keriam reached for her hand and found it ice cold. Beyond her, the cave stretched in fathomless darkness, the sound of rushing water in the distance.

"What can you tell me about her sickness?"

The chief tapped his head. "The sickness is here. Why, we don't know. We must feed her, give her water. She is like a baby." His voice broke and he turned away.

"I'll try to help if I can," Keriam said. If only she could! If she could resurrect her powers, those she had suppressed--

"How can you help, woman? What can you do that we can't?" A look of belligerence crossed the chief's face.

Keriam chose her words carefully. "I have . . . special powers. Often I can tell what a person is thinking just by touching him. Sometimes I can tell what has happened or will happen to that person."

Dorn's eyes widened. "Magic!"

"Magic!" his wife echoed.

Keriam smiled. "Some may call it that. I think of it as an extraordinary talent." She drew her legs behind her and settled her gaze on Lina again. "Is she your only child?"

The mother tore at her hair and scratched her face. "Ah! We had a son, but he died before you came." She pointed to the girl. "Now this!"

"Talmora!" Keriam's eyes misted. "Let me see what I can do. I'll touch her head, see what images I can pick up."

"Yes, if only you-"

"Quiet!" the chief admonished his wife. Chastened, she nodded and covered her face.

Closing her eyes, Keriam leaned over and placed her hands lightly on either side of Lina's head. Only darkness emerged, no visions, no thoughts. Keriam remained that way for countless minutes, stifling all other concerns, all her energy and power focused on the girl.

Long moments passed and pictures gradually emerged. She saw a young boy of eight or nine lying in the cave, his face shiny with sweat, a high fever causing delirium. She saw the girl bathing his brow with cold water, her face troubled, her hands shaking.

The scene shifted. She saw the boy reposed in a deep grave as the villagers threw flowers on his body. Pottery jars and deerskin pouches lay by his side, food and prized possessions to take with him on his spirit journey. The chief and his wife wept beside the grave. The daughter stood motionless, a stunned expression on her face.

Back in the here and now, Keriam sat in silent absorption, concentrating on every impression, every vision she received. The girl's thoughts gradually penetrated, and Keriam surmised her mental illness had been building inside her for a while.

"Ah!" Keriam sank back on the floor.

"Woman! What is it?" The chief's wife wrung her hands. "Tell us!"

Keriam pushed herself to her feet, searching for the right words. "She blames herself for her brother's death."

"But why?" the mother asked, her forehead wrinkled in bafflement. "It wasn't her fault. Our son . . ." She struggled for composure. "Our son died of a sickness. He had a high fever."

"But Lina was alone with him when he died?" Keriam looked from one to the other, full of sympathy for the grief they shared, but also, needing more information to help heal their daughter.

"It couldn't be helped!" Tears streamed down the chief's face. "If only we had known how sick . . ." He swiped his hand across his eyes. His wife sobbed, her shoulders shaking. "Many of our people had this same illness, and they all recovered. We didn't know . . ." He took a deep breath. "I had to go hunting with the men, and my wife--"

"I had to deliver a baby, and--"

"Please." Keriam raised her hand. "The circumstances don't matter. What is important is that she blames herself. What we must do--what I must do--is stay with her for a long time every day and try to make her understand your son's death was not her fault." Could she do it? She had never performed this feat before, had never projected her thoughts into someone else's mind. But she had to try.

Day after day, Keriam sat for long moments with the comatose girl. She caressed Lina's face and spoke soothing words meant to comfort. She repeated again and again, Your brother's death is not your fault. After one nineday, the girl remained catatonic. Keriam despaired that she would ever cure her.

She must rid her own mind of problems, of her hatred for Balor and anxiety for the kingdom, for such distractions would prevent her from healing Lina. But she couldn't drive Balor from her mind. She wondered what evil he was devising now.

* * *

"I fear a revolt, sire."

"What?" Balor sat back in his chair, giving his Minister of War a long look across the desk. Recently finished with sword practice, Balor wiped a silk handkerchief across his sweaty brow. A human head, embalmed in cedar oil and mounted on an ivory stand, gazed out from his oaken desk. "What makes you think this?"

Duncan Cuillaigh squirmed in his chair. "Perhaps I should say 'possible revolt'. I've heard of much discontent among the soldiers and officers. Sire, I fear they are close to a mutiny. They haven't been permitted leave since--"

"A leave, pah! Are we training soldiers, or supervising a nursery? They must learn the virtue of abstinence. Round up the ringleaders, make an example of them. One-hundred lashes for each. That should prevent further trouble."

Cullaigh shook his head. "Too many, sire. The discontent is concentrated in the fifteenth and sixteenth battalions, over eighteen-hundred men."

"I see." Balor pondered long and hard. "So, two battalions." He scratched his scar, still searching for a solution. "Here's what I want you to do. Send them to the northern border. I want them to build winter quarters there, practice maneuvers. Tell them we must counter Elegia's aggressive moves."

"Aggressive moves, sire?"

Balor slammed his fist on the desk. "Use your imagination, man! Tell the men Elegia is preparing for war. Let them think we're in danger from that country. We'll have the disgruntled men out of the way."

"An excellent plan, sire." Cullaigh sat forward. "I suggest we send them north under cover of darkness, when the stores are closed and few people crowd the streets. No doubt some will hear them, but the fewer, the better. No point in arousing the populace now. Later--"

"Later, I'll tell the people Elegia is making warlike moves against us." Balor reached over and caressed the human head on his desk. "And I tell you, Cuillaigh, come spring, we will march against that country. If--when--we conquer Elegia, we will acquire their seaports and sources of wealth. Emerald mines!" His eyes gleamed. "And after Elegia, we will move on the other countries. Soon the whole continent will be ours!"

* * *

These visits are getting to be a habit, Keriam mused as Roric joined her one evening, visits she anticipated, never needing to question the reason why.

"We were speaking of magic not long ago," she reminded him, wanting to lead into the subject again. Heavy rains had soaked the ground for days, and now winter approached with a cold, northerly wind. The first light snow dusted the ground outside her cave. She blew on her hands to warm them, mindful that she must make mittens for herself soon.

"Ah, magic!" He smiled. "Perhaps we can use it for good."

"My feeling, too. There is good magic and bad, don't you agree?" At his answering nod, she went on. "I've had much time to think on so many things during these past few ninedays. I see nothing wrong and everything beneficial if I permit the practice of good magic in the kingdom. And," she said with a question in her voice, "something tells me you feel the same."

Frowning, he ran his finger along the frozen ground, then looked her way. "Once, not so long ago, I feared magic, kept my distance from Radegunda. But you are right, madam. Such enchantment can do much good. However, as Avador's ruler, you must ensure that bad magic never takes hold again."

"Of course. Here's what I plan to do. I intend to employ several druids to rule on what is good magic and what is evil, then codify their finds, have them recorded in a volume. I'll encourage the good to flourish, but anyone caught practicing black magic will be punished, not," she said, holding up a hand, "as severely as Balor has decreed for any transgression. But harshly enough to show those who employ the craft to apply only the good.

"I'm sure my plan will work. Something else–even though I don't practice witchcraft, I've found within the past year that I can use my special abilities to advantage. I will continue to do so, and if I can learn the craft, so much the better."

"You said something about special abilities?"

She nodded. "Often I can tell what a person is thinking just by touching him."

He smiled, a teasing tone in his voice. "Touch me and tell me what I'm thinking."

She hesitated, wanting to do more than just touch him, wanting to be held in his arms, feel his lips on hers. Goddess, she wanted him now, this very moment, more than she'd ever wanted anything or anyone.

"Madam?"

She touched him then, letting her hand rest on his, loving the feel of his skin. "Ah." Her face warming, she drew back, the heat spreading throughout her body. She'd never known a man could arouse her this way, and to read his thoughts, to know that . . . "You think I'm beautiful."

"You have always been beautiful to me." He leaned closer, a look of deep purpose on his face. "Madam, I . . ."

Outside the cave, children laughed, their mothers calling them to bedtime. Men shouted and joked, and the golden moment with Roric faded, never, she feared, to be repeated. She wanted to cry from disappointment. She caught the expression on his face and dared to hope he felt the same.

Their gazes locked, a long moment of silence stretching between them. Then Roric spoke again, as if nothing special had happened between them. Did she mean so little to him? "Tell me, madam, how would you define good magic?"

Inwardly, she sighed, a hundred regrets roiling inside her. Did he feel the same as she, or was that only wishful thinking? Wrenched back to the moment, she frowned. "Well, that's easy. Any spell that helps others, such as healing an illness or saving someone's life. I should think that would be obvious," she said, raising her eyes to his.

"Ah, then, how would you define black magic?" He kept a level gaze on her.

"Any bewitchment that hurts someone, or worse, murder. If it causes pain or hardship to others, it's black magic."

"Well, suppose someone has an incurable illness, such as the deadly sickness that eats away at your body. What if that person is in terrible pain and slowly dying? If you could give the sufferer a strong dose of foxglove that would end his misery forever, would you consider that good magic or bad? Or would you consider it magic at all?"

"Oh, I see what you're getting at. But many people mistake healing for enchantment. For example, look how Radegunda healed people of so many illnesses. That is not magic, but many called her a witch because of her knowledge. This is aside from her actual magical ability." She sighed. "There are no easy answers, are there?"

"Madam, take it from one who's seen much suffering in life, there are rarely any easy answers."

"Then I must leave it to the druids to determine what is good magic and what is bad."

"The druids," he mused aloud, " rigid old men not known for their compassion."

She sat up straight, a look of resolve on her face. "Then I shall charge them with codifying the rules, but I shall have the final say."

"That would be best for the country," he said. "Madam, never underestimate your good judgement." His face assumed a solemn look. "And never doubt you will be restored to the throne. Together, we will make it happen."

328

Night Secrets

Chapter Thirty

She had to keep on trying. She couldn't lose hope. Every day, Keriam kept vigil by Lina's side, holding her hand, speaking comforting words. But nothing happened. And I suppose it will be the same this day, she lamented, discouraged and heartsick. On the limestone floor, she knelt beside the young girl and placed her hands gently at each side of Lina's head. Her parents sat in the shadows, their heads bowed.

"Lina," she murmured, searching for the right words in the torathors' language. She knew she spoke brokenly but prayed that the young girl would understand her words. "Your mother and father are so worried about you. Please believe me that you are not to blame for your brother's death. It was no one's fault. He was taken away by the Goddess, to live in the Otherworld. It was meant to be." She squeezed the child's hand. "Come join us again. We want to see you rise from the floor, hear you talk and laugh. Do it, Lina! Do it for your mother and father, for me!" Goddess, she prayed, please help me develop my ability to the fullest, so that I may cure this sick child.

The young girl's right forefinger moved, then her hand. Turning her head slightly, she opened her mouth, then closed it again.

"Lina!" Keriam whispered, afraid to hope. "Your mother and father love you. No one blames you for anything. Please come back to us." She squeezed her hand again. "Please!"

Dorn and his wife rose from the floor. They inched closer, their eyes wide with anticipation.

"I . . .I . . ."The girl licked her lips and sighed. She shifted her left leg, a look of confusion on her face. "Where am I?"

"In your cave, with your mother and father! They want you back with them, the way you were. From this moment on, she vowed, she'd never suppress her abilities. She wanted to sing with happiness but feared to hope too soon.

The young girl blinked her eyes, then crinkled her eyes at Keriam. "Who are you?"

The chief and his wife stood, their faces infused with joy. "Is she--"

Keriam lifted her hand to stop them, afraid they would spoil this fragile moment. Tears brimmed in her eyes. "I'm a friend of your mother and father, your friend, too. Dear Lina, you have been asleep for a while, but we are happy to see you awake again."

Bracing herself on her elbow, the girl sat up and gazed around the cave. "Mother, father . . .?"

"Ah, daughter!" They rushed over and drew her into their arms, kissing her again and again. "You are well now. You are back with us!"

Keriam departed the cave quietly, leaving the family to share this golden moment. Outside, she blinked in the bright sunlight and leaned against the cave wall. Overcome with emotion, she took deep breaths, then walked away to rest by the river.

She met Roric along the way as he chopped a tree for firewood close by the river, using an axe with a polished stone head. "The chief's daughter is well again," she told him. "All it took was patience." And perhaps help from the Goddess.

Wiping his hand across his forehead, he leaned the axe against the tree, a look of relief on his face. "Princess, you have performed a miracle. The outlanders will never forget this."

She sighed, bracing herself against the tree. "Enough for now that I helped the chief's daughter throw off her sickness." Mentally and physically exhausted, she sank to the ground, where Roric joined her. She stretched out her legs, bracing her elbows behind her, staring up at a gray sky. "Soon winter will be upon us. So it will be months before we can start an offensive against Balor.."

He gave her an encouraging smile. "And we will win."

She returned his smile, unsure if he spoke those words only to encourage her, or if he really meant them. They must defeat Balor; they had no choice.

* * *

A fire smoldering beside her, Keriam slept soundly that night under her thick bear robe. She mumbled in her sleep, her body stiffening. Numbness crept over her body, and a tingling sensation erupted over her arms and legs. Her body paralyzed, her spirit rose, at first only a few feet above the cave floor, then gradually escaping the cavern. Face down, she floated far above the forest as she stared at the countryside, the bare trees, the farmers' fields, and far to the south, the capital city.

Arms outstretched, she drifted toward Moytura, the buildings, spires, and monuments spread out below. Although it was the deepest part of night, everything had an eerie glow, as if lit from within. Tree branches tossed in a cold wind, and dust blew along the cobblestones. Here and there, a vagrant wandered the lonely streets, the taverns alive with talk and laughter.

The clop, clop of horses' hooves jerked her attention to Warehouse Street, and she gravitated downward, seeking refuge in an alley that separated two large warehouses. With the cavalry in the lead, mounted officers, their plumed bronze helmets gleaming in the moonlight, rode alongside hundreds of soldiers who trod past. Marching two abreast, the soldiers spoke in low tones. Above the clink of armor, she clearly heard every word, as though they shouted from the rooftops.

"--get us out of the way."

"King's afraid of a mutiny."

"And well he should be. Haven't had leave . . ."

". . . build winter barracks."

". . . fight Elegia."

The soldiers trooped northward, clad in winter uniforms of a black wool tunic and trousers, black leather boots. Each carried a shield, a javelin resting on his shoulder with a bundle attached to it. This bundle, Keriam had learned long ago, held spare clothing, food rations, and eating utensils. Archers marched with the others, and besides the bundle, each carried a quiver over his shoulder. Horse-drawn wagons rumbled past, laden with tents, blankets, and all necessary supplies. The soldiers' ages ranged from fifteen to forty, Keriam guessed. Half in and half out of the vast wooden building, she stayed motionless until the soldiers marched past.

She must tell Roric her news.

* * *

Mounted on his chestnut, Fintan Davies rode alongside his men, on the way to the northern part of the country to build barracks and prepare for a war with Elegia. As if Elegia posed a threat to Avador! Only Balor could concoct such a lie and expect the people to believe it.

And a revolt of the army? Ah, yes, that threat was real, at least among the two disaffected battalions headed north. Only look at how Balor had promoted his favored friends over more deserving members of these two battalions, making them generals when they couldn't even wield a sword.

Leaving Moytura behind, the soldiers marched along the Bearn Gap through the Orn Mountains, keeping to the west of the Gorm Forest. Here and there, clusters of trees dotted the rocky cliffs. More a path than a road as it wound through the woods, the pass left enough room for two men to march abreast.

As his horse skirted the oaks and hemlocks, Davies's mind spun in different directions, his thoughts on Roric Gamal. Where was Gamal now? If he, Fintan, could instigate a mutiny--and that remained a question--Gamal was the one to contact. But Roric Gamal and Conneid Delbraith had escaped the palace some time ago. He recalled a time long past, when the major had spoken of his family in one of the southern provinces. Had Roric returned to his family? Possibly, but not likely. No, he would stay near the capital, if only from a sense of duty. It wasn't like Gamal to avoid responsibility, to shirk his duty when the country needed him. And the country needed him, indeed.

Davies glanced to the east, to the forbidding Gorm Forest, a sinister land of mystery and monsters. Would Roric Gamal go there? Did monsters really inhabit the forest, or was that only a tale to frighten children? If no monsters lived in the forest, it was a good place to seek refuge.

Fintan Davies's incisive thinking led him to another quandary. Was there a connection between Roric's disappearance and that of the princess? Now that was an interesting possibility. If he found one of them, would he find the other? But did the princess still live? The last he'd heard, the druids had accused her of witchcraft, a charge no doubt initiated by the king, and one in which she'd been found innocent. The Goddess herself had appeared before the people to proclaim her innocence, a miracle everyone still talked about.

To think Balor held the throne! Men were out of work, the people starving. And a fiend ruled the country, one who cared nothing about his subjects, nor the soldiers in his army. The people could not endure Balor much longer, could not continue to suffer such hardship that prevailed in the kingdom now.

One thing Fintan knew: he must contact Roric Gamal.

* * *

"I saw them, major," Princess Keriam said the following morning. Her breath frosted in the cold air, and a strong wind blasted from the north, bending tree limbs. Storm clouds clustered in the distance. She wrapped her cloak closer about her. "Hundreds of soldiers."

"Heading north, you say?"

"Yes, I heard them talking about building winter quarters close to the border with Elegia."

Roric pursed his lips. He and the princess stood within the shelter of a tall spruce. A cold current rippled the waters of the river a few yards away. How he wanted to hold her close in his arms to warm them both, but what would she think of him then? She was the princess, for the Goddess's sake, and he was her servant. She'd sought him out a few minutes ago, having found him outside, chopping a tall spruce. All the adult outlanders were involved in the same task , and the ringing of axes resounded through the forest, everyone preparing for the winter. Just look at how much firewood we need for the coming winter, he thought, gazing around the settlement, something he'd never had to worry about. Even children had their own special tasks, gathering cut firewood and setting the wood inside the caves, making a game out of their chores, seeing who could make the largest pile.

Surprised at her news, Roric rested the axe against a tree trunk and wiped the back of his hand across his perspiring forehead. Despite the cold weather, sweat beaded his forehead. "This was late at night?" he asked.

She gave him a level look, a slight smile on her face. "Spirit travel. Happens only when I sleep." The wind whipped her hair across her face, and she shoved the strands aside. Shivering, she hugged her arms under her cloak.

"Ah, yes." He paused, thinking hard. "But you don't know where on the northern border they're heading."

"No, but I'll attempt to discover the location." She smiled. "Spirit travel again. However, it's not something that I can just call up whenever I want to. Often I may go more than a nineday between my nocturnal trips. Sometimes it happens unexpectedly, and other times no amount of willpower will bring it on. But I'll do my best." Her expression hardened. "I must find out."

"That's all I ask, princess. But one thing I will say--not much time remains before the winter snows arrive. And when heavy snows come, mounted travel will be very difficult, if not impossible." He rested his hand against the tree trunk, his hand brushing against sharp needles. "The border with Elegia is rugged, not many places for constructing winter quarters. But there are a few places I can think of--Mag Rath--do you know where that is?"

"I've been there, major."

"Yes, of course. And Clondalkin?" he asked with a raised eyebrow.

"There's not much of Avador I don't know, sir."

"Yes, well . . . So there are two places you can investigate. Uisnech, also. The rest of the northern terrain is too mountainous for barracks."

"Even if you can lure these men away from Balor," she asked, "how can they possibly defeat his army?" Depression weighed her down, a heavy load she often wondered if she could ever dislodge.

"They–we--can't defeat him in a pitched battle. Assuming I can persuade these men to join me, we will have to use hit and run tactics." Frowning, he stared down at the ground, then quickly looked up again, not wanting her to catch his doubts. One problem after another rampaged through his head. Here he was, a fugitive from Balor and stuck in the Gorm Forest, as much a prisoner as if he were confined to a cell, and no hope of release from his prison, let alone any chance of conquering the fiend.

Her face fell. "Hit and run? How can those tactics work against Balor's disciplined army?"

"Such strategies often work quite well," he said with more optimism than he felt. "Better than doing nothing." Yet she expressed his own misgivings. Would career soldiers be willing to employ such a strategy? And if they did, would these tactics work?

Nothing in life was easy; he'd learned that long ago. And nothing ever worked out as planned, another lesson in life. Nevertheless, he had to try, had to make contact with these disgruntled elements and lure them away from Balor. And he must help Keriam, this woman who meant so much to him, this woman he wanted to hold next to his heart, tell her all he'd kept hidden inside for so long. But his hopes and dreams would forever remain an impossibility. He must focus only on defeating Balor and placing Keriam on the throne.

This is what he planned to do. This he would do . . . or die trying.

Chapter Thirty-one

"The village of Uisnech," Keriam told Roric a few days later inside her cave. "I went first to Mag Rath and saw nothing there except the village itself. But hundreds of tents are spread out to the west of Uisnech, not far from the village. Many felled trees. Barracks should be going up soon, I imagine."

"And the soldiers?" Roric asked, his mind absorbing this information.

"All sleeping, sir. This was the middle of the night."

"Ah, yes. I forgot." He smiled her way across the small fire in her cave, a fire that did little to dispel the cold, obliging them both to wear bear robes. Damn Balor! The princess should be at Emain Macha now, where she belonged, with servants to attend her needs and fireplaces to keep her warm. Even in her crude deerskin clothing, she looked lovely, a woman any man would desire. And he desired her, he realized with a sense of hopelessness, this woman so far above him. Firelight flickered between them, shadows playing across the walls. With an inward sigh, he brought his mind back to the kingdom. "Too bad you can't spirit travel during the day, princess."

Her slender fingers smoothed over her fur robe. "I've always considered my special talents a curse. After healing Lina, I know I can use my abilities for good. If I can help you--and the kingdom--by using my powers, then I should think of them as a blessing. However, night travel is enough, major."

"I can well understand that, madam."

She smiled then, a smile that helped erase, if only for a short while, all the worries that had besieged him for more moonphases that he cared to count.

"I don't feel much like a princess now," she said, indicating her dark cave with a wall of bearskins at its entrance. "Why don't you call me Kerry, as my father always did."

337

He sucked in a breath. "I could hardly call you that, madam. You are the princess, the heir to the throne. In only a few moonphases, you'll be queen." Let it be so.

"Then as queen," she said with another smile, "I shall condemn you to the dungeon if you don't call me Kerry."

He spread his hands. "I have no choice, do I?"

She shook her head. "No choice."

"Then, pr--uh, Kerry, you must call me Roric."

"I've always liked that name," she said, a moment of silence ensuing. "Well! Now that we have that little problem settled, perhaps we should move on to weightier matters. I know better than to dismiss the question of Balor. How do you propose to fight him?"

"I won't lie to you, pr--Kerry. It won't be easy. What I'm aiming for is to gather all the disgruntled elements in the army and persuade them to defeat Balor. In truth, the only men the usurper can depend on is the elite guard."

"Fierce soldiers, intensely loyal to him."

"True, but there are many more men in the army who I feel are ready to revolt. You discovered that yourself when you saw the soldiers marching north. If I can contact some of these men and build on their dissatisfaction, that's a good beginning."

"And from there?"

"From there, I'm hoping the entire populace will eventually rebel." He raised a hand. "Yes, I know I'm being optimistic, but I've heard the people's complaints. I don't think they'll put up with the fiend much longer."

She drew her robe closer around her shoulders, the gesture spawning a myriad of wishes inside him, to take her in his arms and keep her warm for all the nights they would share. Her words jerked him back to the moment. "But any action must wait until spring."

"Any military action," he said. "I intend to leave for Uisnech tomorrow, see if I can contact any of my former men. If I find one, I'll sound him out, discover how he feels about a revolt. We have a long way to go from there, but as you say, it's a start."

338

"You're taking a big chance. What if they return you to Balor?"

"I know whom I can trust. I'll reconnoiter the encampment, see how many of my former men are there. For all I know, there may not be any." He gave her a quick smile. "Don't worry. I've learned to employ a bit of ingenuity. But it may be at least one nineday before I return."

"I'll miss you." Kerry bit her lower lip. "What I mean is, I've enjoyed these talks with you."

"So have I. And I'll miss you, Kerry." If only he could tell her how much. And suddenly, he wasn't sitting across from her any longer, but had moved next to her, as though his body had a will of its own.

"Kerry?" Roric looked into her eyes then, hoping to see that her need matched his, that she wanted him as much as he desired her.

"Ah, Roric!"

He reached for her, needing to hold her close as he'd yearned to for so long. Willingly, she went to him, her body close to his. First tossing their robes aside, he drew her into his arms, and all but cried with pleasure. His every heartbeat, every breath revealed how much he desired her, a deep and aching thirst that pulsed throughout his body. He kissed her passionately, a kiss that conveyed all his pent-up longing. Feathering kisses on her forehead, cheeks, and the hollow of her throat, he whispered her name again and again. She responded, returning kiss for kiss, drawing him ever closer, her breasts pressed to his body. He never wanted the kiss to end, never wanted the night to end. Pressing ever closer, he eased her down on the cave floor, his body stretched out beside her.

Ah, to make her his own! To become one with her and know all the joys her supple body promised. He kissed her again and again, as if he could never get enough. Driven by a desperate yearning he could no longer deny, he touched her body, from her breasts to her stomach and hips. His fingers caressed that most secret part of her, touching, probing, watching her face by the firelight.

"Ah, Kerry!" He wanted her as he had never craved anything in his life, aching to join his body with hers, to satisfy this longing that had taunted him for so long. He had to have her, had to take her now! He could not bear to wait any longer.

She moaned, and reality hit him like a blast of icy wind. There could never be anything between them. She was the future queen, and he was but her loyal servant. With every willpower he possessed, he drew back, a deep ache inside him, his body on fire. His breath came in gasps, and he didn't know how he could bear this unfulfilled passion, this throbbing inside him.

Keriam blinked her eyes open. "Roric?" She reached for him, but he eased her hands away. "Don't do this to me!"

Fierce disappointment sent his spirits plummeting, as if all the joys of life, everything wonderful this life had to offer, had been denied him. A dull ache settled inside him, a need he feared with always remain unfulfilled. "I fear I forgot myself. Forgive me, madam."

"Stop calling me that! Why did you stop when we . . . when we--"

"When we both wanted to make love?" He raised himself on his elbow, looking down into her eyes, and saw his own need reflected in hers. "And then what, Kerry? You'll be queen some day, and I . . . I intend to return to Mumhain, see my family again, then hire myself out as a mercenary," he said, the last declaration a sudden decision, although he'd considered such employment. He breathed deeply, trying to forget all they'd relinquished, all the joy that would never be theirs to share.

He sat up, then helped raise her, wrapping the bear robe about her shoulders, drawing it close around her body. It took all his willpower to drop his hands when all he wanted was to let his fingers linger on her shoulders and feel her warm breasts, to discover all the beautiful secrets of her body.

"I fear I forgot myself, too." She brushed strands of hair from her face and tucked them behind her ears. A look of resolve captured her face, prompting him to wonder if she felt the same despair as he. "You must miss your family."

"Very much." A painful silence followed, then he rose, drawing his robe about him. "It's getting late. I must arise early tomorrow to set out for Uisnech. Goodnight, Kerry," he said with a long look her way. Sacred shrine, how could he leave her!

She smiled up at him, a picture he would carry with him on his long trip, one he would remember for the rest of his life. "Goodnight, Roric."

He stooped low at the cave entrance, removing the posts that held the bearskin cover in place and returned them to their former position. After the bearskin wall had closed behind him, Keriam lay back and closed her eyes, reliving every moment of their embrace. She touched her mouth, recalling the feel of his lips on hers and how those lips had aroused her like nothing she'd ever known. She still throbbed from wanting him in her most feminine part, and moisture dampened her dress. To think what they had almost shared, to think they'd come so close to making love! She touched herself there, imagining him inside her, and could hear his voice in her ear, could feel his warm breath on her neck. Gladly would she give up the kingdom if she could only live as she wanted to, married to the man she loved. But she'd known all along it was a foolish dream. When had a member of the royal family ever put personal happiness ahead of royal duties?

Still, it had been a nice dream, for the very short time it lasted.

* * *

Three days, Roric fumed as he lay face down on an outcrop of cold limestone, surveying the soldiers in the valley below. Three days he'd stayed hidden in the forest, on a hill overlooking the small village of Uisnech. A sharp rock that jutted up from the ground cut into his thigh, forcing him to change his position. So far, he'd had no luck in recognizing army acquaintances. Even if he did recognize any, could he trust him? Despite his brave words to Kerry, he knew he must tread warily.

He'd bought a spyglass before leaving Moytura, and this he swept across the encampment below, where a detachment of men felled trees while others constructed barracks. Hundreds of brown tents in neat rows covered the ground, with cook fires spaced farther to their right and long trestle tables for eating. Latrine ditches were dug downwind from the camp and away from a stream, the camp's water supply. A cold gust whistled through the trees, bringing the scent of pine, ruffling his long hair. The sorrel foraged among the grasses and nibbled on the pine leaves, the mare's coat already thicker within the last few days. Roric set the spyglass aside and blew on his hands for warmth, then picked up the glass again.

A fading sun lit the sky with an amber glow and revealed the dirt road that wound through the rich farmland, leading to the village. Dark wooded hills rose on all sides, and in the valley below, farms intersected, like patches on a quilt. Far to the west stretched the vast Orn Mountains, their lower levels dotted with evergreens, fluffy white clouds hiding the peaks.

Between clusters of pines, Roric focused the spyglass on a new movement in the camp, a man striding toward his horse. Something familiar about the officer caught his attention, the man's walk, the way he favored his left leg, how he gingerly mounted his bay before he spurred it into a canter. Ah, yes, Fintan Davies, a good, steady man, one he'd known for many years in the past. And one he could trust, of that he felt certain.

Snapping the spyglass shut, Roric tucked it inside his deep cloak pocket and raised himself to his feet, then rushed to untie his horse's reins. He mounted the sorrel and trotted through the thicket of trees, his aim to meet Davies along the dirt road to Uisnech. Among bracken and twisted tree roots, he cantered down the rocky, tree-dotted slope, keeping to the right, soon reaching level ground. Once on the road, he increased his speed, narrowing the distance between them, his cloak billowing behind him.

The clatter of hooves drew Davies's attention. He turned in the saddle, his hand on his sword hilt. A look of alarm flashed across his face.

Roric rode alongside him. "Ho, there, Lieutenant Davies!"

Davies slowed his pace, his jaw dropping in surprise. "Major Gamal, in the name of the Goddess, what are you doing here? And it's Captain Davies now, by the way." He reined in his horse, his hands resting on the pommel, and gave him a close look. "I didn't recognize you at first with that beard. But you are a fugitive!" His eyes narrowed. "What makes you think I won't turn you in, claim my reward?"

Roric's heart beat faster. "Will you?"

Fintan clapped him on the shoulder. "Banish the thought, Roric."

Inwardly, Roric breathed a long sigh of relief. "Heard some of the army was sent north. Wondered why." He relaxed his hold on the reins, not realizing until then how panic had gripped his body.

"Major, you can do better than that. Do you mind if I ask why you want to know?"

"One question for you first," Roric said. "Why are you riding into town?"

"Tired of camp food. Found there's a tavern here that serves excellent meals and has pleasing entertainment most evenings. One night off for me." He jerked his head in the direction of the army camp. "Other officers in charge."

"Fintan, do me a favor, will you. Let's stop here in the woods for awhile and--"

Davies frowned. "Roric, what is it?"

Roric motioned toward a grassy knoll. "I need to speak with you. Let's tie our horses here, talk for a few minutes. Then you can ride into town." He smiled apologetically. "I'll try not to take long."

"Of course." Both men led their horses up the rocky hill and tied the reins to a tree branch.

Indicating the camp in the distance, Roric settled himself on the cold ground, drawing his legs up, resting his hands across his knees. "I need to know the reason for this encampment." The cold wind picked up, rustling dead leaves on the forest floor, and he drew his woolen cloak closer about him.

Fintan paused, his mouth working.

"Come now, Fintan. You can trust me. Why would I betray you to, when I'm a fugitive from Balor?"

"You want to know the excuse for the encampment," Fintan asked, "or the real reason?"

"Both."

"Well, the excuse is that Elegia is preparing for war with Avador--"

"Which we both know is false. So what is the real reason?"

Fintan's gaze shifted again. Switching his attention back to Roric, he lowered his voice to almost a whisper. "The soldiers haven't received leave in moonphases, not allowed to see our families. I have a wife and children, for the Goddess's sake!" He shook his head, as if clearing it of negative thoughts. "And . . ." He hesitated.

"And?" Roric held his breath, then let it out slowly.

Davies spoke quickly, as though relieving himself of a burden. "The king fears a revolt."

Now they were getting somewhere. Roric nodded. "A justified fear, I'm sure."

"Damn right!"

Roric stretched his booted feet out. "So this was his means of getting a couple of battalions out of the way to prevent trouble. Complete frankness now, Fintan. How do you feel about a revolt?"

"You want the truth?" Fintan asked

"That's what I'm here for."

"That's what I don't understand," Davies said with a cool, appraising look. "Just why are you here?"

"Fintan, you've been frank with me. I'll return the favor. Suppose we had a chance to restore the princess to the throne--"

"The princess? Is she still alive? Haven't heard anything about her since the Goddess appeared at her execution site. Then Princess Keriam just . . .disappeared."

"I have reason to believe she's still alive. But--"

Fintan held up a hand. "Wait. How do you know Princess Keriam still lives?"

Desperate thoughts raced through Roric's head. No one must know of the princess's whereabouts; yet he needed Fintan's help.

"Roric?"

"I've been in contact with the princess."

Fintan's face registered shock. "Then where is she?"

"Fintan, let that remain a secret for now. Yes, I know this isn't fair to you. I'm asking you to confide in me, yet I won't do the same for you. Later, you'll learn all there is to know. But if we want to restore her to the throne, we must first overthrow Balor."

"Which won't be easy."

"Which won't be easy," Roric agreed, "but not impossible, if we have enough of the army behind us. Now, what I want to know is how many men you can depend on if--and this is a big 'if--we rise up against Balor.."

"We have almost two-thousand men here in Uisnech, and--"

"Before you go any farther, explain the organization of these battalions."

Fintan closed his eyes for a moment, then opened them again. "The fifteenth and sixteenth battalions. Together, we have two-hundred cavalry, four-hundred archers, one-thousand javelin throwers, and not quite three-hundred swordsmen." He paused. "Twenty scouts, not to mention cooks, armorers, farriers, and such."

Roric nodded. "But Balor will still outnumber us about four to one. We can't defeat him in a pitched battle. It will have to be hit and run."

"I'll have to agree," Fintan said, "much as it hurts to say it. I am a military man, used to fighting in the open. So are you. But I fear such tactics won't work against Balor's army." He sighed, looking down at the ground. "So hit and run it is. Anything to defeat the usurper. I hear the soldiers' talk, their complaints about being denied leave."

"And the fiend is spreading lies about imaginary dangers from Elegia?" Roric shifted his position, trying to get comfortable on the cold, rocky ground.

Fintan snorted. "I doubt if any soldier believes that Elegia is preparing for war against Avador. The men hate Balor's guts. So if they know the princess is alive, I'm sure most of my men would rally to her. But how do you propose to instigate this uprising?"

"Fintan, you have just asked the question that has kept my mind occupied for more moonphases than I care to count. But I

345

think I have the beginning of an answer. Of course, we can do nothing until spring. Something else I'll tell you, since we're being frank with each other. We have no assurance of success." He swallowed hard, hoping against hope events would prove him wrong.

"You don't need to tell me," Davies said. "But we must try."

Roric nodded. "The alternative is unthinkable. We can't permit Balor to continue as king. Already, I've seen the hardships in the country, people starving, men out of work. So when warmer weather returns, I'll contact you again."

The sun sank toward the east, shadows dappling the land. The temperature dropped, and Roric drew his cloak closer about him. Soon, darkness fell and the forest became alive with the sounds of night animals, clucking, squawking, and screeching.

Roric's mind worked hard. He understood all the arguments, all the pitfalls they faced. "I'll attempt to persuade the princess to accompany me northward in the spring. She can speak to the officers and men."

Davies jerked with surprise. "She would do that?"

"I'm sure of it," Roric said, well aware that Keriam would take any chance if it would help her gain the throne . . . and help Avador. "Who is the officer in charge at the camp?"

"Colonel Riagan."

Roric thought a moment. "Ah, yes, I remember him. A fine, conscientious officer." And one of the few who saw through Balor. He glanced Fintan's way. "Do you think you could arrange a meeting for me to speak with him tomorrow?"

Davies drew back, giving him a close look. "Don't you think you're taking a big chance?"

"We must take chances, Fintan. We have no choice." Yet he knew Fintan spoke the truth. He'd be lucky if he got out of this conspiracy alive.

* * *

The following morning, Roric sat across a wide oaken desk from Colonel Riagan, in an office that led off from the man's bedchamber. The colonel had a small frame house to himself, which consisted of a sitting room and bedchamber, a small kitchen completing the structure. The office's lone window permitted scant light, and the room's oil lantern created a stuffy, smelly atmosphere.

"Major Gamal, you are a fugitive--"

"A fugitive, yes, sir. Turn me into King Balor, and you'll get enough gold to support you and your family for years."

Riagan waved his hand. "Don't worry, major. I wouldn't betray you, not for one-thousand gold pieces." About forty years old, he wore a single gold eagle on his collar that designated his rank, his long brown hair tinged with gray at the temples.

Roric repeated the facts he'd presented to Major Davies yesterday. He chose every word carefully, not knowing if the colonel would support his scheme, or arrest him on the spot and send him back to Moytura in chains, despite his assuring words.

Fingering a sheet of vellum, the colonel looked thoughtful. "The princess is alive, you say?"

"Yes, sir," Roric said, "but I fear I can't betray her location."

Riagan frowned. "Can't or won't?"

"Sir, I beg your indulgence. For now, the princess's whereabouts must remain a secret. In the spring, I hope to bring the princess here, to persuade the army to ride south to Moytura and overthrow Ba--King Midac."

A brief smile flitted across the colonel's face, and Roric reminded himself to speak of Balor with more caution in the future. A knock on the door brought in an aide with a wine flagon and two bronze cups. Roric exchanged glances with the aide, Mogh Nuadath, a man he knew from long ago, one he had never trusted. Why in the name of the Goddess had the colonel, a good judge of character, employed this man? Then he remembered. Many of the army officers had been forced to use relatives of Balor's toadies. And Nuadath was a cousin to the Minister of Forests.

After the aide left, the colonel poured wine for them both and handed him a cup, then set the flagon on his desk. "The princess would come here, to Uisnech?"

"Yes, sir, I believe she would." Sipping the wine, Roric found it too sweet for his taste but wisely said nothing.

"Major, doubtless you are aware that King Midac sent us north here because he felt he could no longer depend on our loyalty."

"I heard something to that effect, sir."

"Then I believe the princess can depend on our allegiance." The colonel shook his head. "But that doesn't mean that all the men will immediately rush to her support. I fear we have a few men--I don't know the number--who would flock to King Midac should a clash occur." He fiddled with a quill pen, his expression thoughtful. "As for the rest of us, we stand behind the princess. I met her once at a palace reception, talked to her for a few moments. She impressed me as being an intelligent, capable person."

"Indeed, sir." Relief swept over Roric., coupled with a longing to see Keriam again. Goddess, how he missed her.

For now, he'd done as much as possible, an easy task compared to the difficulties that loomed ahead.

Chapter Thirty-two

"You see, Roric? It is easy to use." On a cool day in early spring, when patches of snow still dotted the hard ground, Mord bent low to demonstrate use of the sling to Roric. "You get a stone the size of a caracob egg and place it in the pouch, like so," he said, following his words with action. "Then you whirl the ends of the cord--stand back, now," he instructed. Clad in deerskin, Roric moved aside as Mord swung the pouch several times over his head, building up momentum. "Then release it!" He hurled the stone through the air, hitting the center of the target he'd carved on a birch tree one hundred yards distant. Mord turned to him, a triumphant grin on his face. "You see how easy it is?"

"That remains to be seen." Roric looked up at the giant, thankful he had these outlanders on his side. After much persuasion, he had convinced the cave dwellers that ridding the kingdom of Balor would benefit them, too. "For if Balor continues with his harmful policies," he'd said, "he may well drive the people from Moytura, and they, in turn, might chase you from the forest. I know the people fear you, but desperate folk do desperate things." Roric considered this scenario quite likely, for the Avadorans had suffered under Balor's depredations for too long.

"Here, you try it." Wrenched back to the moment, Roric took the pouch from Mord and whirled it several times over his head. He released it, the missile hurtling through the air, missing the target by inches.

"Close," Mord said, frowning. "But you must practice."

"Right." Roric strode toward the tree to retrieve the stone. Practice, he agonized, as he'd practiced sword fighting with Conneid, both men using wooden swords, ever since his return from Uisnech several moonphases ago. Winter had only recently released its grip on the land. Purple crocuses popped up among snowy patches, and forsythia embellished the ground with yellow blossoms. Flocks of birds filled the sky overhead, returning from their winter sojourn. Soon, he and Keriam must ride to Uisnech to convince the disaffected battalions to join them: a gamble, despite his optimistic words to Fintan Davies.

"Here, let me try it." Having left her cave, Keriam strode their way, surprising Roric with her request. Her gray woolen dress clung to her legs, her long hair billowing behind her.

A shocked look captured Mord's face. "But you are a woman."

"The future queen!" Roric exclaimed at her side, in agreement with Keriam's request. After she'd cured the chief's daughter, the outlanders had worshiped Keriam, proclaiming her as their queen. Although they accepted her as their ruler, old attitudes had died hard. They had imbued her with a near-divine status, reluctant to permit her to perform any task. It had taken some time and much argument, but she had convinced them otherwise.

"And one who must learn to defeat the evil usurper, by every means possible," Keriam added. Tilting her head back, she smiled up at the giant. "Mord, let's see if a woman can do this as well as a man."

Mord demonstrated the sling's use again. He indicated the target and moved aside, looking doubtful. Roric stood a few feet back, hands on his hips, silently cheering her on. His respect for her rose even higher, his pride never greater than now.

She nodded to the giant, then swung the pouch by the ends numerous times, releasing the stone. It fell on the ground with a hard plop, several feet from the target.

Mord's mouth drew down but he said nothing.

"Just give me time!" Keriam nodded to Roric. "Your turn, then I'll try again."

"As you wish, princess." Roric scooped up the stone and returned to the starting point. He swung the pouch over his head and let go of the stone, this time hitting his target.

"See?" Mord beamed. "You do better now."

Better, Roric mused. But could they defeat Balor's army?

* * *

"I still wonder how we can defeat Balor's army," Keriam said days later as they rode north to Uisnech. The horses clambered up a steep, rocky cliff on the outskirts of Moytura, the city laid out like a panorama below them. The draft horse, carrying their necessities, was connected to the sorrel by rope. They had packed breads, dried meat, fruits, and vegetables, to be supplemented with wildlife Roric would find along the way. Keriam rode pillion behind Roric, her arms wrapped around his waist, her breasts cushioned against his back, her nearness a sweet torture.

"Balor," Roric said over his shoulder, his face shaven now. "We must defeat him. We have no choice."

Since the weather remained chilly, he wore his long-sleeved tunic and woolen trousers. Dressed plainly, Keriam was clad in the gray woolen dress but had packed finer clothing with their supplies. It would not do for a princess to appear before the soldiers dressed as a chambermaid. But no matter her attire, she would always be beautiful to him, a beauty that shone from within as much as her outward appearance.

Before departing their forest home, he'd chanced another trip to Moytura, buying as a surprise for Keriam a sidesaddle and a dress fit for a queen, leaving him but little coin. When they reached their destination, she would ride the sorrel, and he the draft horse. He'd said nothing to her about his depleted money supply, but she had guessed his expenditure.

"But Roric," she'd protested, "I still have my amethyst ring. You could have taken it to a pawn shop and gotten a good price for it, I don't doubt."

"Kerry, in the first place, the ring is yours, part of your royal heritage," he'd replied. "Don't even think of selling it. In the second place, it might arouse suspicion if I attempted a sale."

"Ah, you are right." She smiled. "But some day, we must have a reckoning. You have done much for me."

"Which I am pleased and honored to do." He would give her the kingdom now, if he could, would give her anything in the world . He would love her for the rest of his life, a love that kept him awake at night, aching for her. As he ached for her now, she with her arms around his waist, spawning a hundred desires that he'd tried so hard to suppress.

He returned his mind to their journey, ever worried that they might fail in their mission, be arrested and sent back to Balor under guard. Perhaps one of the soldiers at Uisnech had defected and told Balor of his presence there. A hundred things could go wrong.

Signs of spring were everywhere, the birches and hemlocks showing new green leaves, wildflowers sprouting up from the forest floor. Marigolds flourished among hay-scented fern; here and there splashes of sunlight glinted through the thick forest canopy. Still, a cold west wind pelted their faces and shook bare tree branches.

A flock of ravens flew overhead, then landed in the trees alongside the travelers' route, one after another, until more than one-hundred ravens blackened the firs and birches. The birds sat in silent surveillance, their beady eyes fixed on the travelers. Wings fluttering, they shifted from one foot to another.

Roric pointed in their direction. "Look at that, would you! Never saw so many blackbirds in one spot."

"Fancy that," Keriam murmured. She didn't sound at all surprised.

Sidling among thick tree trunks, the horses struggled up a rocky slope thick with shale and limestone and blanketed with the white-flowered dogwood. The snow was gradually melting in the sunlight but the ground remained hard.

At a promontory, Roric turned around for a last look at Moytura before it disappeared from sight.

Keriam followed his gaze. "The Goddess willing, soon Balor will be gone from Emain Macha."

"Yes." It will take more than the Goddess to rid the kingdom of Balor, he agonized.

They continued northward, mile after rocky mile, up steep hills and down into deep, verdant valleys. Often they had to backtrack, losing precious time, but it couldn't be helped: in places the woods proved impenetrable. The wind gradually shifted to the north, bringing cold, moist air with it. Both riders drew hoods over their heads and tied them at the throat.

Tired, with aching muscles, Roric reached a wide meadow, the sun at its zenith. Luxuriant with undergrowth, the meadow extended for several acres. The glade was bursting with daisies, yellow violets, and bright red phlox. Green velvety grass rippled in the wind.

"Let's stop here." Roric swung his leg over the horse's back and slid to the ground. He reached for Keriam, too well aware that this was the closest he would ever hold her, and glad to be on firm ground again. He held her for a moment all too fleeting, when he wanted nothing more than to ease her ever closer, to kiss her sweet lips and run his fingers through her luxuriant hair. Her gaze met his, and he wondered if she shared his yearnings. With an ache that bordered on despair, he released her and turned away.

The Deuona River beckoned, and Roric released the horses so they could have their fill of water. While the horses drank from the river and munched on the grass, Keriam and Roric settled down in the meadow for a short repast, feasting on dried venison and wild wheat bread, finishing their meal with wild strawberries that flourished in bushes on the meadow's edge. Sparrows sang from the trees, and daddy long-legs crept along in the grass. How peaceful everything is, Roric thought. If only life were this serene. If only Kerry and I were farmers, resting from our labors on our vast land holdings.

Mindful of the passing time, they finished their meal, then mounted their horses again.

Hours later, as the sun disappeared below the horizon and shadows crept over the woods, they searched for a place to spend the night, eventually finding shelter at a cave opening. Leaving Kerry to feed the horses, Roric gathered dried twigs and bracken and carried them back to the opening, then made a windshield from large stones placed around the fire. From his leather pouch, he withdrew his tinderbox and a flask of lantern oil. After dousing the twigs with the oil, he lit the flint and soon had a fire going, one to warm them and keep wild animals at bay.

While Roric had collected twigs and bracken, Keriam led the horses inside the cave and fed them oats, giving them but a small amount so their stomachs wouldn't cramp. Several yards from the cave entrance, water trickled from overhead, forming a pool, a good source of water for the horses. Now, the sorrel and the draft horse rested inside the cave, content for the night.

He retrieved their bear robes and flipped hers out on the the cave floor. "Get some sleep, Kerry. We have another long day ahead of us tomorrow." Night sounds echoed around them, insects buzzing, wolves howling, smaller animals squeaking and clucking. Under the light of a full moon, the dark forest extended as far as the eye could see, miles and miles of wooded hills.

They lay down on either side of the smoldering fire, each wrapped warmly against the night chill.

* * *

For the longest time, Keriam lay sleepless under her robe, wanting Roric to lie beside her and take her in his arms. And if he did? She was a princess who must remain chaste before marriage, as was the custom of her country. What if she were married to Roric? she wondered with a quickening heartbeat. The kiss they'd shared in her cave moonphases ago returned to taunt her, warming her body. So what if he wasn't of royal blood; he was everything she'd ever wanted in a man . . . and more. Roric, come to me, she silently pleaded. Hold me in your arms and tell me you love me. Kiss me and caress me, make love to drive me out of my mind. She could only dream of what lovemaking was like, but she knew it would be wonderful with Roric, all she had ever imagined and more, oh, so much more.

She recalled the words she'd uttered to Balor long ago. If she couldn't marry the man she loved, she wouldn't marry at all. But you must consider the royal line, her conscience nagged her. She turned onto her back, reluctant to dwell on marriage. Yet she realized she must pledge herself to another once she was restored to the throne, to provide the kingdom with an heir.

She sighed and diverted her mind to the approaching encounter at Uisnech. What if the soldiers at the encampment refused to serve her? Suppose the soldiers joined their cause, as she and Roric wished. If Balor defeated them, the kingdom would be worse off than before. She knew Balor and his vengeful nature. Everyone would suffer because of their failure.

* * *

Unable to sleep, Roric forced himself to lie quietly as he considered the problems ahead, of persuading the battalions to unite with them, of the coming war against Balor. Above all, he thought of Kerry, this woman who reclined close by, her tempting body turned away from him. What would she do if he threw aside his robe and joined her? Would she welcome him, or would she spurn him for the lovelorn fool that he was?

He raised himself up on his elbow, wanting to go to her, his body aching for her. Did she want him, too? Yet he would never take her as a man used a pleasure woman, couldn't make love to her without a commitment. After moments of intense longing, he sank back down, his mind ruling his heart. . . .

Night after night, Roric fought this ache deep inside him, this burning need for Kerry that drove every other thought from his mind. Did she desire him as much as he wanted her? Go to her, his heart urged him as he lay across the fire from her. The worst she could do was refuse him, a possibility he feared to consider.

On the last night before they reached Uisnech, he tossed and turned under his bear robe, struggling with his need for her. No longer able to fight his desire, he threw his robe aside and went to her. "Kerry? I have wanted you so!" he cried. Lying down beside her, he tried to gauge her reaction. She stared at him, an unreadable expression on her face. Had he made a terrible mistake? Would she spurn him and forever disparage him as a lovesick fool?

"Roric! I thought you would never come to me," she said, drawing him close. She wrapped her arms around him, and the touch of her fingers on his bare skin, the pressure of her pliant body against his, sent all his doubts fleeing and inflamed him like the most passionate kiss. Never mind that she had mysterious powers. Never mind that she was a princess and he only a palace steward. The here and now was all that mattered, this woman in his arms all he wanted.

"How I have hungered for you," Kerry whispered between kisses. "And how I have wanted you all these nights."

"Ah, darling, then we must make up for lost time." He kissed her as if they would have no tomorrow, and indeed, they might not. All this time they could have spent making love, all these chances he'd missed! Why had he ever doubted her? He breathed in deeply, inhaling her lavender scent, reveling in her very essence. He touched her as he'd wanted to for so long, learning all the pleasures her supple body offered. Night sounds reverberated around them, a cool breeze rustling the trees. The flickering firelight cast her lovely face in light and shadow, a face he would never forget. Despite the cold, her breasts were warm beneath his exploring fingers, his body aroused beyond endurance. She opened her mouth for him to explore, and he welcomed the invitation, his yearning for her so great that he couldn't even think of stopping.

She drew back, and for just a moment, he felt cold, bereft, as if denied everything wonderful in life. "Wait, darling . . ." She raised herself and eased her dress up, a look of sultry encouragement on her face.

He needed no more inducement. Quickly, he eased out of his trousers and undertunic, his fingers clumsy with impatience.

"Roric," she said, hesitation in her voice. "I . . . I am unschooled in love, but I can no longer deny what you . . . what we both want."

"Kerry, sweetheart, I will try not to hurt you." He raised himself over her, helpless to deny his need, even if the world had stopped turning, even if he would die tomorrow.

"Ah, darling!" She welcomed him inside her, waiting for she knew not what, knowing only that her life would be empty without this man, without this moment between them. She reveled in his every movement that bound him to her, so happy to share this intimacy with him. Goddess! How she loved this man! She felt his warm breath on her neck, heard his whispered endearments in her ear, as she had always imagined. Ah, what was happening to her–a joy beyond anything she had ever dreamed of, a desire to know and give pleasure to this one man who meant more than life to her. A slow heat built within her, a longing not to be denied.

"Ohh!" Rapture exploded inside her, waves of heat rippling over every inch of her body, their two hearts beating as one. And when his cries of joy blended with hers, she knew she would remember this moment forever, that she would love him until death.

Later, as he lay next to her and held her in his arms, he breathed a long, slow sigh. "Kerry, all these nights, lying so near you, wanting you so . . ." He sighed again. "Torture! I couldn't fight my need for you any longer. But I should never have taken you—"

"Ssh! Don't say it, sweetheart. I don't regret a thing."

"But I do! What if I've gotten you with child?"

"You haven't. It is not the time."

"Thank the Goddess! I would never have forgiven myself had I gotten you pregnant."

She leaned over and kissed him on the cheek. "Let there be no misgivings between us, no recriminations. This wonderful moment between us was meant to happen." She smiled in lush contentment, so happy that she'd had a fragile barrier, that she hadn't known any pain with their lovemaking. Now, she wanted him again and again, all through the night. She swallowed hard, reluctant to think beyond this night. If she lost him in the struggle against Balor, she would have this time between them to remember for the rest of her life. And if she lost him, how could she bear to go through life without him.

* * *

Roric and Keriam crested the wooded hill that overlooked the Uisnech encampment where wooden barracks now stood in place of tents, and a sentry guarded the palisaded entrance. Below them, soldiers practiced warfare, some with sword and shield, others hurling javelins or shooting arrows at straw dummies. A natural obstacle, such as a cluster of trees or a stream, separated each group from the others.

Would the men rally behind him? Roric worried. Would they accept Keriam as their future queen? Or would he and Keriam face arrest and a painful death for treason?

Leaving their supplies in the woods, Keriam rode sidesaddle on the sorrel and he mounted the draft horse. Clad in the dress he'd bought--a cerulean blue velvet long-sleeved dress with a gold chain circling her waist--she looked elegant, her dark hair now drawn into one single braid that swung with every movement. Thoughts of last night warmed his body, memories he knew would stay with him for the rest of his life. They had made love again and again throughout the night, a beautiful blending of hearts and minds and bodies, and when the first lavender glow lit the western horizon, he wanted to make love to her one more time, as if the hours behind them had never existed. He'd gazed at her lovely face and kissed her, then drew away from her to face the new day. Sighing now, he brought his mind back to the challenges that faced them this day.

Kerry glanced his way, a look of determination on her face; yet he suspected she shared his misgivings. And was she, too, filled with memories of last night? Surely she was!

"Shall we go?" she asked. Not waiting for an answer, she urged her horse down the rocky, tree-dotted slope. He followed, his gaze on her ebony tresses that shimmered in the sunlight. He pushed tree branches aside, picking his way carefully among the thick tree clusters and dense understory. Within minutes, they reached the camp.

Dismounting at the entrance, Roric spoke to Keriam in a quick aside. "Best you wait here for now. Let us see how the wind blows." He reached up to squeeze her hand, throwing her a look of encouragement.

She smiled down at him, and it looked to him as if she had projected all her love in this one moment. "May it blow our way."

"Let us hope so."

In front of the wooden fence, the sentry approached Roric. "Sir, state your business," he said, his gaze sliding to Keriam.

"I'm here to see Colonel Riagan." Roric held his breath for a moment, every muscle tense.

"Is he expecting you?" he asked, fingering his sword hilt.

"I believe so, yes." Although his stomach knotted, Roric forced himself to relax, his hands held loosely at his side.

The sentry glanced at Keriam again. "And the lady?"

"She will wait here for now."

Doubt still clouded the sentry's face, but he acquiesced. "Very well, but leave your sword with me."

Stifling his displeasure, Roric drew the sword from its scabbard and handed it, hilt first, to the sergeant. After the guard opened the gate, Roric made a staying gesture to Keriam. He caught the worried look on her face and noted how her slender fingers gripped the reins. More than anything, he wished he could tell her she had nothing to fear. A reassuring smile was the most he could offer.

Inside, his gaze absorbed the puzzled glances of the men. Over twenty evenly-spaced wooden barracks occupied the level ground, set among evergreens and birches. Upon seeing him, the soldiers halted their practice, swords, javelins, and bows in their hands. They stood motionless, as if rooted to the spot.

Colonel Riagan separated himself from a group of soldiers and strode forward. "Major Gamal!" He addressed the sentry by the open gate. "Sergeant, I can vouch for this man."

"Very good, sir," the sentry said, returning Roric's sword to him.

After sliding his sword into the scabbard, Roric inclined his head and placed his hands across his chest in the traditional soldier's salute. "Colonel Riagan."

The colonel returned the salute, then stared at Keriam, his eyebrows raised, mouth open in surprise. He looked Roric's way and spoke in low tones. "Major, I must introduce the princess."

Roric thought quickly. "If you will only wait a few minutes, sir."

The other soldiers remained where they were, muttering among themselves, exchanging confused looks. With hesitant glances at Roric and receiving permission from their officers to halt their practice, the men inched forward along the hard, open ground, until they stood only a few feet from Roric.

"Will you excuse me, sir," Roric muttered to Riagan and headed back for Keriam at the open gate. He reached for her, his hands at her waist, helping her off the sorrel. "So far, things have proceeded well," he murmured. "But it's time to introduce you to the men. We won't gain anything by waiting."

She nodded, her feet on the ground. "I agree. I'd just as soon find out now how they will accept me . . . or if they will."

And if they didn't? He didn't dare consider the consequences of failure.

The colonel snapped his fingers at another soldier. "Leinster, take care of their horses."

"Yes, sir."

Fintan Davies emerged from one of the barracks, heading their way. "Ah, Gamal!" He looked Keriam's way and bowed low. "And--"

"The princess!" The colonel raised his voice, addressing all the men. "I present to you the future queen of Avador!"

With excited murmurs, the soldiers came forward, looking at one another, talking among themselves. Hundreds of soldiers gathered in clusters, some elbowing their way through the crowds, trying to see over their fellows' heads. As one, they started to bend to one knee.

"Wait!" A voice rang out among the crowd. "How do we know she's the princess?" Rumbling erupted among the men, many of them looking more confused than before and straightening up again. "Yes," others bellowed. "How do we know?"

The colonel spoke, his voice loud and clear. "I've met her. I assure you, she is Princess Keriam. Let us have no more of this talk."

"Princess Keriam!" The warriors bent to one knee, their heads bowed in respect.

"Major." Keriam nudged Roric's arm. "Help me stand up on this table so that I may address the men."

He did as requested, touching her with a reverence that befitted her station, so proud of this woman he loved more than life.

After Keriam stood atop the table, Fintan Davies spoke in an undertone to Roric. "We've had twenty desertions, including Colonel Riagin's aide, since you were last here."

Alarm slammed through Roric's gut. "Desertions or defections to Balor?"

Davies sighed. "Who knows?"

360

From her position on the table, Keriam motioned for the men to rise. Hundreds of soldiers stood, a look of admiration on their faces. None speaking, they gazed at the princess, middle-aged men and young, tall and short, men from all walks of life. All wore simple black tunics and trousers, with no insignia, every one of them a steadfast Avadoran soldier ... she hoped.

Keriam's heart pounded until her head throbbed, but she spoke in clear tones. "Soldiers of Avador," she began, "at long last, I can address you, a privilege denied me for too long. For many moonphases, I have remained a fugitive, hiding from the tyrant, Balor. The time has come to overthrow this tyrant. With your help, we can do it, but I won't lie to you. It won't be easy." The sun emerged from the clouds, a sudden clearing of the sky. Keriam raised her face upward. "See? A sure sign the Goddess is on our side. If you are all with me--and I pray to Talmora that you are-- remember that Balor's army in Moytura outnumbers us four-to- one."

The men frowned and murmured among themselves, all aware of the odds against them. As Keriam paused, they gazed up at her, approval written on all their faces. Fierce exultation burst inside her. They were with her! She could count on every one of them.

"We know we can't defeat the usurper in a pitched battle," Keriam continued, turning now and then so that she faced every one of them. "We must use devious methods. Destroy his supplies, deprive his army of food. We must strike him from different quarters so that he never knows where the next setback will come from. We won't defeat him overnight, but with the Goddess's help, we will succeed." Her voice rose. "Men of Avador, are you with me?"

A soldier raised his fist in the air. "We are with you, princess!" The others joined in, raising their swords and javelins high, all of them shouting, "Queen Keriam!"

* * *

During their journey southward, hundreds of men slept on the open ground, spread out among the forest trees or slumbering in the meadows along their route. They had left their tents and much of their supplies behind, their aim to make haste in their trek southward. The officers had decided before leaving Uisnech that the soldiers would depart the encampment one-thousand men at a time, one day separating each group. Thus at present they had almost a thousand men with them. The other thousand, along with Colonel Riagin and the cavalry, followed close behind. Sharing the odyssey's discomforts, Keriam slept apart from the others, while sentries took turns keeping watch every night. Several miles from Moytura, she lay sleepless on the cold, hard ground, staring up through the trees. A multitude of stars mantled the sky, and the constellation of Moccus the Horse glittered overhead like a diamond bracelet.

She drew her bear robe up to her chin, wondering if Roric slept, or if fears kept him awake, too. She smiled to herself, recalling their last night together. Her body heated, his kisses, his lovemaking still fresh in her mind. Running her hand from her breast to her thighs, she relived Roric's every touch, remembering the feel of his body on hers. Ah, to have him again this night and for every night to come. But not once had he spoken of love, and she wondered, as she had so many times, if he wanted her only as a man wants a pleasure woman. But no, she knew it was more than that, knew that his love matched hers.

Around her, snoring, sneezing, and coughing sounded from the trees, further distractions that prevented slumber. Unable to get comfortable, she continually changed position. Insects buzzed around her and nocturnal animals stirred with screeches, clucks, and howls.

After a consultation among them and after seeing the lay of the land at this point between Uisnech and Moytura, Roric, Captain Davies, and the other officers had decided they would proceed no farther, but would make this part of the forest their base of operations.

"And don't worry about the torathors," Roric had emphasized. "They are not monsters, and they are our friends. On our side!"

Separate companies were grouped according to battle plan and would spread throughout this area of the forest, each company with its own mission. Roric had informed her of their intention, and she realized it made sense. The scheme sounded plausible and workable. Why, then, did doubts assail her? Why did a sense of doom hang over her, erasing her earlier optimism?

"I'll escort you back to the outlanders, then return here to take part in the operations," Roric had told her earlier this evening, after their meal. They'd spoken among themselves, far from the others.

"You'll do no such thing--I mean about escorting me back," she'd retorted. "I want to know what's going on with our army, and I can't do that from my cave home. No, I'll stay here with you and the men."

He folded his arms in front of him. "This is no life for a princess. You can't stay here in the woods among these rough soldiers, sharing in their hardships."

"Who says I can't? Major Gamal, please don't tell me what I can and can't do." Irritation warmed her face, but depression, too. Had he so quickly forgotten their last night together?

He threw up his hands. "Very well, have it your way."

And that's how the matter had rested, with no questions or arguments from any other officer. Apparently, Roric had convinced them of her determination. Now, in the deepest part of night, she closed her eyes, aware that only a few hours remained before dawn. After a while--minutes or hours, she knew not which--she surrendered to sleep, her body rigid. A sense of helplessness overtook her, as if she couldn't move a limb. Tingling spread from her head to her feet, and she floated upwards, then flew south in this heavenly journey that always filled her with ecstasy.

Raw power surged inside her. Nothing was impossible. She could conquer the world! For once, it didn't matter that the tyrant occupied her home and ruled in her stead. She would soon rid the country of the fiend. Skimming the trees, she looked below her, absorbing every detail of her domain: the vast forest, every hill and valley, the streams and rivers that wound like blue silk ribbons through Avador.

Movement and talk jerked her attention below, and she gravitated toward the Royal North Road, then drifted downward to hide behind an oak tree. Preceded by the cavalry, hundreds of soldiers, thousands! marched four abreast in one long, winding column, quivers or javelins slung over their shoulders. Meadow and gently-rolling farmland flanked them on both sides, sheep and cattle sleeping in the distance.

What was happening here? Mounted officers rode alongside the warriors, urging them on. Keriam pressed her hand to her heart, eternally surprised when her hand passed through her spirit. The tramp of feet sounded like thunder in her ears, boots scuffling on the hard soil. As in Moytura many moonphases ago, she heard the their talk, as if she stood next to them.

"We'll get those traitors."

"Bound to be hiding in the forest somewhere."

An officer took four mounted soldiers aside and spoke to them. "As scouts, I want you to ride ahead but leave your horses tethered before entering the forest. Probe for the traitors' army, then come back to me when you have found their position."

The men exchanged worried glances, prompting a string of curses from the officer. "There are no monsters in the forest! Only a tale to frighten children!" He gave further instructions about the direction each was to take, then joined the other officers.

In her concealment behind the tree, Keriam heard every word.

Who had betrayed them? How in the Goddess's name had they learned of Roric's plan? Never mind! No time to lose!

Keriam willed her spirit back to her body, where she slumbered on the cold ground, arms flat across her chest, her long hair unbraided, the locks spread out on the grass. Her soul restored to her body, she tossed and turned, a vague worry disturbing her repose. She awoke with a jolt, painfully reminded of the danger that threatened. Throwing her bear robe aside, she rose and walked a few yards, stepping over sleeping men, heading for the spot where Roric slept.

She knelt, shaking his shoulder. "Roric!" she whispered.

He jerked awake, then raised himself on his elbows, staring at her, wide-eyed. "Kerry, are you all right?"

"Balor!" She clenched her hands. "Balor's army is headed this way! His entire army! I just spirit-traveled to Moytura, heard the soldiers' talk. Roric, they know about us!" She shook his arm. "They've sent scouts ahead to find our position. We can't disperse as we'd planned!"

"Sacred shrine, no! Obviously someone betrayed us. We must act!" He shoved his robe to the side and jumped up to search for Fintan Davies, finding him a few minutes later with his company.

Roric shook him awake. "Davies! Balor's army is headed this way. Scouts are already searching for us."

Davies blinked the sleep from his eyes. "How do you know this?"

"Never mind! It's enough that we do!" He'd worry about explanations later.

Fintan sprang to his feet. "What are we going to do?" he asked with a helpless look at all the sleeping men.

"Head south and fight. What else?" Roric clapped Davies on the shoulder. "Never let it be said that we are cowards. But if we are going to die, at least we will die with honor."

Chapter Thirty-three

On a sparsely-wooded hill that overlooked Moytura, Roric viewed Balor's army massing on the Plain of Sorrows below. The hill extended for about a mile, gradually sloping down to a valley on either side: an ideal place for defense. All around him, men talked and joked nervously, fingering swords, scuffing booted feet on the hard ground.

Loud chanting and banging of swords on shields echoed from the battlefield. In front gathered Balor's archers, armed with short bows. Behind them came the foot soldiers, equipped with short swords and protected by shields. Last grouped the cavalry at the far end of the field, the horse soldiers wielding swords and javelins, the horses unarmored.

Dawn was breaking, and a grayish blue glow tinted the western horizon. A chill hung in the air, a cool breeze from the north, flapping banners and pennants. His spyglass raised, Roric recognized a few officers from years ago. He gripped a branch so hard it snapped in his hands. To think he must fight--and kill-- many of his former comrades . . . or be killed by one of them! Glad he held the high ground, he snapped the metal tube shut and set it in the crook of a tree limb.

Upon learning of Balor's approach during the night, he'd sent a courier to the one-thousand men who followed behind with Colonel Riagan, advising them of Balor's advance. But even if the men moved at breakneck speed--and he knew they would--they'd never reach Moytura in time. Keriam had ridden to enlist the aid of the outlanders, whose home claimed a small portion of the southeast corner of the forest. Roric sighed, knowing that if the outlanders joined the princess's army, it would forever end their isolation, their way of life.

At a hastily-summoned war council only a few hours ago, Roric, as senior officer, had devised a battle plan in conjunction with the other officers. Everyone was painfully aware of the slim chance of defeating Balor, but they must try. To ignore the challenge didn't bear consideration. In order to distinguish his men from Balor's, Roric's soldiers had tied a strip from their black undertunics around their forehead. Roric and the other officers wore helmets, and so tied the strips around that head protection.

Discouragement clutched him like a band around his chest, tightening, tightening, until he feared he couldn't breathe. Despite the chill, perspiration trickled down his face and dampened his tunic. He clenched his fists until the muscles ached. Relaxing his hands, he tried to convince himself the princess's army would win this day. But sacred shrine! How could they?

On each side of him, behind every tree, faces hardened with tension. Row upon row of archers stood at the ready, their gaze focused on the enemy below, each man prepared to loose his arrow in unison. In dense formation, they spread out for over eight-hundred yards, with others behind them, every man anxious to defeat Balor. Roric had been forced to weigh the possibility of congestion--so many men within such a small space--against the real fear of lack of coordination.

His foot soldiers had already loosened boulders, their aim to stop as many men as possible.

A bugle blared below. Roric stiffened, his arm raised to give the signal to his men.

Grim faces set in single-minded purpose, Balor's warriors advanced up the hill.

"Release boulders!" Roric shouted. His men sent the rocks rolling down, the onslaught crushing many in the first wave. Screams tore through the air. The enemy continued to climb, stepping over bodies of their fallen comrades.

Roric raised his arm. "Archers! Prepare to shoot!" The archers nocked their arrows, a look of fierce determination on their faces. Despite the chill, their faces shone with sweat.

He dropped his arm. "Looseen arrows!"

A rain of arrows fell on Balor's men, stopping many. But they still kept coming!

Balor's archers shot their arrows upwards. Screams sounded from Roric's men. A quick glance around showed Roric how many had fallen. Too many. Talmora's bones, too many!

As soon as one row of Roric's archers shot their missiles, they knelt to notch their arrows while the row behind them let loose. A continual shower of arrows poured down, so thick they blotted out everything else. Boulders tumbled down the hill, crushing everyone in their path, slowing Balor's archers.

A bugle sounded again on the plain. Balor's foot soldiers advanced noisily, yelling their war cries and banging weapons against shields. Swords flashed in the sunlight. As Roric's archers fell, more came forward to take their place, assuming position behind the trees. From both sides, a never-ending rain of arrows whizzed through the air. Blood soaked the ground and ran down the hill, a stream of death.

Weapon raised, his face infused with blood lust, a foot soldier rushed Roric. Roric lunged forward, his shield protecting his body. The swordsman slashed, but Roric parried the thrust. He stood his ground, meeting each thrust, sending the man staggering back. Ever watchful for a weak spot, he met each parry. With one unexpected movement, the soldier slashed at his arm. Just in time, Roric swayed back, the blade merely grazing his skin. The man raised his sword again, but Roric was ahead of him. One quick thrust sent his sword through the man's belly.

"Ahh!" The warrior crumpled and fell to the ground. Another swordsman menaced, but Roric met each strike, soon dispatching him with a jab to the throat.

Screams and cries merged with the clash of arms, the evil thud of weapons.

Bellows to his left jerked his attention from the fighting. Keriam had returned with over one-hundred outlanders, who advanced on foot. A bag at their side held stones for slinging; wooden clubs were strapped to their other side.

"Look at them!" Balor's men screamed and fell back in fear, many of them racing downhill again.

"What are they?"

"Monsters!"

Climbing up the hill, an enemy officer rallied his men, throwing taunts and encouragement in equal measure. The outlanders wound their arms overhead and released their stones. A stone struck the officer in the chin, knocking out his front teeth, breaking his jaw. Flinching for a moment, he proceeded up the hill.

Yelling, he swung his sword in defiance, but another stone smashed him in the forehead. Silently, he fell to the ground.

Keriam, too, aimed a stone. It found its mark, hitting a warrior in the throat. Dispatching another foot soldier, Roric dashed to Keriam's side. Fear for her churned inside him. Discarding protocol, he grabbed her arm.

"For the Goddess's sake, stay out of harm's way. You've done more than enough!"

Her eyes flashed. "No one gives me orders! I'll stay here, where I'm needed."

"We need you alive, Kerry. We can't afford to lose you. I beg of you. Move farther back up the hill, away from danger."

"Very well. It will be as you say . . . for now."

Roric nodded, relieved to accept her temporary capitulation.

By now, the people of Moytura had gathered to view the battle, scattered close to the treeline that separated the meadow from the plain. Vendors moved among them, hawking their goods, selling cider, honey cakes, and other refreshments. "Princess, princess, princess!" the people cheered, yelling in desperation. "Kill Balor, Balor, Balor!"

Despite all obstacles, Balor's men continued to charge up the hill. Stones, arrows, and swords thinned their ranks. But Roric, too, was losing men, fighters he couldn't afford to lose. Balor's men still far outnumbered him, a ceaseless pool the fiend could draw from. At the far end of the plain, Balor's cavalry waited, pennants flying, horses stamping their hooves. And our cavalry is still miles away, Roric lamented. They would never arrive in time.

* * *

Balor raised his spyglass to view the action on the hill. Mounted on his horse, he thought furiously. Despite his abundant numbers, foot soldiers were falling at a rate he couldn't afford. He'd already lost too many archers. If he were willing to wait long enough, he would win the day. But patience was not his strong point, and Gamal's army was proving more resilient and cunning than he'd ever imagined. He still had his cavalry, horse soldiers he kept in reserve. But even they might prove vulnerable to the archers who held the hill. And the torathors! Shocked to find they weren't monsters after all, he realized their slings had proved deadly.

Thank the demoness for Mogh Nuadath, Colonel Riagan's aide, who'd told him of Gamal's visit to Uisnech moonphases ago. It paid to have loyal spies placed in strategic positions, else he would never have known of Gamal's southward advance.

He focused his spyglass again, then swung it all along the hill. Oh, he knew war; he'd fought his share of battles. But he couldn't permit this loss of life, not if he wanted to fight Elegia. In spite of his bold words to Gamal, he knew that country had a large, well-equipped army.

An idea jolted him, a means of ending the battle.

He snapped his fingers at an aide. "Tell the bugler to sound retreat."

The man stared at him. "Retreat, sire? But we are win--"

"A trick, you fool, as old as time!"

Within minutes, the bugle blared retreat, a sound carried to Balor's men on the hill. They paused, looking confused. Roric's men took advantage of their puzzlement, slashing and killing many. Balor's men raced down the hill and were sent to the rear.

"Stay here!" Roric yelled to his men, aware of the ruse. But none heard him. Pounding footfalls on the hard ground shook the earth. His men dashed downhill, screaming war cries, brandishing swords. No! Roric pressed his hands to his face and shook his head. After surrendering the high ground, how in the name of the Goddess could they win this day?

The outlanders, too, raced downhill, swinging their clubs in barbarous excitement. Dozens of enemy soldiers drew back in fear, dashing from the battlefield. An enemy officer rushed his horse in front of the deserters to stop them, but they ignored him as they ran for safety. Another blare from the bugle sent Balor's retreating foot soldiers back into the melee.

With little time to spare, Roric hurried to Keriam on the hill. Fighting for breath, his tunic soaked with blood, he handed her

370

the spyglass. He must disregard his despair, must not give up. "Here! Use this to follow the battle. I must join the others."

"Roric, please take care of yourself." Lightly, she touched him on the cheek as she grasped the spyglass. "I don't want to lose you."

He took her hand in his and kissed the palm, smiling in a vain attempt to make light of their dilemma. "You know I'll be careful." He left her then, hastening down the rocky slope, sidestepping rocks and gnarled tree roots.

In the fray again, Roric fought as he'd never fought before. He parried, thrust, and hacked, dispatching several of the enemy. Still they came on, a constant barrage he must face. His arm ached, blood and sweat drenching his tunic. But there was no retreat for him.

* * *

Alone on the hillside, her heart pounding with fear for her men, Keriam raised the spyglass to watch the battle on the plain below. Her hands shook, and she stopped to take a deep breath, then raised the glass again. Hundreds, thousands! of men fought with desperation, swords flashing, headless bodies toppling to the ground. Even with the outlanders, Roric's men were terribly outnumbered, fighting a losing battle. Balor's cavalry, too, had joined in the struggle, the soldiers raised in the stirrups, slashing with deadly effect. How could her army win?

Ravens lit on tree branches around Keriam, at first a few score, then more than a hundred, and soon, hundreds more. Ravens everywhere darkened tree branches, their beady eyes fixed on her.

What was their purpose here? Were they visiting her, as they had in the past? Or did they have a helpful motive? Optimism burst within her, but doubt, too. Looking at all the birds, she pointed to the battlefield, then at her forehead. She shook her head, her intention to advise them not to attack her men. The birds sat silent and motionless, as if absorbing her information. Were they here only to watch? Would they not help her? About to give up hope, she saw them lift off the tree limbs, then fly toward the battlefield. Her breath caught; she prayed that they understood her.

* * *

A noisy flapping of wings and a darkening of the sky jerked Roric's attention from the scene of carnage. Hundreds of birds flew overhead, then plunged downward. His stomach clenched. Talmora's bones! Why were they here? As if by augury, they dived at Balor's men, striking their heads, pecking eyes out. Screams and cries rent the air, louder than ever. Enemy soldiers pressed their hands to their eyes. Blackbirds aimed at throats, tearing at jugular veins. For the enemy, minutes seemed like hours. Black feathers floated through the air and littered the ground. Then, as though by signal, the birds flew off again with a clamorous flapping of wings. Heads raised, Balor's men followed their movement, crying with relief.

The fighting resumed with a clashing of shields and swords, the screams, cries, and moans of battle. Wounded horses reared and screamed, falling among the warriors, a death rattle in their throats. Soon the ground became wet and slippery with blood. Everywhere, the dead lay three deep, a jumble of missing limbs and headless bodies.

* * *

Next to a hemlock, Keriam edged closer to the battlefield, spyglass raised to her eyes. Her heart thudded, her hands clammy with sweat.

Out of nowhere, ghostly warriors materialized on the rocky hillside, hiding behind trees. To her right, Keriam caught a movement. Panic flared inside her, quickly doused when she saw it was yet another spirit. Clutching phantom swords and javelins, other ghosts joined the first group, soon dotting the hillside. Why were they here? And where was--

A man in a long black robe approached.

"King Malachy!" She pressed her hand to her heart, surprised to see him, wondering why his force had gathered here.

He inclined his head. "Always at your service, princess, especially this day." He indicated the warriors behind him. "It occurred to me that we could help you."

How could they help? These ghostly warriors could do no harm.

King Malachy pointed toward the battlefield. "Confusion, madam! We can spread such confusion among Balor's men, they won't know whom they are fighting."

"Ah, yes, I see. But King Malachy, your men must remember whom they are fighting. My soldiers wear a black headband."

"Yes." Malachy addressed the men on the hill, his words in a language from ages past. Faces set, they nodded in unison. Then Malachy motioned to these spirit warriors. "Follow me."

Silently, they dashed down the hillside, swords and javelins raised high. Within moments, they appeared on the plain, swords poised to strike, shields held close to their chests. Phantom javelins whizzed at the enemy. Hacking and slashing at Balor's men, the warriors did no harm but caused incredible bewilderment.

"Who are these men?" a warrior cried.

"Fool! Can't you see they're ghosts?"

"Ghosts! But they are attacking only our men, not the other side!"

Crying in terror, dozens more of Balor's men rushed from the field.

At first, Roric's men wrenched back in fright, but upon seeing the spirits attack none but Balor's men, they rejoined the fray with fresh vigor. More enemy fell, dead and wounded. The usurper king's soldiers stepped on top of their fallen comrades. Puzzlement hindered their movements, their strikes directed at apparitions.

Then the ghostly warriors disappeared as abruptly as they'd arrived, returning to Otherwhere.

Balor's men watched their departure with relief, a relief that was short-lived. The ravens returned.

"No! Not again!"

Warriors threw their javelins at the birds; many swung their swords wildly, all of them missing their target.

"Goddess, save me, save me!" Screaming soldiers raced from the field to hide behind trees in the meadow. Others remained, covering their eyes, clutching their throats. Striking the fighters from all directions, the birds stayed longer this time. They whirled and dipped and dived, aiming for eyes and throats, pecking at arms and legs. After endless minutes, they flew off again, leaving dead and sightless soldiers behind. Screams and cries rent the air, a relentless assault that pierced Keriam's eardrums.

She caught Balor in the spyglass. The fiend rode everywhere, dashing from one spot to another, his sword raised in the air, yelling encouragement and threats to his men. The fighting continued, the odds much better for her army now. Injured from both sides screamed and cried, begging for help. Wounded and dying horses cried in agony, blood spurting from throats, steaming entrails pouring from their stomachs.

Balor's cavalry rode among her warriors. Raised up in their stirrups, they threw javelins and struck with their swords. Grimacing with purposeful determination, they hacked at heads and arms, maneuvering their horses among the fighters.

Keriam's hands shook; nausea roiled in her stomach to see her men suffer so. Hours had passed since the fighting had begun, the sun now sinking in the east. Would the battle never end? She swept the spyglass across the field, ever on the lookout for Roric. Talmora, please take care of him, she prayed. Sudden guilt swamped her for praying only for Roric. If only the Goddess could protect all her men!

Roric! There he was! He fought like a madman, wielding his sword as if he'd been born with it in his hand. He dispatched one of the enemy, then turned to struggle with another.

Spyglass focused on Roric, she saw Balor ride his way. Sword held high, the demon raised himself in the stirrups. On foot, how could Roric prevail against him? No! She couldn't let Balor get away with this! Blood throbbed in her ears. Fear collided with fury inside her, a painful amalgam that made her head pound. She clenched her fists, every breath, every beat of her heart concentrated on the demon. She prayed to the Goddess as she'd never prayed before. Help us!

Power surged in her blood, stronger, stronger. She lifted her arms to the sky and shrieked. Focusing her gaze on Balor, she centered all her attention on his horse. She must unseat the fiend. She could not fail!

There!

Balor's horse threw him to the ground, and the fiend fell on his backside, looking stunned. Dragging its reins, the horse raced from the battlefield.

Waves of relief rolled over her. Was it indeed magic she had possessed all along, this wonderful force that had enabled her to unseat Balor? Or was it just her preternatural ability? Never mind! It didn't matter! She had accomplished something vital this day, something that might well affect the kingdom for ages to come. . . . if only Roric could defeat this evil despot. And from this day forth, she would not fear using her talent. Only look at the good she could accomplish with it!

* * *

Balor jumped to his feet, staring about him. Sword clenched in his hand, in murderous fury he looked everywhere.

Roric spun around and saw the king killer. Damn the bastard! Damn him to the Underworld!

For long minutes, they circled each other, Roric gauging Balor's strengths and weaknesses.

Malice burned in Balor's eyes. "Traitor!" he hissed. "I'll cut you to pieces!"

"You're the traitor, you king murderer!" Roric launched an attack at the fiend, but Balor swayed back in time, the sword barely grazing his shoulder.

The field was silent now, save for the clashing of steel on steel, all eyes on Roric and Balor.

Their swords lanced again and again, Roric fighting as he'd never fought before. He struggled as if the hours past had never existed, as though Balor were his first opponent this day. Kill the fiend! Kill him! Yet even in the desperation of battle, he knew he must keep a clear head, must not let anger and hatred betray him. His sword arm ached as if it would fall from him, but he ignored the pain. "You son of a bitch!'

Balor aimed a furious thrust, but Roric blocked it, always keeping his balance on the blood-slippery field. The fiend directed his sword at Roric's throat, but Roric deftly parried, twisting and turning his blade around Balor's weapon. Then he lunged at the usurper. Balor sidestepped, nearly losing his balance but recovering in time. The swords clanged and hissed, the weapons flashing in the sunlight. Circling each other, the swordsmen lunged, thrust, and parried, Roric always looking for an opening. Minutes passed, and he could see the fiend was tiring as Balor gasped with each breath.

"Give up!" Balor cried. "Can't you see you're losing?"

"Don't count on it!" Roric lashed again, aiming his sword at Balor's throat. A startled look came over his face, and blood spurted from the fiend's neck. Balor pitched to the ground. He struggled and tried to rise as blood streamed down his neck. With one last effort, he fell back to the ground and lay still, his eyes closed, head lolling to the side, his body unmoving.

Roric stopped several minutes to catch his breath, wiping his hand across his sweaty forehead. Moving back from the fray, he raised his blood-stained sword high. "Balor is dead!" he exulted. "Pass the word!" Soldiers on both sides paused, a look of caution on their faces as they stared at the prone body. Then they shouted with joy.

"Balor is dead!"

* * *

From the hill, Keriam silently bowed her head. Tears streamed down her face. Too much bloodshed! Too many men on both sides wounded and dead. Cries and groans assailed her eardrums. Men tossed and writhed in pain. Hundreds of dead and wounded littered the battlefield. And the horses! With human-like sounds, they twisted on the ground and wailed in agony.

With Balor gone, the struggle must stop. Despite her grief for each dead and wounded Avadoran, a tremendous relief swept over her, an unbridled joy that the tyrant was defeated. And Roric still lived. She thanked the Goddess, again and again.

The sun was a bright orange ball in the east, firing the sky with a golden glow. The air chilled, a fierce wind sweeping through the trees, bending tree branches.

Brushing the tears from her eyes, Keriam left her spot on the hill, her goal to rally the men to her side. Surely they would join her now; surely they would support the House of Moray.

And Roric--what about him? Never had she loved him as much as she did now, this very moment. Never had she been so proud of him. How she wanted him to stay with her for the rest of their lives.

Balor's men, too, viewed the fiend's body. They lowered their swords and javelins, all the fight gone from them. Quiet had settled over the plain. With Balor dead, why continue the battle? From the first, their allegiance had been to the country, not the man.

Roric raised his sword again, all eyes on him. Sweat soaked his tunic and plastered his hair, his face and body covered with blood. He opened his mouth to speak, his chest heaving. No words came. He took a deep breath and tried again.

"Soldiers of Avador! The usurper is dead! Let a new day dawn for our country." He stopped talking as the soldiers' gaze shifted. Descending the hill, Princess Keriam approached the battlefield, her step quick but purposeful, her dress fluttering around her ankles. She skirted the dead and disabled, a look of brave acceptance on her face, but sorrow, too.

Roric smiled at her tenderly, projecting all his love and emotion in one heartwarming expression. "Princess Keriam!" He lifted his sword again. "Princess Keriam! Your future queen!"

Shouts reverberated across the battlefield. "Queen Keriam!"

* * *

Two nine-days later.

With her coronation scheduled for the following day, Keriam welcomed Roric in her office, a hundred thoughts churning in her head. Now that the battle had been won and Balor dead, she had so many things she wanted to say to him. She wanted to hold him close and tell him of her love, to ask him to never leave her side, for the rest of their lives.

Instead, she stood before him like an awkward schoolgirl. "You'll stay on as palace steward, won't you, Roric? You know I need your help and advice." And she needed him. How she needed him! .

His face spasmed and he opened his mouth, then closed it again. "I fear not, Kerry. I–"

"What! But of course you'll stay. Didn't I just tell you I need your advice?"

"Madam," he said, and she winced at his formal address, "now that Conneid has returned to the palace, he will serve you well as steward. I'm riding south very soon to see my family–it's been months since I visited them–then I will hire myself out as a mercenary." He smiled. "I am not without military experience."

"But, Roric . . ." She reached her hands toward him, then let them fall to her side. Tears brimmed her eyes, but she brushed them away. She would say no more, for there was nothing left to say. He must not see how much she wanted him, how her life would be so empty without him, as if the sun would stop shining, or the world would stop spinning.

"Kerry, I . . ." With one quick movement, he drew her into his arms, her breasts pressed against him, her lips joining his in one long, soul-wrenching kiss. She covered his face with kisses, her body alive with that beautiful, familiar longing for him that would survive all obstacles, that would never end. Surely he would stay now; surely he would see that she wanted him in oh, so many ways.

He drew away the, pain and misery plain on his face. Or did she only imagine his look, her perception spawned by wishful thinking?

Roric clasped her shoulders. "Goodbye, Kerry." Then he turned and was gone, his footsteps echoing down the hallway.

She struggled against her sorrow, stifling her tears, reluctant to surrender to any weakness. From the first, she'd known there could never be anything lasting between them. So why was his departure so difficult to accept? Unable to fight her misery, she pressed her fist to her stomach and cried, all the pent-up tears streaming down her face. After countless minutes–or was it hours?–she straightened up and brushed her hand across her face. A spirit of resolution heartened her. She had lived her life before she'd known him so well, before they had shared so many experiences, before they had made love. She would live her life without him and manage quite well. As her father would have wanted, she'd marry a nobleman, from Elegia, perhaps, or Galdina. She would bear that man's child to carry on the royal line, as was her duty. Never would she let her heart rule her mind and never would she let her mind dwell on Roric. From this day on, she would devote her life to the kingdom of Avador

And Roric? Her heart whispered. Would she ever forget him!

* * *

The next day, Roric left the solemnity of the celebration behind and headed for the stable, his booted feet crunching on the gravel outside. Only yesterday, Keriam had been crowned queen, the delay giving time for envoys from other countries to arrive for the ceremony. Now she held a reception for the ministers and dignitaries of Avador, along with the ambassadors from other countries on the continent.

Seeing Keriam engrossed in conversation with the envoy from Galdina, Roric had departed the Blue Reception Room, easing past dozens of guests. Hundreds of voices filled the room, ambassadors and their wives in splendid attire, drinks in their hands. But it was time to leave for his native village, dispensing with any awkward moments between the queen and him. They had both known from the beginning that their love would gain them nothing. Goddess, how it hurt. More than anything, he wanted to stay with her and never leave her side. But his wish could never be.

He left the gravel path and entered the stable, his eyes adjusting to the darkness inside. Grooming Keriam's horse, Traigh had his back to him. He caught the smell of hay, dust motes floating through the air.

"Traigh." Roric stepped closer.

Brush in hand, the stableboy spun around. "Major! I thought you were still at the reception."

He shook his head. "Going home now, leaving the kingdom in good hands."

Looking puzzled, Traigh set his brush on a pile of hay. "You're leaving us, sir?"

"Indeed. I'll miss everyone," Roric said, resting his arms on a stall door. Keriam, most of all.

"We'll miss you, sir." Traigh shoved his blond hair from his forehead, his face downcast.,   "It's best that I depart now, my family." He clapped the young man on the shoulder. "I hear congratulations are in order. Now that you are handfasted, I'm sure you and Maudina will be very happy together."

"We already are." The stableboy's face reddened and he glanced around, as if seeing the stable for the first time. "She's back at the palace now, you know."

"Yes, I talked to her last night."

Traigh rubbed his hands up and down his sides. "Well, you'll want Donn saddled. Only wait a few minutes, sir."

Happy to have his own horse restored to him, Roric walked out into the sunshine again, his gaze covering the trees and flowers on the palace ground, the lake in the distance, the general's mansion and army barracks beyond the palace grounds. Soon, all this would be a part of his past. He swallowed hard, an ache in his throat.

Shortly after the battle, he'd returned the sorrel and the draft horse he'd 'borrowed,' in the same manner he'd taken them, in the middle of the night.

Squinting in the bright light, he thought about the days after the battle. The wounded from both sides had been taken in horse transports to the city hospital, there to be cared for by druids and druidesses. Keriam and Radegunda had tended to the wounded

there, using their herbal skills and, he suspected, a little magic. The dead from both sides lay buried in a special place, now sanctified, on the Plain of Sorrows.

Soon after her return to the palace, Keriam had established a special druidic tribunal to codify laws on magic and have them recorded in a holy book. As long as it was good magic, never again would the craft be considered a crime in the kingdom.

Equally important for the outlanders, the new queen had declared their forest territory forbidden to others, so that they could maintain their isolation, their way of life.

"Sir." Traigh came out to meet him, holding Donn's reins.

"Ah, yes." Roric stepped forward and placed his foot in the stirrup, then mounted. "May the Goddess watch over you and Maudina,." he said, easing himself into the saddle.

"And you, sir."

Roric swung the horse around, heading for the path that led to the Royal South Road. It would take him several days to reach his family in Mumhain, but the wait was worth it.

After leaving the palace grounds behind, he leaned forward in the saddle and cantered, then galloped along the dirt road. The horse's hooves pounded on the ground, a cloud of dust enveloping him on this warm day. Feeling the bunch of his mount's muscles gather and pull beneath his thighs, he rode past meadows luxurious with springtime growth, where farmers worked the fields and horses pulled plows. A slight breeze brought the glorious aroma of lavender from a field to his left, a reminder of Keriam. He met few travelers along the way, his thoughts his own, his mind, as always, on Keriam.

Now slowing to a canter, Roric covered many miles, his mind grappling with his heart. .He recalled her crestfallen look when he'd told her he was leaving, and a painful stab struck his heart. Had he read too much in her eyes? Could she feel for him all the love he felt for her?

If she did have special powers--and he knew that she did--he would love her just the same, love her for the endearing woman she was.

Her words came back to taunt him. If I loved a man, it wouldn't matter what station in life he held.

He slowed his horse, his mind in turmoil. He would take a chance. What did he have to lose? Later, he would visit his family; he had another matter he must settle first.

Roric maneuvered his horse around and headed back to Emain Macha.

To Keriam.

~The End~

Shirley Martin books also published by
Books We Love, Ltd.

Fairy Tales
Avador
Night Secrets
Night Shadows
Enchanted Cottage
Allegra's Dream

Wolf Magic
Destined to Love
Forbidden Love
Shirley Martin Special Edition

About The Author

Born near Pittsburgh, Shirley Martin attended the University of Pittsburgh. After graduating from 'Pitt', she taught school for one year, then obtained a position as a flight attendant with Eastern Airlines. Based in Miami, she met her future husband there. After raising three sons, she devoted her time to writing, something she had always wanted to do.

Her books have been sold at Amazon and most major book stores and have garnered great reviews. A widow, Shirley lives in Birmingham, Alabama, with her two cats.

Published by Books We Love Ltd.
http://bookswelove.net

If you're looking for something Spicier visit
http:// spicewelove.com